Archie Chamb   ation,
and a nice job teacl   n easy
chair, a nice cuppa   ɔstacle
to this quiet life   .nded,
genetically-modifiec   uristic
City of West Meg.

MW01536599

Archie recognized the signs of executive temperament when he saw them, and pulled back. "There's more to this racket than we thought. Let Robinson show you what he's got. I think he's one hundred per cent right," Archie told Gennaro. "You must let—"

Robinson's hand went to his holster. "What's that?"

Archie realized he'd been ignoring a background noise. With a sinking heart, he knew he'd ignored it because it was a sound he associated with the ordinary buzz of the Gee-9 lab, with virtual war games that did not interest him: the *zat, crack, thung* of weaponry.

Robinson recognized it, too, and moved. "Behind the bar," he ordered the two Gamemasters, turning toward the door with his gun drawn.

The door smashed inward. Archie saw weapons. The Gamemaster Security personnel jumped into action, toward the door. Immediately Archie closed his eyes, threw himself against Gee and knocked him behind the rude wooden bar. There was the deafening sound of weapons fire, a burnt smell, noises of men yelling—and the grunt of men being hit. Blinding flashes of light coruscated about the room.

The bar wasn't much cover at all. Archie knew it. No miracle would save them.

"Max—" said Archie, too late. A final bright blast knocked him into darkness.

PLAY
THE GAME

By Linda Tiernan Kepner

Flying Chipmunk Publishing
Bennington, NH

Play The Game, Copyright © 2008 by Linda Tiernan Kepner.

Play The Game

Published by Flying Chipmunk Publishing
162 Onset Road
Bennington, NH 03442

ISBN: Softcover: 978-1-60459-481-2
     1-60459-481-0

Cover Photo Courtesy NASA/JPL-Caltech
All graphics are Copyright © 1991-2004 by ValuSoft®, a division of THQ®.

First Flying Chipmunk Publishing edition: September 2008.

Acknowledgements

Many thanks to the Wilton Writers sf workshop (also known as the WWF, just because), for putting this manuscript through the mill. Many fine suggestions for improvement came from WWF members Elaine Isaak, Jim Isaak, Deb Jelley, and Mike Joy.

Thanks also to Maureen Tiernan Goetze, who originally suggested the three-part riddle.

Others I would like to thank for encouraging words: Kate Phillips, Ann Geisel, Warren Lapine, Bob Liddil, Allen Steele, and Marie Isham.

Highest thanks to Terry Kepner, who provides manuscript setup and moral support.

The research for Tibet came mainly from guidebooks, and a little help from the Mariposa Museum. The Gamemaster Inc. Labs originated in the halls of the now-defunct *Instant Software, Inc.* Archie's England came from a plethora of old English mysteries and information about the National Trust from the late Margaret Priest.

The independence of mitochondria was suggested by Dr. Paul Curtis a few years ago at Eisenhower College (all right – so it was more than "a few").

Many details of Bet's persecution and the Alpha's response to the attack were suggested, alas, by the daily news.

Table of Contents

-1-
Opening Moves

"Chamberlain. Isn't that your home the SWAT team is attacking?"

No other college student would get that greeting at the end of the day, Archie Chamberlain reflected. Not in Oxford, half a world away from the ruckus. He sighed and leaned his cricket bat against a wall where no one would trip over it. He stepped into the lounge and examined the news screen critically. A dozen fellow students watched the screen and his reaction.

Archie could hear the chuk-chuk-chuk of soldiers' feet as lines of well-armored men ran through the streets of the City of West Meg and into the front doors of a great tower marked GAMEMASTER INC./ MEDICAL/ BLDG. 3 EAST. The doors received them hospitably. He sighed again, and helped himself to a mug of tea from the sideboard. "No, that's an office building. What is it this time?" he asked resignedly.

"Treason. The Earth Combined Military found that the Clarke Mercury Station rebel government is a Gamemaster Ten client. They're raiding for military information. The Clarkes have been pushing for independence from Earth for almost twenty years now, and they're finally getting money enough to bankroll their own weapons. Why on Earth are ECM raiding a medical building?"

"Even I can answer that one," Archie's friend Prentiss snorted. "They expect it to be less protected than the Gamemaster Inc. central offices because it's a research building. As if the research they've done in genetic modification would be in the least protected building on their campus."

Archie nodded. "A lot of the archives are there, you're right, but the building makes no difference to Max." Nor did he feel like explaining Max, the ubiquitous Gamemaster Inc. computer system, in detail.

"Does this happen much?" Prentiss asked curiously.

"Only once or twice a decade," Archie replied. "I remember being in my Mum's office one time when the U.N. Inland Revenue came with armed men. I was perhaps five." *I was going to be five in a week*, he remembered. What a birthday celebration that was.

"The Gamemaster really thumbs his nose at 'em, doesn't he?" Morison queried.

"Stands to reason," Prentiss argued, "if they've got confidential contracts with non-U.N. governments, or rebels, they can't just go dropping information to the ECM on anybody's whim, can they? Besides, it's always fun to see what the Gamemaster will use to boot them out."

Markham was a stodgy conservative at age 20. "West Meg is a United Nations member the same as anyone else. Earth Combined Military is their military. If he's got problems with ECM, Gamemaster can go to the U.N. the same as anyone else."

"Oh, yes, with half of them dying to get him by the short hairs so they can hijack his products. Fat chance of that."

Archie had listened to discussions like this all his life. Usually, the participants weren't naïve academics, but it didn't matter. He was already tired of the conversation. He gathered up his cricket gear and went back to his room. The constant air of debate at Oxford tired him. But he liked his fellow Englishman's wit. Archie was reading in Classical Literature, and in one more term would probably take his First and be done with it. Some friendly soul had recognized that fact. It could have been Prentiss or Markham, but just as likely one of the girls in Lady House. Tacked to his door was an old quote from a late twentieth-century American source that made him chuckle: *Everybody thinks they had a normal childhood, but I think I'd recognize normal if I saw it.*

The Gamemaster blew them into the street from a third-story window, which is why Archie didn't want to work for him, the way the rest of his family had done for three generations now. The dark man's imperial callousness was another reason Archie didn't want to be an employee, as his parents were. There had been some broken bones. Two soldiers died. Gamemaster, all the business but especially the old man, was single-minded, tyrannical, and just plain tiresome.

One would think that after three hundred years of dealing with the line of princely technopirates who owned the North American West Coast the ECM would catch on, but that's what made them the military— persistence, and certainty in their own superiority. That was what had touched off the Sandhurst Military Academy scandal in England, as well, so many years ago, but his parents still talked about it. Archie watched the news summary alone, from the privacy of his own desk monitor. The SWAT team had charged through the Gamemaster Inc. building as if it were a contrabands raid. They bypassed the common herds of lower-level Gamemasters, heading for the Gee-Ten Lab. Somehow, they missed it and ended up in the Gee-7 Lab. At that crucial moment, when the red-faced SWAT team was trying to figure out what they'd done wrong, all the interior doors slammed shut. Gamemaster's own personnel were locked safely in their offices and the military in the corridors.

The air system, easily capable of simulating pressurization or depressurization, blasted an entire ECM division out a window like so much jettisoned cargo.

Archie winced. At least now they'd take the old man to U.N. court, and fight him on the level. Both sides could afford the best lawyers on earth. Let them hash it out.

It's not my business, Archie told himself. I came to Oxford. I'll be finished in another term. Then I'm going elsewhere. I want a life of my own.

Still, he almost reached for the terminal, to call Gennaro and tell him his dad even made the BBC. His hand drew back. Young Gee was almost as impervious as his father. He would be as unaffected by any bad publicity. Besides, it was time for class. He grabbed his academic robes (In the interest of education, Oxford was exempted from many Historic District requirements, but the robes were still required garb) and tore across the college grounds, making it with time to spare. It *would* be a course on Ethics.

He felt that feeling of flight again, and did not yet feel dread. Firm hands pressed against his ribs as he swung through the air.

"He's one handsome little guy, Peggy!" one of the women in Personnel cooed. "Hi, Archie, sweetie, remember me?"

"I'm sure he remembers you all, the way you treat him," Peggy laughed. Compared to the bland West Meg accents around her, Peggy's bold English stood out like a firecracker. He remembered the big green earrings, remembered being drawn against her, into the auburn hair, into the perfume. She held him in her arms. He saw himself reflected in her eyes— blond moppet with big blue eyes. Most of all, he remembered the warm feeling of being held. He saw the joy in her eyes as she held her "only one" in her arms.

"How do we rate?" someone asked.

"George will be here in a while to pick him up. He had an errand to run for Accounting." She gave Archie a cup— apple juice, and sat him in a chair near her. Four. He was four years old. He could still taste the tartness of the juice.

Other people passed by and spoke to him and his mother, sometimes touching him. He couldn't remember what they said, or if he answered. And somewhere, deep inside, he felt the fear start to build.

He saw his mother turn her chair at her terminal. Her head and face were now in the angle he remembered— and she said what he remembered next: "Shelly? What's the noise?"

"I don't know," a voice from nearby replied in a curious tone. Then the tone changed. "What the hell— ? It's a breach. Breach, people, breach! Lockdown! Lockdown! This is NOT a drill!"

He saw fear in his mother's eyes for the first time in his life as she scooped him up, and left her chair spinning empty behind her. "Oh, my God. Baby— Baby— " she forced her voice to be calm as she poked a combination into a touchpanel on the wall, and a door slid open. "I'm going to put you in here where it's safe, love. I'll bring you out after the other men leave. Don't be scared, all right, darling?"

He must have spoken, must have agreed trustingly, although he never felt himself say anything in the dream. He remembered the door sliding shut, his mother disappearing quickly from view, and suddenly understanding that he might never see her again. Now the panic started. The room had some machines in it, no people, a small room— he ran to the door and shoved against it, then tried to reach up to the touchpanel, calling out for his mother. That was when he started crying out in the dream— maybe in real life, he never knew.

As he cried and threw himself against the door in his dream, he also knew what happened next, and waited for it. Again and again he launched himself at the blank white door. One time, when he pulled back, ready to throw himself forward again, the door slid open and he stopped, relieved.

Then he cried out in terror. It was not his mother. It was a huge monster, with something over its face and eyes, carrying a gun. There were one, two, three of them. He screamed, and heard his mother cry out, "My baby!"

They had all stopped in their charge through the doorway, and seemed to be staring at him, as astonished to see him as he was to see them. Then there was a blinding flash and an explosion that blasted them into his chamber. He felt the heavy body drop on him. He saw the dead face. The door slid shut. Their masks had been blasted off. Three men— three dead, bloody men—

He screamed, screamed, screamed... no, it was a buzzer, again and again... Archie Chamberlain woke, sweating, to the buzz of his own desk monitor. In it, he saw the face of the school on-duty, and gasped, "Wh-what time's it?"

"Three a.m. Sorry to wake you," said the on-duty. "You've got an emergency call from West Meg. I'll put it through."

"Oh, Lord." Archie struggled into his bathrobe with a sinking feeling in his stomach. Mum was due to retire soon, but her last heart attack had made it imperative. "Please don't let this be it," he prayed. His screen sprang to life.

Anxiety replaced relief in an instant. No, it wasn't Mum. He knew this face almost as well as his own, however. It belonged to a young man, his age, genetically perfect, skin pale but everything else as dark as a yard up a chimney. Sometimes Archie called him Gennaro, because that was his name. Very often he called him Gee, as if in anticipation of things to come.

"Sorry about the time difference," said Gee, in his clean West Coast American accent. He seldom smiled, rarely laughed, and was incapable of really looking sorry.

"Is my mum all right?"

"Your mother is fine. It's my father I'm calling about."

"Oh Lord," Archie breathed. "Gentian's dead."

Brief nod. "Out testing ship reactors with the Clarke rebel government, amid blazing publicity. The magnetic dampers failed. They flew into the sun."

"Lord help us." Archie stared. "I didn't see anything on the news. That's a slow burn, Gee."

Another brief nod. "By necessity, The Gamemaster's affairs are always in order. We had a last-minute conversation, but just on details. They jettisoned the black box. I have it. I am, of course, suppressing it. I don't need *that* kind of blazing publicity. Max just gave me the word of final death. I've been The Gamemaster for— " he glanced offscreen— "twenty minutes now. I wanted to tell you in case there was a communications freeze later."

"Understood." Archie knew there was no one even to tell. Gee had no family. "Shall I come?"

He blinked. "Why?"

"Because, dammit, you're alone and your father's dead."

That brought the slightest of smiles. "West Meg is my city, with three hundred fifty million inhabitants, and you want to come visit me because I'm alone."

"That's about it," Archie agreed.

"I'll never understand you. But I suppose it's the same reason your mother sent me cookies."

"It's in the blood," said Archie.

"Aren't you in exam time?"

How did he know that? "Death in the family."

The new Gamemaster, the most powerful man on the planet, cocked an eye at him. "Going to take the GCODE while you're at it?"

"Not if it was the last job on Earth."

Now Gee did smile. "Take your exams. Visit when you're able. Perhaps the dust will have cleared by then. I've got the Federal Law Enforcement Agency at the door with guns and search warrants."

"It's a great life," Archie agreed. "Can I say something? Just an opinion, you understand."

"Go ahead."

"I thought the old gent was out of line on that ECM thing. There was no reason to kill those soldiers."

"Why not? They were invading." In his own way, Gennaro sounded as conservative as Markham.

"So smack 'em on the nose with a couple of lawyers and send them on their way. They were just obeying orders. West Meg isn't at war with the ECM. We're supposed to be working with them, not against them. It wasn't necessary."

Gennaro appeared to think. "They attacked and we defended."

"Well, hooray for our side. It wasn't right, Gee."

His immobile face glanced suddenly at something offscreen. "FLEAs at the door. I have to deal with them," said the Gamemaster. "Keep in touch." The screen went dead.

"We're the same age, and all I have to do is find a job," muttered Archie, feeling a pang of something annoyingly like guilt.

Archie lay down again on the bed, letting the guilty feeling fade, knowing from experience that he had to attend to the dream first. It was watching the raid on Medical Building 3 East that had brought it on, no doubt of that, but he knew that he would not feel calm until he finished the entire sequence.

He closed his eyes, remembering what happened next, and fell into a half-awake, half-asleep state. He remembered the pressure again of the body atop him, and felt something wet— blood? His tears? He never knew.

"God in Heaven." A deep English voice, not his Mum's, but even more welcome. The weight shifted. Arms lifted him again. He was looking into a pair of eyes as blue as his own. "Here, let me get you out of here. Don't look. You don't need to see that." In a blur, they were back in the office, the door shut. Archie felt the linen as his father wiped away his tears, smelled the clean smell of his dad's handkerchief, and saw his frown.

George gathered a sobbing Peggy Chamberlain into his other arm and brought her close, too. "There, there," he soothed them both, "it's all right. If this is the worst that ever happens to us in life, we should thank God."

"Those bastards!" sobbed Peggy.

"Not in front of the child," said his dad, and meant it. He lifted Archie a bit more, and looked into his face with concerned blue eyes. "You remember, son, that no matter how bad it felt to be in there, it ended well and you were back in our arms. Remember that. Promise?"

He had nodded then, and he nodded now. No matter how often the nightmare returned, he kept his promise.

Archie found the job, on a suggestion from Prentiss, who had successfully followed his own advice. Good jobs were hard to find on Earth but plentiful elsewhere. One simply had to qualify to travel to them.

Archie twisted and turned, getting used to zero gravity. He felt an itch inside his spacesuit and realized there was no way to scratch it. Sweat ran down his leg. The breeze that he felt against his cheek was cool and soothing.

There was a sudden blast of air. Everything went black.

He was standing in the middle of an empty room, in his own clothes. "What happened, Louis?"

"The breeze, Monsieur Chamberlain. You should have slapped your helmet shut that moment."

"Oh." Archie frowned. "So I should have. Earthbound breeding will tell, won't it?"

The small, dark man said nothing, but smiled politely. "Shall we give it another try? You must pass this simulation if you want to go to Mars."

"We'll do it one more time," Archie said.

Louis demurred. "We'll do it until you pass, sir."

"That's one more time," Archie said firmly. "Let's go." Archie turned his attention completely to the business at hand. Again they went through the simulation. Archie watched the right dials, responded to the right cues, flicked the right switches. When they finished, he was satisfied. So was the examiner.

"That simulation is just like being there," said Archie.

"Bound to, monsieur. That's a Gamemaster product, the top level of Gamemaster Inc. They put a lot of good research into everything. In the old days, we lost hundreds of people in space and air accidents, when all they got was a speech. Now, they're *there*." Louis smiled. "You're cleared for any Mars ship for the next six months, monsieur. Bon voyage."

"Thanks," said Archie. Once again, Gee and Gamemaster Inc. After that one call, nothing else had happened. Archie hadn't gone back to West Meg, hadn't spoken to Gee.

"What are you going out for, monsieur?"

"Teaching assistant."

"Well, good luck, monsieur. You do seem a quick study."

Those parting words bothered Archie.

Archie entered the headmaster's office, still damp from his shower. He wore a comfortable, slightly out-of-date suit, but that didn't bother him. Mars wasn't big on fashion. "Sorry I took so long, Mr. Pemberton. You caught me at an awkward moment." The men had risen from their seats. Plainly, they had been discussing some of the pictures and medals on the walls, the pleasant academic clutter of headmasters' offices anywhere.

"Quite all right," the headmaster reassured him. "We saw you with the students. Mr. Arrow, Mr. Chamberlain. Mr. Arrow's son may be attending next semester."

Archie shook hands, wondering why the son wasn't here. Mr. Arrow was perhaps in his early forties, but there was a timelessness about him. This feeling was reinforced when he spoke. "We watched you trying new soccer plays with those kids, Mr. Chamberlain. You were as involved as they were. It's been a long time since I'd seen a group of people having that much fun." Vague accent— maybe American, maybe English. It wasn't exactly peace that Mr. Arrow radiated; but this was a man who had found answers. Something in his eyes made Archie think, Bomb squad.

"I enjoy teaching and learning, wherever I am. The exercise is as good for me as it is for them." It was a stock answer to give to a prospective enrollee at Isidis-Mars Preparatory School. Observation and deduction, as Gentian used to say, don't disparage the skills you have. Unthinkingly, Archie found himself taking stock of the visitor just as old Gentian used to coach him. Boots not very worn, clothes don't have an air of regular use, hair never gets too long, very little callusing on hands but that ring is quite dented. The old Gamemaster also said, a suspicious nature isn't a bad thing, either.

"James Arrow is recovering from the flu and cannot travel," the headmaster explained, "but he wants to be a writer. Since you teach classical literature and run the writing workshop, perhaps you should give Mr. Arrow a tour of the academic areas."

"Certainly." Archie accompanied Mr. Arrow out of the Headmaster's office.

They walked out of the building, back into the watery day as seen in the school pressure dome. "Seems dark, after Earth," said Mr. Arrow.

"I joke about it being 'just like home,' England in winter in the rain," Archie agreed. "You probably know that the grass is a modified tundra grass, more brown than green. The trees, too, are modified tundra trees, for the most part. They're well-watered, artificially of course, but have the advantage of being naturally used to erratic sunshine."

There was a glint of humor on Mr. Arrow's face. "And the oaks and the elm?"

"Synthetic, sorry. The Headmaster just felt that no true English school should be without them."

"Do you ever get back to Earth?"

"Oh, yes. As a matter of fact, I just brought a group of Fifth Years back from an architectural tour of Rome."

Mr. Arrow's eyes widened for a moment, and he spoke respectfully. "I have to admit, taking a bunch of teenagers on a spaceship isn't my idea of a good time."

"The kids understand that horseplay on spaceships is fatal. They usually overcompensate with horseplay on the ground. The trick is to see that they get plenty of exercise when they can, especially after being bottled up on a ship." Archie added, "My favorite technique is to run them ragged with new soccer plays. Then we all sleep well."

"Do they keep up on current events at home, nonetheless?"

"If you mean issues like the Recover movement and the Isolationists, yes, but their interest is academic. Except, of course, they hope they're not going to be on a ship home that Recover hijacks, which isn't likely unless it's a military ship, or something the Isolationists blow up. But this is Mars and the Isolationists are primarily Venan, so the predominant risks for the children are the ordinary risks of space travel. Not to demean the risks, nonetheless."

Mr. Arrow's questions were standard parent questions. "Do they explore much outside the dome? It seems rather dangerous for kids, yet the opportunity to be on Mars..."

"We have a Climbers' Club, managed by a Mars-sider, Mr. Gregorian. Usually there are several teachers along, including myself. You know the dust storms are what one watches for here, I presume. They can do tremendous damage to a suit, and brownouts are like being lost in tar. The students get a lot of dust practice right here in Isidis Planitia, because we certainly have our share. They've climbed in both Syrtis Major and Terra Tyrrhena. Mr. Gregorian hopes to take them on a serious climb to Elysium Mons by the end of this year. Of course, they all want to climb Olympus. Start at the top, that's their motto." Archie gave him the standard answers to his standard questions.

"Do they play day and night games here?"

"The kids like to play Moonlight Cricket and Moonlight Football, which are the same games with the field lights off and luminescent bands on the equipment. It amazes me we don't have more injuries than we do, but they're quite careful. Over there are the dormitories, coed in alternate suites, separated by years. The classroom buildings are over there— " he pointed and kept his voice neutral, hiding the resentment he felt at wasting his time on this tour. "The science labs and library over there." As they walked along, various students and faculty passed and greeted them. They weren't alone until they reached the Common Garden, a little square of benches and gravel designed for privacy and meditation.

"How long have you worked here?" asked Mr. Arrow.

"Three years now," Archie replied. "I came out on a teaching practicum, and stayed. The academic atmosphere's good, the kids want to learn, and I work fairly cheaply. A great deal of the work here is human-driven rather than robot-driven. The kids supplement their scholarships with student jobs. That's also fine by me, because I have always disliked robots."

"You married?"

"No," said Archie. "I had three proposals to stay happily in Oxford the rest of my life. I was sure I'd go mad within the decade if I did. They still write to see if I want to come back."

Mr. Arrow chuckled. "You're frank."

"If you were really a parent I'd be more polite. The idea, coming here with such a crock." Now, in private, Archie's voice hardened and his eyes blazed. He faced Arrow, blocking the garden exit.

Arrow gave him a straight, hard look. Then he relaxed. "They said you were pretty quick on the uptake."

"It's been tried before. I'm surprised at you. The ECM even attempted to draft me. A teacher. You'd be laughed out of court. What I really resent," said Archie, his voice shaking despite his best efforts to steady it, "is all the people who think I'd make some kind of grand hostage against the Gamemaster. First off, you know he refuses to deal with hostage situations. That's policy. In addition, I don't work for him, I don't know anything, my folks are moving to the England Historic District, and I'm off-world. Period. Besides, the idea of forcing him to do anything he doesn't want to do is laughable."

"You grew up together."

"Not true. I was allowed to play with the boss's son. He was trained, privately, from birth, to be the Gamemaster. I attended grammar school in West Meg and then went back to England, to public school. A few years at play— *that's* all we have in common. So you can take your draft papers, or your patriotism speech, or your Secret Service speech, and go to hell."

"Archie." Arrow's strange, calm voice cut easily through Archie's irritation. "I never had a speech. I wanted to see you and hear you. That's all."

"Not much of a show, is it?" Archie said furiously. "Give the wedding band back to whomever you borrowed it. What are you when you're in uniform, anyway?" He turned to leave, but Arrow's voice stopped him.

"Archie. Look at me." He met Archie's glare in that same patient, peaceful manner. "It's true that ECM wanted me to do something about the Gamemaster. They didn't specify what. They give me plenty of leeway because I get results. Right now, I can only see one thing. This killing has got to stop."

It brought him up short. Archie had never heard an army man say the killing had to stop.

"Gamemaster takes out a couple of soldiers, we hit a couple of his Security squad. We all go to court and let the lawyers spin tales that end up with no bearing on reality. We each throw our weight around and insist that ours is the only method to co-exist, chalk something else up to the grudge list. And we do it all over and over and over again.

"Command came in with a laundry list of writs they'd issued, actions they'd taken, assaults they'd mounted, pages of them. Against the Gamemaster in his own home nest of 300 years? Talk about needing a reality check." His eyes were an odd shade of hazel. "I asked them if they'd ever said please. They looked at me like I'd just dropped in from Venus."

Unwillingly, Archie asked, "Why pick on me?"

"You tell me," Mr. Arrow challenged, in that same peaceful tone.

Archie lost the staring match. "Oh, hell." He plopped down on a nearby bench and focused on a wall instead.

Archie thought of his Mum. Peggy Chamberlain was in the Personnel Division, one of the dozens of personnel and human-services employees who catered to the company's needs. Yet, the old Gamemaster had called her, to her teeth, one of his most valuable employees. And what he recalled vividly now was the old man, sitting at his desk looking up at her attentively, while she walked up and down his luxurious office and raged and yelled and read him the riot act.

Archie had been seven years old. Gennaro's brother had just died. Archie had gone to play with Gennaro, and Gee had told him his father said they were not to play together any more. When Archie came home, crestfallen, and told his mother, he hadn't expected her reaction. His father sighed philosophically and said, "Ah, well." However, Peggy Chamberlain's face hardened, she took her little son's hand in hers, and she marched them both up to the exclusive penthouse.

Even then, Archie understood that his mother's rage was not focused on himself, but on something or someone else. Many of the words she said didn't make sense until years later. At the time, he was just a little tow-headed boy, staring up at his mum with big blue eyes while she yelled at the most important man in the world.

"You can't send the whole world away because you find it inconvenient. You will lose the ability to deal with the world if you do! That little child in there has no mother, and doesn't know why. His brother's not coming home, and he doesn't know why.

"Oh, don't tell me how you told him a test failed! Who gives a good goddamn about tests? They are dead. Dead, dead, dead. They're being ripped away from him. Dammit, Gamemaster, you hired me as a personnel officer and a personnel officer is what you're getting and there were only three goddamn members of your staff who didn't have a choice but to work for you. Do you know what not having a choice is called? It's called slavery.

"And now you only have one, and you're telling him it's his brother's own fault, he failed a test, aren't you? How's that supposed to make him feel? Don't feed me one *gram* of that bilge about Gamemasters not feeling, I don't want to hear it because it's not true.

"If I have to, I will fight to the inch for the one employee who has no choice. He's just a child, he's seven years old! Give him the same damn rights you'd give any employee! If you had a manager who treated an employee the way you're treating that child, you'd have him cashiered! *I'd* have him cashiered! I'd have him in court for abuse!" She pounded the desk. "How *dare* you treat a child like that! Not just any child, your own! How dare you treat any Gamemaster Inc. employee like that! How dare you treat any human being like that!"

In there, somewhere, the old Gamemaster must have said that he wasn't any human being, he was the Gamemaster. It didn't even slow her down. Peggy Chamberlain met him on his own ground, with spirit. "How can he be the top human on earth if he has to give up his humanity to do it, then?" she raged on.

What was amazing was that the Gamemaster let her, and listened to her. Well, his mum was making a coherent argument in full sentences, despite her anger. His mum was always sensible. At the time, the only effect on Archie was that he and Gee still played together on some afternoons, and remained friends. But he remembered Peggy Chamberlain's words, as clearly as if it were yesterday: "If I have to, I will fight to the inch for the one employee who has no choice."

At last Arrow said, "You know something I need to know, Archie."

In a very changed voice, Archie replied, "I can't tell you why the SWAT missions always fail."

"Oh, I figured that one out. That's not important."

Archie stared. "Well, tell *me*."

"He moves the rooms," Arrow said matter-of-factly. "He's got a sophisticated conveyor system inside every building, and moves them around like puzzle squares. The employees don't notice or don't care, because the signs and walkways adjust automatically. But anyone with a map, bypassing those, is done for."

"I've always wondered. I think you're right." Archie stood. "But look. You're asking me to expose some weakness for you to take advantage of. — No, hear me out.— First, there isn't any weakness. He's a fifth-generation gene-mod, bred just to run the company. Second— and I realize how loony this sounds— I wouldn't if I could, because Gee is my friend."

"I never asked you to expose a weakness. I only want an entree to— well, to an ambassador, from us to him. To establish relations. You might be able to get us in the door, after a hundred years. Peacefully. To talk."

Archie warned, "He's been dealing with diplomats all his life."

"I meant for me to talk to him."

"You could have just called."

"And got the military brush-off. No, you have to say I'm OK and it's worth trying. He listens to you."

"He does whatever he damn well pleases."

Arrow shook his head. "What were you thinking about, there on the bench, Archie?"

Archie sighed. "I need to think. Go away. If I need you, I'll find you."

"I hope you will," said Mr. Arrow.

Archie got the bat across his shins during the cricket match, which served him right. He always felt games should be played with full attention, or not at all. Mr. Pemberton walked with him to the edge of the field. "Mr. Chamberlain," the elder teacher said quietly, "I am quite aware that Mr. Arrow said something to upset you. If you don't wish to talk about it, that's all very well— but I only hope he didn't cast aspersions upon your teaching ability. That would be, quite honestly, a lie."

"Thanks for the vote of support." Archie managed a smile. "Actually, he questioned my taste in friends."

"Gamemaster, you mean." Pemberton nodded at Archie's surprise. "You're certainly not a braggart. Quite the opposite, in fact. So much it shows. I have met others who worked for Gamemaster Inc., or grew up in West Meg. They always mention their flamboyant ruler, at least occasionally. Not you. It has always seemed to be a source of strong emotion for you."

Strong emotion, thought Archie ruefully, as he kicked stones on the tired little Common Garden. Who am I kidding?

John Arrow actually looked surprised when he opened his guestroom door and saw the young English tutor there. "Do you play chess?" Archie asked, without preamble.

"Yes."

"Well or poorly?"

"Well."

Archie took the gamebox from under his arm. "Play me a game and show me that you're worth a letter of introduction to another player I know."

John Arrow smiled as he let him into the room. "Test me first. Spoken like a true Gamemaster."

"That's as may be," said Archie Chamberlain, tight-lipped, setting up the board.

The letter came over the terminal as Standard Packet, in among Archie's regular mail, not live or attracting any special attention. "Archie, just a note to let you know I played some games against your chess man. What a first-class mind! I appreciate your introduction to me.

"You were, of course, aware that he was an officer in the Special Services Division of the Earth Combined Military, and that his current assignment was to improve relations between Gamemaster Inc. and the ECM. Somehow you neglected to mention that in your letter of introduction. Please don't omit such details in the future.

"I thought I should at least drop you a line and let you know that the shooting's stopped.

"Remember that you have an open invitation to test out. I understand from Arrow that you've proven yourself to be a good teacher, and good at spaceside life. Those would be especially valuable qualities here.

"Gee."

Not Gennaro, but Gee, what Archie always called him. A Standard Packet, not to embarrass him. A Thank You, unheard of.

"Gee,

"I realize it's bad manners to say thank you for a thank you, but I was glad to hear from you. I must be getting soft.

"Archie."

Time passed at Isidis-Mars Prep. It was frightening to Archie to realize that the First Years who came in with him were preparing to graduate. He had now watched six classes go their separate ways— jobs, university, on Earth, on Mars, Venus, the Jovians, spaceside. He himself received early tenure. No longer was he a green teacher at his first job, but an educator with over six years spaceside experience.

He was glad for Prentiss, too. Charlie Prentiss was due for tenure and a dead certainty to get it. Like Archie, he felt vindicated and complete at the school. Unlike Archie, however, he was ready to give his whole life to it, to the point of making plans to marry and settle at the school. Sheepishly, he announced this to Archie at the bar they visited on their days off, in a different dome from the school. His intended, Sylvia Phillips, was one of their old girlfriends from Lady House. Truthfully, the knowledge that two of his old friends had made cheerful plans to spend their lives together, doing things they enjoyed, made Archie feel there was something especially right about life.

His parents sent the best news of all. They both retired. They left West Meg and did what they always wanted to do, gone home at last. They had a little house in the England Historic District. They were touched that Gennaro had hosted their retirement party. Truthfully, so was Archie. He was proud that Gee had let the world know George and Peggy Chamberlain made a difference to him.

Gee, also, seemed to thrive. In truth, the transition between Gentian and Gennaro was almost unnoticeable, as they both would have desired. The plainest difference was that Gennaro was more likely to litigate or evict, rather than send out a security squad. Apparently he did listen to advice. When Archie watched the news and it mentioned Gamemaster Inc. policy and predicted how the Gamemaster would react in light of it, the analysts were often correct. Gennaro did not balk established policy just for spite, as Gentian might. If the policy was unfair, Gennaro consulted with his company experts and changed it. This did not mean he was a sucker. He had proven himself just as hard as his predecessors on many aspects.

Archie watched the news. ECM or the FLEA or the UN did this. Gamemaster Inc did that. Setbacks. Through it all, John Arrow somehow managed to maintain his tenuous chess connection. Once a month, Arrow and Gee had dinner together, played chess into the night, sometimes conversed, sometimes didn't. Both sent occasional messages to Archie, mentioning each other. To Archie, it seemed that they forgot, for a few hours each month, that they were on opposite sides of the fence.

One day, Archie received a Standard Packet from John Arrow. It was brief: "Archie, I'm afraid I'll be gone by the time you read this. I'm being transferred to Rejalta, one of the Venan colonies, to deal with some problems there. I don't know when I'll be back. What you go through to align all factors to land on Venus, or leave it, fills a large computer. Good luck with your teaching. I'm glad to hear you got tenure— it's tough to do these days."

The sons of bitches transferred Arrow. To some Venan colony, where their specialized, erratic atmospheric pocket-stations, seeded liberally through the Venan atmosphere, kept him virtually incommunicado. Being sent to Venus was the equivalent of the Foreign Legion, as far as Earth was concerned.

For the first time since Archie had met Arrow, he was afraid. He always felt that Arrow was the buffer. If Gee had only one sensible man to talk to in tight times, peace would be maintained. Now they'd blown it. There would be hell to pay.

Hell started right away. The original ECM request wasn't on the news, but whatever it was, Gee refused flatly to honor it. The Earth Combined Military raided Gamemaster Inc. They had caught onto the moving-room trick, but it hadn't helped them much. Gamemaster Security took them on, with weapons. For the first time, innocent bystanders— Gamemaster Inc rank-and-file employees, not the specially-trained Security Division— were killed.

There was no mercy now.

Gamemaster simply evicted the Earth Combined Military from all their offices on the West Coast. As their landlord, he was well within his rights. Where they did not leave peaceably, they were ejected by Gamemaster Inc. Security. It was war.

Archie actually spent money trying to contact someone in the ECM Special Services Division, and got Arrow's commander. He looked like he was not far out of officer training school. Plainly he was not interested in any help some teacher from the outback might be able to give, and certainly wasn't willing to take advice.

Coldly he regarded Archie Chamberlain over the video screen. "This is a difficult situation, sir," he said, in the tone of voice that meant You're a Civilian and I'm Not. "Unfortunately, Gamemaster has allowed it to escalate beyond limits imposed by the government."

"Gamemaster allowed it?!? Now you're going to tell me that John Arrow didn't tell you you were making a mistake and that if you transferred him, you would break the first peace West Meg has known in a hundred years," Archie interrupted. "Let me tell you something, Commander Marsden. I may be the same age you are, possibly younger, but one skill I *have* mastered is admitting when I'm wrong and trying to remedy the situation. You killed civilians. That's inexcusable."

"You have no authority to tell me anything, Mr. Chamberlain. Good day. I am severing this connection." The officer reached out his hand and did so.

No authority, Archie fumed. He would like to give that pompous little fart a good dose of authority.

He found himself in the Common Garden, where he had once kicked stones thinking of his Mum. *"If I have to, I will fight to the inch for the one employee who has no choice."*

All right, Archie told himself, I am a teacher. I've proven myself. I didn't need Gamemaster or West Meg or anyone else, to do it. I made a difference in some students' lives, and they in mine.

But am I doing enough?

John Arrow had guessed ages ago that Archie Chamberlain had a method to get the authority he needed to make that ECM captain roll over and play dead. Gamemaster, too, for that matter. Archie had consciously chosen not to use that ability. Was he wasting his gifts?

His mum— She'd been in Personnel. These were all her babies. There was no need to spend the night agonizing over his decision. He had spent many nights doing that, in the past. Fat lot of good it had done.

Archie paged through the School Bulletin Board, looking for the exam listings. ASVAB, 1200 hours Tuesday March 10. LSAT, 1300 hours Tuesday April 17. MCAT, 0900 hours Saturday March 14. Here it was— GCODE, 0900 hours Tuesday March 3. Tomorrow.

-2-

Endangering the King

Prentiss was proctoring the placement exams. When Archie showed up at the door, he grinned and waved his fellow to a seat near his. "Chamberlain, what brings you to Examland? Thinking about taking one?"

"As a matter of fact, I am. Got an extra?"

Prentiss sobered. "Good Lord, man, that was a joke. You haven't preregistered."

"Check your rulebook. Unlike every other examination in the universe, the GCODE doesn't require preregistration. It's free and voluntary."

The look on Archie's face worried his friend. "Archie, if you're that upset about something, you should see the Headmaster."

"He couldn't help. He's probably already guessed. Fork over the exam."

Prentiss handed him the tablet with the extra copy, eyes bulging. Archie sat amid his own students, their eyes also bulging, and filled in the forms.

After that, he didn't let himself think about what might have been.

His shuttle made a wide arc over the City of West Meg before it pulled into Port Authority West Meg. It was an ordinary landing, from a regular Mars-to-Moon-to-Earth connection. He was just another disembarking passenger.

"Mr. Chamberlain?" a soft feminine voice said.

He turned to stare up into the lovely face of a tall African woman wearing a Gamemaster Inc. badge. She smiled. "Welcome. I'm Malasha Masere, from Personnel." They fetched his luggage together. She asked him how his trip was. Archie had the absurd feeling that he was coming home. This is what his Mum would do.

"I wonder if you know Peggy Chamberlain," Archie said.

Malasha smiled. "Trained under her and took her job. She told me if I didn't take proper care of you, she'd come back and slap me up, personally."

"Atta girl," said Archie.

They hadn't yet told him where he'd tested out. That was a privilege reserved for the Gamemaster. That was Archie's next stop, after assuring his escort that no, she wasn't needed.

Silently, he entered Gamemaster Inc. Residential Building 1 West, also known as the Alpha. At this time of the afternoon, there were tourists in the public areas, dining in the Alpha Tea Room and gaping at the museum-quality furnishings in the public areas of one of the world's most famous buildings. Probably they were also hoping for a glimpse of its most famous resident, who lived in undocumented luxury in the penthouse apartment. Archie hardly looked at the artwork or tapestries as he made his way to the end of a corridor. There, an elevator stood open and untouched. Occasionally, tourists wandered in, not realizing the lovely little room was an unresponsive elevator. They sat on the ebony-wood bench or admired the golden mirror or the redwood paneling before they realized their mistake and wandered out again. Archie had been using this elevator by himself since he was six.

He stepped inside and said, "Hello, Max. It's Archie."

"I recognized you, Archie. Please stand by." The doors shut. Archie felt the motion upward.

The doors opened upon another gracious corridor. This one was less Classical than downstairs. Gee had made quite a few changes. The furniture and wallcoverings were elegant and traditional, but there were Pacific touches. Pacific Indian masks, a painting of fishermen, a tiny totem pole, and other such surprises peeked from various places. It made Archie smile. Archie was not another George Chamberlain, but neither was Gennaro another Gentian. Archie walked a few meters down the corridor, not on the well-remembered path to the penthouse, but to the office. The great ebony double-doors swung inward as he reached it.

Gee was waiting for him.

They shook hands.

"I suppose I should say welcome back," said the Gamemaster.

"You don't have to. Tell me where I tested out."

"Gee-Nine."

Archie stared.

Gamemaster caught the look. "Didn't expect that, did you? Frankly, neither did I. I had no idea you possessed that much ability. There's only a handful of you in the universe." Gee held out his hand. A little metal badge rested on it, the Gamemaster logo and the number 9 clearly visible. "Put it on and let Max calibrate it."

Numbly, Archie Chamberlain pinned on his new badge.

"Now tell me what changed your mind."

"You'll find out quick enough." Archie met his employer's gaze squarely. "As a Gee-9, I have even more push than I expected. Here is what you are going to do for me. You are going to get me a contract job with the Government of Eastern Seaboard. Then one with the Parliament of Ontario. I intend to chip away at every employer of the Earth Combined Military until I have a quorum under my thumb."

"What about me?"

"You're already under my thumb. That's your job."

"Perfectly sound," Gee agreed. "Glad you understand that. So many employees have to learn that managers and I are here to provide what they need."

"Goddamn it, Gee, we are going to make this peace permanent. Not only is a peacetime situation nice to have around, it's good for business." That argument ought to stick, if nothing else would.

"Agreed. I'll help you where I can, but it's up to you. You've got a desk waiting for you in the Gamemaster Nine Lab. Trann is the manager. You'll take your assignments from him. But, as you know, you pick the job, he smoothes the path." Gee slid behind his desk and consulted his console. "Get yourself settled in first, before you take on the government. I see a couple of jobs on Trann's standby list that look ideal."

Quietly, Archie said, "You knew I'd do this, didn't you? You knew that sooner or later, I'd give up and let you rope me in."

Gamemaster looked up. Equally calmly, he replied, "I think it's a question of who roped whom. I believe I just heard you give me marching orders."

"I did, didn't I." It was a statement.

Archie had met Trann, the Gee-Nine lab manager, on various social occasions like the Christmas party. The best summary of Trann was that he was about four feet high, brown, and square. Trann was a Marianan, a genetically-modified citizen of the underwater Marianas City. What were virtues on the ocean bottom were almost handicaps here: a throat designed to accommodate breathing equipment, a solid body to resist the bends, a duplicate circulatory system, a slightly different chemical composition. An almost unexpressive face, because who could see it through a mask? A voice that spoke with an effort and broke between syllables. But the best managerial brain in the business, still trying to figure out if having one of the Chief's friends in his lab was an asset or a liability.

Archie promptly did his part to prove to Trann, and himself, that it was an asset. He spearheaded projects that were making their way up through the ranks, and initiated projects of his own. By the end of two years, the Eastern Seaboard had refrigeration units that could reach two degrees Kelvin; the Canada transport system followed the route of the old Canadian railroads; the Confederate States of America had its virtual museum up and running; and these were just the highlights on Archie Chamberlain's list of accomplishments. With each job, he dragged in Gee and promoted the peace.

He was proudest of the liver cell business. This was one of the few projects he had started from scratch, so it was special. In Archie's opinion, liver cell medical research had never gone as far as it could. When colon cancer was virtually eradicated, liver cell cancer seemed to take up the slack. Only a true Gamemaster, someone capable of thinking "outside the box," could have put together the virtual-surgery enlargements and manufacturing processes that Archie and Trann did. They had drafted (without much difficulty) surgeons from Walter Reed West, the branch of the renowned ECM hospital located in West Meg. They spent many hours in virtual reality, working on liver cell nanites to combat cancer and diabetes by non-chemical, non-radiation methods. Archie told Trann this was a good piece of work that would go far, and Trann agreed. It was the one job that Archie had Trann leave unwarranteed— in other words, open for any researcher to improve on what Archie started. There were stipulations that further research had to be documented at Gamemaster Inc. Medical and had to be for medical use only, and were otherwise a violation of contract. Gamemaster's Contract division was the only division more dangerous than Security, with lawyers that could smell a violation even before it was committed. But it looked like great things could happen with these medical breakthroughs.

He had planned to celebrate his two-year anniversary alone.

Archie sat in his apartment, feet up, watching the evening news. He was alone, by choice. He'd rapidly made friends at Gamemaster Inc., but he'd wanted to watch this night's news by himself.

On his wall screen were six Presidents, four Generals, and one Gamemaster, announcing joint ventures in medicine and education. The truce had been sealed.

Archie had had invitations from six Presidents, four Generals, and one Gamemaster to be present at the ceremonies. He declined all offers as graciously as possible.

He felt satisfied.

"Archie, Major John Arrow at the door. He says don't get up, just let him in."

Archie smiled and didn't move. "Do it, Max."

John Arrow was in uniform, but a bottle of brandy under one arm gave him an off-duty look. Archie waved a negligent arm toward his small bar. He hadn't expected Arrow or the brandy, but he wasn't surprised. "Didn't think you drank."

"This is a special occasion." Arrow unstoppered the bottle. "Besides, I didn't buy it."

"Oh?"

Arrow waved one snifter in the direction of the screen. "One of the people in that picture did."

"Anyone I know?"

"Quite well. You never bullshitted him, you know."

"Never thought I did," said Archie truthfully. He swirled the snifter, savoring the aroma. He watched the patterns form on the insides of the glass. "Never thought we'd both be able to keep within the system either, and we did."

Arrow sat down in a comfortable chair near him. "What now? Ready to take on the rest of the universe?"

"No, this job's big enough." He continued to stare into the glass. "When I first met you, I thought you were bomb squad."

"I was. They didn't expect an ECM soldier to play with him without getting killed."

"Mmph. I see. And now?"

"Now? It's a success."

"Without you being there?" Arrow's transfer had been the wrench thrown into the smoothly-flowing peace process, the crisis that had forced Archie to let the system suck him in.

"I was there," said Arrow. "And to think that you play chess. Did you forget that, in order to castle, one must endanger the king?"

Archie sat back in an overstuffed chair against an antimacassar right out of a storybook, and sipped real English tea.

His father, George Chamberlain, sat in the opposite comfy chair. He, too, sipped tea. The sun shone through the windows, through the lace curtains, into the cluttered living room. Most of the loud Jacobean-style floral wallpaper was obscured by picture frames and a jumble that only its owner could love. "Quite a mishmash, isn't it?" Dad said fondly, gesturing around the room with his teacup. "We can't change much. It's against Historic District regulations, you know. We have to maintain a certain tone."

"Does this 'tone' have a name?" Archie asked with a grin.

"Early Twentieth-Century English Bad Taste, unless I'm very much mistaken," his father rejoined. "Your mum's in her glory. There's a Women's Institute and a nursing home and a home for unwed mothers, all within a block. Not to mention C of E. Last time I was in a C of E church is when I married her, and I won't tell you when the next time will be." His eyes, as blue as Archie's, twinkled. "Are you going to stay with us for the week?"

"Love to, if I won't upset the tone."

"We'll manage. How's the shop?" George Chamberlain, like Peggy, was retired from Gamemaster Inc. However, he had been an accountant in the Finance department. He had not dealt with the flamboyant Gamemasters on a daily basis, as his wife had done. It enabled him to provide a steadying influence in their household on even the worst days. George had been a Person at the company; Peggy had been a Personality.

"Still standing." Archie drank more tea. Muffins, too. A "daily woman" to do much of the housework. And no robots. That made it Heaven, especially, for Archie. The West Meg mechanical staff was programmed to complete their household chores during Archie's absences. Even after all these years, he couldn't bear to see the living dead vacuuming his upholstery.

"And young Gee?"

"Still standing, too."

"How is he getting on?" Dad's tone gentled. It probably had something to do with having a son of his own.

"Gentian's already just a memory."

"Your mum says you have a lovely flat."

"Yes, well, it's one of the Rhodalia Row buildings. Only the best for a Gee-Nine, you know."

"Want to talk about it?" asked his father. At Archie's startled look, he explained, "If you'd wanted to talk to your mother, you'd have done it over the phone. If it's me, then you always want a quiet corner and a cuppa."

"Now you make me feel too foolish to ask," said Archie guiltily.

The noise his father made was noncommittal. "There's always tomorrow. You don't have to broach whatever-it-is today."

As usual, it was just the right thing to say. Archie found himself telling the long tale about John Arrow, Arrow's trip to the prep school, the chess games, and the cease-fire. Dad listened without interruption. Archie talked himself hoarse. The only time his father moved was to turn on an ugly fringed lamp when darkness set in. Archie finished telling his tale, concluding with, "It all seems like it has a happy ending. But the power I have... it scares me sometimes."

"Rightly so," said his father.

"How can I do it? I'm not... not genetically engineered, like Trann and the Venans, and the others." He paused, and felt breathless and afraid. "Am I?"

Dad set down his cup, and sighed. "No," he said mildly, "you are not." He shifted in his seat. The light from the lamp lit him fully, so that Archie could see his expression well. However, Archie knew by now when he was getting the truth from his dad. This was it. "You are scratch-fed and organically grown. When Peggy got pregnant— she wanted a child so badly, and the stress of that job was too much— I stepped in. Asserted my authority, as they say. I cut her off, cut off Gamemaster, put my foot down, and said, That's it, we are moving to the Historic District until the child is born. And that we did."

"You stayed at Aunt Lacey's."

"Yes, we did. No surgical suite, a nice birthing room, real milk for you. Eggs and cheese and green grass and fresh air. We can laugh at the jumble sale, here, but the National Historic Trust was Miss Beatrix Potter's gift to the world, as far as I'm concerned. We came back to Britain, into the England Historic District, and pushed the Off button on Earth. I wouldn't even let her take memos. When the shop tried to contact her, I fielded the messages. It was not a bad call, Archie. From the moment you took in your first lungful of air, you were a healthy, robust child that would put those West Meg gene-jobs to shame. Best thing I ever did."

"And you didn't do it just to get her away from the old man."

"Old man?" Dad blinked. Then, in an altered tone of voice, he said, "Ah. I see."

Archie felt his face burn. He was glad the light pointed away from him.

"Gentian was a thief, a liar, a murderer, a con man, and the best manager I ever met, but he was not a womanizer. He kept it in his trousers, where it belonged. He knew how important that was to a good business. That was the cause of one of their rows about Gennaro, as a matter of fact. Peggy said he had to get him out and into a social life. That's when we started seeing him at public events, with attractive young things on his arm. Who were taken chivalrously home and never saw the inside of the penthouse, as they expected."

"Gentian was in love with Mum." Archie thought he would shock his dad, but nothing of the sort happened. He merely nodded and set his cup back on the table.

"Head over heels," George Chamberlain agreed. "The fact that she had standards— which, by the way, did *not* include him— was one of the things he liked best about her. Gentian always knew where he stood with her. He knew it right down to his stone core. Peggy always had his best interests at heart, especially where it concerned the youngster."

"She's probably the only mum Gee's ever known," Archie mused, "and that, at a distance."

"Cookies and milk in our flat," Dad concurred, "a comfy chair, a nice cuppa tea, and people to talk to. What more could one want?"

"Can't argue that." Archie tipped the pot one last time. He had one more question to ask. "Still, though— were you ever afraid for your life?"

Again, his father's mild and truthful answer astonished him. "More than once, my boy. There's a long history of that. Trace it back to Uriah and Bathsheba, if you like."

Archie laughed. "I can't exactly picture Mum as Bathsheba."

"Nor can I. Nor could he, which is more to the point. Gentian had enough enemies without stirring up dust among his employees. After all, he hired them because they were capable self-starters."

"Was there dust?" Archie wanted to know.

His father's mouth tightened. "There was dust," he replied grimly.

The week's vacation, and answers to long-standing questions, refreshed Archie immensely.

Now, they were in the simulation, standing ankle-deep in pulsating liver. The greatly-magnified right lobe surrounded them and filled the space.

"All right, I'm moving slowly," Archie said, in his quietest voice. "Talk me through this, Doctor."

Dr. Bane, beside him, spoke in the same level surgical tones. "We're right on target. These nanites are a different color, aren't they?" They watched the little fluorescent-blue-colored "machines" scramble through the virtual liver cells on Archie's signal.

"I colored them deliberately. I want Gamemaster Inc. Medical to try a different alloy. I've been in touch with WMIT. We'll see if we can tweak these little bugs almost to invisibility."

Bane smiled through the clear surgical mask. "All right by me."

"Excuse me, Archie." Max, too, had gentled his voice to match what his receptors had gathered. "Gamemaster wants to cut in but you have the walls up."

"They're staying up, Max. I want to concentrate. Bane and I will finish this up and I'll be back in touch with him. Now go away and let me think. And remind me later."

"Affirmative, Archie."

"That's a wonderful computer," said Dr. Bane.

"Mm-hm. Gee's house pet. Now— what am I seeing over here? Is this all right, or some kind of growth? What does the nanite need to accommodate, here?"

"Oh. Yes. That's an abnormality, but a fairly common one." Dr. Bane launched into a description. They reabsorbed themselves in the surgical problem. At last, Bane said, "I'm sweating as much as if I'd been in surgery. We've been standing here at least six hours, judging by my feet."

"Oh. You may be right. Shall we call it a day, then?"

"Yes, let's."

"All right, Max, save and file and exit."

"Doing it now, Archie." The room shifted. They were no longer in an operating theatre, but standing in Archie's cubicle.

Dr. Bane sighed appreciatively. "And the patient lived, even though we spent eight hours walking through his insides."

"I'll send these files over to Gamemaster Inc. Medical tomorrow, and tell them to construct some beta-test nanites. Reed West will find a liver cancer patient willing to try it. Contract will get in touch with Reed West Contract, or whatever your equivalent is, to handle the business end. It's not my problem, or yours."

Bane sighed again. "That makes me almost as happy as the nanites."

Archie grinned sympathetically. He was as footsore as the surgeon, from standing at the magnified virtual body. It wasn't necessary but it was the surgeon's habit. They preferred to be as realistic as possible. "Go home and get some sleep. Pleasant dreams."

"The same to you," Dr. Bane said warmly. Trann escorted the visitor out of the Gee-9 lab.

After they left, Max prompted, "You have eaten no lunch or dinner, Archie. You also must return a call to the Gamemaster."

"Oh. Um. Yes." Archie rubbed his eyes and sat down. Immediately, his legs told him this was where he ought to stay for a while. "Anybody going to Scottie's for supper?" Scottie's was the nearest restaurant, the common hash-house for many busy workers from this building. Archie's feet were telling him to keep his walking to a minimum tonight.

"I'll check. Malasha Masere 1600 hours. Shiera Walton 1700 hours. Andy and Diane Andrews 1730 hours."

"Shiera going alone, or has she got Alan with her?"

"Alone."

"Buzz her, give her my love, ask if she wants dinner company. And give me Gee."

"Doing it now."

The room faded. Archie seemed to be sitting in front of Gee's great black desk. Gee looked up. "What's on your mind, Gee?" asked Archie.

"What have you got on for New Year Day? I'm going to Monte Carlo and need a spotter."

"I've got a date, thank you. What do you need a spotter for? That damned airgame?"

"Yes. I'm still getting bad reports on that amusement park. I have heard that people are being threatened if they use the airgame, and the police are not responding to complaints. I will bypass the local administration by putting the fear of Me into some of my employees."

No one could accuse this Gamemaster of having no sense of humor. "Well, have fun. Go pick on someone else."

"I will not. Who's your date?"

"Shirley from Contract."

Gee made a sound suspiciously like a snort. "I thought even you had better taste than that."

"I'm a quart low on my gossip. Besides, she's a fantastic dancer."

"Her other good points are that she's nosy and stupid. I'm leaving on the 30th at 1200 hours. Either pack your bag yourself or I'll have a robot do it."

"You send a bloody robot into my flat and we *will* have words. All right, but you'll owe me big time for this. I *hate* spotting for you."

His boss was obviously unimpressed. "You and every other Gee-Ten and Gee-Nine in existence. See you on the shuttle."

The scene shifted and Archie was back in his office. Max was reporting.

"Shiera Walton says she would love to join you for supper but she's been unexpectedly called away."

Alan. That stupid git. Someday, even Shiera Walton, the most tolerant manager of all, would have enough of her annoying husband, Archie bet himself. "Repeat my invitation to Malasha." Archie tidied up his desk.

A moment later, Max reported, "Malasha says she'll meet you there."

"Good enough. Thanks, Max." Archie hauled his tired body vertical and headed toward Scottie's Restaurant.

A day or two later, Archie looked up from his mail to see Trann standing at the entrance to his cubicle. "What's up?"

"Do you know the name Bet Berensen?" Trann demanded.

"Not to speak of," Archie replied evasively.

Trann nodded approval. "Not to speak of. Two of your good points are that you never lie, and you never break confidences. Malasha Masere from Personnel told you about Bet over dinner. She said so."

Archie relaxed. "Oh, well, then. Yes. What's happened?— Oh, Lord, let me guess. Bet's tested out as a Gee-Nine." He stood up, sensing urgency.

"Your third point is your intelligence." Trann paused meaningfully. "You know perfectly well that only the Chief discloses a ranking, first to the candidate, and only on the premises. Also that Bet Berensen cannot possibly have taken the exam, because it is illegal and impossible for her to obtain one where she is. So, of course, you must only be theorizing that she might be a Gee-9."

"But of course," Archie agreed. "I must be only imagining that it might possibly be so." Malasha had, in fact, described her amazing new find at dinner, and how they had managed to smuggle an exam to her in installments. Scottie's was a safe place for talk like that, in a quiet corner, in whispers, between people with Gamemaster badges.

Then Trann said, "Your fourth point is your tact."

"Shit. Don't tell me Gee himself is stepping in."

"Madder than hell," Trann confirmed. "He's meeting with representatives of the Confederate States of America later today. Malasha did not mention names, but began the application for working papers. She was told quite emphatically by the CSA to drop the subject. No decent Christian girl may work for money." There was a hardness in Trann's voice Archie had never heard. "I want that girl. I want her out of that hellhole, and I want her here as a Gee-Nine. I need her desperately, to work on the solar probe project. Get her here. That is your assignment."

"You're even sounding like him," Archie objected.

"Have you seen pictorial documentation of that area? It is ruled by Christian fundamentalists who rob and rape at will. The CSA frankly admits that the 'sheriffs' there have all control. Some wart in CSA actually told the Chief that 'the local feeling' is that no girl of theirs will whore for him, they would kill her first."

"Isn't that special. Were they trying to provoke him deliberately?"

"I do not know if it was deliberate. But he was certainly provoked. I would rather you be on hand before we catch ourselves invading the Confederate States of America."

Within an hour, Archie found himself entering a meeting room across town. Men were arranged around an oval conference table. Further back, at a seat against the wall, sat Malasha Masere. She was the only woman in the room, and the only non-Caucasian.

Gee glanced up from his paperwork at the table. "What are you doing here?"

"Trann sent me." At Gee's nod, Archie took a seat against the wall, near Malasha. Her hands were folded tightly together. A quick scan of the room confirmed Archie's worst fears. Among Gee's conference team were his Chief Security Officer and Intelligence Chief. On the other side of the table were civilians and Earth Combined Military Peacekeeping Forces— obviously stationed in the CSA. These were not diplomats. They were all fighters.

The man opposite Gee, obviously a mediator, spoke in a soft drawl that was very pleasing to the ear. "Gamemaster, I would appreciate it if you would summarize the background, for some of the members here who are unaware of the situation."

"Certainly, Mr. Sommerlin. I received a letter which had been smuggled out of the Delay region of Georgia, in the Confederate States of America." Already, they had reacted— two men, opposite, glanced at each other in clear dismay. "It was, for lack of a better term, a fan letter to me. Just a girl, wishing she could see the bright lights and big city. Under ordinary conditions, I would treat it as such. However, also in the letter— her 'last hurrah,' as she put it, before she would be forced out of high school— she laid out plans for a radical extra-solar probe. Most remarkable was her suggestion how to avoid losing lives in such probes. I have had my research teams look into her suggestions. Her theories are possible. With her work, we could move beyond the solar system, without loss of life. The girl is obviously a talented researcher. I want her here."

"She would have to take the GCODE test and prove herself qualified to work in your organization," said Mr. Sommerlin.

"You know perfectly well," said Gee, in that same quiet voice, "that Delay is at least two hundred miles from a GCODE testing facility, the population is too poor to travel more than 50 miles, and that any girl traveling that distance, alone, has a high probability of being raped or murdered, with no punishment for the rapists or murderers."

Again, the silence, the exchange of glances.

"I also know, as well as you, that even if she were to brave those distances and survive the trip, she would not be allowed to take the GCODE when she arrived. Some excuse would be found to prevent a 'girl' from taking it."

"What do you propose?" asked Mr. Sommerlin.

Archie stepped over to Gee and whispered in his ear. "Student exchange program through the University of Georgia."

Gee nodded and repeated the suggestion.

"Certainly, I don't see any difficulty with that. Give us the girl's name, and we'll make arrangements."

"You will do no such thing," said the Gamemaster.

Sommerlin stared. Then he said, "Forgive me if I point out that you came to us with this request."

"Forgive me if I point out that you are completely incapable of insuring one girl's safety out of Delay. The local organized criminals have already beaten you back twice. Then you stopped trying, because Delay has nothing you want. If her name gets into their hands, she will be dead by nightfall. True, she will be told by her tormentors that it's for her own good, but she will be just as dead."

Malasha gripped Archie's arm, hard. He understood her entire argument in that grip. Gee was ready to drop in his own security people, effectively declaring war on the Confederate States of America. If Bet wasn't dead now, she would be by then.

"I am willing to drop a Security team into one unspecified area to pick up two people. Then I will transport them to Atlanta, where processing and testing can begin." He did not mention that, somehow, Bet had already taken the GCODE and hit the genius level. There would be no transport to Atlanta.

Sommerlin shook his head. "Impossible. Raiding Delay would start a firestorm. Our hold over that area is loose as it is."

The ECM officer nodded confirmation. "It's rural, spread-out swamp, some old tobacco fields, smuggler's country. Even your boys would have trouble with it."

"Suggestions, then?" Gee inquired.

The officer said, "I think this deserves further study."

Mm-hm, thought Archie, so what if one girl dies? "You have strong hands," he whispered.

"Sorry." Malasha released his arm.

"If you move your men in," the officer was telling Gee, "it will be considered an act of war. Pitting the ECM against you just because of one girl is a little ill-advised, Gamemaster."

Gee was completely unmoved by the threat. "It would not be the first time I have taken those odds, and I am still here." Archie felt certain this immutability was reinforced by the hellfire Christianity behind the government of the Confederate States of America, which was invariably one of Gee's examples of why he loathed religion.

"May I say something?" Archie asked. The Gamemaster nodded briefly. "I think we might need to take the lid off a bit."

"I will not give up the girl's name."

"Not about the girl. About the tobacco."

Gamemaster paused. One beat, two. "No, I think not." He stood. "Gentlemen, good day." They left, as a group.

In the transport, Gee chuckled. "Thank you," he said to Archie, "that was very, very good."

"You are most objectionable when you chuckle," said Archie, not for the first time.

"I don't understand." Malasha frowned. "What about the tobacco? I thought her idea of 'living pilots' for the probes, plants instead of humans, was confidential information."

"And I never gave that away. I just mentioned tobacco. It's a tremendously vulnerable spot for Delay. Delay's a tobacco-growing area. It was their only crop, ages ago. They never replaced it with anything else. That's what ruined them, do you see? They still tell stories of the grand old tobacco plantation days, as if they just happened yesterday. So suddenly, we're hinting that there are gold fields in Delay," Archie explained. "You told me Bet did her theorizing on the 'plant pilot' probes and suggested tobacco, didn't you? 'A plant we know inside and out.' So now it will be worth money for them to go in and clean up and organize Delay."

"Have you written to Bet?" Gee asked Malasha.

"I was going to, tonight."

"Just tell her to hang on a little longer." He turned to Chief Robinson. "How quietly could you get her out?"

"Like pulling a loose tooth," Robinson replied.

"Do it. If you need spadework done, be sure it goes in 'Molly's' pen-pal letter tonight."

"My pleasure," said the Security Chief. "But you'd better realize they'll be checking the mail now. Molly's letter may not be from West Meg, but it's a letter. They'll tag it sure as shootin', now that they're looking for it. Even this one might not make it."

Gee turned to Malasha. "We'll take our chances. All right, one more 'Molly' letter and you will see the little girl you've kept alive. It will be a quiet kidnapping, I promise. The greatest contribution probably came from Archie, however."

"From what I understood," said Archie, "Bet was dead serious about using tobacco plants in her space probes. She was right, too, that Tuskeegee had a complete file on every possible aberration of the plant and every microstep of its growth. There are people in the CSA who literally know tobacco inside and out. Think of a plant as a universal space probe pilot, the various stages signaled by its growth cycle! It's mind-boggling. A plant we know, growing and dying and recycling for hundreds of years in a sealed system, piloting a probe to other stars."

Gee had a different slant. "Tobacco in demand again, for scientific experimentation. That could easily put Delay and much of the CSA into a Renaissance, if it's done right."

Archie nodded. "Very likely they'll forget the aspersions cast on their morals and character if they're rolling in tobacco money. It might work, Gee."

"That will be part of Bet's project, also," said the Gamemaster. "After all, she is a Gee-Nine."

-3-

Arrow Hits Target

Rather than fix a boring supper at home alone, or hit up an on-site cafeteria, Archie and other single Gamemasters and employees patronized Scottie's and other local restaurants a great deal. They saw much of each other at these meals, so they tended to be social occasions. Occasionally, a group of them got together to go someplace unusual for dinner, just for fun. Which explained why, two nights later, Archie and a group of friends had still been shooting the breeze and drinking their last drinks at well after two o'clock in the morning, somewhere in western Canada.

It was no excuse, but it certainly contributed to Archie's morning fog as he rolled out at 0800 to the sound of Max calling his name. Also, because he was so regular, he knew that if he hadn't shown up by 0900, Trann would be demanding loudly to know the reason why. He heard Max repeating, "Call for you, Archie. Wake up, wake up."

"All right, I'm awake," he groaned. He slid into his place at his desk and snapped on the viewer, expecting to see Trann. Instead, he saw a young woman. His first thought was, Thank God she can't smell my breath. "Good morning," he said.

She was staring. "Good morning. I'm... sorry to wake you."

Too late he saw the shoulders of the olive-green uniform. Just recover the situation as best you can, he told himself, forcing a smile. There was absolutely no point in telling an ECM soldier that this wasn't his normal behavior. The two industries dealt with each other in a civilized fashion now, but bad opinion could be so easily cultivated. "You didn't. I was being lazy today. How may I help you?"

"I'm Lieutenant Sheila McAllen from the Office of Public Relations. I'm getting in touch with you about some publicity for the liver cell work being done at Walter Reed West."

"Ah, excellent!" Archie sat up straight. "I had thought, perhaps, a virtual tour, but a little less blood than the tour I do with the surgeons."

A tight professional smile. "Soldiers are used to blood, Mr. Chamberlain."

So she was going to take the high road, he thought. "Yes, but not inside, where it belongs. They're used to seeing it in all the wrong places."

"I suppose that's true," she admitted.

"That's where I like it best, myself, inside where it belongs." He had no intention of forcing any confrontation of ideals.

"I agree." The Lieutenant had dimples. Her sun-blond hair framed a tan face. She looked like she might have grown up along the California seashore. Her accent sounded like it, too, as if she could be warm and relaxed in the sun. "My superior officers are very interested in our involvement in this project."

Archie nodded. "It makes us all look good. I'm sure your higher-ups want to be on the scene as much as mine."

Again, she agreed. "That's where the longest delays will occur, I'm afraid. It's difficult getting approval and making arrangements."

Archie considered her words for a long moment. He stared so long, in fact, that she asked, "Mr. Chamberlain? Is something wrong?"

"Oh, no. It just sounds so pompous for me to say that's not a problem on my end, because I'm in charge."

"Oh, but you have supervisors, not to mention the owner," she countered.

"There is an office manager, a handler, if you will. His job is to fill the inkwells and make sure we haven't triple-booked our appointments. The Gamemaster owns the business, not the projects. He knows if he stuck his finger in most pies, he'd slow down the work, so generally, he doesn't." Archie was reasonably certain he was making full sentences. "A decent cup of tea, Max." Max, who had been anticipating that request, slid a mug of hot tea out of the desk-hatch. Archie took a sip. "So. If this will be a committee meeting, why don't you set it up on your end, somewhere on your turf, and just assume I can make it?"

"So would our first meeting be to set up a virtual tour, or to arrange the press announcement, or would we meet to go over to Gamemaster Inc.?"

Archie blinked. "I'm sorry? We're not communicating. None of the above."

She flushed. "Mr. Chamberlain— "

"We wouldn't 'set up' anything. We would take the virtual tour."

"Until we meet, I can't get clearance for outside equipment. Or movers, or a room to set up virtual reality equipment."

Archie took another long drink of tea. He no longer felt like his tongue adhered to the roof of his mouth. To himself, he said, "Yes. I am making full sentences." To Lieutenant McAllen, he said, "We are not communicating. There will be nothing to set up because I am there."

"If you plan to facilitate the equipment— "

"I'm sorry, I'm being rude. I never interrupt, and I've interrupted you twice. I am not the facilitator for the equipment. I am the equipment."

"You're hard-wired?"

"Nothing so crude. Make your arrangements. You'll see."

Her mouth tightened. "I'll take you at your word, then."

"Very well. Looking forward to it. Thank you."

That over, he cleaned up, dressed, got one piece of toast, and set off for the office, to make his promises come true.

The next day, Archie walked carefully along the corridor of a game simulation, examining the rocky walls of a castle dungeon. "So why does it look so phony, Max? This is an excellent game. We ought to be paying the author a fortune for this simulation, instead of receiving complaints from every tester."

"To my receptors it is technically perfect," Max replied. "You made notes on the testers' comments, saying 'Human receptivity issue.'"

"I did, did I?" Archie touched the wall and felt smooth, warm, cut, polished stone. "Hm. For one thing, it's scent-free. We could give it a cold, damp underground scent. We don't have to go to any great depths, not to the point of mimicking real dungeons, just a clean underground smell." He ran his hand along the wall thoughtfully. "Oh. Got it. They look fine, but the feel is wrong. These are tombstones, Max. Worse than that, modern American graveyard tombstones."

"Explain, please, Archie."

"The author's from North America, and took his data on stone for the virtual walls from computerized measurements he took of tombstones in his local suburban graveyard. He even went to the graveyard on a sunny day to record the tactile data. The stones are polished, they're warm, and they're clean. This isn't what a stone wall in a castle should look like, nor what it should feel like. Send him some data on stone from— Glamis Castle, that ought to do. Tell him to interpolate from it to this, and throw in some random variations." Archie touched his lapel badge. "We're done. Save, file, and exit."

"Noted, saved, and filed," said Max, as the walls of Archie's cubicle appeared around him once again.

Trann was at the partition entry, waiting. "Do you know a Lieutenant McAllen?"

"Sure do. ECM Public Relations."

"Glad to know they realize they need it. She checked your credentials, the newbie," said the Gee-Nine Lab Manager disparagingly. Seeing that Gee-Nine badge was all one needed to know.

Archie chuckled. "She hasn't seen me do any tricks yet. I'll educate her."

"Liaison for the Walter Reed West business?"

"Yes. First big job, I think. And I don't inspire trust by saying I'll be alone without equipment or an entourage."

"You might have an entourage, unless you can talk him out of it. I gather their brass has been in touch with our brass."

"So that's why you're hanging around. I didn't think it was my credentials. I don't care if he comes or not, Trann. He hasn't seen the whole show, either."

"If you don't care, then I don't care. It looks like 1500 hours today is the time, then."

"What time's it? 1330 hours. Time enough for lunch."

"You are eating too much. If you do not start scheduling yourself for the gym on a regular basis, I will. You will also ditch the cookies with your afternoon tea, and I have told Shiera Walton that the next time she drags you along for drinks with her idiot husband and his friends, I will make her life a living hell." Shiera Walton was the Gee-Eight Lab Manager, and no one knew how to make life hell like a fellow Manager.

"I hope you didn't call Alan an idiot to her face, or his," Archie commented, amused. "He's an AC-tor."

"If he can act, then I can train elephants to tap dance," Trann contradicted, then added, "I didn't. But do stay clear of them off the job, Archie. When they blow, he would be stupid enough to try to blame you for alienation of affections. There's no limit to what he might try."

"I've never understood why Shiera can't see what a boob he is."

Trann shot back, "What makes you think she can't? What makes you think she ought to stay home alone, not doing anything and not having fun? You know Sheira Walton is not a fool. You can't be a good manager if you don't have insight on plenty of people. You don't get an insight on other people if you don't get out there and live life yourself."

"That's a hell of a way to do it," Archie objected.

"To each his own. I admit, Shiera's way is not my own. Don't for a moment think she doesn't know that the fun will end some day. But right now— there's a lot of fun."

Lieutenant McAllen met him at the guardhouse. She glanced behind him, obviously looking for the rest of the parade.

"Nothing here but me, Lieutenant. Why, wasn't Trann very comforting?"

"No. I had understood that the Gamemaster was coming."

"Schedule conflict. He'll see it later."

Her voice was sharp. "This is a fine time to tell me, Mr. Chamberlain. I've got General Carpenter here, and some other very important people, and he doesn't show."

"Lieutenant." Archie opened his blue eyes wide. "You're going to make a terrible egotist of me if I must keep repeating, 'This is my show, not his. You have me and you do not need anything else.' You trust your specialists in their own areas, don't you? Now, please trust me, in mine."

She pulled herself together. "I'm sorry. You must think I'm an awful greenhorn."

"I never said so." But Trann did, he thought. "Now come on, it's showtime."

A smile broke through for the first time. "Break a leg, Mr. Chamberlain."

She showed him into a room with a rectangular conference table and about twenty people, all in uniform. Six were on one side of the table, the rest in seats back against the walls. They had left an entire side open for Archie's non-existent parade. The setting was actually perfect for what he intended, so he remained standing.

"I must apologize to you, and to Lieutenant McAllen, for false pretences," Archie said to them all. "The Gamemaster, as you may know, planned to attend this session, and I told him he wasn't needed and that he would only be in my way. He booked another meeting and he will see this on computer delay in an hour or two."

"Monte Carlo Amusement Park?" General Carpenter asked, with a dry smile. He had met General Carpenter before, at another joint-venture conference.

"Oh, so that made the news. Yes, he's been gathering reports in case he needs to do a little housecleaning. I think he's drawn walking papers for everyone from the CEO to the janitor." He turned back to his hostess.

Lieutenant McAllen introduced him to the officers around the table, and mentioned that they had received Dr. Bane's published information on the new techniques.

"Well," Archie said, launching into his talk, "I refer you to Dr. Bane's work for the medical aspects. What I want to show you is how we use non-invasive nanite probes to gather data for a room-sized enlargement, where one or many specialists can confer on a specific liver problem with no damage to the patient. The specialists view abnormalities and map out the path for physical repair nanites to enter and exit the system without doing it in real time. We've been calling the nanites the Tourists and the Road Crew. We're also using a third type of nanite for cleanup and carrying out excess materials. These nanites are most similar to the military microbots with which you are familiar."

General Carpenter spoke. "The Truckers." Yes, he had done his homework.

Archie nodded. "In fact, I adapted them from models of your biological-warfare cleanup microbots. If you think my demo is getting too gory, just sing out, all right?"

General Carpenter nodded. "Go ahead, Mr. Chamberlain."

"All right. Max. What news of the world?"

"Standing by, Archie," Max replied from the conference table speaker.

"What the hell— ?" one officer said. Another newbie, Archie realized. "I thought we just bought a new firewall to keep out invasive software!"

"And a very good firewall it is, too," Archie agreed, "some of Gamemaster 8 Tenian's best work." He saw Carpenter stifle a smile. "Begin the liver simulation demo, Max."

The entire room shifted. Those at the table now sat on a fold of liver, with the gall bladder to their right and its duct apparently running across their laps to the hepatic artery nearby. Those near the walls found themselves sitting and standing in more of the liver's right lobe, while it trailed away to the left lobe (on Archie's right).

Archie did his spiel, introducing the nanites and explaining their mechanical functions and sources of power. He enlarged his presentation to the cellular level and had the nanites enter to show samples of their work, highlighting various types of liver cancer cells and accommodations the nanites made for them.

Once they got over the initial shock of sitting inside a human liver, the conference attendees asked intelligent questions. Archie answered some and referred some to the physicians, lawyers, and contract negotiators. He finished his presentation, and answered a few final questions. Then he told Max to clear the simulation. The room returned to its original condition. He heard Lieutenant McAllen breathe deeply.

They got down to the business of press releases, operations, research rights, and access to information. Archie answered technical questions, asked Max about contract questions, and guaranteed open rights to information. Out of the corner of his eye, Archie saw Lieutenant McAllen scribbling away busily in her wordpad, taking as many notes as the others.

Finally, General Carpenter thanked Mr. Chamberlain for his time. Archie knew it was his cue to leave. Lieutenant McAllen escorted him out to the main entrance.

As she walked with him, she stared straight ahead and said, "I think I owe you about a dozen different apologies."

"Not necessary."

"...but I'm amazed that you're not arrested for violating almost as many security rules."

"Max, you mean."

"Max most of all. He took over part of a government facility and turned it into a giant liver, and back again."

"You don't seem to have any idea how many components of your daily work are off-the-shelf technology from Gamemaster Inc. and its subsidiaries, not original ECM research. No one asks and we don't tell. I hate to burst your bubble by informing you, but probably seventy per cent of the technology of the Earth Combined Military is purchased off-the-shelf from Gamemaster Inc. Another twenty per cent is contract work, done by same. I hope, by the way, that explains the resentment of many Gamemaster Inc. employees, when they feel ECM is biting the hand that feeds it. The Gamemaster Inc. computer, Max, can slide through almost any electronic or electric technology, but of course, he slides through our own best. He's invasive, but not malicious. He leaves nothing behind him unless asked to do so."

"Does he take?" she asked dryly.

"I have no information on that point."

"But you. The virtual presentation. No goggles, no special suit, no gloves, no wires, no special room..."

Archie tapped his Gee-9 badge. "All right here." He let her touch the little metal badge.

"It's set to me. No one else can use it."

"Which is why kidnapping Gamemasters never works," she said thoughtfully.

"Exactly. Or stealing their badges. When you have Max, the Gee-9, and the badge together, you have Archie Chamberlain's traveling road show."

"Well, I have received quite an education today. Thank you."

"You're welcome. No doubt, if you hang around West Meg long enough, we shall meet again."

"I doubt it," Lieutenant McAllen replied. "One of us lives on the wrong side of the tracks." Her dimples returned. "I'm not saying which one."

"Naturally not," said Archie.

The little shuttle labeled GAMEMASTER INC. BUSINESS parked unobtrusively at the edge of the pad set aside for spaceship landings. The pilot waited with the ship as two figures emerged to join the Adults Only section of the theme park.

"It was a good presentation," Gee said. "I think you covered all the basics, and you were well-received by West Meg ECM. That is hopeful."

"It is," Archie agreed. "Speaking of ECM, what was that message you were listening to on the way here?"

"Too cryptic to unravel." He slipped a memory chip from his pocket, and once again clicked the tiny "on" switch with his thumbnail.

It spoke in a masculine voice. "'In view of recent events, your presence is requested in Commander Scott Marsden's office 1100 hours 2 January. Office of Special Services, West Meg division.'"

"Marsden," said Archie thoughtfully. "I should know that name. It'll come to me. I hate to rely on Max for everything. I've got a memory, poor as it is sometimes. What have you got going beside the liver business with them?"

"Several projects. We've been getting along fairly well. It could refer to any of them."

Parts of Parc Monte Carlo stood empty and dark, although it was the evening of New Year Day and the sun had not yet set.

Archie grumped, "It's still a fault of humanity that we want to kill ourselves for fun."

Gee was dressed in his finest black evening clothes. The cloth and the cut spoke money, although black was always black. It was his signature color and style. "For me, it's in the job description."

"That's as may be," said Archie. "The rest of us sign liability waivers to compensate for our own stupidity."

"That is for human error. They can still sue if the equipment breaks. However, it's personally more cost-effective to keep the money, avoid the maintenance, and hire your relatives."

"Pretty sure that's what happened, aren't you? And what about law and order?"

"It gets paid by the hour here, from what I understand."

They strolled toward the Airmaze.

The barker in front of the Airmaze saw them approach. Apparently their nationality stood out enough for him to speak to them in English, for he said, "We don't encourage that ride, gentlemen."

Archie stepped forward, and his companion dropped back into nearby shadows. "Oh? Why not?"

"It's dangerous. Often fatal. We don't cover insurance."

"Can't I sign something?" As Archie's blue eyes flicked around the area, he spotted the observation cameras, emergency speakers, fire hoses, and electrical lines. With all these materials available for Max to back him up, he was in no physical danger.

"No," said the barker flatly.

"Suppose I want to take the risk, anyway?"

"I'll actively discourage it." There was a dangerous tone in the barker's voice.

Archie pulled out his credit bar and prepared to push it in the slot. The man's hand slapped over the slot. Archie said levelly, "I think you'd better send for the park manager."

"I am the manager."

It was not surprising to find the manager defending the biggest ride, after the expose' on this park that had just appeared on worldwide news. "It's a

Gamemaster ride in one of the most famous amusement parks in the world, on the busiest day of the year." Archie did not move. "There should be a line for it, dangerous or not."

The man's other hand made a motion behind the post, obviously summoning assistance. Two large burly men appeared almost immediately. "I think you should move on," the barker said menacingly, "and go break your neck somewhere else."

"Oh, no, Signor Ravenna," Archie contradicted, "I want to see this ride."

The barker froze at the mention of his name. He noticed the little pin on Archie's lapel for the first time. The Gamemaster had sent someone here! It was that damn reporter, talking about the darkened rides and the number of employees here who seemed to be relatives and friends. Ravenna's tone changed. "Did you come from the home office?"

"What would you expect? The Gamemaster does watch his own people."

"Look here," Ravenna said persuasively. "We should have a little talk about this. It's due for some maintenance, you see? I'm worried about a serious accident." He waved off the bruisers hurriedly.

"According to your report, it received its regular maintenance work Monday," said Archie.

A shrug. "The guy didn't come. I couldn't tell West Meg that."

"But you did. And had receipts for a maintenance man who seems to be a half-brother of yours."

"Look, don't ride the ride. It's not safe."

"It should be safe."

"But these dumbheads don't know how to pilot a ship. I've lost three this year."

"That's the average. You know that's a perfectly ordinary figure in an aging report." Archie paused. "Which is why you used three. How could they have died in a ride that wasn't operational? I wonder if the local hospitals could match your figures. Which hospital did you take the casualties to, Signor Ravenna?"

"Now, let's not get into that. Just take my word and don't take the ride."

"Oh, I wasn't planning to." Archie had led the barker through all the preliminary questions and answers. He stepped aside. "He is."

Gee stepped out of the shadows and into the light. Archie had never considered how terrifying the dark figure might appear, especially to someone with a guilty conscience. It was as if the devil had come to Monte Carlo. Gee's eyes bored into the manager's. The Day of Reckoning had come.

Worse than that, Armageddon spoke Italian. "You have taken my money and violated the contract."

"I swear I didn't! I swear I didn't!"

"Then this ride should be open and in use!"

"They are bad pilots! They will kill themselves!"

"They cannot learn on a ride that is closed! You have taken my money. You lied about maintenance! You have hired— *these*— " his voice was contemptuous as he regarded the other men and pronounced two or three adjectives and a noun that were not in Archie's Italian repertoire— "to make my business fail, my name worthless. This ride will come back to life, or you shall pay."

"I have broken no law."

"How many officials you bribed is not my concern. You have broken my contract. You will repay what you have stolen from me. *You will repay.*"

Hell, thought Archie, he is theatric! And he's got it just right. By the time he's done, they'll be convinced he's Satan on Earth. Archie walked over to the main panel and hit the switches. The Airmaze lights and panels went from Standby to Operational. Archie muttered into a tiny speaker, "Max? All OK?"

In an equally tiny voice, Max replied, "Running diagnostics now." In a moment, he said, "Routine maintenance items have not been replaced, but all parts are functional at the moment."

Archie turned and nodded at Gee.

The Gamemaster climbed into the Airmaze ship with the easy swing of long experience, slipped on the helmet, and reached for the canopy latch. The lights and activity were attracting people from all over Parc Monte Carlo. "Let us see if this is as maladjusted as you claim, or whether it is the staff that needs adjustment."

Archie shoved his credit bar into the slot, and registered payment. Two other toughs appeared, probably signaled by the use of the credit bar. With Max at his back, Archie was perfectly capable of dealing with them, and intended to. However, it was unnecessary. They looked at his face, then at the Gee-9 badge on his lapel, then decided they had business elsewhere.

Behind them, the ship took off.

Archie knew what was going to happen, or he would have screamed like Signor Ravenna. The ship did not enter the Airmaze; it went straight up.

There were gasps on the ground as the spectators got a stunt show they had not even paid for. The little ship rolled loop-the-loops, made some mean curves, then shot high into the sky and headed toward them in a tailspin. Someone squealed. The ship pulled out nicely and made another lateral curve around the park.

"God in Heaven, what's he doing?" gasped the barker.

Archie, who was not a pilot and found flying simulations boring, watched the little ride turn into a stunt show. Max was making a recording of this, to be used in future promotions. "He's testing the ship. I certainly hope it passes," Archie said. "What a pity to be responsible for the death of the Gamemaster in a ship that failed to function properly. It would mean the end of life on earth— at least for a park manager."

The retros kicked in unevenly. The ship twisted. As it should. The ship settled daintily into its dock.

The canopy popped open. Gee climbed out. He might have been disembarking from a leisurely boat ride. "The mechanism needs cleaning, but it is certainly in good shape. The fault is not with the equipment. That much is certain." He looked around, at the faces he saw, secure in the knowledge he would make the news.

Ravenna slowly dropped to the ground.

"Fainted," said Archie in disgust.

Harry Goto piloted them back to West Meg. "I *hate* spotting for you," Archie repeated. "Is there anyone back there you did not sack?"

"Is there anyone back there who was not a relative of Ravenna's?" Gee countered. "Of course I sacked them. If there was anyone I missed, he or she will get the pink slip tomorrow. There's enough people looking for work that I can rebuild that park from the ground up. Why should I keep deadbeats?"

Harry cut in, interested. Like Gee, Harayuki Goto was a good pilot, and his boss was his favorite passenger. There was a familiarity among pilots that even Gennaro shared. It was perfectly normal for the correct Japanese to cut into a conversation about piloting, although he would have blushed crimson to interrupt any other topic. "How could they have the nerve to screw up the Airmaze? That's a joy. Everybody's crazy over that. In Yokohama, you have to get a two-week reservation! Cut that for cash? It's crazy! That's how I got my training, before I could get out into space for the real thing."

Gee nodded as if Harry's opinion only proved him right. "I don't mind a little greed. I want my people to have initiative. However, they are not welcome to the Maintenance, Publicity, and Insurance line items in addition to their salaries. If they want money for nothing, they can hit up the temples and the churches, not my business."

"Don't worry," said Archie. "There were journalists there whose feature stories in the Entertainment section just turned into the first news story of the year. The sun will have to go nova to shake you off the front page tomorrow." Harry, eyes intent on his panel, grinned and nodded.

"That was, of course, the idea," Gee said grimly. "According to Max, I have already received six applications for Ravenna's job. He's history, and his bad management of one of the most famous amusement parks in the world is on the news. He may be decent at managing something smaller than an ice-cream store, or he may not. I think I had an effect upon him." Well, a dead faint could be called an effect, Archie supposed.

Harry said, "I've got a brother-in-law who needs work."

"Does he speak Italian?" Archie wanted to know.

"He would if he had to," Harry replied, flashing that grin again.

"Well then, tell him to get his application in," said Gee, with one of his rare smiles.

Harry dropped them off at the Gamemaster Inc. pad on the top of Alpha Building, where the penthouse was located. As they walked across the sunny platform, Max spoke. "Welcome back, Gamemaster. I have a packet from John Arrow waiting on your desk."

"Good. I'll be right there."

"How is Arrow, anyway?" Archie asked.

"I have no idea. I haven't seen him for two months. He was working on a Special Operations project, I believe."

"You *believe?*" countered Archie.

"Actually, he's somewhere breaking code. The Venan Isolationists seem to be doing a lot of illegal buying and selling lately."

"Ah. I think I read somewhere that the Isolationists are stepping up their publicity efforts and becoming a hot item. Not as bad as Recover, though."

"Not as bad as Recover," Gee agreed. "The Isolationists are stodgy and conservative. They have a clear agenda, to make the rest of the universe go away and leave them alone. Journalists have a good idea who the leaders are, unlike Recover. Recover just seems to be at war with everything military."

"Speaking of military. See if Arrow's in the area. I think I could tolerate dinner with the two of you."

"Sounds good," Gee agreed. "Come to the office."

They descended to the top level, and into the corridor. The thick Oriental rugs, the artwork on the walls, the tapestries looped back occasionally to display a vase or sculpture to its best advantage, now looked familiar. The heavy ebony doors swung open as they approached. The homely little packet seemed out of place on the immense black-glass-topped desk.

A strange little wrinkle appeared on Gee's brow. "Paper," he said.

So it was. Archie watched, as puzzled as Gee, as he untied a string and unwrapped it from a tiny paper packet. Inside was a rough notepaper. Gee unfolded the paper and smoothed it out. He read it, then frowned and passed it on to Archie.

In equal puzzlement, Archie read:

"My only wish was to leave you the greatest gifts in my power. Promise me only that you will never give up."

"What the devil?" Archie frowned and turned over the paper wrapping. He saw LASCOMB & SWEENEY, ATTORNEYS AT LAW, and his heart sank.

Gee's lips were tight. "L and S."

"Probate." Archie sank onto a chair. "Love of God. He's dead."

Apparently, Gee's thoughts were on another track entirely. "Why did a career military man arrange to send me a final message through civilian lawyers instead of ECM Wills and Probate? They take care of their own."

Archie was not listening. He took a deep breath, and rubbed his hand across his mouth. It felt numb. For some reason, he could taste brandy. "Wh-what?"

"I said snap out of it and use your brain."

"Oh. Yes. Because of the deep love the ECM has for you, I'm sure. He probably decided years ago they would accidentally forget to tell you he died." Archie started. "Marsden! That incomprehensible robotic message you had on the memory chip in your pocket. That's Arrow's commanding officer, the one that shut off on me when I was back in Isidis Prep. That message was not his voice. It was ECM Standard. But he must have sent it."

"He must have," the Gamemaster said briefly. Only the shortness in his tone indicated how much he had been moved. "Tomorrow. We shall be there."

The two men quietly took a Gamemaster Inc. transport cross-town to ECM Headquarters. It was perhaps a quarter-hour until the time named in the official letter, for what was obviously the reading of John Arrow's last will and testament. They presented themselves at the main gate. There, they hit a snag. No one was expecting them. No, Commander Marsden was out, on assignment. Archie had visited Arrow here, once, but didn't know his peers very well. Casting around for an alternative, he suggested, "Well, could you see if Lieutenant Sheila McAllen from Public Relations is around? We've worked together, and perhaps she could find out for the Chief where the mixup is." It was the mention of the Chief, standing ominously silent nearby, that made the guard move a little faster. In a moment, they were escorted to the main gate of the West Meg ECM HQ.

Lieutenant McAllen waited for them. "Gamemaster? We haven't met, live. I'm Lieutenant McAllen. Mr. Chamberlain. To what do we owe the honor of this visit?"

Gee, who made a point of never looking surprised, let one eyebrow raise. "The meeting involving John Arrow, of course. I received a communication notifying me that it was today at 1100 hours. Now, no one seems to have heard of this meeting, or of him."

Now it was her turn to look blank. "Excuse me. I'll find out." She stepped to an intercom toggle. She spoke for a moment, listened, then turned back. "Gamemaster," she said, "the reading of the John Arrow's will was scheduled for January 2nd."

"Yes. And— ?"

"That was yesterday."

-4-

A Puzzling Legacy

For one stupefying moment, Archie thought she was telling them they had traveled forward in time, or been unconscious for a day. Surely they hadn't gone through a time warp while Gee was garnering publicity in Monte Carlo.

Then, the answer hit him. New Year Day fell between the last day of December and the first day of January on the New Solar Calendar. His relief at not being insane was overshadowed by the awareness of the battle they would be forced to undertake to unseal a dead soldier's possessions— if they hadn't already been destroyed. The expression on Lieutenant McAllen's face showed that she saw the problem as well.

The third party present had reached the same conclusion simultaneously. His tone showed that he was not amused. "Do not tell me you Neanderthals are still operating under the Gregorian calendar."

"It will correct itself on Leap Year Day," Lieutenant McAllen said automatically.

"It never will," Archie contradicted, just as automatically, "and you know it. No one else in the solar system except Earth Combined Military still uses it."

Lieutenant McAllen opened her mouth to argue. Gee overrode them in a clear voice. "I want the information I was supposed to have. I want it within ten minutes." He never said or else what, which made his statements even deadlier. "We shall wait."

"I'll find it," she said, and took off.

Archie turned to Gee and muttered, "The Gregorian calendar!"

"Don't start. I am keeping my temper in check." His sphinxlike face told nothing.

"What I want to say would reduce this place to a cinder!" Archie exclaimed.

"You and I are so used to the 'Left Coast,' as they call it," said Gee, "that we forget there are people out there who will oppose any idea we set forth, no matter how good, simply because we suggested it. It was my grandfather who pushed the New Solar Calendar through, because it separated the year into months of equal length."

Archie admitted, "I've already got fundamentalists opposing the liver research because replacing cells on the microscopic level is against the will of God. But it's hard, Gee."

"That it is," said the Gamemaster.

The kid officer had grown up in the past two years. And to think that Archie had almost forgotten his name. "Hello, Gamemaster. Mr. Chamberlain, we meet again." Commander Scott Marsden grimaced. "The last time I saw you, I thought I was showing initiative by giving you the brushoff. I hope you'll accept my apologies."

Archie shook his hand. Lieutenant McAllen, unaware of Marsden's profound influence on Archie's life, looked on puzzledly. Archie demurred, "We were both manipulated by an old pro."

"It was a pleasure and a privilege to work with that old pro, I assure you." Marsden turned to the Gamemaster. "When I saw you on the news at Monte Carlo, I didn't connect the date shift, but I did assume you wouldn't make it back in time for the reading. It never occurred to me that since I sent the message to you as standard text from my apartment, not from the office, the header was New Solar Calendar and the Gamemaster Inc. computer wouldn't pick the military date discrepancy out of the text. It didn't hit me until McAllen 'phoned me that I'd cross-timed. You have my sincerest apologies."

"What happened to Captain Arrow?" Gee was unsmiling.

"Classified," Lieutenant McAllen murmured, before her superior officer could speak. If she issued a warning, it was too weak; if she meant to shove the stranger back in his corner, it was futile.

Gee's voice turned to ice. "Then go into the corridor so it won't hurt your ears."

In a nicer tone, Marsden nodded toward the door and said, "On out, McAllen."

"Yes, sir." She saluted stiffly and exited.

He motioned them to seats before his desk, then touched a speaker toggle. "Tell Behrens to bring in the box I put in storage yesterday, the sealed one with Arrow-slash-Chamberlain on it," he told it. Clicking it off, he explained, "He left something to each of you. I figured the name Chamberlain on the box would make less noise."

"Sound thinking," said Archie. "Thank you."

Marsden returned his attention to the Gamemaster. "You probably have a good idea what Venus is like. Those pocket stations are legendary. The technological sophistication the Venans have fused necessarily into their stations and by choice into their everyday lives have put them a quantum level above anything else in the solar system."

"I have heard that many of them are matriarchies, and many are repressive."

"True enough. I heard you have Gamemasters who are Venan runaways."

"One Gee-8, three Gee-Sevens, one Gee-5, and a number of first readers."

"I've met Tenian, the Gamemaster-8. Brilliant man. Ready to slash his wrists, I heard, when you picked him up. That life is all they know. They can't imagine not being Venan. I imagine Tenian could tell you or me a great deal about their underground."

"I suspect not. He made his way to Earth by conventional means. But I concur that their underground probably consists of men and women who feel they have nothing left to lose, and are consequently more vicious and desperate."

Marsden nodded. "The matriarchs are just as vicious putting down rebellions. The U.N. has objected so much to their tactics that an anti-Earth movement has started in retaliation."

"The Isolationists. I know."

"So. If a Venan bomb floats toward Earth, you can expect it to be technologically sophisticated and yet have no idea who launched it, Isolationists or underground. John went after it because he had a good idea which side was responsible, and therefore what resources they'd had available. He diverted it from populated centers, but was still defusing it when it went up. We lost four good officers, including John Arrow."

"Why didn't they leave it?"

"Who knows what it would hit eventually? A live bomb with Venan technology. Anything they do is so far beyond us— " Marsden rubbed his eyes. The door opened, and a man entered, pushing a floating trolley. It held a box about a meter on each side, labeled ARROW / CHAMBERLAIN in bold black letters. After he left, Marsden opened the box.

He lifted out one book after another. "These go to you, Mr. Chamberlain. They're antiques, and surely very valuable, particularly— " With an effort, he pulled out a leather-bound Bible. "This beauty." He added it gently to the pile of twenty or so books on his desk. Then he reached in with both hands, and pulled out a large wooden case.

Marsden opened it to reveal classic jade chess pieces, in green and white. The last item from the box had lined the bottom, a matching inlaid jade chessboard.

With everything out of the box, Marsden turned and said, "His will said his books go to Mr. Archie Chamberlain, who would appreciate them. The chess set goes to the Gamemaster, 'to help him remember all my little aggravations,' as he put it. There's a hard-copy of the will in the bottom of the box."

Gee remained silent. It was Archie who said, "Thank you. I'll cherish these." They re-packed the box.

Gee turned suddenly to the soldier. "Did anyone object to us taking these?"

"Not to my knowledge," Marsden replied.

Archie comprehended. "He means he didn't ask, Gee. He just took them and sealed them, rather than destroying them."

A little motion of Gee's head indicated that he understood. The intent look in his eyes told Archie something else as well. Gee was not silent due to emotion. He was silent because he was thinking hard. "We shall be honored to accept John Arrow's last gifts," he said.

Lieutenant McAllen was waiting for them outside. Archie, knowing whatever Gee said to her would be rude, cut in first. "Lieutenant, can you line up a transport for the front gate? Then we can give you back the trolley on the spot."

"I am perfectly capable— " Gee began.

"Be quiet," Archie told him, and turned again to Lieutenant McAllen. "Please."

She nodded, moved to a wall intercom, put in a call, and caught up with them. "On its way. I'll escort you to the gate."

"I am able to find the gate without your help." Gee's very tone was an insult.

Her eyes flashed with anger, but she replied neutrally, "You're a visiting dignitary, sir. It would be a pleasure to escort you out."

I daresay it would, thought Archie in amusement, seeing the offended flash in Gee's eyes as well. However, the Gamemaster made no reply.

At the gate, Gee loaded the box into the transport while Archie thanked Lieutenant McAllen. "I owe you one, and I hope you'll remember to collect."

She sounded as though she meant it when she said, "I'll be glad to do you a favor any time, Mr. Chamberlain. These cooperative ventures are beginning to work out rather well. Until we meet again."

They stopped first at Archie's apartment. Archie had empty bookshelves, enough for Arrow's books as well as his own. Gee watched him sort and shelve carefully. "I don't understand your fascination with them," he said. "They are static."

"They are timeless," Archie contradicted. "And, what you keep says a great deal about your thoughts and values. Look here." He ran his hand along one spine. "From Arrow, I might expect a Bible. But a copy of 'The Book on the Bookshelf' is a surprise. I'll have to think about 'Journeys in Tibet.' And they're all leather-bound, all keepers."

Gee was always willing to listen to information on how people thought. That went with his job. He regarded the books in a slightly different manner. "See if they tell you why John Arrow left me a chessboard. I have a finer one. He knew it. He used it. I don't collect chessboards."

"Perhaps it was all he had to give."

"*Why* was it all he had to give?"

"Perhaps you're making too much out of a last gift." Archie felt his temper rising.

"Perhaps you are too wrapped up in sentimentality to realize there is something wrong about that gift. That is why I had Marsden state, before a witness, that I had clear title to it before I left." His tone was meant to be a cold shower on Archie's mood.

It had exactly the opposite effect. "Dammit, Gee, just for once, can't you accept the gift without criticizing the giver?"

"You are being maudlin, which makes you ridiculous."

Archie growled, "I'm going to enjoy escorting you out of the building as much as McAllen did."

Gee was unimpressed. He hefted the half-empty box. "You and she are two of a kind. Hang up on your fancies and shut off your brains. When I find out why Arrow left me this, you will eat your words."

"Go be objectionable somewhere else."

"With pleasure." He left.

Archie suppressed an urge to call Lieutenant McAllen and offer to join forces in kicking Gee's well-tailored bottom.

Naturally, Trann was at his partition in less than half an hour from Archie's arrival at work that afternoon. "You are cordially invited to tell me why you and the Chief are in such rotten moods."

"We've just had too much of each other for a while."

"I gathered that," said Trann dryly, not moving.

Archie told him about Arrow's death. Then the trip to ECM HQ, the mixed-up dates, the meeting with Marsden, the row about the legacies. Usually, Trann stood and listened. This time, as Archie spoke, he pulled up a seat in Archie's cubicle and made himself comfortable. He continued to sit in thought as Archie finished his tale. After a moment, Trann said, "It does make one wonder."

"Not me."

"Well, you know I look at things from the Chief's point of view. As well as my own selfish interest, as far as the Chief is concerned. If there is no puzzle, it's a harmless diversion for him to exercise his ingenuity, and who knows what great ideas may be borne from it. If there is a puzzle, knowing the quality of Arrow's mind, it will be a whopper." Trann regarded Archie thoughtfully.

Knowing that a manager's job was to nag him worse than his own mother about his health, mental and otherwise, Archie warned, "Don't start."

"About your fear of death? Hadn't crossed my mind," said Trann with, for him, a broad smile. "Since I've already got you watching your weight and your social life, I won't lay more burdens upon you." Trann paused as if listening to a voice only he could hear.

Belatedly, Archie realized this was indeed happening; Trann kept Gee-Nine Lab business private by means of communications implants. "All right, chief. Shall I send Archie, or not?— Of course. He's on his way." Trann's attention was again on Archie. "Something has happened to Bet Berensen, and whatever it is, we didn't do it. Robinson wasn't in place yet. Go to the deep-level elevator next door, and to Security Ops, the map room. Security Chief Robinson and Malasha Masere from Personnel are there, trying to find her. But they are having trouble. They need a Gee-9 point of view."

"I'm on my way."

Archie took a lift from the Gamemaster 9 Labs to the ground floor of Building 4 East, and out the front entrance to Early Street. He ran along Early's moving walkway, dodging other pedestrians. Only some buildings had deep-level express elevators, and Building 4 East was not one of them. He ran inside Building 2 East to the Express elevator. It closed the moment he entered. Max said, "I am taking you to the Map Room, Archie."

"Thanks, Max." He felt the elevator changing directions, rising, dropping, as it left Building 2 East (possibly) and took him to Gamemaster Inc. Security Headquarters, wherever that was. He emerged in a well-lit cavern, almost as busy as the street had been. In tone, personnel, and general busyness, Gamemaster Inc. Security HQ was no different from ECM West Meg HQ except for being entirely underground.

Archie entered the Map Room. It was a control center staffed by about twenty grim-faced Security people, with sophisticated control panels and monitors in every direction. The technology surrounding them looked fully capable of starting Solar War Three, or stopping it. However, the technology was not Archie's concern. He glanced at the personnel as they stared mainly into maps on various monitors, but Archie himself went immediately to Gee. "What happened?"

"You tell me," Gee retorted. "We were fifty-five minutes from pickup when we lost contact."

"Did Bet have specific instructions?" Archie asked Robinson.

"Yes," the security chief replied, just as grimly. "Malasha sent 'em in her letter. 1700 hours, they were to be on their back porch, her and her grandmother."

"When the squad arrived, Bet was gone and her grandmother was dead on the living room floor," Gee continued. "It was a heart attack."

"Yes. But what caused it?" Archie stared intently at a map screen.

"I would guess— unwanted visitors," Gee replied. "Bet was also supposed to keep the letter with her. It's on the kitchen table. We had a tracer in it."

"Then she's being tracked, so she ditched it," Archie said.

"Thank you," Gee growled. "I'm with you so far."

Robinson slapped a console. "*No* tracks in the grass. *No* motion detected. *No* animals scuttling away. *Who's* chasing her, and where the *hell* did she go?"

Archie stared at the screen and imagined himself in Bet's place. It was far too easy to do, and probably beyond the ken of most people in this room. A place without Max, without mechanized help, where awareness of the world was a sin that could lead to a painful death. Harsh men who wanted to kill you, to punish you simply for surviving, nothing but your wits to protect you. Your family gone, or afraid to help you. In almost a trance, Archie replied, "She's being chased by people she knows well, who grew up with her, and know every trick in the region."

"Jess Quilter's gang," Malasha said suddenly. "We know the members' names from her letters, don't we? Hunt them up."

A Security operator had already placed an aerial view of a dirt road on the screen. It looked like an old-fashioned film— a motorcycle gang, overhead view, dust rolling around their wheels, on the road after something. A voice sang up to them, over the engines, "Where the hell is she? Thet gal is mine!"

Another voice called back, "She can't have gone far."

"Her Granny was the only relative who stood up for her," Malasha was saying in the background. "Her older sister has already been gang-raped by this bunch, and is living with an uncle who I suspect is picking up where they left off. Her father is a CSA vet who died of his injuries in a Vets hospital. Her mother was the subject of a family conference where she was ordered to marry the head of the house, this same uncle, after the father died. She put a gun to her head instead."

"Does Bet read?" Archie asked.

"Of course she does," Gee snarled.

"Not like that. - Max, does Delay have a public library?"

"Yes," Max replied.

"Is it open now?"

"No. It closed at 1800 hours, Archie. It is now 1830 in Delay."

"What's conventional communication there, videophone? And does the librarian have one at home?"

"Yes and yes," said Max.

Archie remembered the rigmarole Malasha had used to communicate with Bet via postal-service mail. She had created an artificial white-female-Christian persona that would be acceptable to the other family members who read the girl's mail. The uncles had thoroughly read everything, all right, not knowing the real messages were underneath the postage stamps. The tricks that worked for Malasha would work for him. "All right. I want to put a videophone call through to him or her, but the librarian must see and hear the simulacrum of a 14-year-old Caucasian girl named Molly— " he waved fingers at Malasha.

"Molly Miller," Malasha prompted.

"Molly Miller, with a West Meg accent, when I talk. And I want a full-range view of the librarian's apartment or house, in case of eavesdroppers."

"Standing by, Archie."

Archie glanced at Gee, who gave a brief nod. "Commence, Max."

A monitor shifted to show an antique little room full of collectible clutter. It reminded Archie of his parents' place, but tattier. An old woman entered, limping, and picked up the receiver. "Hello?"

"Hi," said Archie. "Sorry to bother you, but they said Bet Berensen was there."

"I haven't seen Bet all day," the woman said nicely. "Are you a friend of hers?"

"I'm her pen pal," Archie replied. "I'm visiting my cousins in Atlanta. My aunt said I could call, but Bet doesn't have a phone. But I know she liked the library a lot. I thought she might be there."

"Oh, no, Bet would never be here after dark," the librarian replied. "It's not safe. But I ought to see her tomorrow. I could give her a message."

"Just tell her Molly said hi. She'll know. What do you mean, not safe?"

"Oh, dear, you aren't from around here," the librarian sighed. "It's a dangerous place at night."

"Oh, you mean wild animals," said Archie, like a good ignorant West Megger. "I imagine Bet's a good runner, huh?"

"No, she has a bicycle and— and a club," said the librarian, biting her lip. "I-I won't run up your phone bill any longer, dear. I will be glad to tell Bet you phoned. If you want to plan ahead— When should Bet be here to take a daylight call from you?"

"I'm headed home tonight. Just give her my love," said Archie, "and God bless you," he added, like a good Christian.

"God bless *you*, Molly," said the librarian, "good-bye." After she terminated the connection, the librarian spoke to what she thought was an empty unhearing videoscreen. "And God help Bet, because I can't."

Gee's hands were flying over a console as Archie turned to him. "Club. Club. Here it is. A young man attacked a week ago in a tobacco field off a lonely road. Concussion. Just woke up today in the hospital. Name of Quilter."

"Jess Quilter, the sheriff's son. God *damn* it," Robinson swore. "Bet defended herself from an attack by the gang leader, and she's been waiting for the other shoe to drop for a week."

"The attack was on the direct route between the library and Bet's grandmother's house. Does the librarian know?" Gee asked.

"Of course she knows," Archie replied. "She's terrified. But she's not hiding Bet. She can't risk it. For a long time, though, the library's been Bet's safe haven." Archie stared at the screen some more, thinking.

"Max. Scan the area for a rusty Schwinn bicycle, two gears, at least fifty years old, red and white," Gee was saying.

"Scanning." Max paused. "Gamemaster, Mr. Sommerlin wishes to speak to you."

"Voice only, Max. – Mr. Sommerlin?" Gee yawned. "What may I do for you?"

"Sorry to wake you, Gamemaster." Apparently the CSA Consul was one of those misguided folk who thought rich men took afternoon naps, or something viler. It was men like Sommerlin who reinforced Gee's immense distaste for organized religion. "I was calling to tell you that I just received report of a disturbance from Commander Derleth. Delay is stirred up, for some reason."

"If you are asking if I have stirred up something in Delay, Mr. Sommerlin, the answer is no. I haven't had time. What sort of disturbance?"

"It looks like a manhunt. The entire county seems to be in on it. There's a motorcycle posse on the road, and sheriffs' patrols are out. Commander Derleth has indicated that he is going to send troops into the area to prevent a bloodbath. The Christian Council has armed vigilantes for a 'cleansing,' directly against mandates from Confederacy government. It was only local news, but the son of one of the Delay sheriffs was nearly bludgeoned to death last week."

"I saw that, yes. Where he was lounging inoffensively behind a tree with a knife and some rope."

"At any rate," Mr. Sommerlin continued stiffly, "it is not a good occasion to interfere in local politics."

"I have no intention of doing so. I only involve myself in situations that have some hope of success and improve my public image, Mr. Sommerlin. Good day." He shut off the connection. "Robinson! Have you found that bicycle?"

"I've found six." Robinson sounded sour.

Water! Archie felt a sudden inspiration. "It's smashed or in a tree."

"Got it!" Robinson exclaimed, "in a tree. Fifteen point seven kilometers northeast of the area we've been searching! No wonder we couldn't find her. She dodged us *all*!"

"Give me the map and be sure to include the river and the dam," said Archie.

Another technician stared superstitiously at the Gee-9 as she pulled up a map of the new area, complete with river at the top running southwest to northeast. There was a dam, a hydroelectric power station, and, further downstream, an abandoned lumber mill. Gee leaned forward, intent on the screen. "The lumber mill?"

Archie shook his head. "The turbines."

To his credit, Gee understood at once, and looked startled for a scant moment. Then he barked, "Robinson! How close have you got anyone? I need immediate action."

"We're almost there now."

"I want a diver out of sight in the water at the dam. For all we know, she may have already jumped."

"No," a woman spoke up, "I've got her on satellite pic. Ten minutes to the dam at her current rate of speed."

"The posse?"

"Way behind her."

"Good news. Blodgett's team was already in the area," Robinson announced. "He anticipated me asking them to start a quadrant-by-quadrant search." He paused. "Blodgett's in the drink. The dam crew didn't see him slide in from the other shore. He's got an extra mask with him, too. The rest of the team is in the woods, standing by."

"Now we wait," said the Gamemaster, "to see if Archie guessed right."

"Oh, I guessed right," Archie said softly. Bet Berensen's last hurrah; she said so.

"This will be cake," said Gee in a satisfied voice.

It is a matter of record that he was also right. The girl evaded the barricades at the top of the dam as if they weren't there, and jumped. By the time the dam's warning klaxon sounded, Blodgett had grabbed her from below, shoved a mask on her, and taken her to the bottom of the reservoir, far beyond the turbines that would have killed her. An escape outlet brought them through viaducts into the trees, where the little Gamemaster Inc. shuttle jetted the team out of an area they weren't supposed to be in.

Bet Berensen was officially deceased.

Archie and Malasha left with Gamemaster. He was almost purring in the lift. "I'm still on time for the Olympic Association dinner. I shall attend that, then get myself invited to someone's private home for after-dinner drinks, and not return to Alpha until around 0400. That ought to convince Mr. Sommerlin of my virtue— at least as far as the CSA incident is concerned."

"Some day, you'll have to introduce him to Bet," Archie said.

"Some day," Gee agreed. "Atlanta my ass." He stepped out of the elevator, into the corridor of his own penthouse. The lift doors snapped shut again.

Archie looked up at Malasha. "Where shall we dine?"

"We don't," she replied apologetically, "although I would love a rain check, you know that. But I will wait for Bet to arrive here, for the rest of my life if I have to."

"Drop us off at street level, Max."

"Very well, Archie."

Malasha's soft, reedlike voice rose and fell as she asked, "How did you know, Archie? Don't tell me it's because she's a Gee-Nine. I won't believe it. The bicycle— and the river. You *knew*."

Archie shook his head. He felt tired, and somehow sad. "I only hope Bet likes it here."

"What's not to love, after the life she's led?" Malasha asked, surprised.

"Well, it might not be the paradise she's expecting. There could be some big culture gaps. Starting with Gee and his attitude that all religions are pestilential epidemics that should be squashed like beetles."

"Oh, don't talk to me about culture gaps," said Malasha sharply. "My father is still keeping six cows and a bull on standby for the day when I meet the right man." At Archie's tired grin, she softened. "In all seriousness, Archie, I understand what you mean, and I will do everything I can to keep her from being sorry the lake did not get her."

"That's all I ask, love. Sorry to be a wet blanket."

"You really don't look well, Archie."

"I know. It's been a strain. I might take it easy for a day or two. I think I'm coming down with something." They reached street level. Malasha touched his cheek and he smelled her perfume, that odd sweetgrass scent he always liked, for just a moment. Then they parted company. Archie went home for the night.

He arrived to a neat and clean home, since Max was in charge of all cleaning operations, and did them while Archie was absent. One of the first rules he had laid down at Rhodalia Row was that no robot was to enter his presence, because it was too much like a zombie. Archie had a horror of dead bodies or items relating to them. It was one of his few true handicaps, to bolt from the room at the sight of a robot as others did from spiders or hornets. By the time he arrived, the flat was clean, classical music was playing softly over his sound-system, and the smell of a chop and potatoes wafted in from the kitchen hatch. Nothing could have been more calculated to dispel his pessimistic mood.

Sitting in a comfortable chair, his after-dinner coffee and brandy beside him, Archie stared idly at the beautiful leather book bindings. Like his own, Arrow's books were well-used. He rose, hauled out the great Bible, and drew it down into his lap. The scent of fine leather wafted up as he refreshed his memory from its pages. Water. Where was that? "On the willows we hung up our lyres and wept, For our captors taunted us, saying, Sing us the songs of Zion..." No, that wasn't right. He was mixing up the words with a hymn. Did this Bible have a concordance, and what did it say about willows?

The Bible fell open to an entirely different place. Apparently it was creased there, for there was no bookmark or turned-up page. Archie read the random passage, and wondered if it was coincidence that the book fell open here. Why had this particular passage meant something to Arrow? Archie felt himself dozing off. Oh, well. If Arrow had indeed left a riddle on this subject, Archie hoped he would be able to recognize both the riddle and the answer when he saw it. If there was a sign that the riddle had something to do with threes, this passage would be a warning that it would be especially prolonged and drastic.

Whether it was the brandy, the early night, or the solace of the beautiful old book, Archie slept a peaceful sleep.

Archie felt much better in the morning, and changed his mind about taking a day or two off. Besides, he had other plans. Trann's badgering about exercise had had an effect. Archie scouted around for a cricket club and found one. Inevitably, it was called the West Meg Players. The name may have been trite, but they had a good record among the North American amateurs. Archie's personal record was not spectacular, but it was not bad, either. They welcomed him. As a new player, he felt he had to make at least a presentable show. Saturday they were playing double innings, which would take most of the day, against a team called (just as inevitably) the Gorham Cliffs Gentlemen. With Trann's blessing, Archie left after lunchtime to go downtown to the indoor pitch owned by the club. Other equally interested Players had taken time off from their work for the same reasons. They practiced their bowling, batting, and fielding. By the end of practice, Archie was convinced that none of them would make history, but neither would they disgrace themselves. They needed a good bowler, not one of Archie's strengths, to become outstanding.

He was replaying the day's practice in his mind as he walked the last distance to his flat, his bag of gear over his shoulder. The winter darkness fell early and there was a threat of snow in the sky. It never snowed much, this far south, in this climate, but the promise was there. He would almost like to see some snow. A day or two with his folks, that would be nice. Then, to come back here, away from the snow, back to Gentlemen and Players in an indoor arena. It would be the best of both worlds.

In the lift to his flat, Max spoke. "Gamemaster would like you to join him for dinner at 1800 hours. Cocktails at 1730 hours. He knows that you have no conflicting appointments. It will be at his penthouse, dress for dinner, please."

Archie sighed. That meant someone who needed to be impressed, most likely a foreign dignitary. "Ask Trann if I can get out of it."

"Trann has already said under no circumstances are you to skip this dinner."

He sighed again. "All right, all right. Let me clean up and I'll be there."

"Very well, Archie. I shall notify him of your intention."

Archie showered, shaved, and dressed for dinner. He had finally forced himself to buy new black-and-whites when his outfit from Isidis-Mars frayed at the edges. He hated trotting out dinner dress, envying Gee's ability to be cutting-edge classy without apparent effort. He made the familiar trek to Alpha, took the lift to the top floor, and walked down the carpeted corridor to the penthouse. He rang the bell, and stared when the door opened.

There was no question in his mind that he was seeing a butler. Without thinking, Archie exclaimed, "Great Heaven! How much did you cost?"

"Good evening, Mr. Chamberlain. You are expected," said the man, with a trace of an English accent.

Archie recovered himself. "My apologies. That was rude, no matter who you are. Thank you for taking it so well."

"Of course, sir."

"And your name is— ?"

"Haviland, sir. May I take your coat, sir?"

Archie handed his topcoat to the butler, unobtrusively bumping his hand. To his embarrassment, Haviland understood the gesture.

"The Gamemaster informed me of your aversion to robots, sir. Please be assured that I am flesh and blood."

"Again, my apologies, Haviland."

"Certainly, sir." Haviland showed him toward the smaller lounge. "We will use the Puget Rooms this evening, sir."

Archie was familiar with that little salon and dining room, with its white walls, simple dark furniture, and tasteful Pacific Northwest artifacts. "I take it this is a small gathering, then," said Archie.

"Indeed, sir. There are nine guests." He ushered Archie into the salon. Several people stood with drinks, and turned at his entrance. Apparently, Archie was the last to arrive.

Archie declined a cocktail, and took a good look at his fellow guests. Trann and his wife, Delora, he knew. This was not the first function he had attended with the two natives from the underwater Marianas City. Malasha Masere was dressed in her finest Maasai dress and jewelry, always saved for special occasions. The well-perfumed aggressive blonde in rustling blue satin with Chief Robinson had to be Mrs. Robinson, and proved so upon introduction. Danny Blodgett, Security rank-and-file and uncomfortable in the presence of so much brass, introduced his girlfriend, Selina, who had plainly read too many fashion magazines. She was overdressed and over-make-up'd as only the magazines encouraged. That left only one introduction.

A quiet, dark-haired girl with large brown eyes looked up to him. There was great weariness in those eyes. The Gamemaster Nine badge she wore was extraneous information. Archie smiled and quoted softly, "'So this is the little woman who started this great war.'"

Gamemaster looked blank. Not Bet Berensen. She recognized the quotation. It had a place in Confederate history, what Abraham Lincoln had said upon introduction to Harriet Beecher Stowe, the author of Uncle Tom's Cabin. Her lips parted in a genuine return smile. Her face, still clear and beautiful, looked like it belonged to a different person now. "Hello, Mr. Chamberlain," she said, in a very attractive CSA drawl. She held out her hand. "I'm glad to meet you at last."

He clasped her hand. It was warm and equal to the pressure. She wore a plain black dress and simple slippers. Nonetheless, she was the center of attention, and seemed to be able to handle it. "Welcome to the Left Coast, Miss Berensen. I hope you enjoy living and working here as much as I do."

Such an intimate gathering in Gee's own penthouse was rare. Archie rightfully guessed that he was trying hard not to overwhelm his young acquisition. Bet was silent most of the time, and smiled rarely. Her silence did not seem gloomy, but rather, she was listening and taking everything in.

Sitting on opposite corners of a table for ten at dinner, Archie did not get a chance to chat with her. On the other hand, with Malasha to his left in the hostess position and Selina immediately to his right, he felt assured of pleasant company. He and Malasha soon put Selina at her ease, and chatted like old friends. The food was good, of course. It was novel to see Gee, who never kept servants, being waited on by a butler. Archie suspected it was a concession to humanity, and wouldn't dare say anything to put Gee's back up. It relieved Archie, who loathed robots.

Selina was indeed a West Meg High graduate now trying to make a living as a dancer. She was surprised to find these strangers talking intelligently about dance, and soon learned that their friend Shiera Walton, the Gee-8 Lab Manager, was also a dancer in her limited spare time. She knew Shiera's teacher and troupe. Across from Archie sat Delora, and next to her, Security Chief Robinson.

At one point, Delora took a sip of her drink and said, "So. Archie. Both my husband and Chief Robinson tell me they set a thief to catch a thief. Or rather, a Gee-9 to catch a Gee-9. And you came through with flying colors."

"That he did," Chief Robinson confirmed.

"I asked him how he did it," Malasha interjected, in her softest voice, eyes upon Archie, "and he would not say."

He realized that table talk had eased off. They were all looking and listening now. He met Bet's gaze. He asked her, "Do you know?"

"Yes," she said simply.

He shrugged. "No one else needs to, then."

"It's all right, Archie." She called him Archie, he realized— not Mr. Chamberlain, as she had. Even across a table, without conversation, she recognized a like mind. That was the quality the GCODE searched for. In a short sentence, she had sealed the link.

"Well— " Archie leaned back uncomfortably, blue eyes intent on his wineglass. He felt like he was undressing in public. "It struck me that the bicycle was Bet's only freedom. She would deal with her freedom or its ending. I had to look it up later. Psalm 139."

"Oh, the Bible?" Malasha asked interestedly. "I have never read it."

"The more shame you, then, pretending to be Molly Miller. Depending on what version of Psalm 139 you read, on either the willows or the poplars there, we hung up our lyres, our harps, or our lives, because our captors taunted us, saying 'Sing the songs of Zion.'" Again, Archie felt unclothed. "Beside the waters of Babylon. So I looked for churned-up waters that would finish me off and no mistake. I mean, finish Bet off."

The Gamemaster sighed, and spoke to Trann. "This is why we have Gee-Nines."

"Amen to that," said Trann happily.

Archie brought his after-dinner coffee into the Gamemaster's office. "Haviland told me you wanted to see me in here for a moment?" He saw Arrow's chess set. "Have you got something, then?"

"Yes, I do," the Gamemaster replied. "Prepare to eat your words."

"Cheerfully. What have you got?"

"Arrow's will said, 'Remember my little aggravations.' Losing a game was aggravating. So, I started thinking about the games I had lost to Arrow. Usually, if he managed to nail me, it was a knight that came to his rescue."

Archie lifted the knights, palming two of them at a time. He lifted one green jade knight carefully.

Gee nodded confirmation. "I asked Max to compare the weights of matching pairs, but yes, that's the one. Go ahead. I've left it loose."

Gently Archie pried loose a thin bottom shell of green jade to reveal a cavity in the knight's base. A rough paper— like the note— was rolled to plug the gap. Carefully, he pulled it out, unrolled it, and read Arrow's familiar handwriting:

> "Bravo, G.!
> If you have got this far, then I am unmistakably dead.
> For my sake, Find these three things, *in order*:
>   - a stone monkey
>   - a dead bird
>   - a brass mouse.
> Solving this riddle will enrich your life in a way I cannot describe."

After that was his signature, John Arrow.

Archie's heart sank as he thought of the warning passage in the old Bible. Threes.

Gee saw the dismay on his face. "Any ideas?"

"Not any concrete ones," Archie evaded.

"Then some non-concrete ones?" Gee's voice had an edge. "After all, you are a Gee-Nine. And a good puzzle solver, as you've proven."

"I have no idea how to solve Arrow's riddle," Archie replied.

"You have the answer," Gee accused.

"No, I have not."

"Give me what you have, then!"

Archie's mouth tightened. "*No.*"

Gee glared at him. Then, he acknowledged the obvious fact that Archie had no intention of yielding. In a very mild tone, Gee asked, "Why not?"

Archie matched his tone. "It would confound us both, rather than help. It's not the answer to the riddle, it's a clue to keep you from going too far wrong." Gee was satisfied with that answer. It's as much as he's ever going to get, Archie promised himself.

They rejoined the others in the lounge. Archie meant to mingle, but Bet stopped him. Apparently she did not like what she saw in his eyes. In a quiet voice, she asked, "Archie? You all right?"

"I should be saying that to you."

"I'm as all right as I'm ever goin' to be," she said.

Archie regarded her with new vision. "There are mighty few people I would take at their word when they said that, Bet, but you are one of them. You make me feel ashamed— " he took a breath— "because I hate keeping secrets and I hate telling lies."

Bet was listening to him, her head slightly tilted, her gaze somehow going through him or beyond him. Then she asked, "Is it temporary, though?"

"I think so, yes."

"Then don't lose sleep over something that will pass. 'Fear not him that killeth, but him that hath the power to cast thee into hell.'" That quiet drawl was comforting. If ever the voice of experience spoke, it was Bet Berensen. "We can put up with anything if we know it will end."

-5-

The Stone Monkey

Peace and quiet reigned for ten days. Figuring out Arrow's riddle was just one of the many projects on Gamemaster's plate, and had to take its place in the queue. Archie was by no means deluded into thinking he had heard the last word.

Archie saw Bet around the Gee-9 Lab, mainly in passing, not to converse. She kept busy, too. She was taking high school courses at West Meg High because Trann felt the socialization was good for her. When she finished, she would have a high-school equivalency degree. Apparently she preferred simple black or grey dresses, but either Trann or Malasha had exerted some influence there, for they were in different styles and fabrics. Her hair was trimmed and styled— again, simply but elegantly.

She worked on Gee-9 projects, especially her original proposal. Project Green Pilot, which had first brought her to Gee's attention, was a "generational project." This was an oft-used euphemism at Gamemaster Inc. that meant the project would take several generations of Gamemasters because it moved slowly. There was no race with any competitor to complete it. The project had to have every crack filled before it could even be tested, which might take years. In her "fan letter" to the Gamemaster, where she had said goodbye to the outside world, Bet had outlined an idea that had never been considered by conventional scientists. She had given more details to the fictitious Molly in the secretive follow-up letters. Gamemaster technicians had found her ideas plausible, causing the rescue mission to be kicked into high gear. Bet had proposed using the well-documented growth cycle of plants— such as tobacco, the best-known and best-tended plant in Delay— as triggers for sending space probes to other stars. In a self-contained biome, the rise and fall of their life cycle could initiate different phases of the progress of the probe. There would be no loss of life, and a self-contained biological unit could operate, theoretically, into infinity. It was almost a pure scientific experiment. There was no urgency. While Bet learned the ways of Gamemaster Inc. and kept Project Green Pilot on her burner along with other more urgent projects, Trann, Malasha, and the rest of Gamemaster Inc. simply followed SOP— standard operating procedure. Bet was neither the first nor the last employee to take a wild ride to get here.

One day, Archie dropped by Bet's cubicle with his morning tea, just to say hello and shoot the breeze. When she eyed his tea longingly, it occurred to him that Bet might not know how to conjure up something from the corner dispenser. He took her to it and showed her. He helped her tell Max how to memorize her favorite settings. "Thank you so much, Archie," she said. "I'm used to a water pan on a gas stove. There's just so much happening at once."

The comment encouraged Archie to ask another question. "Is it proper to invite you to my place for tea on Saturday, or do you need a chaperone?"

Again, he got the smile she seemed to save just for him. "I'm not that back'ard. You're just about the closest thing I got to family here, you know that."

"The truth is, I do know that." He gave her his warmest smile in return. "Will you come over, then? About 1600?"

"I'm looking forward to it. My work schedule is full, but my social schedule fits on a blank page right now."

Archie gave Bet the grand tour when she came to his flat. Bet clearly liked what she saw. Archie's flat was geared toward warmth and comfort. The lighting was indirect, save for the reading lamps. Bet felt the fabric of drapes and curtains that let in the bright light of day or the softness of subdued light as the owner wished. Archie's father, or even his grandfather, would have known where to find the comfortable chair, a desk to work at, and the location of the brandy. They talked about wood and mock-leather being so much more welcoming than chrome-and-clear. Bet sunk her slippered toes into comfortable rugs and ran her hand along smooth mahogany paneling. She smiled at Archie's framed etchings that would have done an 18th-century gentleman proud, the contrast of light prints, black frames, and dark wood half-paneling. Archie knew Bet was picking up pointers for her own place, bigger than anything she'd ever owned, hers alone. It probably felt empty. "Your grandmother was supposed to come with you, wasn't she?" Archie asked.

"We were finally goin' to be happy." Bet stared beyond Archie's walls, to a place only she could see. "I could finally give her back somethin' for all she'd done for me, standin' by me when it got tough." She shook her head. Her eyes closed for a moment. "I don't really want to talk about it, Archie. Still too fresh."

"I understand." He leaned against his desk. "I'm going to say something heretical and sacrilegious, and I only hope you won't take it the wrong way. I preface it by reminding you that the Gamemaster himself exists only for the good of the company, above all." Bet watched him attentively, so he took a breath and said, "Gee let you reach the river before he picked you up."

Her head gave that little peculiar tilt, for just a moment. "He didn't know where I was going."

"He asked me. You're a Gee-9, Bet. I had deduced a river with a power plant without even knowing the terrain. You were ready to die."

"'Whoever loseth his life shall save it.'" She was staring hard at nothing.

"Exactly," said Archie. "In one way, he was a skunk, for posing as your savior when you were most vulnerable psychologically. In another, he picked you up at the exact moment you'd cast it all behind and were ready for a new life. And you woke up in heaven."

"Oh, no," Bet contradicted him. "I wasn't that far gone."

"Well, I'm relieved you realized it wasn't heaven," Archie said with a smile.

"True enough." They went to his living room. She slid into one of the comfortable overstuffed chairs. "Did you say something about tea?"

"Great Heavens, I did." Archie addressed the computer. "Pot of decent tea, Max, in my Mum's pot with her cups and saucers, sugar in the sugar bowl, fresh cream in the creamer, and Mum's silver to match." In a few minutes, he fetched the tea tray from the kitchenette hatch and brought it back. "I've been told it's bad manners to invite a lady to tea and make her pour, so I'll do the honors." Bet watched him, smiling, as he did so. Archie hadn't mentioned biscuits; Max used his initiative to add them. Bet ate and drank silently as Archie talked about his Mum and Dad and tea in the little jumbled house in the England Historic District. He kept it light. She was silent for so long Archie asked, "Am I prattling?"

"Not really," she answered, in that soft drawl. "You're letting me think, which I appreciate."

Archie sipped tea in receptive silence and suddenly felt like his Dad.

"Don't give me that look," she said. "You ain't no father confessor."

"Perish forbid," Archie said with a grin.

"An' I appreciate the attention, Archie, really I do. I've got a lot to think about, though, an' I don't like puttin' my thoughts aloud."

"I am not trying to put the moves on you," Archie objected.

"Now, stay in the cart. I never said you was."

"— Were."

"Were," she corrected unblinkingly. "You wanted to put me straight because I am a Gee-9 like you. And I don't mind the cold water, Archie, true I don't, an' I hope you keep doin' it. I've only been here a short time an' I'm processing an awful lot of information from a cold start." The drawl faded when she spoke academically and returned when she spoke casually. "I'm meetin' an awful lot of people here, an' I have to get the slant on each an' every one of 'em, real quick. It's a lot to do. An' I shy away from men specially."

"I know." Archie's face was serious. "You may be only sixteen, but you are the oldest sixteen I know. If you care, you have seven years before you reach my minimum age requirement."

Brief smile. "Thank you, that's good to know. Truth is, I didn't really care. I'm pretty sure where I stand with you. I wa'n't worried. 'Bout the only man around here I *do* have figgered out completely is Gamemaster. I thank you for pointing out a spot I missed. But it's just a spot." The head tilt, pause. "It's not that he played the Savior that bothers you. It's that he played God without a pang of conscience."

Archie felt his face redden. Bet saw through him like glass.

"Don't ever change, Archie," Bet Berensen said. "You are a pearl of great price."

He didn't know what to say. His face still burned.

"Gamemaster's got blind spots bigger'n a star cruiser, but he compensates by being aware that he has 'em. An' hirin' people like you and me to cover. An' he wants us to think his thoughts and breathe his air."

"That's it." The painful flush faded. Archie knew she saw. "I was afraid you'd think I was badmouthing him. Nothing is further from the truth." He drank tea. "But the entire truth is, I'm quite taken with you, too. I don't know what it is you've got, but you've got it. I'm wondering if it's the real thing, or if I too have a mad crush on you."

Bet grinned widely. "It's a mad crush. Trust me on this."

"How do you know?"

"By how red you got. You need to marry somebody who i'n't goin' to make you that uncomfortable daily."

"Do you read palms, too? How do you know my infatuation isn't going to last? And I did notice your struggle to avoid 'ain't.'"

"No, I don't read palms, that's heathen. Your infatuation will not last because that i'n't my kind of luck. And yes, I will kill 'ain't' or die tryin'." She smiled. "You know what I was thinking about? That book you gave me about the primate researchers. You know, the one that said after a while, the researchers interacted with their educational panels at their universities the same way their study animals interacted in their groups? Gorilla researchers interacted more like gorillas, orangutan specialists more like the orangutans, chimpanzee behavior students like the chimp hierarchy?"

Archie laughed. "When I slouched down in this chair, I thought, the ocean is the motion. I was very casual and fluid, just like a soft-walled animal cell. I rolled with the cushions. You were sitting in that chair, looking so stiff, I could see your cell wall. I would almost expect you to grow toward the light."

"The human version of a plant cell." She nodded. "I guess that, at times, I really have grown my own cellulose protective layer, in a manner of speaking. I never thought what we researched would affect how we thought and acted on the levels that it does," Bet agreed. "No wonder we need people

232504

Ms. Linda Kepner
162 Onset Rd
Bennington, NH 03442

603-588-3232

CUSTOMER'S ORDER NO.				DATE		
NAME *Sharon Baum*						
ADDRESS						
CITY, STATE, ZIP						

SOLD BY	CASH	C.O.D.	CHARGE	ON. ACCT.	MDSE. RETD.	PAID OUT

	QUAN.	DESCRIPTION	AMOUNT	
1	1	PTG	10	00
2				
3				
4				
5				
6				
7				
8				
9				
10				
11				
12				

RECEIVED BY *LJK*

A-3705
T-46240/46250   **KEEP THIS SLIP FOR REFERENCE**   01-11

like Trann to give us second opinions of ourselves. We really do get caught up in what we do. Between me growing cell walls like a plant cell, and you sneaking mysterious undocumented mitochondria out of the great wide oceans and into your animal cells, we are turning into quite an amazing mix. We're lucky we have such a good place to do it in." She curled up in the leather chair, looking slightly more relaxed – less plantlike and more like Archie. "You know what I would really like you to tell me about? Gee-9 guarantees. That's information I really *do* need to know."

"Oh. Guarantees." He shifted into a more comfortable position in his chair. "Rather like the opposite of a lawsuit, you know."

"More like a contract, I thought."

"Contract as in its original definition, a gentleman's agreement. As a Gamemaster 9, I give a guarantee to someone I don't want to suffer the indignity of a lawsuit for something I have asked them to do or refrain from doing. If I'm dealing with someone who is scared to death of litigation for some reason, I may give a guarantee to get them to stop trembling and start acting rationally."

Bet laughed. "So a guarantee is psychological, too."

"It is also very, very legal. If you give one for a silly reason, someone from Contract or the Legal Division will be on your doorstep, asking why. Always keep that in the back of your mind whenever you feel like giving one: you had best have a very sound and logical argument for Lucretia Danvers and her myrmidons. However, they will not countermand a silly guarantee. They cannot. That is why we are Gamemasters and they are not. They have only one court of appeal, Gamemaster himself, and he usually won't overturn a guarantee."

"How do I give one?"

"Exactly the same way you'd give your word to someone, Bet."

She looked very serious. "Or swear to God."

He nodded. "About the same. Only people who truly believe their word is their bond can give good guarantees, and the rest shall never be allowed to."

"No wonder lawyers aren't allowed to countermand them. They'd be countermanded six times before breakfast," she commented, thereby displaying a prejudice against lawyers as strong at Gee's against Council Christians. To each his own.

"Exactly. Now, you arrange it with Max by setting up a communication box..."

So they sat back and talked guarantees until dinner, then adjourned to the Bread Factory for the best sandwiches in West Meg, and had a very happy time.

Life settled into a comfortable round of work and games. Archie had perhaps a dozen projects on his "To Do" list at any given time. The variety was stimulating. Then he might go over to the fitness room (he had yielded to Trann on this, too) or go to cricket practice. The Players worked together well as a team, and it was fun.

Archie, who was used to winter in England and the dim daylight of Mars, still found himself lethargic occasionally. He was tempted to volunteer for a project in some sunlit area, something on Trann's "deferred" list, just for the change. However, he knew he was perfectly capable of weathering out the winter, and he didn't want to spoil himself. January in West Meg was simply dull, even amid the bright dome lights of the cricket field. Over the years, he had learned to be careful what he wished for, because the wish was often granted with a vengeance.

As far as he was concerned, this was exactly what happened with his unguarded wish for a little snowfall.

He sat in Gamemaster's office, staring at him, unable to believe his ears. At last, he managed to say, "No, I will NOT go with you, and no one but a goddamn *lunatic* would even consider such a thing! January, in the Himalayas! Are you *mad?*"

"I am not going to wait six months," the Gamemaster stated inflexibly.

"Oh, for Christ's sake. The riddle's waited this long. It can certainly stand another six months!" Archie argued.

"I won't have free time then. People live there, even in January, and have for centuries. Traveling there is not extraordinary. This is a project I am going to work on now."

"Why Tibet?"

"Stone monkeys are more common in Tibet than elsewhere. John Arrow has, or had, a brother, somewhere in the Himalayas. Max cannot pinpoint exactly where. So, I must go there to find out."

"But you have no idea where in the Himalayas," Archie countered, remembering fully as well as Gamemaster that one of John Arrow's books had been *Journeys in Tibet*. "This is not the season to be wandering around asking questions. For God's sake, at least wait until the second quarter. Wait until spring."

"No." The tone was non-negotiable. "And you are going with me."

"Then I hope to hell we find Richard Arrow fast, preferably in downtown Lhasa."

"He's not there. He's somewhere outside the city."

"Then you *are* out of your mind. Gee, it is *January*— January in the Himalayas! Thermal clothing won't do you any good under a hundred meters of snow at the bottom of a kilometer-deep chasm. Not even a magnetic-field floater can buck those winds! We've done a lot of climbing, but we're not professionals, for God's sake! Even pros wouldn't work those hills in January! And may I remind you that you don't have an heir to all this, should you happen to breathe your last somewhere in the mountains?"

"That isn't my fault. My father instructed me to marry a stupid woman, and I haven't found one stupid enough yet." Gee did not even look up from his work, and seemed unaware of the magnitude of his atrocious statement.

"What?" Archie stopped short.

Now Gee looked up. He explained almost patiently, "My mother was stupid. She was beautiful, but an incredible imbecile." It was a callous thing to say. But, come to think of it, Gee's mother had been a gracious, beautiful moron, at that. At least, that was how she had impressed young Archie, the few times he'd seen her before her death. Dumb or doped, one or the other. Perhaps that was the only way to put up with seeing your children regimented like that, and even killed.

Archie sighed, and thought, Let's not go there. "Why do you want me to come along?"

"You had a classical education. I didn't. While I was learning Advanced Business Analysis, you were studying Latin, and soaking up Oriental literature and art. Also, unfortunately for you, you are the only one who knows anything about Arrow's riddle."

"All right, I'll do it," Archie said doubtfully. "Even though I know that the only transport station in the Himalayas is in Lhasa itself, and that's only a halt-on-demand stop. And even though we don't have the slightest idea what Arrow's brother looks like or where he is."

Gee was satisfied. "Tibet is feeling the pinch financially. In fact, they are backsliding. Some of the Chinese services are pulling out, after hundreds of years. The entire Chinese Reconfiguration is retrenching from Zero Growth rebound. The ratio of elderly to youth is roughly 37 to 1 right now, in some of the most populous areas. Tibet's not as badly hit as far as the workforce ratio is concerned, but there's no money coming from Peking."

"Which means a lot of old, broken-down equipment and no place for Max to come through in a pinch," Archie reminded him. "Please reconsider this."

"No. I can clear time now, and I can't later. The second and third quarters will be extremely busy. It is now or never."

Archie hoped fervently this wasn't "never."

"Pack tonight," Gee directed. "McKinney from Cold Region Research will supply us with warm suits and traveling gear. It will not be a problem, Archie. We leave tomorrow morning."

Harry Goto piloted them to Tibet. There was doubt in his voice. "I'm glad you're landing at the Lhasa space pad, chief. Lhasa's flat, but it's the only place that is. If you have to use choppers to get around, you're going to be at the mercy of the wind, but you can land in a smaller space— maybe. They say that when the winds pick up around here, you can't tell vertical from horizontal, not even with instruments."

"So if I must go outside the city?" Gee inquired. Harry's opinion was one that Gee would respect, Archie thought in consolation.

"Do it the old-fashioned way, on two feet or four." Harry shook his head. "Stay away from those goddam mechanical choppers they've got— they're an accident that's found a place to happen. I read that three crashed last summer, and that was in *summer*. The choppers are as old as those Land Rovers they use, but at least if a Land Rover crashes, you have a chance of ending up alive in a ditch."

Gee flashed a quick smile and glanced at Archie. "At least, if we must take a Land Rover, our practice in the England Historic District will stand us in good stead."

"Yes," said Harry, "as long as you remember where the controls are once they're relabeled in Tibetan for 150 years. If you tip over a Land Rover, what happens to the company?"

"It is provided for." That was a stock Gamemaster line. Harry asked for no more details than anyone else ever did, and Gee gave none.

Archie had expected tight little buildings nestled in a small river valley, all dingy and grey in the January light, and found nothing of the sort as they dropped easily to a soft landing on the open spacepad. Everything around them was full of color and beauty. The Lhasa River meandered through several splits and branches here, creating a wide valley for a busy city. The sun was blindingly bright. The sky was as blue as the Pacific Ocean they'd left half a world away. Gold ornaments glittered on the top of a distant building, which Gee informed him was the Jokhang Temple, one of the places on their itinerary. Strings of prayer flags flapped and fluttered in the sunlit breeze, each flutter the repetition of the prayer imprinted upon the flag.

The Gamemaster Inc. shuttle made a vertical landing on the flat little pad, with the afternoon sun at their backs. Archie could see Tibet from the panels on three sides of the landing shuttle. Lhasa City was to the east, before them. To his left, almost immediately to the north of the pad, Archie could glimpse part of the Drepung Monastery amid the mountains, looking flat and brownish in this light. Rising out above Lhasa were the great white walls, hundreds of little dark windows, and the great red and gold roofs of the Potala Palace. To the south more mountains rose suddenly to immense heights, beyond a river he couldn't identify. He checked his little map. Lhasa river— that could be the Brahmaputra, he'd have to check. Gazing at the glorious mountain scenes surrounding them, Archie felt strangely humbled.

Gamemaster, apparently, felt nothing of the sort. "At least it isn't snowing," was all he said, as he hefted his duffle bag over his shoulder. The hatch popped open, the steps dropped down, and Gee led the way outside. Archie stood, every joint aching for some unknown reason, hefted his own gripsack and followed him down the steps onto the busy little landing pad. The first thing Archie saw was blindingly bright sunlight and blue sky; the first thing he heard were prayer flags flapping in the stiff breeze. Archie wondered if a stiffer breeze would be an advantage or not— it might make travel difficult, but they could certainly use the additional prayer power. Each flap of a prayer flag was another prayer offered to God. Despite the sunny day and his thermal clothing, the breeze chilled him. Two other tiny shuttles were loading and unloading eight or ten passengers each, and other Tibetans were standing around. Their size made Archie, at five foot ten, feel quite tall.

Archie scanned his surroundings, as was his defensive habit. There was something to say for Gee's pessimism. Everything in sight looked old. Equipment had been neatly painted, but one could see that this layer of paint covered many others. He could see where broken bolt-holes once existed, now welded instead. Everything was sturdy, but repaired in an antique fashion. In fact, there was not one single camera, sensor, or even an emergency fire hose housing to be seen. There was nothing he could tell Max to use to their advantage in an emergency. Lhasa was completely mechanical. There were no Gamemaster Inc., ECM or any other modern devices here. Archie was used to the England Historic District, which prided itself on antiquities, so he did not feel as naked and disarmed as other Gamemasters might. He could make do with mechanics. But it reinforced his original foreboding of no backup via Max in emergency situations. He was not going to be able to make a seamless connection with Max merely by raising his voice and making a demand for information or protection. In fact, he did not see a single method to speak to Max at all.

They watched Harry rise skyward again. At first, Archie thought he was feeling even more foreboding, then realized that clouds were passing over the bright sun. It would not be long before the Himalayas cast their shadows over the valley with the passing of noon.

A man standing only to the height of Gee's shoulder stepped out of the dozen or so bystanders and greeted him. Despite his name, Mr. Zhaba was Chinese, not Tibetan. He was as cheerful and compact in size as the Tibetans around him. "Welcome to Lhasa, Gamemaster! Mr. Chamberlain, welcome!

It is an honor to host you." He grabbed their bags and arranged them in the boot of a Land Rover that looked as old as he was. "I am the host of Red Door Hostel. We are still in business, even if CITS has pulled out."

Even Gamemaster looked surprised. CITS, the China International Travel Service, had been a fixture in Tibet for centuries, managing all foreign travelers. "What? Are things that serious?"

"Well, Beijing says not." Mr. Zhaba climbed into the driver's seat while Gee took the other front seat and Archie scrambled into the back. Mr. Zhaba turned a key, and the engine rumbled to life. They began a slow, jolting journey toward the older portion of the city, further east. To Archie, in back, main streets were indistinguishable from ruined side-alleys. Archie felt shaken around in the back seat like a pea in a bottle.

"I came out here to manage the Red Door Hostel for CITS," Mr. Zhaba was telling Gee, "after I came back from service. We're just off Chingdol Don Lu, near the bookstore, a prime location. Almost fifty years ago! Even I don't believe I'm that old. It was a good job, and I had veterans' points. Now it's still a good job— no reason to go back east. And we meet such interesting people."

"I suppose so." Even Gee had to hang on to the frame for support as the old Land Rover swayed and creaked over ice, or bad pavement, or potholes— or whatever it was that made Archie feel like he'd been slapped into a centrifuge and spun.

Archie paid no further attention to the conversation. He was becoming thoroughly ill. Mr. Zhaba drove slowly, because there were more pedestrians as they journeyed further into the city. There was ice and snow in the roadways to dodge, as well. The ride took forever. Every jolt sent his stomach in a new direction. He wasn't sure whether he felt sweaty or chilly inside the thermal clothing. The vehicle's interior smelled of age and an old stale heating system— not objectionable, but not pleasant. Archie concentrated on keeping the contents of his stomach where they belonged. When the Land Rover stopped, Archie climbed out gratefully.

Mr. Zhaba shot him a sharp look and said, "Comrade, the altitude has attacked you."

"I am certainly aware of it," Archie agreed. "I never had this happen before. I hope it is not part of growing older."

Mr. Zhaba laughed. He hefted Archie's bag and left Gee to pull out his own. "Did you bring simple medications, like aspirin? It should be all you need, if you have never been troubled by altitude sickness before."

"Yes, I did."

"You will be all right." They entered the hostel's brightly-painted red front door. It might have been anyone's comfortable house. Cooking smells wafted toward them. There were some pictures on the wall (one of Mr. Zhaba in the uniform of ECM China, and a wedding picture), and other Chinese and Tibetan decorations. "I shall show you to the room you will share. Medicate and rest." Mrs. Zhaba stood in her kitchen doorway, welcoming them with a bright smile. She was wearing a bright printed apron over several layers of clothes, and was still wiping her hands on a towel. "My wife shall call you for supper."

The wind whistled in through cracks around the old windows. Archie realized that although this hostel was heated, it wasn't going to be very useful. He was thankful for the lightweight and warm Survival Thermal blankets and clothing which McKinney, the head of Gamemaster Inc.'s Cold Region Research Lab, had given them. There was an old-fashioned oxygen tank beside his bed, always available for foreign guests in Lhasa because of the altitude. He wasn't sure if the dampness he felt inside his shirt and pants was sweat, fever, or his imagination. Taking a breath was difficult. His ears rang in a fashion he associated with the flu or a high fever. He hoped the aspirin would take care of the annoying ringing. Archie had been in spacesuits and space stations before, but he had never felt like this.

"I'm going out to look around," said Gee. "Are you coming?"

"No. I'm not going anywhere, Gee. I'm really having trouble adjusting. This is the worst I've felt in ages." Archie saw Gee's annoyed look but felt too ill to care. Gee left. Archie took his aspirin. He had learned that, because of financial and weather issues, even the hospitals were self-sufficient and mechanical-based. Max was unavailable anywhere. He lifted the O-2 mask to his face, cranked the creaky old mechanical valve until he heard it hiss, took a few deep breaths, and felt better. That must be it, he thought, the altitude, but what a strange time for it to start! He had never been troubled by mountain sickness before. He shut down the valve, took off his boots, lay on the bed, and fell asleep.

The sun had set when he awoke. Archie felt the true darkness of a place without monitor lights, power indicators, or street lights. Max might as well be a million miles away. Archie felt much better, although still not his best. He had trouble re-fastening his thermal vest, and couldn't force himself to care much about the problem. He put on his boots and wandered out to look for the Gamemaster. He met Mrs. Zhaba instead, who informed him that Gee had gone to make an appointment to meet the Dalai Lama. Archie felt very tired. "Doesn't anything ever slow that man down?" he asked his hosts, in passable Chinese. They laughed. He was glad Gee decided to go along without him.

The Zhabas set a groaning board for their only guests, important guests at that. It was everything the scent had promised. Even Archie's wonky stomach settled at the sight of the appetizing spread. There was fruit compote, homemade barley bread, prawns, abalone soup, and good hot Chinese tea. It was tourist food, especially the seafood, but Mrs. Zhaba was an excellent cook. She admitted with a giggle that she wanted to show off. Gee joined them just as supper started, having made his appointment at the Potala Palace and also making a brief visit to the Jokhang, a good couple of miles away. He certainly had been around.

Mrs. Zhaba, who, like her husband, had a good nature which seemed to be altered by nothing, asked, "How did you find the Jokhang? It is beautiful, is it not?"

Gee sat on a mat. He took up bread, and slapped butter on it. His response was scornful. "Today I have watched mindless peasants grovel upon cold stone floors before wooden statues. I have seen broken human skulls with candles planted in them, upside down and jewel-encrusted. I have seen altars thick with stuck pins, planted in the hope of some magical aid to wisdom striking the supplicant so that he can avoid the hard work of studying. I have seen food rotting in piles, left by nearly-starving farmers, to feed golden statues whose gold would have at least served the people much better by use in medical machinery. For this privilege I have paid money for a ticket, to the music of 'The East is Red' in seven different varieties over a very bad loudspeaker. The gentleman with whom I finally spoke, a representative of the 'Fountain of Wisdom,' couldn't remember if I was supposed to make a left turn or a right to get back to the main street."

Archie scolded, "Maybe it's my good old C of E upbringing, but you really shouldn't run down people's religions when you're just visiting, Gee."

"I'm not shocking anyone here."

"Not us," said Mr. Zhaba with a smile. Mrs. Zhaba's smile dimmed. Archie realized that her feelings had been hurt, even if she pretended along with her husband. It reinforced what he'd gathered from the portraits, that Mr. Zhaba had come out a bachelor soldier and married a local girl all those years ago. Nonetheless, their host prodded, "Religion is indeed the opium of the people, isn't it?" Archie had the absurd impression that Mr. Zhaba was egging Gee on, to see what he would say.

"I have always been very anti-religion for that very reason," Gee said. "Throughout the history of West Meg, you won't find churches involved. As Archie can tell you, I have been combating religious fundamentalists and other 'holy groups' on my own continent for as long as I can remember. Religion is a poor excuse for bullying by people who would be otherwise treated with contempt. I give them no more than the contempt they deserve. I'd rather have the Earth Combined Military than organized religion. The ECM and I fight viciously but rationally."

"You do not believe in a higher power? Do you find any other use for religion, besides as a weapon used by thugs?"

"Not in the least."

"And yet, you risk your life, daily if necessary, for your business and your city. As I once risked mine, in the Mars One Wars."

"In my family," said the Gamemaster, who never talked about what went on behind closed doors in the penthouse, "we merely say – End of Game."

"Ah." Mr. Zhaba was thoughtful. "You know there is continuance. It is provided for." Archie was a little surprised to hear Gee's oft-used phrase here.

"Yes, it is provided for."

"So, your own death is not really a concern for you."

"Indeed not."

"Mine is." Mr. Zhaba sat back, comfortably and seriously. "Rather I would stick pins in myself and pour yak butter over my head than indulge in such silliness as what you saw today, for I am a good Communist. But still, I hope something protects me, something more than Beijing, when I go into battle. You have never feared for your life, nor for someone else's."

"People die, that is all," Gee agreed. "End of game." He rose. "If you will excuse me, I wish to sleep. I didn't have an afternoon nap, and my body is still adjusting to the altitude."

"By all means. Good night." Mr. Zhaba watched him thoughtfully as he left the room.

"I am sorry," Archie said uneasily. He had always been uncomfortable expressing himself in Chinese. "I should have warned you. He does not see things quite the same way others do. That is just the way he is. Please do not hold it against him."

"But he should have at least enjoyed the beauty," Mrs. Zhaba said sadly, making Archie feel even worse.

Mr. Zhaba, however, still looked thoughtful. "No, wife, do not be upset with our guest. It is rude to both him and Mr. Chamberlain. In my mind, it is a very good sign, and I like him more for it. He has a good heart. What he saw was ugly because it helped no one."

"It is good of you to see him that way. Many do not. I find him— " Archie searched for a good word— "exasperating. But, as I keep telling people, he is a fifth-generation genetic modification. He really is made that way."

Mr. Zhaba, still thoughtful, smiled. He said something that surprised Archie, something that was obviously the experience of an old soldier. "Sometimes the most amazing things pop unexpectedly out of gene mods. I expect some day it will occur to him. I only hope the rest of the world is ready to withstand the explosion when it happens."

The incident left an unpleasant impression in Archie's restless mind. It was one of the many things that disturbed his sleep that night. It was bitterly cold, a cold which seemed to creep into Archie's flesh beyond the heat-retaining thermal clothes and blankets. The business of the day had fatigued him beyond sleeplessness. In addition, the thin air took its toll. The oxygen tank gave no relief. Archie spent a cold, sleepless, comfortless night. He must have dozed off sometime, because he had a vague recollection of Mr. Zhaba coming into the room and waking Gee up, telling him to let Archie sleep. He had taken Gee for a walk, or something, in the wee hours.

That morning, Archie was plainly ill. His pale face and the rings under his eyes testified to that. He ate little. Mrs. Zhaba fretted over him. The only note in the Gamemaster's cold voice was one of annoyance. "Haven't you kept up your vitamins and supplements?" he demanded, as he sat down to breakfast.

"I thought I had," Archie mumbled.

"Well, we can't leave for a couple of days, while I make inquiries," Gamemaster said ungraciously, "so you will have the time to recover. You were in full health when we left, Archie— I don't have time for this."

Or the patience, Archie thought, with anyone else's weaknesses, or your own. He knew how Gee was chafing at being stymied by John Arrow's riddle. The longer he was forced to spend being stymied, the worse his mood would become, and the more impossible it would be to slow him down when he found a clue. "Where have you been?" asked Archie.

"Taking a walk, with Mr. Zhaba. He told me about the old Communist days, and about his childhood. He told me I had a fine sense of values and a good heart. I would make a good Communist." Usually, he would smile when he made such a comment, but not now. "If I have to listen to debates for many more days between Red Hats, Yellow Hats, Poms, Communists, Indian Catholics, and at least ten other religions, I will be driven out into the snow as surely as if they brandished rifles at me."

-6-

A Good Dump of Snow

Mr. Zhaba said, "My wife loves organized religion. Some of those candles in the Jokhang are hers. Her way is different from mine."

As Mr. Zhaba had the tact and grace to tell his guest he'd committed a social error, their guest had the grace to acknowledge it, to Archie's relief. Gamemaster turned to her and said formally, "I apologize for hurting your feelings." She smiled and waved the incident away.

"My feelings recover easily," she said. "My husband does not go to the temple, but still, he knows there is something beyond us. He says that he found his moment."

"His moment?" Archie asked, savoring the warm Chinese tea. He had tasted bhoja, the Tibetan version of tea, full of yak butter and various spices he couldn't name, and much preferred his tea unadulterated.

Mr. Zhaba said modestly, "You wouldn't know it to look at me, but not that many years ago, I was part of the First Battalion of the Earth Combined Military, China, in the Mars One skirmish. I think, perhaps, I found my moment there."

"Mmph. The old adage, 'There are no atheists in foxholes' comes to mind," said Archie.

The old man's easy manner made him good company. There was never any malice in Mr. Zhaba's tone or words. "I think that is true. Certainly it is true in Tibet. People tend to forget that the Dalai Lama is not the ruler of Tibet, and never has been. What unites Tibet is oral and written language. There were always political subdivisions, changing throughout the centuries. The Communists were the first true unification, and they are fading. Tibetan Buddhism is hardly the only religion. The Dalai Lamas certainly weren't spotless saints, either. When the Dalai Lama returned to Tibet, only seventy-five years ago, he was not welcome. People like me— good Communists, who had tasted the work of their hands— distrusted him immensely. There were bombs, attacks— " He shook his head. "But he worked— truly worked— to win the love and respect of these people, Chinese and non-Chinese alike. They took nothing for granted." He used that curious dichotomy they had found common to so many Tibetans to speak of the series of Dalai Lamas as a single man in one sentence, separate men in the next.

"Good publicity," the Gamemaster commented.

"Quite good. Religion at work, so to speak. In these difficult times, the results of his efforts are outstanding. The Chinese government has pulled out of this land, yet look. No civil war. Everyone is working together, Buddhist, Communist, Muslim, Christian, and agnostic. Together, we are being Tibetan. The Dalai Lama, acting as no more than an advisor, has kept us intact through this strife." Mr. Zhaba gestured in the general direction of the Potala Palace, once again the Dalai Lama's residence after so many years vacant. "He reminds us that the day must come when each of us, no matter how great or small, must face impossible odds— and we will always be unprepared."

Archie focused on his health. He had never felt this weighty and breathless. He felt an occasional sharp pain which passed easily. No doubt it was the altitude, since he was a flatlander born and bred. Neither West Meg nor the England Historic District were more than a few hundred feet above sea level at their highest points. Aspirin seemed to dissipate the pain, and he was adjusting to the altitude. Three days, Mr. Zhaba told him, was what it usually took for a visitor to adjust, and Archie was fitting right in.

Mrs. Zhaba fretted over him. On the second day after their arrival, she took him for a walk through urban Lhasa, on what she called the Lingkor. He found it was a traditional pilgrim's circuit along some of the main streets of Lhasa, and a nice two-hour walk with his hostess. They kept to the left of every road, as pilgrims do. His hostess laughed as she taught him Tibetan street names, and had him toss stones into the Kyi Chu (Lhasa River) for luck.

On the third day of their stay, Gee and Archie met the Dalai Lama. To Archie's great relief, they walked to the great white Potala Palace on the hillside. Gee also admitted, to Archie alone, that riding with Mr. Zhaba was like being dropped into a blender.

Archie hadn't known what to expect, of either the residence or the religious leader. A young monk, acting more secretary-like than monk-like, met them at the front gates and escorted them through rooms in the White Palace portion of the Potala. Their footfalls echoed throughout empty rooms as their escort explained in Chinese that this area was still half-museum, a relic of the Communist days when most of the order was destroyed and the Dalai Lama's former quarters made into a curiosity. It reminded Archie forcibly of a tour he'd taken in France, visiting castles that had suffered under the French Revolution. Like France, Tibet had not re-filled the emptied rooms with cheap replacement "facsimiles," but left the space empty. They passed through large rooms with white walls and woodwork painted in bright primary colors, through gilded rooms with red highlights. He could smell incense and sandalwood. Also, as in France, the furniture might be gone but the walls were filled with every sort of imaginable art. Any of these rooms would rival a museum collection, he suspected. If he weren't so tired, he would dig in his heels, and tell Gee he wanted at least two weeks to look at the art. As it was, he just wanted to get this adventure done with, and back to his comfortable rooms on Rhodalia Row.

One room held comfortable rugs, and Archie could see low tables at the sides holding office supplies. There was not a great amount, more like someone's attached home office in an earlier era. He saw card files, paper, and notebooks, as well as a desktop computer and— could that possibly be a rotary-dial telephone? A young man in full religious robes stood as they entered and walked toward them, smiling. Good heavens, Archie realized, this is the Dalai Lama himself!

He spoke excellent English, and was pleased to have the opportunity to use the language. He motioned them to seats before him on soft, comfortable rugs.

"Gamemaster, you are well-known," said the young lama, "even in Tibet. Some of your products still find their way here." His very tone of voice was refreshing. "I was intrigued by your riddle of the stone monkey. I have given much thought to it. As you said, stone monkeys are common in Tibet. The Monkey Cave of Chenrizik is a popular pilgrimage destination here, as you probably know. But, perhaps, a lama named 'Arrow' is not as common."

The Gamemaster leaned forward in the intent fashion of a Western businessman. "You have found him? When might I meet him?"

"You cannot," the Dalai Lama replied serenely. "Not in this season. He is at Karpo Gompa, the White Monastery."

"Where is Karpo Gompa?"

"Karpo Gompa," said the lama, "is wherever the Karpo Drapa, the White Monks, are. You see, there is no Karpo Gompa."

Another puzzle?, Archie wondered. Even sitting on a mat, here on this tiled floor, he could feel the cold seeping through his clothes.

"The Karpo Drapa are nomads, or so it is said."

"Nomads? In the Himalayas in January?" Archie exclaimed.

"Their monastery was destroyed during the First Chinese Reconfiguration, when so many of the old orders were destroyed. The order survived without a monastery, in the mountains, living as they do now. They make a home in some cave or abandoned fort in the northwest, and change it from time to time. Now, of course, it is more tradition than necessity— except to remind themselves that nothing is permanent."

Gamemaster sat back again, his dark features set in a frown, clearly dismayed. "Surely this cannot be."

"It is so. I am sorry."

"How do you communicate with them?" Gee persisted. "You knew his name. What knowledge do you have of them, or of their whereabouts?"

"Occasionally, travelers come to the city who have seen one of them in the mountains, or their marks in the snow. They are like the— what are they called?— the monks of Saint Bernard, yes. They rescue travelers in distress, risking their lives, and they meditate. Among them is a giant called Arrow."

Among the tiny Tibetans, a well-fed, good-sized Westerner would seem a giant, Archie thought.

"Surely they fall under your rule," said the Gamemaster. "Can you not command them to appear?"

The Dalai Lama shook his head. "They are free, and answer only to God. In theory, yes, to me. We returned here only seventy-five years ago. It has taken hundreds of years for the Chinese government to decide that we might be good for Tibet. Even then, there were doubts. Who knows for certain that there will never be another Chinese Reconfiguration?" It was disconcerting to hear him speak as though he and previous Dalai Lamas were a continuing unbroken person in one sentence, then revert easily to his own personal experience in another. "The Karpo Gompa saw no reason to change, and good reason to continue as they were. Most news of them comes from Keilan village, seventy-five kilometers northeast of here, as the crow flies— but long, hard travel in this weather. Once there, I have no idea how you would contact them. They rarely mingle with villagers."

"They must buy supplies."

"Occasionally. I presume in Keilan. It is a city of ridges and valleys, of mountainside farmhouses. Even a chopper is out of the question." Good, thought Archie, remembering Harry Goto's warnings about the choppers.

"That could be our link for finding them."

"You do not understand," said the young lama. "Seventy-five kilometers is nothing in North America, but it is many days' dangerous travel here, in winter. The road to Keilan does not exist in this weather. Winds cause difficult whiteout conditions. The climb is almost vertical. The ridges in the northwest run contrary to the direction you wish to go. The *la*, the passes, are few and difficult in this weather. The area is formidable. Yaks or *bung-gu*— burros— might fall into difficulties. A man must take his own provisions, as well. Keilan has perhaps fifty residents. They could not be expected to provide completely for an additional party for as long as it would take them to stay through a possible blizzard." He indicated a window. "You see how the sky is turning grey. In another day or two, the sun will vanish even here in Lhasa."

"Then I had better get started. I certainly will not wait around here for weather conditions to lighten up."

Archie knew the futility of opposing Gee when he got like this— three days of sitting around without work to do, in the midst of people he could not respect because they were involved in religion, an activity he despised. He would go on without Archie if necessary, which made Archie feel even more obliged to go. If there had been someone else from the company with them, if a blizzard would keep them holed up in Lhasa, that would alter things. But not Gee on a tear, getting impatient. It wouldn't matter if Archie had the key to the ages, let alone half a clue to a strange riddle with a hidden meaning that he could only guess at.

The Dalai Lama looked surprised. Then he closed his eyes, in meditation or thought. When he opened them, he stared straight at Archie. An additional pang shot through Archie's stomach. For a moment— just for a moment, he thought the Dalai Lama was going to solve the riddle on the spot.

Instead, he smiled. "I never met a city man who really understood snow. I can also see that you do not understand why Lhasa is called the Sunshine City— because it alone has great sunlight and warmth in this season. Are you sure you wish to make this journey?"

"I am certain."

"I wish you good luck and good journey, then. Now, be patient, Gamemaster, for a moment longer. I am going to give you a blessing that you don't particularly want, for your safety and for the future of your own kingdom. Then I shall let you go on your way, I promise."

The blessing was in Tibetan. The parish priest was taking a last crack at an unrepentant heathen. The thought made Archie smile, despite his misgivings. Then the young secretary-monk escorted them out of the Presence.

Archie woke with a pounding headache, feeling ice-cold and bloated. His first thought was, *I can't possibly be hung over, because I haven't had anything to drink.*

He groaned and sat up, his pulse pounding in his ears, and reached for his bottle of aspirin. The water in his cup wasn't frozen solid, but it felt as though it should be. It was just light enough to distinguish shades of grey in the morning shadows.

"*You* sound ready for a strenuous day," observed an acid voice from the other bed.

Archie restrained an impulse to tell his boss where to go and merely observed, "Yes. If this is where good food and clean living gets me, I might as well go back to West Meg and carouse with Shiera's stupid husband and the actors."

"That'll larn you," Gee copped one of Archie's own wisecracks as he stood up and began to dress. Dress! Archie was wearing all of his clothes already, and shivered as he watched him. The prospect of action had plainly put Gee in a better mood. "Mr. Zhaba said he would try to round up a couple of guides for us and they would meet us at breakfast."

Archie felt cold to his bones, but this chilled him further. "Did he say *try?*"

Gee, folding clothes, missed the point. "No matter. Are you packed?"

"It won't take long," said Archie truthfully, since he was wearing most of them already. He didn't like the cold feeling of dread that had just settled on his stomach, either. "I'm going to go get a cup of hot tea. I need a warm start. Back in a jiff."

He shut the door behind him, and trudged down the carpeted corridor with a sinking heart. He examined exactly how rotten he felt: a headache alternately pounding and sharp, that wouldn't go away; a bloated feeling that gave him sympathy for pregnant women; weak knees and tired feet; tired eyes; and a fever that seemed more like a low-grade infection than anything else. Oh yes, he was in a perfect shape to go hiking seventy-five kilometers uphill in the direction most roads didn't go. In Tibet. In winter.

He met the Zhabas in the hall outside the dining room. "There's no guides, are there?" he asked resignedly.

"I told him yesterday," Mr. Zhaba sighed. "If I could get you a guide now, it would be someone not worth the money. It's the New Year, you know, four days. And it coincides with the Return. Of the Dalai Lama to Tibet. Everyone will celebrate one or the other or both."

Archie sighed, and offered, "I'll tell him. You shouldn't have to take the heat for this." He trudged back down the carpeted hallway, back to their room.

"Everything ready?"

"Gee," said Archie resignedly, "you didn't listen. You know perfectly well that when someone here says he'll try to do something, the implication is he'll probably be unable to do it. This is not West Meg, this is China."

Gee demanded, "Are you saying Mr. Zhaba did not supply us with guides?"

"I'm saying God couldn't supply us with guides. It's both the New Year and The Return of the Dalai Lama to Tibet, a double festival." As Gee strode toward the door, Archie blocked it. "You will not give our host hell about being unable to produce the impossible."

"Get out of my way."

"Make me. I already feel rotten enough, I don't care." He knew perfectly well that Gee could pick him up and throw him across the room if he felt like it. *Maybe I do have the death wish upon me,* he thought.

"Then you will go with me, with or without a guide, or pack animals. I have a computerized orientation system, and there is no need to wait for guides or other baggage."

"My, that was predictable," Archie snarled, almost nose to nose. "You are going to owe me incredibly for this. So much that Mum will think I've got early retirement."

Gee closed his converted backpack with a snap. The glance he bestowed upon Archie was not friendly. Since he was getting his way, he had not continued the argument.

Archie said nothing more. He slipped his pack over his shoulders and buckled it in place. He sent one more glance around the room he and Gee had shared, taking care not to forget anything. In his present frame of mind, forgetting things was very likely.

Archie had taken all the medication he dared, and did his best to appear normal. He had grave misgivings about his abilities when the drugs wore off. He tried to avoid drugs for that reason, because the rebound was so debilitating, but there was no way out of it now. *All right, you wanted me here, I'm here,* he told Gee's back in continuing silent revolt. *Have it your way. I'll trudge along in your footsteps until you're sick of me.* It was probably a good thing that they had stopped speaking to each other.

Mr. and Mrs. Zhaba stood at the door, wishing them a polite but concerned bon voyage. Like Archie, they recognized all the signs of executive temperament, and were no more capable of dealing with it than Archie. So they merely wished their guests well.

Against the advice of the Zhabas and the Dalai Lama, they began the trek toward Keilan. It seemed to be seventy-five kilometers straight uphill, moving perpendicular to most ridges rather than parallel to them. Archie hauled up ridges and squeezed through minuscule passes behind Gee. Archie was slogging. It was all he could do to put one foot in front of the other, and keep the forward momentum.

They carried packaged food, a small tent, and basic hiking tools. Seventy-five kilometers— roughly forty-five miles— was, as Gee put it, "hardly an Olympic stretch." It might take them a couple of days, and meant camping out in the tiny tent overnight, only an inconvenience if the weather remained fair. If the weather turned foul— well, that would be unpleasant, certainly.

Archie kept his aspirin in a handy pocket, and swallowed them with a sip of tepid tube-water from a hose in his backpack at noon. By then, they could no longer see the Lhasa river valley behind them. The ridges cut off views in most directions. The sky was dark grey and threatening.

They had climbed mountains before, in all seasons. They knew that hostile weather could pop over a ridge suddenly. However, the blizzard dropped six inches of snow on them before they realized it. Faced with the choice of down or up, they chose up, and kept climbing. McKinney of Gamemaster Inc.'s Cold

Region Research Lab had given them his best boots, with a good snowshoe surface and, if needed, popout crampons for a grip on ice. Their hiking hammers could pound a clamp in place quickly and easily for their safety ropes. They were about halfway to Keilan, so there was no difference between going ahead or going back. At any time, Archie told himself, they could cross over the next ridge. The snow could stop as suddenly as it started.

It was getting harder for Archie to climb. His leg muscles seemed weak, as if they were pulling more weight than mere body and pack. The snow was not crusty, but it was stiff. It was still an effort to make an original footprint. Thankfully, he was behind Gee so he could step where Gee had stepped. Archie was becoming unable to find his footing easily, even following, and worse yet, not really caring if he hit his mark. Archie slipped and almost went down. His gloved hands acted on instinct without him, grabbing and twisting the cord. Vaguely he thought, *I'm sorry I don't feel more concerned about this. I really should be.*

They fought their way to the next ridge, to find snow more intense and visibility far decreased. Moving on was a struggle.

Then he felt a sudden stabbing pain in his side. Pressure gave way in Archie's gut and he knew. All the symptoms he'd been ignoring fell into a complete pattern. "Gee. Stop. It's no good. I can't go on."

"What do you mean, you can't go on?"

"I've got appendicitis, Gee. My appendix just burst." Archie meant to sit down on a ridge, but melted into a small crevasse between two ridges.

Gee came back to lift him up. Archie cried out in pain. Now, he was in agony, doubled over, the blurred mental curtain gone. "Oh, Goddamn it," he cried out, "don't touch me, don't touch me, let me curl up and die. Oh God, God, I've never felt anything like this for pain."

Quickly, Gee found their medical pack, and gave him some painkiller.

"That won't stop it," Archie sobbed. "Gee, I'm done for. I can't walk. You're going to have to leave me and go on to Keilan."

"Are you insane? I'd never find you out here again."

"Then you have to go on without me. This is not a joke, Gee. My insides have ruptured."

"Under no circumstances am I deserting you." Gee's voice was firm. "I brought you out here. I pack out what I pack in."

"You can't— " Archie cried out in pain again as Gee lifted him up onto his shoulders. Then he passed out.

A jolt made him cry out. Time must have passed. He was still over Gee's shoulder. Gee's voice said, "At least you're still making noise. You've been silent for so long I was worried."

"Not good noises," Archie gasped, and passed out again.

When Gee shifted him on his shoulders, the pain woke him again. He thought, *I never realized how strong he is*, and faded out.

Again, he reached consciousness. He was lying down. "Gee— "

"I'm taking a breather." Gee's voice was subdued, but otherwise normal. "We're getting closer to Keilan. Go back to sleep." It was impossible to see. Gee's hands touched him, finding his mouth, and tipped a little liquid down his throat. More of the painkiller, probably. Archie didn't have the strength to ask. He closed his eyes.

A blast of icy wind brought him around. The thought occurred, *No chance of putting up a tent in this wind.*

Another painful shift on Gee's shoulders made him groan. He heard Gee's voice. No idea what he was saying or how he said it. Odd to think of Gee even speaking aloud, without an audience. He thought he heard him say, "Hang in there, Archie, just hang in there." But the voice didn't sound like Gee's. More desperate, perhaps.

The painkiller was meant for broken legs and similar catastrophes. It kept out pain but also rational thought. Archie could barely appreciate what Gee was attempting: Trying to haul his only friend to safety, knowing that he had endangered Archie's life and probably killed them both. Agonizing miles of carrying Archie, refusing to leave him behind.

A tremendous drop brought him to sudden consciousness. He felt himself flying, just like the dream. As he did in the dream, he grabbed hold. So cold, so hard. Not Mum.

He felt Gee's arms wrap around him. "I've got you. I've got you. Let go." Oh. It was Gee. The mountain. Gee pried Archie's hands loose from the rock spur.

It must have been a long time before he responded, though. "Sure?" he gasped.

"What? Yes, I'm sure." There was a blinding red light, for just a moment, then total darkness.

Archie woke up in the snow, in the dark. "Gee— "

A stirring in the snow. "Sh. Don't talk." Barely able to sense Gee bending over him, grasping his shoulder, brushing off snow. "It's an ice wall. I can't get around it or over it. I can't go back. I am sorry."

"Don't be, Gee. I'm sorry I let you down, too. I never meant to. I am dying." Archie examined this experience with new interest. Nothing hurt. He wasn't cold any more. Nothing could be done. It was not worth worrying about. Regrets about his life? None to speak of. Pretty calming, actually. *You know, I'd been doing all right so far*, he thought. "So this is what it's like. Queer. Not such a bad feeling, at that."

Gee was silent for a long moment. "I never meant this to happen. I am to blame. I never even looked at you. I am so, so sorry." There was more emotion in his voice than Archie could ever remember hearing.

Archie knew his words slurred. "Caring for only yourself is easy."

Archie could not imagine what Gee was doing or thinking. Another man, here in the dark, might be either weeping or praying. Archie thought disinterestedly: *I wonder at which exact moment Max will tell the world that our badges have stopped functioning?*

Archie closed his eyes, and felt great peace.

Noises. Warmth. Not worth stirring for.

Warmth again. Sweating. Thirsty. Damp cloth on his lips.

Soft noises. Men's quiet voices. He groaned. Gentle words, not in English. Something or someone sliding or moving on a floor. Damp cloth across his face and lips. Someone said, "Water," and held up his head for him to sip. He trusted the familiar voice.

His stomach hurt.

His stomach. Appendicitis. He couldn't open his eyes. He was lying flat, on something hard. He tried to speak, but knew he only made a noise.

"Easy, Archie. Don't rush it," said a voice he knew well.

He felt like his brain was a dusty, dead thing. He grimaced, tried to think, tried to move.

"Easy, Archie."

"Gee— " he managed— "Wh— "

"We're safe, Archie." A damp cloth touched his lips. He heard Gee's voice. "We're safe. Go back to sleep."

Obediently, he passed into a peaceful sleep.

For the rest of his life, whenever he was very ill, Archie heard that voice, felt that soft cloth, and slept the sleep of a trusting child.

Waking again. This time, he heard echoes. He heard the sounds of soft boots or slippers swishing against stone, the murmuring sounds of men's voices, sweeping, and something else— chants?

That was what made him open his eyes. The glare of the lamp was painful.

He was on a padded mat in a cave. It was warm and well-lit. The figure near him shifted position to see him better in the lamplight. Archie did not know the face— a dark-bearded man in rough native clothes. When he saw that Archie's eyes were open, he reached for a cloth and dampened his lips. It was a gentle motion, as compassionate as the look in the man's eyes.

"Thanks," Archie said weakly. "I think I'm here for good now." He had no idea if the stranger spoke English.

The stranger smiled and settled, cross-legged, near the mat. "I think you're right," said the stranger, but the voice was undoubtedly Gee's.

Archie started. "Good God!" He winced at the pain in his stomach as he tried to sit up, and felt the resistance of a pad of bandages.

Gee leaned forward in alarm. "Easy, easy!"

"How long have I been unconscious?"

"Ten days. During which time, I might add, I have learned to make a proper bowl of tea, a decent helping of edible rice, learned to sweep floors properly, how to speak, read, and exercise properly, surgical nursing practice, and how to be a general carry-all man for the Abbot of Karpo Gompa. Besides learning some Tibetan, and improving my colloquial Chinese wonderfully."

"God in Heaven," Archie breathed.

Gee promptly proved that he was no liar by changing Archie's dressing. The incision was still pus-filled and repulsive, but Gee never turned a hair. He changed the dressing as if he had done it all his life, certainly many times before this. The gentle care Gee gave Archie was as stunning as anaesthetic.

Gee changed the dressing, quickly and competently— yet gently. His entire stance and attitude was so uncharacteristic that Archie could find no words. "How— ?"

"I'd been firing the flare gun from time to time, although there was no hope of anyone seeing even a laser in that uninhabited region. The patrol spotted my very last flare before I went down, too."

"The red flash! How stupid of me."

"Mmph. Well, then I won't tell you how far I'd gone before I remembered I had it." Gee face actually reddened slightly. Normally, he would not confess to such a failing.

"Moot, since they wouldn't have seen it earlier, anyway," said Archie.

"True, but not particularly consoling. I remember wondering how long before Max would register our deaths."

"So did I," Archie interjected.

"The next moment, a man hovered over me. He said get up, and I did."

"Arrow?"

"I think so. Those moments are rather confused. I explained what had happened to you, in Chinese, and accompanied them here. I helped them set up their makeshift surgery. I assisted— while they sliced you open by candlelight. There was a prayer group chanting the entire time— that's what I remember best." Gee was obviously putting an effort into keeping a commonplace tone. As he spoke, Archie reflected that lesser men would have melted into a pile of jelly long before that. "They said they'd cleaned you out and sewed you up to the best of their ability and now it was all in the hands of you and God. That was when I slept."

"Must have been a hell of a night."

"And a day and a night." He shook his head, as if to chase away an unpleasant sound or vision. "You took a long time to pull through. I was numb by the time you passed into a normal sleep. I could have slept on bare rock. In fact, I think I did. When I woke up, everything that happened before seemed unreal."

"Like a dream?"

"I don't dream, at least never that I can remember. So I have no standard of comparison." He stared at the wall for a moment, then added, "I can't explain to you what I am seeing now because I don't have the vocabulary for it."

Archie's instincts warned him not to probe that statement. There was something unusual in Gee's current mental state. "But since we've been here, you've done the daily drill the way the Karpo Gompa does it."

Gamemaster finished cleaning up the food and bath materials. Then he sat down beside Archie again. "We are going to be here for a long time, Archie— at least long enough for you to travel. In that time, the Abbot has informed me that I am responsible for our room and board, not you. The medium of exchange is not North American cash."

"He wants your soul," Archie guessed.

There was surprise in Gee's eyes. "He is convinced I have one, some-where. He intends to teach me some religion. And— perhaps he can do it."

"Perhaps he can. You need it." Strange how it didn't bother him to make such an atrocious statement to his boss, either.

For a moment, Gee was silent. Then he said, "I think so, too." He did not meet Archie's gaze. It was the closest Gee had ever come to abject repentance for an error. The Gamemaster always took the blame for his own mistakes, but not in such humility. Of course, this had been a whopper, a stupid impulse caused by his own stubbornness and then forced upon another human being. It really wasn't that important, Archie thought. They were both alive. It was incredibly easy to forgive him.

Archie reached out and gripped his hand. The Gamemaster returned the grip. Then, wordlessly, he gathered up his materials.

"Ahfternoon tea," said the rough-bearded giant with a smile, in a very English accent that was meant to be a put-on.

Archie gripped the mat and shoved himself up to a sitting position. The incision hurt as it folded with the bandage. He lifted the bowl to his lips, and stopped. "What, no yak butter and milk?"

The giant seated himself comfortably. "No, plain ja-ngamo. I thought you might be tired of additives."

Archie sipped the hot black tea with sugar. "Well, I was, thank you. Bhoja is an acquired taste, but I am aware that it's good for me." The steam felt good on his face, and wholesome. He breathed in the aroma of plain black tea. Usually Gee came in with the smiling Tibetan cook-novice, Chenni, for afternoon tea. Archie was being especially honored today. Now that he was recovered enough to sit up and was beginning to understand who was who and what was what, he knew Arrow's importance here.

Richard Arrow's regular speaking accent was very mild, but English nonetheless. "Here's some bread, too. That's where you'll find the butter. Chenni said you must have it on something."

"Chenni and the others are spoiling me rotten and I deeply appreciate it." Archie sipped tea. "I only wish they'd let me stand up and tend to some of my own business."

"That will come with time," Richard Arrow replied. "Our surgery was primitive, and you were very badly poisoned by your own wastes. When I found you in the snow I expected your corpse. I thought Gennaro merely hopeful when he said you were alive. And tending to you is good penance for Gennaro. He freely admits his irresponsibility in bringing you to Keilan."

Silently, Archie drank tea and waited. There was a point to this visit.

"Why were you going to Keilan, Archie?" Richard Arrow asked quietly.

"I was accompanying Gennaro. You should ask him that." As Archie had suspected, they did not know that Gennaro and the legendary Gamemaster were one and the same.

"The Abbot has asked him. Pride clamps his jaw. He will not speak of who he is, or why he is here, until he sees that you are well and you have not lost your life to his foolishness." Arrow sipped tea he had provided himself on the tray he brought in. Then his tone changed. "Do you have any idea what he is going through, here? He is reviled like the lowest acolyte by the Abbot. No complaint escapes his lips. His humility is perfect. The Abbot says he is a warrior king straight from the storybooks, here to pay a price like any acolyte. He takes his lessons, does his schoolwork, performs as servant to you and the Abbot. Is he paying his dues?"

"I think so," said Archie. "He thinks it's fair. I have no idea if you're making a dent in him or not."

That, apparently, was what Arrow wanted to know. He nodded in understanding. "You met death in the snow. You weren't afraid. But you have no idea what he met, do you?"

"None whatsoever. And you won't find out from him," said Archie.

"The Abbot will," Richard Arrow replied. "He is the wisest man I have ever known."

Archie shook his head. "But Gennaro is a gene-mod."

"That doesn't matter. He's still a man. Interesting that you knew he was a gene-mod. He hasn't said so, although it's obvious. He clears 'em off the mat at martial arts practice, and almost doesn't notice when he's been hit." Richard's eyes were a hazel color very like John Arrow's. He saw Archie swallow. "What's wrong?"

"I've— " Archie took a deep breath. "Necrophobia. I have it badly. Since I was a child, I've had a fear of dead bodies. Even a housekeeping robot makes me faint, or run away. Your face reminds me of a friend who died. I'm trying to maintain eye contact with you. And I can't."

"Don't look at me, then. Look down. Here." Arrow patted a decorative design on the tea tray, an entwined flower, elephant, and something leading it that looked less like a man and more like a monkey. His voice took on a different tone, the tone of a counselor. "You must learn to breathe, Archie. You might still feel the fear, but at least you won't faint."

"That would be nice," said Archie. "I don't like this feeling. No hypnotism, though."

"None," Arrow promised, as they started the breathing exercise.

"The infected smell is gone," Gee observed, wiping Archie's incision. "This is clean. You're healing quickly."

"I feel better, too," Archie concurred. "I had noticed the difference in the cut."

"This is very encouraging."

While Gee was changing his bandage, Archie opened a new topic. "We need to discuss something."

"All right." Gee kept working, not looking at him.

"You pinned my badge inside my shirt. I haven't said anything. Richard Arrow was in here today, asking why we were headed to Keilan."

"What did you tell him?" Gee cleaned the wound.

"To ask you. That's not the point. The point is, you're stalling. I need to know why."

Gee glanced at his face while he finished the bandages. "What do you think?"

Archie met his gaze squarely. "Honestly? I don't know you well enough to know if you're hiding classified information, ashamed of doing something stupid, or if you got a genuine scare."

The water tinkled in the bowl as Gee washed his hands and wiped them carefully. "Do you know what they call me?"

"The warrior king. And they don't even know who you are." Archie drew breath. "I think you should tell them."

"I don't want to," said the Gamemaster.

"I know. And I'm asking, why not?"

Gee still wiped his hands with the towel, appeared to catch himself making a repetitive movement, and stopped. It was the first time Archie had ever seen such a gesture from him. Was this true emotion?

Archie pressed, "You're keeping your secret self from them because as long as they don't have it, you're not vulnerable. All right, I will honor that, if you want me to. I won't blow the lid off. But, Gee— you'll never have a better, safer chance to take the lid off, yourself, and look inside. I can't say if that will be good or bad. Mr. Zhaba said— the day something popped on you— he only hoped the rest of the world could contain the explosion."

"Mr. Zhaba said?" The alert look he gave Archie was one he recognized— Gee respected Mr. Zhaba's opinion. That morning walk with the old soldier in Lhasa must have been quite an education. For the first time, Archie was sorry he missed it.

"And he isn't even a Buddhist, like the Dalai Lama. Other people see something we can't see."

Gee sat in thought for a moment. Then he said, "Strange that you, of all people, can't see anything."

"Not at all," Archie answered. "You're my friend. Naturally I have blind spots. In fact, you've commented upon some of them."

"Oh. I have, haven't I?" His tone was so unlike him that Archie felt a sudden surge of wonderment. Had the Abbot made a dent, after all? "What would you suggest, Archie?"

"I'm not going to take responsibility for your decision." How many times had Archie said that to a student?

The Gamemaster smiled, a smile that even warmed his eyes. That never happened, either. "I understood that. What's your wish?"

"My wish?" Archie stared at the wall of his sickroom before he spoke. He wanted to give his most honest reply to this broad question. "To not lose it at the sight of a robot or dead body. Richard Arrow could help me, I think. I would dearly love to react like other people. However— " he focused back on Gee's face— "when he tries, I'm bound to let out that the cause of my phobia is Gamemaster Inc."

Gee watched him intently. Somehow, Archie felt that he had indeed shocked him.

"It was the raid in Personnel, back when I was five. I was trapped in the file room with three corpses."

Expressionlessly, Gee gathered up bandages and washcloths. Then he said, "Give me tonight to think about it before you say or do anything."

"Certainly."

Archie fell asleep in the knowledge that Gee sat on his mat in the corner of the sickroom. He awoke to the sound of the morning chant, expecting to find him either asleep or absent, as usual. However, he seemed not to have moved from his sitting position. He rose and left as soon as he saw that Archie was awake.

The usual routine was for Gee to appear in a few minutes with morning tea. Archie sat up carefully, and waited. Too much time passed. Archie realized that Gennaro had been quite literal when he had asked for the night to think about it. It was a good guess that he had made his decision.

Richard Arrow entered the room, looking somber. Chenni, the cheerful young cook-monk in the orange-yellow robe, accompanied him with the morning tray. Arrow's voice was subdued. "May I see your badge?"

Archie unpinned it from inside his shirt, and handed it to him. Chenni looked, too. "Nine," said Chenni, in Chinese.

Arrow gave it back. "And the reason my face disturbed you?"

"Because you look so much like your brother," Archie confirmed regretfully. "He died recently."

"So Gennaro said." He sat down.

"Drink," Chenni said to Archie. "Today will be a strenuous day. The Abbot wishes to question you. You must walk to him."

Without heat, Archie protested, "I'm like a baby."

"He knows," said Arrow. "There will never be a better time."

Archie willed his legs and feet to cross that rough cave floor without falling. He made it to a rug that awaited him, directly in front of an old man dressed in yellow robes. Archie sat down carefully. Once seated, he allowed himself to look at the cave wall drawings, the candles, the rugs, and the thirty or so men seated or kneeling around and behind him. It was the first time he had been out of his sickroom in two weeks. It would have been impossible not to peek.

When at last he met the Abbot's eyes, the first thing that struck him was that the Abbot was quite aware of what he had been doing. "How do you feel?" the Abbot asked, in standard Chinese.

"I am weak." Archie, not good in this language, felt a further limitation. "Thank you for your aid. I am grateful."

"Does your life matter to you?"

Archie answered, "Not to me so much as to others." The language was a struggle. Neither Arrow nor Gennaro offered so much as an encouraging look, leaving the entire discussion to Archie alone.

"Gennaro said that you were a teacher. You taught ancient literature, and supervised children under your care. Is that so?"

"Yes, it is so."

"Why did you leave that work?"

"I have never left it," Archie replied.

The Abbot understood. Once a teacher, always a teacher. "Here, you will learn more, then you will be able to teach more. You will learn to read, write, and speak the lessons. You will recover your health."

"Thank you."

"That is all," said the Abbot.

-7-

Monkey Games

Archie matched pace with the two other mattress-beaters on either side of him, whacking the dust out of the bedding on racks in the open air near the entryway of the cavern. The fresh air blew away the smells of fires, candles, and three months of staleness in the caves.

Richard Arrow, carrying a yoke of buckets full of snow back to the entrance, cautioned him, "Don't hurt yourself doing that, Archie. You've only been walking around a week now."

Gee, behind Arrow with matching buckets, commented, "You're wasting your breath. He's not here. He's in the crease with the score against him."

Arrow grinned. "Among the things I don't miss about England is that. You make cricket sound almost an interesting game, which it's not."

"A couple of Philistines," Archie panted, and they both chuckled. Then he switched to the pidgin Tibetan in common use so that the other workers wouldn't feel left out. "I want to be useful. I must strengthen my body also." Being outside, in the beautiful sunlight and bright snow, felt miraculous enough. "And, I want to learn to make proper tea and rice. If even Gennaro can learn it, how hard can it be?"

That brought roars of laughter from the monks doing chores. It would be the joke told at dinner tonight. Gee took the ribbing good-naturedly. "That knocks a year off the retirement time I owe you," he warned.

"Bringing it down to nine thousand, nine hundred and ninety-eight years?" Arrow grinned.

"Roughly."

"Ninety-nine," Archie contradicted, aiming a few more great whacks at the mattress. Chenni, still laughing, took it down from the rack for him, since he still could not lift heavy objects, and hung another in its place.

He whacked it single-mindedly until he heard Gee say, "Stop." Gee had brought a cup of water for him.

Archie drank gratefully. "Thirsty business. All that dust." He looked approvingly at housework spread over the mountainside. "Hard to believe thirty-odd men trapped in caves by winter weather could accomplish so much."

"They're having great fun with you," said Gee.

"I'm enjoying it, too," said Archie. "The Abbot reminds me more of my Headmaster at Mars-Isidis daily. Though I think perhaps the hardest thing I've ever done are the open hypnotism sessions with Richard Arrow. It's very difficult, pulling one's defenses down completely."

"I would be both physiologically and psychologically unable to do it. After the reign of Sang Tvar the Torturer in Hong Kong, anti-hypnotism lessons were built into Gamemaster training. It's a regretful necessity, because there are still Sangs throughout the world, so my mind simply folds up or switches to another topic. I've been trained for it. It is interesting to watch, though, as you use the weakness in your defenses to strengthen yourself. The Abbot said it is a classical martial arts move, taken from the physical and applied to the mental."

"The Abbot's as knowledgeable in Chinese and Tibetan as anything I've encountered at Oxford. The men are getting a first-class education." He paused. "Go ahead, say it."

"I don't need to." A smile touched Gee's lips. "I'm supposed to say, 'And do what with it,' and you reply, 'To become better men.'"

"We *have* been here a while, haven't we?" Archie agreed.

The Karpo Gompa, despite its eccentric location, was very Tibetan. Traditionally in Tibet, since the fifth century, the eldest son took over the land when his father died and any other sons became monks. Daughters did not stay at home unmarried, but either became the wife ("the woman") on some farm, or nuns. "No worry about an inherited lot too small to live on, or money going in a different direction from entailed land," Arrow explained to them as they sat, finishing a meal, one evening.. "Since the other sons didn't get anything and knew it all their lives, it was no surprise for them to head for the monastery."

"Suppose the second son didn't want to go?" Archie asked curiously.

When Richard Arrow smiled, a set of sunny wrinkles appeared around his eyes, just above the thick beard. "He didn't have to. But he couldn't get married, either, or raise a family. The boys who remained on the farm were all married to the same one wife that the first son married."

"Whose children, logically, followed the same path as those before them."

"Exactly. That was part of the horror of the Communists, you see— killing monks, forcing them to rape the nuns, throwing them out into the streets. They destroyed centuries of orderliness about both marriage and real estate."

Gennaro had been silent during this conversation. Now, as he drank tea, he murmured, "It was provided for. But you are no Tibetan, Abbot-to-Be."

"I am a second son, though," Richard replied. "John was three years older than I. It was in order for me to be here. I've found a useful place where I am welcome." A cloud passed over that face, well-weathered by the reflection of winter sun on snow. "Which is more than I can rightfully say about the place where I was born." He changed the topic abruptly. This did not surprise

Archie, since John Arrow, too, never mentioned home or family. "I still wonder about your method of arriving here. True, you were in God's hands, as we have all agreed. And yet, at the same time, my mind objects to the purely religious theory. You were traveling by compass. There was no reason you should have ended up going in circles in the storm."

Gee nodded, and frowned thoughtfully at the empty bowl before him. "I was perhaps confused by the blizzard and Archie's desperate condition, but not to that extent. – No offense, Archie."

"None taken," Archie replied good-humoredly. "I'm puzzled, too. There's no reason I can think why your compass should have developed a mind of its own right then."

Gee started. Richard Arrow jumped and looked at him in the same moment.

"A mind of its own!" Arrow exclaimed. "Were you using a computerized orientation system?"

Apparently, Gennaro had been struck by the same idea. "Yes. Not a magnetic one. That's it, of course." At Archie's blank stare, he explained, "Computerized. Do you see? Who was aware of our condition but mute?"

It struck him at last. "Max," said Archie in wonder.

"Exactly. He was speaking to us in the only device available to him, to tell us that you were ailing. He didn't know I was quite aware of that. I was looking at the compass to find north— but Max was pointing continually at you."

Archie began regular trips outside. Hours of uninterrupted sleep, healthy food and drink, and a peaceful mind paid off well. He marveled at how well he felt, how quickly.

The day came at last when Gennaro said to him, "We must leave tomorrow."

They spoke in Tibetan out of politeness for the others, but they also spoke it because they were comfortable with it. "I will miss this place," said Archie.

Richard Arrow— the next Abbot of Karpo Gompa— said to them, "I have been thinking about what you told me. Come."

They followed him to a cave used only by the Abbot and Arrow himself. It was lit with perhaps a dozen candles, a room well-decorated with religious ornaments. There was nothing that would be inconvenient to carry from one mountain cave to another. In this room, a book of meditations rested on a stone base. "I have wondered since you mentioned it which stone monkey could have been the one in my brother's puzzle. My only conjecture is this." He ran his hand down the intricate carvings of the stone— where, certainly, a stylized monkey seemed to hold the book in position. "I wrote him once and mentioned it. This pedestal is used only for resting the holy books of the

Abbot. I don't know if John expected me to have come that far, or if it was merely hope. John and I haven't seen each other since we were teenagers. We wrote a bit, though, back and forth, when he was stationed out in space and I was learning my way here. I feel this is the stone monkey he meant."

Gee looked at Archie questioningly. Archie gazed at the stone carving for a long time. It was beautiful, a greyish marble about a foot and a half tall. The figure was a monkey dressed in Tibetan clothing, holding his hands upward to receive an open book. "I think it is," said Archie. "I'm pretty certain this is John Arrow's stone monkey."

"May I touch it?" Gee asked. Richard Arrow nodded affirmative. Gee ran his hands over the stone figure as carefully as he had examined every chessman. At last, he grimaced and said, "Nothing."

"You expected a clue to the next part of the riddle," Richard observed. "I shouldn't worry. I wouldn't be surprised if you find the middle portion to be the easiest of all."

"You're sure it was the right monkey," Gee said, as they hiked down the sunlit mountains. It seemed so much easier than the trip up, like a brief jaunt in the Alps.

"Pretty much so. It jibes with my half-clue. Apparently this riddle involves items with which John Arrow had personal knowledge." Archie concentrated on his footing. His side still hurt occasionally, and the cold still cut like a knife. He was glad of the Gamemaster Inc. thermals and boots. When they stopped for a meal break, Archie said, "I still have a question to ask."

"There can't be too many questions left that haven't been sieved out of us in the past two months," Gennaro replied accommodatingly. "Fire ahead."

"You never answered, for the Abbot or me, what would happen if you did kick off on one of these adventures, and leave the business with no heir. You just say, 'It's provided for.' Provided for how?"

His dark friend stopped and looked at him in genuine surprise. "You don't know?"

"Don't know what?" Archie asked the obvious question.

"Max taps the Acting Administrator if my signal or vital signs disappear, or if I am otherwise disabled. Since I have no children, the Acting Administrator taps Cryo when I'm dead."

"Cryo?" Archie demanded. "As in cryogenics? Frozen? Who's frozen?"

Again, that odd look. "You really don't know. Genoa, of course."

"Genoa?" Archie barely recognized the name. Gennaro's brother, the dead one. Not the one Mum had raised hell about, but the older one. There had been three brothers.

"Sure. Oldest of each generation goes into storage, the others fight for the title. If they all die, the Acting Administrator pulls the youngest cryo out of cold storage. My grandfather was the cryo of his generation— haven't you read how Gaikin 'returned from abroad to assume his duties'?"

"My God. I didn't know. That's appalling!"

"Your reaction might explain why it was never mentioned," Gee said thoughtfully. "The business ought not to be split up among various factions which might compete against each other, or subdivided into uselessness. It must remain a single viable unit. It's not that much different from the Tibetan land traditions. Perhaps my ancestor was inspired by them. I certainly expected you to take it better. Of course I cannot leave the company without an owner. I exist for that. Naturally there are safeguards."

"Yes, but— " Archie swallowed it. "I suppose you're right. And the Acting Administrator?"

"— is an employee of Gamemaster Inc. who stays completely out of the limelight unless called upon. His or her regular job is not related to the invocation of emergency powers, which may never happen. Although I like to give them a chance to practice from time to time, just in case." Again, that strange look "This is all new to you."

"Certainly it is. I'm stunned. At the same time, I'm thanking God the Acting Administrator isn't me."

Gee smiled. "No, it's not. You didn't qualify. And— hate to sound trite— I'm glad. It would have been awkward."

"Awkward is one word for it," Archie agreed fervently. "Why did you think I'd know? That's not the kind of office gossip that floats around the Gee-9 lab. Apparently the Cryo Manager is even more hush-hush than Acting Administrator."

"It was also not the bulk of his work. Cryo Manager for three or four chambers wasn't a full-time job."

Past tense. Archie licked dry lips as he asked a question whose answer had already occurred to him. "What did he do the rest of the time?"

Gee knew he knew. "He worked for Accounting, for forty-five years."

His father, George Chamberlain.

Archie voiced his first thought. "Mum doesn't know, does she?"

"I don't think so."

"All right," said Archie. "It stops here."

"Very well," agreed the Gamemaster. "So it does."

Mrs. Zhaba was standing in front of the red door, stringing some new prayer flags across a shutter, when she turned and saw two men she took for strangers. But it took her only a moment— "Aaaaiiiihaaaiiieee!" She dived off her stepladder and into Gee's arms.

Archie and Gee had only thought they'd been treated well here once before. Now, they were welcomed like lost orphans. They spent the evening in a riotous dinner with half of Lhasa packed in the house. Mrs. Zhaba kept touching their hair and faces as if to believe they were real. There were tears on her cheeks. Archie was sure she'd had a religious moment when she touched Gee. Mr. Zhaba beamed as if someone had promoted him to District Administrator. There was much they didn't tell about their harrowing time in the mountains, but they told tales that made the mysterious Karpo Gompa look better than ever.

Harry Goto was there to pick them up in record time, but was also welcomed like a wandering hero, much to his astonishment. He ended up staying the night in the comfortable Tibetan house with the red door. Clean, shaved, and looking more like themselves, Gee and Archie flew back to West Meg in the morning with Harry. Archie felt the absence in his bones as they left Tibet behind. For him, it would always be the most strenuous, beneficial vacation of his life, and certainly worth while. Nonetheless, Archie steeled himself to face forward, to greet West Meg and the new day.

It saddened him to watch Gennaro— the Gamemaster— face it also. His impregnable shell reappeared as the miles passed beneath them. Archie watched him sit straighter in the seat of the business shuttle, look more attentively at his papers, and dictate answers to letters in an ever-sharpening tone. By the time they reached West Meg, the twinkle in his eye had vanished. His voice had recovered most of its old dry tone. They had one week to finish quarterly deadline. March was almost over and April about to begin. Little could they have imagined, Archie thought, what they would tally this First Quarter.

Plunging into two month's accumulated mail, Archie regretted how quickly they had completely re-immersed themselves in the same old routine. If only, he thought wistfully, they could keep a piece of their experience. If only, somehow, there could be a memento of their journey here in West Meg. At last, he turned his thoughts into action. He sent a telefax, the best method of communication to Tibet, to ask a favor.

A few days later, Archie was at his cubicle desk, still trying to shovel out from under a monumental "To Do" list that had accumulated in his absence, when he felt someone at the door. He turned, expecting to see Trann. Instead, it was Gennaro, making an unprecedented live appearance in the lab.

Gee smiled. For a moment, the Tibetan light returned. "Thank you for the gift."

"Oh, good," said Archie, "it arrived. I asked Mrs. Zhaba to shop around for me."

"It's quite beautiful. Have you seen it?"

"No, I haven't."

"I'll be at home tonight. Come up after dinner. I put it in the office. It seems somehow appropriate." He left.

Appropriate, yes, to have a statue of the Bodhisattva of Compassion, the most beautiful of the Buddhas-To-Be, in the corner of the master office. Maybe it would do some good after all, Archie mused.

Archie shut out everything and concentrated on the bowler.

He didn't expect to save the game, but if he only held a respectable bat, the next batter *would* win. Griffith was in position. The ball came speeding toward him. Archie hit it to leg, and ran like hell.

Griffith did his part, too. As they passed, Griffith said, "Give us another!"

"Do my best," Archie panted.

He kept his promise. Another to leg. There were cheers. The fielders started to gather at leg. This time, Archie pasted one to off, and suckered the entire opposing team. The hits were going right where he wanted them today. Griffith was grinning like a fool. Back to leg, one more. Eventually the ball was dead, but Archie had achieved his aim of increasing the score enough for the next batter to win.

The changing-room was full of high spirits after the game. Men sang, showers splattered, bare feet padded around on the changing-room floor. Timberlake, the captain, clapped Archie's shoulder. "Damn good job, Chamberlain."

"Damn good job by all of us."

"You said it. We may not have star players, but we're a star team. By the way, your girlfriend's outside waiting for you. She's a stunner. You never said."

He blinked. "Girlfriend?"

"Oh, now he says which one. The natural blonde in the turtleneck and green slacks. If you don't want her, say so now and let the line form on the left."

"Oh," said Archie, "her."

Another cricketer came in, saying, "Sheila's waiting for you, Chamberlain."

So he saw. Quickly he changed his clothes and headed back out to the stands, where Lieutenant Sheila McAllen stood, minus her olive uniform jacket to avoid attention. She watched him approach and set down his bag of gear. "Hi," she said.

"Hi yourself," said Archie. "What brings you here?"

"I'd never seen a cricket game before. It was an opportunity. And I wanted to discuss something with you."

"Shall we discuss it over dinner, then?" Archie was famished.

"No, thank you," Lt. McAllen replied, "I'd rather not."

"It would be my treat. I'm asking you."

"I'd rather not be beholden to you." The answer was rather stiff.

"Oh." Archie, nonplussed and starving, was moved to say, "Well, if you don't mind then, we've played double innings and I simply must have sustenance. I want to hit up the fish and chips booth over there before they close."

"Sure. Go ahead, I don't mind. I'll wait here at the bleachers," she said. Archie dropped his gear at the stand, and got himself a paper full of fish and chips.

He sat on the stand. The smell of fish and chips and vinegar wafting up to him was overpowering. He sank his teeth into hot fish, then potatoes, again and again until he took the edge off his hunger. "Sorry to be so single-minded," he said at last, "but as you may know, I've been ill. I'm still getting my strength back."

Lt. McAllen sat on an upper bench, looking down at him. "Is this your first long game since you got back?"

"My longest, yes." Archie took another healthy bite of the fish. He saw a look on her face that could be best interpreted as hungry. A thought occurred to him for the first time: *Maybe she's not just watching her reputation.* "Want some? There's more than I can eat. I hate to throw good food out."

Apparently, it was the right thing to say. She accepted a chip, then some fish. "Thanks. They are good, even with vinegar."

"You're welcome. Now, what brings you out here?"

"I wanted to talk with you, and I'm not on the Gamemaster Inc. call list."

"You aren't?" He cast back his mind. "Surely you are. You called me at home."

"That was business. And— I didn't know— I knew you'd been away for quite a while— I didn't know if you even knew that you were suing me."

Archie stopped eating to stare. "That I was what?"

"I did something stupid, Mr. Chamberlain. I don't know how. I could have sworn I'd taken all the headers off the press releases. But I sent out one that still had the ECM boilerplate about restricted use and penalties, and Gamemaster Inc. Legal came down on HQ like a ton of bricks." She swallowed. "And they came down on me. You had a Gamemaster 9 guarantee on it that it would be open-use research, and it really looks like— that I was trying to pirate it, and cut you out. I never."

"Of course you never," said Archie indignantly.

She kept her jaw clenched as she swallowed the remainder of her pride. "When I tried to get through to you, I got stonewalled, because we were now on opposing legal sides. All I could think of was to try to catch you off-site and assure you it was an accident, lawsuit or not. I remembered you saying you played cricket on Saturdays, so I took a chance."

"I'm glad you did. I had no idea."

"When I saw you today, I knew you didn't." Lt. McAllen still had a clamp on her jaw. "I can't believe I did such a stupid thing. Everything was going so well, and then suddenly, bam! There was Gamemaster Inc. Legal, shutting it down."

"Let me see what I can do, Lieutenant. I can step on some bunions somewhere." He hesitated, hating to ask a personal question. "How much did you get hurt?"

She took another chip before she answered. "Demerits and a pay cut." She might have been admitting betrayal of the United Nations, from her tone. "That's not important. I'd rather you didn't fuss about me, or— they'd think there was something unprofessional about it. I'm— a junior officer in that department, and— it hasn't been easy."

Archie suspected loads of understatement in each of those sentences. He also suspected that they were sitting here, munching chips in the stands, because Sheila McAllen couldn't afford to go Dutch treat. She lived from payday to payday on a minuscule paycheck, now further reduced, and was too proud to admit it.

"I work with a bunch of great guys. There's so much to learn. I think I'm getting somewhere, and then— I backslide."

Archie climbed a row to sit beside her, and shifted the fish and chips to his other hand so they could both get at them comfortably. She accepted the unspoken offer to help herself to more.

"So what you're really asking me to do," Archie summarized, "is to focus on the liver-cell research itself and minimize the damage to it on my end."

"Yes, that's it."

"And not to notice that I've given you a monumental bloody nose."

She stopped either laughter or tears. "Bleeding all over the pavement, as you would say."

It was something Archie *would* say. He smiled. "All right. I can do that." He saw a speaker nearby, and raised his voice. "Max, what news of the world?"

"Standing by, Archie."

"I need an override code for Lieutenant Sheila McAllen of the Earth Combined Military."

"Seven seven one, Archie."

"Thanks, Max." He turned back to her. "So. The next time the 'We're sorry' message kicks in, you say in a very normal tone of voice, 'Override 771.' Just until this lawsuit business is over and you're back on the regular call list."

"Thank you," she said.

"You're more than welcome. I don't have that many contacts in the military that I can afford to lose them." Just as he was thinking he needed something to drink, the Lieutenant lifted up a container.

"It's just water. Want some?" she asked.

"If you don't mind sharing germs."

To Archie's surprise, Lt. McAllen laughed. "You didn't have something contagious, did you?"

"Heavens, no." He drank. "Appendicitis, in the heart of Tibet."

"My God!" Her eyes opened wide.

"Mm-hm. Didn't get bad enough to set off Max until we were so far away Max couldn't tell us. It was a jolly mess. I'm all right now, though my side still aches and I tire very easily."

"And you just played cricket all day," she said wryly.

"I can't tell you how comfy and inviting this hard bench looks, so it's a sure sign I'm fading," Archie agreed. "Taxi, home, change of clothes, and out." He yawned. "Now, come on, I'll see you home."

"No way," she said. "You'd fall asleep in the cab and end up in La Paz. *I'll* see *you* to a cab, and then I'll get MilTrans back to the base."

"Sound thinking," he agreed. "Ungentlemanly, but adequate."

"That's me all over," said Lt. McAllen.

Since the next day was Sunday, Archie slept in. Then, morning tea in hand, he sat down at his home console to review the press releases. Yep, that one with the harsh military voice at beginning and end, declaring all the enclosed material to be the property of the government of the United Nations, stuck out like a sore thumb.

He had not shared his uncharitable suspicions with Lieutenant McAllen on the stands, because she was still an idealistic young flag-waving officer. She wouldn't have believed him, anyway. He suspected that, when Sheila McAllen told him she was sure she'd taken those headers off, she was speaking the literal truth.

It also did not take Archie long, using one of Max's sophisticated recovery palimpsest programs, to see that this release had been cobbled together and edited by more than one person, and at various times. It was not McAllen's original work. The same console ID's kept reappearing. There was no means of telling if this was the work of a jealous senior, trying to sandbag young McAllen, or a deliberate effort to spike the liver project, or just a general offensive to get a shindy brewing with Gamemaster Inc. But something, here, was being deliberately sabotaged.

He fought his first impulse, to contact someone in the ECM, and followed SOP instead. Standard Operating Procedure for Gamemasters was quite clear on this. Even if you have given your word or a guarantee, even if it's a private deal, you do not take the law into your own hands. You tell the Lab Manager.

Trann had several Monday-morning brushfires to put out, plus a department-head meeting. Archie was not worried. Being a paid babysitter for thirty-seven primadonnas, as Trann was, would monopolize anyone's time. This was not an emergency, merely an annoyance. He worked on other projects and waited for his turn in the queue.

Trann did not appear at his cubicle until late in the day. He listened attentively while Archie told him about running the press releases through the palimpsest programs, and his results— the releases had been tampered. He kept his silence about McAllen and did not tell of her visit to the cricket field.

Trann gave it the same serious consideration he gave any other problem. "So. Hanging up the research with lawsuits is undesirable. Going ahead, while someone tries to sandbag either you or the newbie, is undesirable. Getting the ECM and the Company fighting again is undesirable. Dropping the project is undesirable. What are our options?"

"Well, my gut feeling is that I don't want to kick it upstairs to the brass on either side. Then they can't help but take official notice of it," said Archie. Trann agreed fully. "What I would really like to know is, Has Lieutenant McAllen had similar problems before, on other projects, and if so, who sandbagged her? That might show it's office politics, or at worst, discrimination by a commanding officer."

"Internal affairs." Trann nodded.

Archie continued, "It would tell whether it's an anti-Gamemaster or anti-McAllen movement. I can't think of any other way to settle that issue."

"Yes, but I can't just waltz into ECM West Meg HQ and demand an internal investigation," Trann pointed out.

"Nor can I," Archie admitted. "I think I'm making some solid contacts there, but this might strain them."

"Then we sit on our hands for now, keep our eyes open, and move forward slowly," Trann concurred. "We know there's something rotten there. We shall be wary. If we bide our time, something will turn up to our advantage." He smiled, a wicked little smile. "That's what makes us Gamemasters."

The second quarter passed into the third quarter. As Gee had predicted, the riddle was temporarily shelved in the rush of ordinary business. Again, Archie did not delude himself into thinking it had been forgotten. In the meantime, he absorbed himself in ordinary work. The Three Rivers game, on the bottom of Archie's lowest-priority list, resurfaced at last like a bad penny.

It was sheer programmers' superstition that caused Archie to declare this program the continual jinx in his life, but there was no doubt he was working on it at the time of the Neptune Shipyard Crisis. Admittedly, this great disaster may have colored his perception of the game.

Archie had no more than looked at the opening screens when Trann's voice cut in on maximum broadcast: "Something's happening, turn to the newsnet, everyone turn to the newsnet, hurry." There was an urgent, horrified tone in his voice.

"Max, save, file, do as he says." Hurriedly, Archie turned his controls to the news. The view he saw was a view of space, somewhere, with ships. "Max, what am I seeing?"

"The Neptune Shipyards, Archie. In the foreground are ships from Earth Combined Military. In the background, at one o'clock, ships from the Federal Law Enforcement Agency. Midfield are unidentified ships which claim to have hostages. Journalists believe it is Recover."

Horrified, Archie saw the laser cannons on the strange ships glow. "Oh, God, they're firing." Shots flashed across the screen.

The FLEA and the ECM returned fire. One of the unidentified ships rolled, glowed, then burst into innumerable pieces.

A journalist's offscreen voice said, "Sensors are beginning to pick up traces of bodies. Some are in spacesuits, some not. Oh, God, it's the hostages. Children, aged— the sensors, say, as young as ten to fourteen years old— "

Oh, please God, thought Archie, finding it hard to breathe. *Not from Mars Isidis. Not from Prentiss's class—*

"We don't have any reports yet where these children came from or how they arrived on the ships— " Pause— "The Earth Combined Military is receiving notification of children missing from the military crèches— "

Archie heard nothing else. He saw the unidentified cruisers move directly backward from the carnage of the destroyed ship. He saw the blast of high-power rockets. The ECM and FLEA lost precious moments maneuvering around the rubble in their way, rather than charge through the children's bodies. That slight delay allowed Recover, if it was them, to get a lead, and vanish. The military ships tore after them.

"They're losing them, aren't they, Max?" Archie's voice was hoarse.

"I predict they will, Archie."

The dead children haunted his sleep for a week. In his dreams, Archie would be teaching class, full of strange children. Then they would suddenly appear in space suits. They would start to float while he spoke about transitive verbs or some other simple language aspect. They would roll, pitch, yaw in place, tethered by air lines, no motion of their features. They were dead, tethered in his classroom, bobbing around like balloons.

After a week, he got in touch with Malasha Masere and told her his problem. Could she recommend a therapist? Very apologetically, she asked him if he could hang on for another week or two. Every therapist in the region was at capacity. He said certainly, and began treating himself, via Max, with memories of his sessions with Richard Arrow. He dealt with the dreams, and they faded. It was the first time Archie felt truly in control of the nightmares.

With great trepidation, he was again working on the Three Rivers game, the continual jinx in his life.

Archie balanced precariously on the raft, and shaded his eyes with his hand. The raft rocked unhealthily beneath his feet. He looked into the sunset, toward the place where the rivers joined. Had he seen something move?

The pirates were still coming around the bend. He checked starboard. There was something moving in the water there, sure enough. Didn't they realize he'd already lost the gold? And wasn't there a sandbar just ahead?

An arm flopped over the starboard side of the boat. He grabbed the boat-hook— where was the boat-hook? it had moved, make a note of that. The pirate was on board, grinning. Archie had no choice but to lay into him with the hook. The pirate, astonished, looked down at his own blood and guts. The combined revolting mess trickled down his legs, reddening the aging wood of the boat's deck. With one foot, Archie pushed him back overboard. The raft rocked from the stern— another pirate tried to climb aboard. No time. There was one shot left in the gun. Archie used it. The result was as gory as the boat-hook had been. Archie could see blood and brains. Damn. That left him nothing for whatever was moving toward him from the direction of the sandbar— surely the river monster.

That dark object moving toward him on the port side was a mine. If he maneuvered the raft around the mine and the oncoming monster— but there was that bloody sandbar to consider, too— An arm flopped over the port side now. Maybe the dead pirate's blood would attract the monster. But why the hell were they all coming after him, with the gold gone? Didn't they realize it? Archie reached for the boat hook again, and stopped, annoyed. The perishing boat hook was gone. He grabbed for what was left of the oar—

His entire vision shimmered and faded. Standing there was the Gamemaster, dressed as usual in fashionable black. "Archie."

"GODDAMMIT, GET OUT OF HERE! I'VE FINALLY FOUND THE BUG, AND YOU SHOW UP!"

Gee smiled. "Heart's in your work. I approve. Come up to my office when you're done here. I'm going to break a few laws and I want your help."

"ANYTHING JUST GET THE HELL OUT OF HERE BEFORE I LOSE THE MOMENTUM AND SCREW IT ALL UP!"

"I'm gone." The scene reappeared, just as it had been. No. Archie looked in disgust at the missing boat hook, and two mines where there had been one a moment ago. He touched a mine with his oar, and blew himself up.

His office cubicle was around him once again. He scowled at the screen before him. "Max, mark that new distance. The clock's wrong at that point. I need to pick up from the new mark in the next session."

"Understood, Archie," the computer replied. "I am marking the Three Rivers game manuscript at the new location now."

"Thanks, Max."

Trann naturally had come over to check out the yelling in the busy office— no regular Gee-9 had looked twice. "*Now* what?"

"The first day in months," Archie growled, "that I get a chance to do something *fun* off the slush pile— a game. No medical technology, no military simulations, no rush engineering jobs— and *he* butts in and blows my concentration. I swear to God I'll become a traffic controller, for the rest."

"What do you think of the manuscript?" Trann tended to business first.

"I think I've found the bug— there's something wrong with the timing in the later stages. I need to feel around and see exactly what." Archie shook his head. "It's not obvious. But this program is definitely marketable. Now— " Archie sighed that patient little sigh that drove Trann to distraction— "I'd best go see what's on Gee's mind. He said something about wanting my help."

"I am not happy about that, I assure you. I've got seven Gee-9's on vacation. The thirty here are swamped. Convey my regards. And Archie," Trann added, "it is budget time. I am trying to get my departmental budget through intact. Please stop swearing at the Chief. What it does to my hearts."

Archie Chamberlain grinned unrepentantly, and headed for the Alpha.

-8-

The Dead Bird

Gee's private office had black wainscoting about a meter high, topped off with dull red-and-black designed wallcovering. Usually he left it alone, but Archie, wandering in today, noticed that a virtual "To Do" project panel replaced the wallpaper projection on one portion of the wall. The panel only contained three listings, in the italicized computer script the Gamemaster generally used for extremely important projects. The three lines read "Stone Monkey," "Dead Bird," and "Brass Mouse." "Stone Monkey" had a check mark beside it, just like any other project. Archie looked at the project list and sighed.

Gee did not look up from his reading. "Make yourself comfortable while I finish this."

Archie nodded, and made his traditional request, "A decent cup of tea, Max." A wall panel slid open, and Archie took the cup. He stepped behind the desk and the man, and stared out the window at the view. The Pacific Ocean shimmered in the western sun. On shore, city lights were blinking on. God's palette of colors, rainbow and dark, luminous and soft, was getting a full workout tonight. Archie drank tea, and felt contented. "Put those hard-copies down, and come take a look at this beautiful sunset."

Gee rose and stood beside him. For a few moments, they just stared at the colors of the sky. Then Gee spoke in a changed, peaceful tone. "I needed that. Something was bothering me."

"What?" asked Archie curiously.

"Arrow." Gee moved to one of the office chairs. He looked relaxed now, but there was a thoughtful frown on his face. "And the riddle," he added.

"What about it?"

"Everything about it. The more I look, the more I am intrigued. There is something significant in the riddle, and I truly want to know what it is. John has left me a challenge unlike anything I have ever encountered. What do you know about John Arrow?"

Archie sipped his tea, and replied, "I didn't even know he had a brother until you dug him up. Arrow was not forthcoming."

"According to Somerset House Central Office, he doesn't exist."

Archie blinked, and settled himself into the opposite chair. "Somerset House Central Office? As in birth, death, immigration, and probate records of the British Isles?" Another thought struck him. "And *you* searched? With Max?"

"Yes. John Arrow simply appears out of the blue at age sixteen as a declared independent adult, no parents listed. I found Richard originally by cross-referencing John Arrows. John's records did not list a brother. Fourteen-year-old Richard listed John as next of kin on his original passport from England to Tibet. In four sentences, I have told you everything the public records have on John and Richard Arrow."

"Impossible," said Archie. "Birth certificates. Church baptismal records. Identity number applications. Pilot's license. Credit applications. Travel tickets."

"None, none, and none."

There was no conceivable way Gee or Max could have made a mistake of that magnitude. Gee's level of computer competence, with Max, was unquestionable. Nothing would have been safe from his scrutiny. At worst, governmental software would have informed them that an item was restricted. Archie considered the situation. "Arrow was good with puzzles and games. He was a superlative programmer. It would not be inconceivable that he hacked out a new identity for himself and his brother. I can't imagine how, not without a trail of some kind. There must be something you missed."

"He would have the military and government access to cover his trail, if he wished," Gee agreed. "I am inclined to think there used to be something, and he eliminated it later, after he reached adulthood."

"But it would be a hell of a good job," Archie agreed. "How about worldwide? There's more to the world than Somerset House."

"Oh, I agree. Max simply used them as a starting point. But cross-referencing records on Earth, the Moon, Mars, Venus (what I could get), and the colonies got me nowhere. I've got possible brother-brother combinations of the right age that I can't eliminate with one hundred per cent certainty. Yet I also have a hunch that none of them are John and Richard Arrow." He shifted comfortably in his seat. "So I gave up looking for brother-brother combinations, and attacked the problem from a different angle. I looked for a relation between John Arrow and birds or names of birds."

Archie sat up. "And you found a match? Arrow and what dead bird?"

"An albatross. Specifically, the *S.S. Albatross.* It's a decommissioned heavy cruiser in the Neptune graveyards." Gee scowled. "It is also off limits, for some unspecified reason. I got the standard runaround from ECM. No one seems to know who can authorize me to board that ship, nor why I can't, nor who can give me any details about its current status. Arrow served on it for almost ten years. He must have known it like the back of his hand. If he left something there— "

"If he left something there, surely the ECM have found it by now," Archie objected.

"With Arrow's brilliance? Not likely."

"They aren't all stupes, you know. There's probably a simpler reason why they're not cooperating. They probably think they smell a rat and they're wondering what devious plot you're up to. Not without due cause, I might add."

"If I were Recover, or one of these terrorist groups," Gee growled, "I could probably get on that ship in no time. That's an idea." He raised his voice. "Max, prepare to do a Recover simulation. We'll test *illegal* means to get us on board."

"What does Robinson say?"

"I didn't ask him," Gee replied with dignity. "This is my party."

"That's hard on your staff."

"They can always quit," he answered. "But, if you like, I can give them a trail that will keep them busy while I'm working on things that are not their business."

Archie sighed. "You said break a *few* laws. Not all of them, all right? Give me an hour or so to see what I can see."

Archie gazed in distaste at the ugly, grandiose gilt eagle-and-shield symbol of Earth Combined Military as it appeared on his screen, and waited for a voice. It was a gravelly male voice, of course— an extremely unattractive one with some indescribably hokey accent. "You have reached the West Meg Division of United Nations Earth Combined Military. Please state the nature of your business."

"Lieutenant McAllen, please."

He waited patiently, staring at the tasteless symbol, until her face appeared on the screen. "Well, Mr. Chamberlain! What can I do for you?"

"I'm calling for a favor, of course," Archie admitted.

"Such as?"

"I want to take a peek at one of the old ships that's up for dismantling in the Neptune salvage yards. Just background for something I'm working on. Can it be arranged?"

"Sure, no problem. Just any old junker?"

"I think it is. The S.S. *Albatross*."

McAllen's expression changed. "That's not funny," she said darkly.

Archie blinked. "What isn't?" he asked innocently.

"God Himself couldn't get on the *Albatross*. That's top-level classified. Not to mention all the litigation. Don't you watch the news?"

"I saw the news," Archie replied quietly.

"Half a dozen peacenik groups are suing to prevent it from being used as any kind of peace museum. The Hague is supposed to issue rulings in a few days, but in the meantime, we don't breathe the name. I'll get you on any other."

"Suppose I wanted the *Albatross*?"

"Suppose I just broke this connection." Her hand moved toward the screen.

"No, wait! I'm indebted, Lieutenant, really I am. You've already told me more than I've learnt in days. As God is my witness, I don't know anything fancy about the old girl and really just wanted to find out." He paused. "And, if it's anything like your job being on the line, I'd be willing to underwrite a guarantee on that."

A Gamemaster 9 guarantee would cut ice anywhere. She was impressed, but nonetheless, she shook her head. "Can't you take my word for it that the ship isn't worth the effort of getting on her? It's not just my job I'm worried about— it's the court-martial and the accompanying execution that bother me."

Archie acted on a hunch. He spoke the same words he'd heard just a few minutes before. "By golly, I wonder how some terrorist group like Recover would handle a situation like this."

The lieutenant jumped a meter. "Mr. Chamberlain! Don't even mention them both in the same sentence."

"I *see*. Recover was after the *Albatross*, weren't they?"

"It was originally slated to be the Earth Combined Military L5 War Museum. I'm going to get into trouble if I tell you any more. I really must go." She broke the connection.

"Double damn," Archie grumbled. "Recover has declared it a target. They're getting bolder every day. The Hague must be damned close to making a decision that's going to hurt the cause."

Archie and Gee rode out alone with Harry Goto, in a small Gamemaster Inc. high-speed shuttle. They traveled without escort, which made Archie wonder if Gee's security unit had been shanghaied or bullied out of accompanying him. At the speed they traveled, a trip to Neptune Yards only took a few hours— like the A1 or an Interstate Highway, but even more boring. There were no tourist sights or billboards along the way, and it took a couple of hours just to notice a change of position.

There really wasn't much difference between mountaineering and spacedogging, Archie reflected. You pounded a clamp into a rock to hitch your ropes and links on a mountain; you waved a magnet or electronic key over a ship's exterior to make the clamp pop up. Then you clipped yourself in place the same way— to avoid falling in one situation, or floating away in the other. Gamemaster products all. The water was just as tepid and tasteless, no matter what kind of tube you sipped it from.

Eight hours later, he was standing on the deck of the small Gamemaster Inc. shuttle, wearing an unmarked spacesuit with the helmet off, checking out the valves and controls. Gee, attired in a similar red suit, had already examined his. Ahead, Neptune shone as brightly as the moon, and in the middle distance slightly larger reflecting dots were becoming junked Fleet ships of the Neptune Yards. The silvery metal of their hulls caught and reflected the moonshiny light.

For a change, Archie heartily wished he was carrying a gun, but guns were absolutely forbidden out here. It was only common sense. The slightest puncture of a spacesuit meant death for your target, or to yourself if an "accident" occurred. You could not merely injure with a gun in space, and warning shots were of course impossible. The only weapon spacemen carried was the little emergency knife Archie had in his belt.

As Archie checked his suit one last time, he tried to keep his hands from shaking. He knew that Gee saw, from the corner of his eye, but had said nothing. Gamemaster's hands were like rock. He was always in control. The hand which tapped the pilot's shoulder was as firm as if he were in a board meeting. "We'll stop here, Harry."

Harry Goto gently put on his retros. "We're a long way from the Yards, though."

"It will be best this way. We'll coast in on our positioning jets." He fastened his helmet, and checked the readings of his collar panel. Harry's radio speaker said, "How's the sound?"

"As good as it gets," Harry replied. "You're coming through fine." He and Archie followed the same procedure. They stepped into the airlock. It slid shut behind them. Tiny status lights kept the tween-hatch area from pitch darkness.

"Once we get outside, we'll maintain radio silence," Gee told Harry. "Don't try to contact us. If you so much as smell a government ship, cut and run."

"What about you, chief?"

"If it's a government ship, we'll have all the air traffic we can handle," Gamemaster said dryly.

"Amen to that," said Archie. "Off we go!"

They dropped, into— nothing. Archie shoved himself away from the unobtrusive four-compartment shuttle— big enough for them, yet the smallest made. There was nothing to distract Archie from examining the controls occupying a three-inch-wide panel around the front arc of his spacesuit collar, below the clear helmet. Orientation compass, suit environment controls, locomotor controls, communication, all fine. It was a good habit to check before the ship was far away. He looked up to realize that Gee had already finished his check and was now turned in the general direction of the distant *Albatross*.

Floating in space, using the positioning jets to change direction, Archie marveled at how good it felt. It had been a long time since Mars. He took a deep breath. One crisis at a time, Chamberlain, he told himself.

They both knew the *Albatross*'s position, roughly. It did not take too long to find her. Out here, floating in the dim light reflected from the planet, she took Archie's breath away. She was beautiful. The *Albatross* was a heavy cruiser that had been on duty for months at a time, in and around the solar system. The metal of her bulkhead reflected pearlesque blues and golds in Neptune's light. The occasional transparent pressure panels seemed almost like champagne bubbles. He could well imagine what she must have looked like, once, when her lights were lit and she rolled through the stars in all her silvery splendor. He felt small beside her. He forced himself to look away from the ship and toward the Gamemaster. "Now what?"

"Now we go inside."

Archie shuddered. "I knew you'd say that. All right, let's hunt up the most unobtrusive entrance we can find."

Even in the space suit, Archie could see the decisive shake of Gee's head as he disagreed. "Bad move. They're the most likely boobytrapped. I vote for the main hatch." Archie sighed, and propelled himself in that direction.

Gee pulled a small probe from his suit pocket, and waved it over a mark on the exterior. An anchor ring popped up. He attached himself to it with a mountaineer's clamp, and concentrated on some serious breaking-and-entering. A crewman of the *Albatross* would have had an ID-badge he could touch to the sensor- plate to open the hatch. As they were Gamemaster Inc. products, the Gamemaster's own badge would have done the job, too. However, he did not use it. It was hidden inside the spacesuit, and it would have left a record of the badge's owner. There was no reason to enlarge the number of witnesses against him. His small electronic probe activated the panel on the fifth try. The hatch popped open.

They pulled it shut behind them. The world suddenly became black. Archie hadn't realized how much light Neptune contributed to the scene. He flicked on his torch, and pointed it toward a panel. He lit it while Gee again employed his probe.

Their intent was merely to open the inner door. They both assumed that, without power, the *Albatross* was lifeless— no lights, air, or artificial gravity. To Archie's surprise, he saw lights and gauges kick in when Gee hit the proper combination.

"What in— ?" He saw Gee's puzzled frown, too, and decided that it would be better to maintain radio silence. The inner hatch opened. Archie gave himself a push toward the corridor.

A ring popped out immediately from the wall.

They stared at it. "Everything in here should be locked down tight and turned off," murmured his chief.

Archie felt hair standing up on the back of his neck. This was not good. He followed Gee down the corridor to a hatch. "Let's keep to ladders," he objected. The ladders were open; hatches could swing and lock shut automatically.

"Good idea." Gee led the way to the corresponding ladder. Archie was beginning to wonder if they were going the wrong way when Gee said, "I need to see the manifests first. They should be on Deck 6. Then we'll head for the control room, if it's still in working order."

At last they found the level containing the information. Gee started leafing through hard-copies, still in cubbyholes. "There should be a copy of the manifests in here somewhere, even though the ship's computer is shut down. Also— secondary control systems usually aren't disabled and dismantled until the very end, in case they are needed in an emergency. At the distance we are from Max, we won't get instant navigation response— it will be around ten to fifteen minutes, and it wouldn't be that fast if Earth wasn't on this side of the sun right now. Better to have both primary and secondary systems and controls functioning. Ah. Here. Repairs, Maintenance, and Engineering. Go down two more levels, Deck 8, and see if the ship's computer is still intact. There should still be some abandoned loose machinery there, too."

"Right." Archie moved back down the corridor to the ladders, and counted his way down two levels, his torch at its very dimmest setting. His light barely illuminated the 8 painted on the bulkhead. He stepped off the ladder, feeling around for a toehold, turned, flicked on his torch— and found himself staring into a dead face. His breath stopped. There was a tremendous rushing sound in his ears.

Archie Chamberlain blacked out.

He felt his cheek being slapped, and opened his eyes. He heard Gee's dry chuckle. Archie was clamped to a ring like an errant balloon. Both men's helmets were off.

Archie's torch was still firmly attached to his glove. He flashed it around. Rooted to the deck on this level were row upon row of robots. "What— ?"

"Part of the Maintenance and Repairs loose machinery. Obsolete repairs androids. Still necrophobic, I see."

"Just a tad."

"I thought Richard cured you of that."

"Debate later. Let's get out of here." Then, both men stiffened.

Without the helmets, they could hear the sounds of the ship. It was *not* tomblike. There was a low hum of ship's power.

"This ship's ready to peel out!" Archie whispered. "It's only on brownout status. That's not what McAllen said!"

"Perhaps the Fleet didn't start the engines. Come on."

Cautiously, they slid among the statues, across the deck to their goal: the main computer.

Archie moved anxiously behind Gee as he stepped out from amid the androids to examine the large machine. He held the torch while Gee searched the control panel. "It's no good," Gee said. "I need area lights. Ah!" He found a switch to turn on the nearest overhead lights while Archie's alarmed heart did handsprings. Gee chuckled.

There was a note, an official ECM document. "RETAINED AS PER FEDERAL ORDER 2715," Archie read. It hit him. "Arrow had this salvaged. It was supposed to go to the Fleet museum if the ship was scrapped!"

"That's it. Whatever was in this computer was supposed to live on. Now let's see what the mystery is." Gee touched the probe to the computer's security key. Nothing happened. He played with it again. Still nothing. It must be keyed to a code different from the rest of the ship's locks, Archie thought. Still, that was no problem. Gamemaster's own badge, which he wore under his spacesuit, would unlock any lock in existence. It would mean unfastening the cumbersome suit and unpinning his badge, which was only an inconvenience for Gee. However, that badge, with his symbol— the symbol of all of Gamemaster Inc.— was the key to all locks.

Gee touched his collar latch.

A voice said, "Don't move."

The voice was youthful and perhaps feminine, but even from behind them, it had the air of authority of someone holding a gun. They froze.

Archie's only thought was, thank Heaven Gee hadn't had time to unfasten his suit. Once they saw his clothes, or either incriminating Gamemaster badge, there would be hell to pay.

The voice spoke over a radio. "Blue 1, this is Blue 5. We have a problem."

They froze for what seemed like an eternity. Then, there was the sound of more arrivals.

"Oh, hell," said another voice. Then, to them, "Turn around. Slowly."

Archie stared in surprise at their first captor. She appeared to be a young girl, with bright blue eyes and short, curly blond hair. She was in a Gamemaster Inc. spacesuit, not as sophisticated or new as Archie's. The others also wore them, eight youngsters in all, with weapons, looking quite capable. None of the group could have been more than twenty years old, Archie realized with a shock.

"Of course," Gee breathed in an enlightened tone.

The young man who led them, Blue 1, was tall and slim. Like Gee, this youngster was used to taking command.

"I heard noises," the girl told him. "They were coming up from below. I think they've been prowling around for a while."

Archie made a very small "I told you so" sigh.

"Who are you?" Blue 1 demanded.

"Uninvited visitors, as you are," Gee replied.

"Cute. Your name, mister."

One raised eyebrow and a frozen look were the only answer he got.

"He was tinkering with the computer," Blue 5 contributed.

Blue 1 eyed him appraisingly, and the probe which he still held. "Oh? That probe got you in, I see. But it doesn't work on the big computer."

"I found that out," said Gamemaster.

"You must be good with locks. So what are you— a scavenger? You're no military man. Neither is your pal. So who do you work for?"

Again, the look. "Myself."

"Oh? And why are you here?"

"Curiosity."

Blue 1's laugh was grim. "You can't be so stupid that you don't know about the ECM ships out there. How did you get by them?"

Gee shrugged. "It was a dare."

"I want the whole story out of you, and I want it fast."

"When you move this ship, the ECM will be all over you. I had credited even Recover with more intelligence than that."

"The *Albatross* is in perfect fighting condition," the young leader said. "The ECM expects us to fight our way on board. They don't know we're already here." He took the probe from Gamemaster's gloved hand, and examined it. "Nice work. Gamemaster Inc. North America, this year's make. That's quality." Although Archie hadn't detected an accent, Blue 1's reference to "Gamemaster Inc. North America" implied that he lived elsewhere.

"So it is."

Blue 1 eyed him appraisingly. "So you've got money. How much would someone pay for you?"

There were very few things that could make Gee smile spontaneously, but that was one of them. Throughout the centuries, the Gamemasters had made themselves kidnap-proof by simply refusing to deal with kidnappers, except to exterminate them. "You could hold an auction, I suppose."

Blue 1 motioned to three of his companions. "Take them down to the brig and lock them up. Make sure neither one has a probe or a weapon. Keep the surveillance cameras on them until we move."

The remaining crew was in too much of a hurry to open up the suits. They found Archie's utility knife, but no other weapons. They were taken at gunpoint to the brig, and locked inside, without helmets. Then their guards vanished.

Gee frowned in thought, and shook his head. "Blue 1 looks like someone I should know. I can't quite put my finger on it. The rest makes perfect sense." He frowned. "Which is precisely why we're in danger. Recover can't let us go, knowing what we know."

"I don't doubt the fact that we're in danger," said Archie. "It's obvious the news was wrong about the Neptune Shipyard Crisis. Those children in the Neptune Shipyards weren't hostages killed in the attack. They were the attackers. Who would understand better how to sabotage military machinery?"

Gee nodded. "A great many ECM soldiers have been killed under stupid conditions, conditions that never would have been tolerated at— other places where we've worked. No wonder their children rebel. And who else could be so efficiently organized as military brats?"

"That computer seal has them puzzled."

"It has *us* puzzled. Why not them?" Gee returned. "They know there must be something in there worth taking. We know that, too. However, without the ability to unlock the computer— they can't navigate this ship. I doubt any of them are crack pilots, the kind that could manually pilot a battleship alone."

Archie thought he saw where Gee was heading. There was a crack pilot on board who could pilot a battleship alone, and Archie was sharing a cell with him.

"I imagine that their plan will now be to blow up the ship, since it's otherwise unusable to them. The explosion will at least be a sign of protest."

"How do they plan to get off?"

"The same way they got on, I assume."

"But you do think they plan to blow it up."

"Of course."

"Can I point out one little drawback?"

"If you mean, had I noticed we're still on board?" Gee said dryly. "That hadn't escaped my attention. I wish I knew how much time we had."

"I can grant that wish," said a voice from a speaker— Blue 1. "You have thirty minutes."

"Now I know," said Gee, otherwise unruffled. Nor was Archie surprised that they had been monitored all along.

"I see you're watching the alarm panel," said the voice. "You weren't born yesterday."

"Yes, I know about fission engines."

"Oh, hell," Archie breathed in horror. "You're going to short out the engines!"

"I'm afraid so. We can't afford to have eyewitnesses describing us." There was a pause. "Unless, of course, Mister Intruder, you are a crack pilot. Your pal seems to think you are."

"I'm good, but not that good. Sorry."

"Just as sorry as I am to leave you here, I imagine. Blue 1 out."

Archie waited patiently, in silence. After a while, he asked, "Are they still watching?"

"I have no idea," Gee replied, watching the alarm panel. A white panel lit beneath the red, amber, and green lights. The number 28 appeared. "But they're still aboard. That was what I was waiting for. In twenty-eight minutes the *Albatross* becomes a memory, along with about half the Neptune Yards." Evidently, he had decided to take a chance. He unfastened his suit, and reached inside for his badge, which had been small enough to escape notice when they were frisked.

The alloy of the Gamemaster badge was special, a house product. It responded to Max and the badge-holder like a second skin— or second mind. In addition, it was almost indestructible. There was, in fact, a joke going around Alpha that Gentian was on his way to put his badge back on the rack, because not even the Sun could hurt that badge, and now Gentian was in a place where fire wouldn't hurt him, either.

Carefully, Gee unpinned his badge from the underside of a lapel, where it had just barely remained out of sight. Apparently he had indeed thought to hide it. He used an edge of it to pry up a corner of a panel near the entryway. Sparks flew, but the spacesuit insulated him. Understanding what he was doing, Archie got out his own badge, and employed it as a prybar on another corner.

Gee plunged his arm, badge in hand, into the hole. It didn't take special instructions for Max to turn the badge into an electronic key; that was one of its basic functions. Archie grabbed hold of the brig's hatch and heaved. It opened heavily. Quickly, Gee and Archie dodged outside.

The signs below the alarms throughout the corridors said 22.

"After 5 it can't be shut off," said Gee. "By then, the power surge will have wakened every ship in the area. Let's move."

Archie stopped Gee in mid-flight at a storage hatch. The *Albatross* had been left half-supplied, presumably for the ease of salvage crews. They both grabbed helmets and fresh air supplies.

They reached the docking level and its observation deck. Archie saw a ship of military design with the Federal Law Enforcement Agency logo, almost close enough to touch. "Oh, boy. We're in trouble."

"We're not. It's neither a FLEA nor ECM design. That explains it. At a quick glance, the military thinks it's a FLEA ship, and FLEA thinks it's an ECM ship. Law versus military. The two don't cooperate any more than military and corporate."

"Of course! So they sidle in and out under the noses of both."

The ship had docked. Gee answered Archie's unspoken question. "We're heading for the docking bay, just to see what we can see. Then the control room, to stop the explosion."

"Shouldn't we reverse the order on that?"

"No. Otherwise, Recover will get off without a scratch. I intend to scratch." Suddenly, he sniffed the air. Archie understood immediately. They both sealed their helmets at the same moment. Recover was evacuating the ship from the control room before they left. Which was supposed to kill them, down in the brig, Archie wondered— the evacuation, or the explosion?

The exit corridor of the docking bay level was lit, ready for action. Gee, apparently, was just as ready. There was a glitter in his eye and joy in his voice, the tone of the pirate. He was tinkering with his helmet radio control. "Don't be alarmed when I jam the radios. You and I are on a different frequency from theirs." Gee opened a storage hatch and left it partly open. He appeared to be setting up a scene.

"Whatever you're up to, you don't need me," Archie told him, "and I'm getting nervous about the time. We still don't know what kind of shape the secondary control room's in, except that they seem to be able to use it. It might help if I could get there and start taking a look at things the very moment they leave."

"Good point. Go down two levels, then go forward and come up again using the forward ladders. They'll be coming down from one level above, heading aft, so you'll miss them. You'll be able to tell when they reach me by the jam, and your path will be clear."

Archie slid down the nearest ladder, two levels, much faster than he'd done before on any spaceship. He dimmed his torch to nothing, kept to every nook and cranny in the darkness, and kept his ears open. Making noise was no longer an issue; with the air evacuated, no one would hear him kick anything from here to Triton, and with his sturdy suit, he wouldn't even stub a toe on it.

He felt his way forward in the dark, to the fore ladder tube, stopped, and waited in the radio silence. There was one chance in a million they would take this circuitous route down to bypass the observation deck, knowing that if they could see out, someone else could see in. Archie found himself a dark niche.

Then he heard other helmet radios.

Blue 1: "They're here. Come on. We've got sixteen minutes."

Another voice: "I dunno. I had a feeling about that guy. I think I saw him in the news, or something."

Another: "He'd probably have made good insurance, Blue One."

Blue 1: "So would the Commissioner of the FLEA, or Gamemaster, for that matter, but we didn't have them, either. All we've got is fifteen minutes. Let's go."

There was a tremendous static crash.

Blue 1: "Blue 5! Blue 2! Red 1! Do you copy?"

Another: "Someone's jamming us!"

Archie grabbed a rung of the ladder and shot up the tube. One level, two, Secondary Control Center. Hatch intact— that was a good sign. He slid in, realizing it was a double hatch. As an emergency control center, it was sealable and self-contained. Outer hatch closed, inner open. He entered the Control Center and the inner hatch sealed behind him. Telltale lights and gauges flickered in the darkness— Archie breathed a sigh of relief. Primary systems had not yet been removed by the salvage team.

He activated a control panel and said, "Max, this is Archie. Respond, please, as soon as you can." It would take Max at least five minutes to reply, probably more like fifteen.

Then Blue 5 screamed, a noisy burst of static that cut off abruptly.

In his mind's eye, Archie imagined what happened: Gee's sudden dive across the corridor, tackling Blue 5 and barreling into the opposite hatch with her. The old helmets these kids had were opaque on three sides. If he moved very fast, they might not even have seen him. He heard speakers who received no responses.

Blue 1: "Blue 5!"

Another: "Blue 5!"

Another: "No sign of her! What happened? Wasn't she behind us?"

Blue 1: "Fourteen minutes. We need ten to get out of range of the explosion. Let's go!"

Another voice, female: "Elsa!"

Blue 1, insistently: "Let's go! Thirteen minutes! Let's go!"

There was a long silence.

Archie took a sharp breath. He found the Control Room light panel and brought the lights to half-power. He noticed with relief that the Secondary Control Room had no pressure panel, only monitors, so he could turn the lights on full without an exterior porthole lighting up. He only hoped there were no exterior lights that increased with the current. He found atmospheric controls, and began giving the room air. The double hatch would keep it inside where it belonged.

At last, he heard the sound of the outer hatch clanging. Then, after a wait, the inner hatch opened. It was Gee. The pirate light of his ancestors still shone in his eyes. He carried Blue 5— now known as Elsa— over his shoulder, unconscious. "Pinched off her air supply and then hit a nerve. They've got the old-time models." Gee secured his captive to a seat with discarded cable. He removed her helmet and his own; Archie followed suit.

"Hello, Archie," said Max. Archie could have kissed the speaker. "Your voice sounds strained. Is there a problem?"

"Max, I'm sitting on a live bomb with ECM and FLEA ships all around me, and an important computer full of data which I have to keep intact. That's why I sound strained! First, would you kindly deactivate this fission bomb? The one made out of the *Albatross* engines? We're going to need those engines to move this ship. Then, start transferring the computer files here— every piece of data you can find— just in case we lose this computer in the scuffle. While you're doing that, open up this ship's computers for full navigation capability." Then, there was nothing to do but sit and wait for Max to respond.

Gamemaster sat in the pilot's seat, and also spoke. "Max, I need to know what kind of shape the navigation panels are in."

The numerals upon the wall read 10, 9, 8. Then the panel shut off. "Deactivation completed." Archie let out a breath he hadn't realized he'd been holding. Then Max said, "They are old, Gamemaster. There are some discrepancies."

"We may go on manual for a while, just to confound our opponents. Continue the data transfer."

Archie turned to look at the slip of a girl, still unconscious and bound, her head lolling to one side in the helmsman's seat. He indicated her with a sweep of his hand. "Why?"

"It presents great opportunities," Gee replied, consulting the boards before him. "Max has powered up this ship, and got that computer running well enough for me to peel out— I have 65 per cent capacity. It will improve the closer we get to Earth." He hit a toggle. "No doubt neighboring ships have sensed the increased power."

Archie sighed, and flicked the switch on a communications panel. He heard what he expected to hear. "— Combined Military. We order your surrender, Recover. We know that you are aboard the *Albatross*. Surrender or be boarded." The message began again. "Attention. This is the Earth Combined Military. We order your sur— " Archie shut it off.

Gamemaster examined the control panel in the same intent, happy, fashion that Archie had seen him regard many other equally dangerous and inviting navigation boards. Archie suddenly felt very reassured.

Elsa was coming around. Her blue eyes focused upon the control panel, then upon the red-gloved hands beside her, the breast of the red suit, the open fastener at his throat, then the face. Her eyes widened. She struggled in her bonds, and started to swear.

"Elsa," Gee said without stopping work at his boards, "If you don't stop that language this instant, I will stuff my gloves in your mouth."

She stared at him, but stopped. Apparently she recognized a real threat when she heard it. "How did you get out of the cell?"

Archie cut in. "Gee, that ECM cruiser is moving in closer. They're getting ready to board."

Elsa glared vengefully at Gee. "You are *dead*. All I have to do is say you kidnapped me— "

"Elsa, you are perhaps fourteen, and your parents must think you're away at boarding school," said Gamemaster. "Now, be quiet, and try to live to fifteen." They watched the ECM cruiser move into docking position. The hatches almost touched when Gee kicked in the engines and dropped rapidly out of the plane of Neptune Yards.

The ECM cruiser shot where the *Albatross* should have been. Elsa's face indicated that she knew something about piloting, and she was getting a good show now. Archie knew, in theory, that a space battle involved 3-D elements not normally considered in ground combat. He also knew, in theory, that your opponent could seem a long distance away, very suddenly. But to see the *Albatross* move out, reappear, or suddenly go in a direction perpendicular to what he expected, made Archie marvel to see the theory in motion.

Apparently, the ECM ships' orders were to keep the *Albatross* intact, if possible. Several times, they tried to box her in. Here, the simple vastness of space defeated them. One, two, three, four ships would move into position— and Gee would simply drop in another direction. The Gamemaster patiently teased them back from Neptune, back past the orbits of Saturn and Jupiter, into the asteroid belt. From there on, Archie knew, it was Max's game.

Gamemaster raised his voice. "Max, I have a priority transmission."

"If you try that radio," Elsa snarled, "every ship in the Solar System will pick up on you."

"Standing by, Gamemaster," Max replied immediately. Elsa's eyes widened and her jaw dropped, Archie was pleased to note. Yep, that guy *had* looked a lot like "somebody on the news."

"Inform Bel Aire Hilo that I'm on my way, and remind them they owe me. I want their security team ready to scuttle the ship I'm in the moment I land, and it must be done in record time. The ship I'm in is a hot ship."

"Is that literal?" Max asked carefully.

"'Hot' as in freshly stolen, Max. Get to it."

"Yes, sir." Max was also programmed to recognize Gee's don't-argue-just-do-it tone. In a moment, the speaker said, "Confirmed reply. Dock Seven, Hilo, is ready."

"Acknowledged, Max. Now, hang onto your helmets, children." He kicked the *Albatross* into high gear.

Archie did not have Gee's or Harry's absorbing interest in piloting. He had no interest in such shows as the stunts Gee pulled at Monte Carlo. Even now, he understood only theoretically that the pilots and gunners of the pursuing vessels were outclassed. It took a while, but Gamemaster lost them. Then he swung in toward Earth. Eventually, Archie saw the Pacific Ocean below them. A space station, clearly marked BEL AIRE SHIPYARDS HILO DIVISION lay ahead. Men in spacesuits floated about as Gee slid into docking position. The speaker said, "Gamemaster, this is the Dock Seven foreman. Do you copy?"

"Yes, I do, sir. Don't ask questions. Get to work."

"We copy. What do we do with the pieces?"

"Scuttle them. If you want souvenirs, take them, but they can't see the light of day for seven years. This is high priority. You'll have FLEAs here within the hour. Hop to it."

"Yes, sir," said the foreman gleefully.

Gamemaster rose and began to strip off his space suit. So did Archie. Gee stood at last, as intimidating as ever in the black suit, and said, "Elsa, you are going to leave this ship with us."

"Fuck you!"

Apparently the Gamemaster didn't hear her. "You have two options. Walk out on your own two feet, or I carry you out, unconscious. The choice is yours."

The blue eyes stared up at him. Then, sulkily, she said, "I'll walk."

He untied her. "Why don't you get out of the suit?"

"Be-because it's all I'm wearing."

Archie stifled a smile. "Perhaps she'd best keep the suit on," he suggested.

A Bel Aire Shipyard shuttle took them back to West Meg. Archie returned to his own apartments, showered, and changed his clothes. He had enough of Gee and dead birds for one day.

And he needed some sleep.

Snakes and Ladders

Archie Chamberlain got his second cup of morning tea from the dispenser in the Gee-9 lab, greeted Trann inside the lab door with his usual cheerfulness, and made himself comfortable at his desk.

Trann was not amused. "What in HELL have you got stored in the main computer banks?"

"Is there a problem?"

"Unless you made an error piping it over," Trann answered, "which I doubt, it is as big as all outdoors."

Archie scowled at his screen. "It is, at that, isn't it?"

"Is this from the *Albatross*?"

"Sure is," Archie confirmed, hitting a few keys. "You're right, it's monstrous."

"What is it?"

"That's what I'm trying to find out."

"So you are unavailable for other work," Trann accused.

"Sorry, Trann." Trann left grumbling, and Archie concentrated on his work. He took a sip of tea. "Can you find the startup program for me, Max?"

"No, Archie, I cannot."

Archie blinked. "Come again? I mean, the start point for this program."

"There is no indicated startup program, or even a startup sequence, as far as I can determine. To the best of my analysis, this program is incomplete."

"Incom— ? At this size?" he asked incredulously.

"Affirmative."

"Is it all program code, or is it in a specific computer language?"

There was a long pause while Max sorted and counted— almost an entire minute. "Neither. There are seventeen different program codes here, and between two hundred thirty-seven and three hundred fifty-nine languages involved, depending on the definition of 'language' used."

"Hm." Archie frowned in thought. "So you can't simply find a start-point and launch it."

"Affirmative."

"That says euphemistic and referential logic to me. Damn. I have to use my brain and eyeballs. Go one-third in, mark, and give me the next ten minutes of code from that point."

Numbers and words flashed before Archie's eyes. He slowed it down, and browsed thoughtfully. Sure enough, he saw words and phrases— in English, in Gaelic, in Tibetan, in something that might have been Hausa. He also saw proper names, which puzzled him especially.

He opened up more code, looking for matches. He cross-referenced and made copious notes, marking his path as carefully as if he were hiking an unknown mountain trail.

At last, he said, "Mrs. Merdle. As I remember from English lit, Mrs. Merdle 'detests a row.' Is Mrs. Merdle possibly a code for the level of difficulty in the related section of the program?"

"Possibly, considering your notes, Archie."

"All right, let's find and cross-reference some proper names. Pick only ones with titles, for consistency."

Patiently, Archie dragged forth proper names, examined, and discarded them. It was a monumental process, because he was using very 'plain-vanilla' search techniques to compensate for his absolute ignorance of the method and technique of the program. Every once in a while, he stood up or stretched as his muscles told him he had spent too much time unmoving in his seat. The tea was long gone. Trann came in once and asked him about lunch, to which he made a vague reply about "being in the middle of something." Mercifully, Trann left him alone after that.

Then he became aware that Trann was speaking to him again— odd! Archie thought he'd left him alone. "I'm sorry. I didn't hear."

"I said you should get lunch before dinnertime hits."

Archie stared at the chronometer. He certainly had been absorbed in this mess! It was 1700 hours. Not that the Gee-9's ever paid much attention to such mundane details as office hours. Trann was only doing his job, reminding him to eat. "And you can tell me about the babe. I hear everything second-hand."

"Babe? What babe?" Archie knew by now that Trann was never deceived by the baby-blue stare.

"Must I hear everything from other Lab Managers?" Trann complained.

"Oh, the babe. Why? Has she been around?"

"Walked through here with the Chief. You never looked up. She has a Visitor's Badge. So who is she? Surely not romantic. Not him."

"True enough. You don't really want to know, though, Trann."

"Try me."

"She's a lieutenant in Recover."

Trann's long pause was downright painful to hear. "Wonderful."

Archie felt no choice but to report his lack of progress to Gee in person. Max said he was back in his office. Archie left his building for Alpha, taking the familiar elevator to the penthouse level.

He was not prepared for what greeted him when he stepped off the elevator. There were enough uniforms in that foyer to secure the entire City of West Meg. The mob, with Chief Robinson, all looked sheepish in the presence of their top brass.

"It would have served you right if she had gunned down the entire force, you parcel of goddamned idiots," Gamemaster was saying, in a tone that carried wonderfully throughout the areaway. "You say if I told you she was a Recover agent you would have been more careful. I told you full fucking security and I shouldn't have to tell you twice, I am your goddamn commander, in case you morons have forgotten. And if you have, you can go join those other assholes on foot patrol until you remember."

Archie simply bailed, back into the elevator. Both tone and vocabulary showed that this tirade was not meant for him to hear. Worse than that, he had accidentally caught Robinson's eye before his hasty retreat. To Gee, idiocy was a crime far beyond treason. The Gamemaster never spoke angrily; he merely grew louder and more distinct. But it was not a pleasant experience to be on the receiving end of his wrath, worse yet to have it observed by outsiders.

Archie bolted into the Tea Room, past the patiently-waiting line of guests. He waylaid the host. "Luki," he said urgently, "find me a corner, any corner out of sight, and something to nosh on. And let me know when the flames die down on the top floor."

Luki Drost was equal to the task. "Right you are, darling. I saw all the boys and girls head upstairs. Are we having a little heart-to-heart with Security over the full-building Alpha alarm a while ago?" He hustled Archie to a corner behind a large potted palm.

"I dare say," Archie bantered, in the same tone. "We had an alarm, did we?"

"Oh, a big one. Lockdown by Max. Something that sounded like gunfire. I don't have any gossip on it yet, so you owe me."

"I can't possibly think of any gossip you wouldn't have got first. Do I owe you a favor for this charming hidey-hole?"

"Absolutely. I have three Brazilian ladies out here, just pining to meet a real live Gamemaster. This is a table for four, you know. I'll bring them over for tea. Now, be charming, and don't get yourself engaged before the end of the meal."

"Hasn't happened yet," said Archie. "Bring 'em on."

Luki Drost fixed a gimlet eye upon him. "One day it will happen," Luki predicted, "and you will fall like the proverbial ton of bricks. I shall be there to cheer you both on, and cater the reception."

Archie ate biscuits, drank tea, and whiled away his time with three Brazilian women having a tourist fling in West Meg. He was dutifully charming until Luki peered around the potted plant and announced, "The earlier visitors have left. It's your turn, Mr. Chamberlain."

Archie paid for the ladies' meal, and departed. "That is the sign of a true gentleman," he heard Luki telling the women. "You're guests of the house, ladies."

Once again, Archie stepped out on the top floor. The contrasting silence was sobering. He walked down the corridor to the office, where the big ebony double-doors swung in as he approached.

Gee looked up from his desk, and chuckled.

"You know," said Archie, "you are most objectionable when you chuckle."

"I know," Gee replied. The shadow of a smile remained on his face. "But I could have shouted for joy when Robinson came in, hat in hand, to tell me they'd barely kept that little slip of a girl from escaping the entire compound. It almost makes up for the insufferable security-cop attitude I put up with daily. Look." He nodded to the space in front of his desk, where he treated Archie to a virtual replay.

The scene was a well-furnished suite on this level. A door opened, and Gee and Elsa entered. "This will be your room, for now," Gee said.

Archie watched in astonishment as the pert little blonde girl turned and pressed her forearms against Gee's chest. Her hands traveled up his shirt and vest, straying toward the top button of his collar, which she tried to unfasten. Gee never changed expression. He wouldn't, although Archie knew exactly what he was thinking. Gee loathed flirtation of all kinds. Elsa sighed. "Well, here I am. And here you are. We oughta be able to do something together." Her hand touched his throat, then went back to play with the shirt button. "Tell me what you're thinking," she said, in a low voice Archie wouldn't have recognized. He grinned.

"I'm wondering how long you'll play with that button before you realize it isn't attached to anything," Gee replied. She jumped as if burnt, and lifted one hand as if to slap him. "Don't even think about it," he warned.

"Lord, this is trite," Archie commented as he watched the replay.

"Isn't it, though?" the real Gee agreed, and chuckled again.

"Max, have you completed that scan on Elsa?" The image Gee addressed the air.

"Yes, Gamemaster. Elsa Anne Grayson, born 15 July 2457, to Commander James Grayson and Lieutenant Maria Hochmann Grayson. Lieutenant Grayson was killed by an anti-personnel mine on Mars One. Commander James Grayson..."

"...was commanding officer of the *Sun King*. Yes, I remember," said Gee. "That's enough, Max. Give the information to Personnel, Security, and Medical."

Elsa melted into an upholstered chair.

Gee stood, looking down at her. "So you watched your father fall into the sun." Then he added, "About a year before I watched mine."

There was a different tone in her voice. "Yes."

"But I was twenty-two. You were six."

"It's not the sort of thing you forget."

"I know," said the Gamemaster.

"What do you want from me?" she asked.

"A cessation of active hostility, for starters," Gee replied. "After that, perhaps, a meeting of the minds, if you have any mind to meet. I thought you had. I needn't tell you that even the thought of a girl half my age, trying to vamp me, is repulsive."

"*And* it doesn't work," she added, looking up at him for the first time.

"And it doesn't work," he agreed, with a slight smile. "Now. You will stay here, in this suite. Fix yourself lunch, change your clothes, take a shower if you wish. You're welcome to do anything within reason— read, catch up on the news, exercise, take a nap. But remain here. I have to deal with FLEAs, but I'll be back."

"Looking for a ship, are they?" she asked.

"There seems to be one missing," he concurred. He left.

As he left, a female security officer entered, and made herself at home against a wall. Else put her head in her hands and sobbed. She spoke to the guard. "What's he going to do with me?"

"Don't know, miss, I'm just Security."

"Please! Can't you tell me anything?" Elsa's terrified little-girl-lost routine would have been worth money in a theater. She truly gave the impression that she had been kidnapped for a harem. She made occasional frightened comments in the same vein to the guard, who began to look uncomfortable. This continued for some time.

"Uh, oh," said Archie. "I can see this one coming."

Elsa fell to the floor in a fit of hysterics. The woman called her partner. They both came over to haul Elsa off the floor.

No wonder Gee had read his staff the riot act, for behaving like such a pack of suckers. Archie was embarrassed just watching it. Elsa's first kick got the man squarely in the groin; her punch in the woman's face laid her out cold. She yanked a weapon from the woman's gunbelt, and disappeared offscreen. There were flashes and noises of armament from the adjoining room.

"A decent cup of tea, Max." Archie stepped over to Gee's office panel and fetched the cup back to the uninhabited display. There was one more large, final flash from somewhere outside the doorway, and silence. The scene ended.

"Was she hurt?" Archie asked Gee.

"Not very."

"The guards?"

"She got two more before Max entered the fray. Nothing was hurt but their pride. One certainly understands how Recover gets away with things. Robinson's eating ashes."

"Is she still unconscious?"

He shook his head. "Down in the infirmary, along with her casualties."

"Uh-huh." Archie sipped tea. "I came up here to tell you how far I've got with the computer program. I've worked on it all day. If you'd wanted me for anything else, you would have let me know."

"True enough. What results do you have?"

"I can't say it's negative progress, but that's about all I can say, Gee. Max is still sorting it all out. You're right— my nose knows there's something there. But there's tons of it. I haven't got a summary, or found any sort of clues yet as to what it is. I've been sifting and sifting."

Gamemaster leaned back. "If this were any other project coming through the door, what would you be recommending right now?"

Archie sighed. The Gamemaster hit the ball at first bat. Regretfully, he admitted, "I'd be telling you to shoot it upstairs to a Ten because it's beyond me. Dammit, I don't want to let go of this one, Gee!"

Gee's face remained impassive. "Let us fetch Elsa and then go see Alec." Alec de Bruyter was the Gamemaster 10 Lab Manager.

"Fetch Elsa? Why?"

"She has a right to know what our trip was about. She would be a valuable addition to our military work here if she would stop playing Mata-Hari and start using her brain. As I have said before, Recover knows things I would like to know."

"Do you think that's wise? Alec's got his hands full, especially with Damiel resigning."

Gamemaster stood. "Until I find out what this program is, nothing around here will be allowed to return to normal." Archie recognized that for the direst threat, and thought, *If Trann were here right now, he'd have a stroke.* Archie accompanied him down to the Alpha building infirmary. As they walked to the elevator, Gee observed, "Elsa, and many children like her, grew up in various crèches and private schools where other military brats also attended— the perfect network for Recover."

The doors closed and the elegant elevator descended. "So did she do her 'name, rank and serial number' routine?"

"No. After all, I don't want to destroy Recover. I want to learn how to use what they have in my favor."

"In what fashion?"

Gamemaster shook his head. "I haven't quite worked that part out yet. I just have a strong feeling that there is something we both can do for— " As they stepped out of the elevator, he shrugged his shoulders. "I can't seem to find the right phrase to convey my meaning."

"For general improvement of the human condition," Archie supplied thoughtfully.

Gamemaster stopped dead, to turn and stare at him in surprise.

Archie shrugged. "It seems a sensible move with the resources available, and just plain right. I admit I'm prejudiced that way."

Gee accepted that explanation, and they walked on. "I gave her a Guest badge, but told her that Max would deal appropriately with security breaches."

"Which he did," said Archie wryly. "She took on the guards, and he knocked her into next Tuesday. And the ship?"

"The *S.S. Albatross* has gone missing. They can't find a trace of her. Apparently ECM sensors at the site noted that the ship's navigation computer was down, so they came to demand a list of my best pilots, and their ratings. Gamemaster Inc. is the single largest civilian pilot employer. I warned them they had bitten off more than they could chew, but they were adamant."

"How many pilots did you list for them?"

"Fifteen hundred and thirty-seven, on the hard-copy," Gee replied imperturbably. "I also pointed out the thirteenth-ranked name on the list."

"You should keep in practice."

"I'll have more time later. I hadn't realized I'd slid out of the top ten." He looked about as worried as a pigeon in the park.

Elsa was on one of the infirmary beds. Gee pulled her to her feet unsympathetically. Plainly, the whole world spun.

"Watch it, poppet. Hang onto my arm," said Archie in alarm. She leaned on his arm and took a few shaky steps.

"Have you made your token escape attempt, and got it out of your system?" Gee inquired coldly.

"Yeah, I think so."

"Then stand up straight and let go of Archie. We're going to the Gee-Ten Lab."

"Um— won't the computer retaliate?"

"It depends on how cooperative you are," Gee responded unhelpfully.

They crossed the plaza to Building 2 West. The sky threatened rain. The breezes stirred their new acquaintance's golden curls. "I like that wind," said Elsa. She looked up at the blue Pacific sky. It was an extraordinary thing for a spacer to say, and she was a spacer born. She was not afraid, Archie realized. She's very adaptable.

"Spacers aren't supposed to like wind," Gee murmured to her. "Perhaps you are human after all."

In the lift, she leaned on the Gamemaster. Archie had never seen any girl lean on Gee before; nor had he let them. "I'm in more trouble now, huh?"

Knowing the continual security tug-of-war between Gamemaster and Chief Robinson, Archie was not surprised by Gee's reply.

"Not really. You proved my point. I said you were dangerous, and they didn't believe me. My own Security people." He looked and sounded annoyed.

Apparently she had caught on right away. "Yeah," she said. "Nobody believes a pretty boy."

Gee's quick smile flashed. Archie chuckled and patted Elsa's arm. "Don't, ducks. His ego's already so big he's unfit for human company."

"I'll try to watch it," she replied, in the same vein. She was recovering fast. Archie found himself warming to her, and thought, *This lass has personality. That's what Gee saw.*

The lift halted. They stepped out into an austere lobby.

They walked through double doors into an anteroom. Max said, "Registering Gamemaster, Archie Chamberlain, Elsa Grayson. You are cleared, ladies and gentlemen," as they passed through.

The outer office of the Gee-Ten lab always looked like an abandoned building to Archie. Elsa looked around at the bare walls, the occasional empty socket, the shabby carpet. Archie caught her glance. "The Tens don't cut much dash on office furnishings, do they?" he said.

"No." Her voice was full of wonder. "I would expect the Gamemaster elite to have the works."

Again, Archie patted her arm. "They could, but they don't. They have the worst desks in Christendom, and never notice. Half the time, they aren't here, and when they are, they still aren't here. In spirit, at least."

"Besides," said Gamemaster, "there are only four of them. This area is meant for thirty, but it has never seen thirty Gamemaster Tens. Once, in my father's time, there were seven." They passed through a large, open, totally empty room to another door. Inside this room, there were desks and people.

One man stood up from his desk immediately. That action alone would have marked any Lab Manager. Gamemaster 10 Lab Manager Alec de Bruyter was remarkable for other reasons as well. He stood a good six foot two, and weighed perhaps a hundred forty pounds. His gaunt face was topped with a mop of bright red hair. Archie had never seen him smile. Then, if Archie were the Lab 10 Manager, he probably wouldn't smile much, either.

Alec moved so rapidly to face his chief that Archie had the absurd impression Alec was protecting his children. Then he thought, *Of course he is; Trann would do the same for me.* The words were what Archie expected to hear, friendly and normal: "Hello, chief. What's up?"

"I put Archie on a personal project that's too big for him. He's kicking it upstairs."

"That's hard on me, chief," Alec objected. "You know I'll only have three Tens after Friday."

"I understand." Gee's voice was bland. "I'm prepared to halt everything except the top-level projects until I get this one untangled. You and Trann will clear as much as necessary to get my project done."

Alec raised a brow. In the meantime, one of the Gamemaster Tens had looked up from his desk, as if his name had been mentioned.

"Halt everything?" Alec checked his hearing.

"You heard me."

Time to play good cop bad cop. "It's like this, Alec," Archie said, in his humblest voice. "We got shot at and kidnapped while obtaining this program, and we'd like to know why. But as near as I can tell, it's a patch job of data files with no executable programs whatsoever, no menus, nothing. I've chipped at it all day with nothing to show." He saw Alec frown in puzzlement. "You know I'm no duffer at this, but I'm lost."

Elsa watched all three as if it was a tennis match and only she could see the ball.

"A man left this to me in his will," Gamemaster added. "I want to know why."

Elsa caught her breath. "This was in the sealed computer?"

Alec looked at her sharply. "What sealed computer?"

Archie did introductions. "Elsa, Gee-Ten Lab Manager Alec de Bruyter. Alec, Elsa Grayson, daughter of Captain James Grayson of the *Sun King*. You may remember the incident."

"Good heavens," said Alec. His entire tone changed. He regarded her again with extraordinary interest. "Of course I do. Jocko Grayson was as worried about that assignment as I was."

"You knew my father?" Elsa stared up at Alec. No one else had known that James Grayson's nickname was Jocko, Archie reflected.

"Certainly. He came here asking questions about the new engines. He was perfectly right in his concerns. I issued a safety warning on those field dampers because they had failed lab tests, and we got our noses pushed in."

"By the same charming gentlemen who tried to raid this lab with a SWAT team not that long ago." Gamemaster moved toward one desk. The other Gee-Tens, now conscious of other presences in the lab, stopped what they were doing to watch.

Archie watched Elsa Grayson meet Damiel Detreuil. He was an enfant-soleil, a sun-child from the Riviera, with two or three generations of genetic modification to make the best of that sunny climate. Archie had forgotten that women found the shy student's golden eyes, white featherlike hair, and coppery skin to be fascinating. Elsa was already getting lost in those eyes.

"Damiel," Gee greeted him. "You will not reconsider?"

His voice was wonderful, too. "I cannot be the cause of such pain. I became a Gamemaster Ten because I felt I could improve the condition of all humanity. I can no longer aid in their destruction."

Elsa blinked, and spoke up as if she belonged there. "You're leaving? Why?"

"Why should I tell you anything?" Damiel asked her. "You are the enemy."

"No, I'm not," Elsa told him. "If you think I am, then you *should* retire and go back to your little hole-in-the-wall. There's only one enemy, and that's human stupidity."

She sounded twice her age. She sounded like an outside consultant. And she wasn't saying anything that probably hadn't been said a hundred thousand times within these walls, Archie reflected. He saw the expressions change on both Damiel's and Alex's faces.

Elsa promptly proved she wasn't stupid, either. "I get it. You invented the Kapi tracking sensor, didn't you? And it's roaring successful. It can track everything, everywhere, and can even note what's around the neighborhood. It's the most successful, least effortless tracking device ever invented. Find your missing keys in an instant, see if your daughter is sitting next to the boy you told her to stay away from. Everyone's switching to Kapi and seeing things everywhere they never saw before and weren't meant to see. Including military intelligence, who are muscling into everyone's business now. So you're embarrassed and bailing out. You're going home and sticking these people with the problems your new product caused."

"That is untrue," Damiel protested. However, even Archie was thinking, *I hadn't put it in quite that light, but she's right.*

Damiel's glance rested for a moment on Alec de Bruyter, whose gaze returned to his desk panel and stayed there. Archie felt quite certain he had seen an entire year-long argument in those two glances.

Gamemaster's face was as expressionless as if he had heard and seen nothing. He continued the conversation right where he'd left off. "A Gamemaster Ten quit in my grandfather's time," said Gee, "but I never thought

I would lose one of my own. Of course you'll have all the rights of a Gee-Ten Retiree, wherever you go, all your life. But I would rather be giving you the rights of a Gee-Ten. You are meticulous, and caring. What happened was not your fault."

"We have been through this," Damiel objected, in the same musical voice.

"I know we have." Gamemaster's voice softened. "I will not bring it up again. My apologies. But Friday is three days away, and I'm hijacking you." His tone had not changed, but the abruptness of his final words was startling.

Damiel glanced at Alec nonetheless. Then he looked at Archie. He had logically inferred that a Nine was passing the buck to a Ten.

"I'm sorry, Damiel," Archie said, still humbly. "I can't get this."

"Then it is difficult, Archie," Damiel replied. Somehow, his voice sounded kind but not patronizing.

"Well, thanks for the boost, but I don't deserve it. I was at this all day, and couldn't even find a directory. Max has the files stored for me, in locations H6 through L7."

"You mean locations H6 and L7," Damiel corrected.

"No. I mean H6 through L7. It's the program that ate West Meg."

Damiel stared at him for a long moment.

"Shall I call it up?" Archie asked.

Wordlessly, Damiel slid out of his chair. Archie slid in. Naturally curious, Elsa came over immediately to stand behind him.

"Max, this is Archie, at Damiel's desk in the Gamemaster 10 Lab. I'm turning over to him all the information I have on the project I've worked on all day today. Give him all my notes and marks, and transfer all material from Project Albatross to Damiel's command."

"Working on it, Archie," Max replied. That was proof enough that it was so large Max had time to chat. "Is there anything else you'd like me to do while we're waiting?"

"Sarcasm ill becomes you, Max."

"It was not sarcasm, Archie. I am not programmed for sarcasm. I really did have twelve seconds to spare for other purposes."

Alec de Bruyter, an arm's length away at his desk, was staring at his terminal. "What in hell did you just transfer into the Ten databanks? The planet Jupiter? It's still transferring."

Archie ignored him. Lab Managers were meant to be ignored. Elsa was looking over his left shoulder. She wasn't going to steal any secrets from him on this, he thought disparagingly. He spoke only to Damiel. "Here's as far as I've got. This is one of the most complicated, intricate programs I have ever seen. Show us what I've been able to find of the Overview, Max."

Damiel was leaning closely over his right shoulder. "Where is the documentation?"

"There is none. That is, none has been found. It was stored on the *Albatross.* Recover tried to blow it up, so if it was ever there, it's gone now."

"*Albatross.*" Alec was paging through something at his terminal. "The *S.S. Albatross.* The future ECM Museum, the missing ship. Max, I want someone from Legal up here *now.*"

"I'm sending Lucretia Danvers up, Alec," Max replied.

"The wise man is permanently suspicious." Archie kept paging through the Overview, Damiel reading over his shoulder.

"Paranoia is an important quality in my Managers," Gee agreed, leaning against Alec's desk, his back to him.

"Ah, there, I thought I'd seen that phrase before. Elsa, what's Desert Shield?" Archie, wrapped up in the problem, shot the question at her as if she were just another consultant.

"Operation Desert Shield," Elsa replied promptly. "Persian Gulf War, 1991. It became Operation Desert Storm after hostilities started. Middle East, petroleum dependency era. Iraq invaded Kuwait. The United States moved in to recover oil territories in Kuwait."

"Did you say United States?"

"Yes, when there were fifty or so separate states. The Restructure didn't occur until the twenty-first century."

"You know your history," Alec said to her.

"It's her job," Gamemaster said tersely.

"You're going at this wrong," said Damiel to Archie.

"Hallelujah. I'm moving out of your chair. *Please* tell me what I'm muffing up."

Damiel slid in. "You're typing these up and looking at lines of program. There's embedded execution codes in here— this line, look— and this line."

"I'll be damned. I thought that was Aramaic."

"You don't speak Aramaic, do you?" Damiel said reasonably. "And if you did, it would look like Serbo-Croat."

"I get you."

"We need to get a grip on these embedded codes. Max. Get me the Typhoon Codebook, the First Squadron Kodebook, and— let's try the first edition of— what was his name— James Joyce. Ulysses."

"Hah. So I did see Aramaic."

"You're aware that the first editions of Ulysses seem so arcane because the printer left out half the copy," said Damiel to the Gamemaster.

"Mmph. That wasn't discovered until the late twentieth century. In the meantime, it had generated more interpretations than any other book in Earth's existence except the Bible." Gamemaster, still leaning against Alec's desk, concentrated upon Damiel's exposition. Elsa's gaze flitted from one man to another, still as if she watched an invisible tennis game and only she knew the score.

"I am seeing snatches of various literary works, sprinkled throughout the programming. I think these embeds have a literary background— something like Ulysses or the Bible. If I can get a grip on them— Max. Stop. Six screens back, Max." There was a pause. Damiel touched his screen, moved things, touched commands. "Hmph. There's several books mentioned in here, mainly allegorical. Whoever put this together had a first-rate mind."

"That's John Arrow all over," said Archie. "Gee's old chessmate. He died."

"I deeply regret the loss of such a mind," said Damiel, eyes still on the screen. "Max, go back two screens— give me a split screen with the Kodebook— mark parallels there, there, and there— Ah. You see, Archie? Nothing stands alone. These quotes match each other in subject, or type of reference— Have you played much with spherical logic? There seems to be some of it in use in these passages."

"Damn. Never crossed my mind. And it should have, when I wasn't getting a grip on these literary embeds." Archie pulled a pad out of his pocket and started making notes of his own. He was vaguely aware of Elsa Grayson staring as Damiel breezed away at the problem which had confounded him all day. Mainly, Archie watched, taking notes, as oblivious to the others as the Gee-Ten. It was true that Damiel got more of Max to play with than Archie did, but it was also true that Damiel's intuition augmented Max's abilities far beyond that of most humans.

"Your notes are good, Archie," Damiel was saying. "I can follow you up to this point— " Suddenly his tone changed. "Got it."

"What have you got?" Elsa asked.

"Virtual reality program. Hang onto the desks, everyone— I'm initiating." The scenery shifted around them suddenly.

"Eeep," said Archie. "This is what gets Gamemasters killed."

"Sorry," said Damiel. "I should have given you advance warning." He looked around. They were on an island about the size of the Alpha Tea Room, with blue sky and bright sun overhead. There was white sand beneath their feet and some palm trees at the opposite shore. "Pacific desert island, yes?"

"Looks it," Archie agreed.

Damiel gestured toward the ocean with a quick smile. Archie caught his meaning. There was no sound of waves, no seagulls diving— a completely silent vista. The bright sun was not warming them. Archie bent down to touch a handful of sand and felt the shabby carpet of the Gee-10 Lab. This scene was incomplete.

Alec had brought his desk with him. "Energy use is minimal for a simulation of this size," he said, peering at his screen. "There's a very nice patch between this program and conventional power sources."

"But why are we here?" Elsa wondered.

"I would say— this is why," said Gamemaster.

They turned to stare at the Gamemaster.

Not the one standing beside them. There was another Gamemaster standing here: a dark, severe, unsmiling twin, staring them down.

"Pretty good VR image file," Archie said approvingly, "but the clothes are a few years out of date."

The image Gamemaster spoke. "You are not authorized here. If this transgression occurs a second time, we will take measures."

The voice brought Archie up short. This was a Gamemaster he didn't know, not quite. Archie silently blessed the Tibetans for some of the changes in the devil he knew.

"Good Heavens." That was the real Gamemaster. "Do I sound like that?"

"No, it's a logical extrapolation of a very old image file. John Arrow did a marvelous job of it. He even guessed what you'd look like in ten years. He was off a bit. We'd better soften that image. No, we'd better not," Archie amended. "I'm beginning to get an idea what this program is, and I think we're going to need an extremely unyielding host."

The image Gamemaster wasn't interested in that. "This simulation does not allow any modification. When you have paid for artillery and players, the landscape and battle conditions become immutable. I have no record of any payment cleared."

Elsa's eyes widened. "It's a war game!"

"Certainly it is," Gee said softly. "The war to end all wars. Imagine governments paying real money to fight their battles here. Bloodless battles, Elsa. They abide by the decision because of the money they've spent."

"Money talks," said Damiel, just as softly.

"Identify yourselves immediately," said the image.

Gee turned to Damiel. "It thinks we are hackers. Don't identify yourself as the Gamemaster in charge of this simulation if you are leaving the company. Since we haven't found any documentation yet, I think changing identifications later will be extremely difficult."

"I concur," said Archie.

Damiel looked at Gee, then at Archie, then at the image Gamemaster.

In his hard voice, the image repeated firmly, "Identification, please. NOW."

Elsa Grayson moved forward suddenly. To Damiel, she said, "Tell them you'll take the assignment. I'll help you."

Damiel glanced at her. "What have you to do with this?"

"I'll fill you in later. Just say yes. Then we'll both have jobs. Don't you see? A way of settling disputes on a gigantic gameboard. We can do this! Go for it!"

"You're in the military," Damiel deduced.

"I've done my time." Standard answer the universe over.

The Gamemaster, apparently, was not held back by any qualms. He inquired, "Ready to partner up on this?"

"I'm shutting you off," said the image harshly.

"You'll do no such thing." From his forgotten desk, Alec de Bruyter spoke firmly to the image. "I am the Manager of the Gamemaster Ten Laboratory, and you are part of a program under consideration by the Gamemaster Ten Lab. If you don't think you are, you had better re-check your config files. You are still in the experimental stages and you will *not* adjust yourself until the appropriate Gamemaster Ten takes action!"

The image accepted his order. "Standing by. However, I have a very short timer."

"I've heard *that* before, too," Alec de Bruyter muttered in the voice of managerial experience. "Just wait." Alec's sharp eyes went back to his own lost lamb. "Are you in or out, Damiel? Do I haul someone else in from the lab, or do you want this baby?"

The pools of gold in Damiel's eyes circled and flashed. He had to make a snap decision. They were probably waiting for him at home. "I shall take it."

"Then stop this pussyfooting around and introduce yourself to the master of ceremonies. Log in."

"I'm doing it now." His hands flew over his console, tapping here and there.

The image turned to look at Damiel. Its expression never changed. The old Gamemaster's wouldn't. Again Archie blessed the Abbot for the changes he had wrought in his friend. "I'm receiving a login transmission and a first password code. Do you wish to make this permanent?"

"Yes."

"You are Damiel Detreuil, Gamemaster Ten in charge of the War Game Simulation?"

"Confirmed."

"Then welcome."

"Take me to the opening sequence showing the requirements of play," Damiel ordered.

The scene shifted around them. They were in a boardroom. A large conference table dominated the central area. Around the walls were countless screens depicting various terrains, maps, and accounting tables. Archie tapped one of the last. "Until your money runs out," he said.

"So I see," Elsa replied. She moved to stand beside Damiel.

In his hard voice, the image Gamemaster began the introduction to the game. "This is the War Game Simulation, the alternative to bloody warfare. This program was conceived, but not completed, by Major John Arrow of the Earth Combined Military. Projections indicate that the main portion of this interactive program may be completed by a Gamemaster Ten within twenty to twenty-five years, with continuing updates beyond the life of the Gamemaster to accommodate technological and sociological updates. Both experimentation and utilization of the program require cooperation of various governments to give adequate results. Among the requirements of play..." The image began outlining the rules of the game to Damiel. Gee turned to Archie and Alec.

"I don't think we're needed here any more," he said.

Alec de Bruyter looked neither happy nor sad. Well, Archie thought, why should he? He kept his Gee-Ten, but didn't get him back to work on Ten Lab projects. It was a draw. Alec bent his face to his console. The lab reappeared around them.

A short distance away, in a separate carrel, Damiel and Elsa stood. They saw only the image Gamemaster.

"I'll tell his folks not to expect him," Alec said quietly.

"I'm sorry, Alec," said Gee. "I will put some personal effort into finding you a new Gee-Ten. I've been neglecting you lately."

"I know how it is, chief."

"No. It's not right. I'll be back in touch. Max, make a note that I'll be back in touch with Alec de Bruyter."

"Noted."

Alec's expression lightened one very small iota. "Thanks."

Gee touched Archie's shoulder. "Let's push on."

Midnight, and their dinner plans had been blown away by the day's activities. Max made cancellations and apologies for them. When Archie said he was just going to have a quick sandwich and call it a night, Gee asked, "Mind sharing sandwiches? I'd like to see those books again."

"Not at all. Come on over." Archie smiled at the memory of his last visit, wanting to kick him out, chessboard and all.

Over sandwiches, coffee, and brandy in the living room, they discussed the books. Sure enough, there had been a copy of *Ulysses* in Arrow's collection, along with the *First Squadron Kodebook* and most of the other books Damiel had mentioned. There was also a history of the creation of the National Trust and some other books which might be future clues, simply because they hadn't popped up yet in current use.

"He was a superb programmer." Archie shook his head. "If he wasn't a Gee-Ten, I'll eat my slippers. I wonder how he kept his abilities from popping up in the GCODE."

"He may have been exempted. Military schools often are, and there are hints of that type of education in his records. It's easy enough to waive the GCODE battery, although I don't publicize it." Gee finished the last bite of his sandwich. "All right, referee, how are we scoring on the dead bird riddle?"

"I do think this is it," said Archie. "The dead bird, the *Albatross*. I think it's solved. John Arrow wanted you to find this program that he started, and keep working on it because it could possibly lead to solar peace. Or at least a great reduction in warfare."

"It feels like the solution to me, too. There's no mention of an albatross or bird within the program, but it does feel like finding it was the goal." For a moment, there was an odd light in Gee's eyes. "He promised me the finest gifts possible, and delivered. Who else can say they've received the promise of world peace as a gift?"

"But what'll you do with it?" Archie asked. "This gigantic program. I can't exactly see governments standing in line to play games to settle wars, not yet."

"Not yet," Gee agreed. "But, we can do simulations. What if we follow this decision, what if we do that. With Elsa's advice, we can show the effects of particular actions. Also with Elsa's help, perhaps we can make the projections dark enough to make factions think twice about employing certain tactics. Or light enough."

"I suppose that's true," mused Archie. "We have all the time in the universe."

"Yes. We do. Even if we do nothing in my generation but make plans for the program, and test it, and ask for input from various factions, we shall have them talking together and thinking. Anything is more than what we had before."

"It boggles me," said Archie, "to hear you speak so blithely of 'my generation,' as though you were saying 'for the next hour or so.' I can't think like that."

Gee shrugged. Archie doubted very much that Gennaro realized he made a face whenever he spoke of his training. The expression wasn't particularly pleasant. "It's all part of the mechanism and the protocol. By now I should reach x percentage profit, by this time I should have started on children. It's all there."

"You're very far-seeing. Can you send that along, too, to the next generation?"

"No," said Gennaro, "I can't. Not the way you mean." He shook his head. "But then, some future Gamemaster may have a valuable quality I cannot imagine."

"You said 'started on children.' When does that come along in the schedule?"

"Pretty soon now."

Archie sighed, put his feet up, and took another sip of the brandy. "And you just cast your line into the pool and hook a wife."

"Do you have any idea how many women are out there, angling for me?" Gennaro asked mildly. "Max handles most inquiries after my health, and the love letters, and the fan mail. Not to mention the outright marriage proposals, and proposals that would probably scandalize even me if I ever bothered to read them. My opinion of the opposite sex— with, I admit, a few notable exceptions like Shiera Walton, Elsa and Bet— drops daily."

"I don't envy you that," said Archie. Then he added, "Come to think of it, there's not much about your life that I do envy. Except, possibly, how the tailor gets it right in one fitting."

It was rare that the laughter reached Gennaro's eyes, but it did this time. "Well, that would explain one aspect of your life that's always been a mystery to me."

"Takes me five years to work up nerve for another trip to the bloody tailor," Archie agreed. "Seriously, though, will I walk in some day and Haviland will say, 'Mrs. Gee is waiting for you, Mr. Chamberlain'?"

The laughter faded. "No. Nothing says she has to live with me or take part in my life. If she has any sense, she won't. My mother committed suicide, you know."

"No, I didn't. But I suspected it."

Gee swirled his snifter, breathed the aroma, barely touched his lips to the golden liqueur which he had paid for. "Pills and liquor. Truthfully, not much of a loss to me. She was trying her best not to be close to her children. We kept killing ourselves off. What brought this topic up, anyway? Were you thinking about yourself? The same rules need not apply."

"I know." Now it was Archie's turn to stare into the drink. "I was thinking about the unfairness of life in general." Again, there was a long pause in the conversation. Maybe the letter he just got that day from Prentiss and Sylvia at Isidis Prep, telling him their first baby was on the way, really had affected his mind. Archie felt frustrated by the rank of the person sitting in his guest chair, sharing his liquor. "Sometimes I do wish you were just a fellow I knew at school, particularly when I want to talk about a subject that would piss off the management at Gamemaster Inc."

Gennaro looked surprised. Then, he seemed to realize that Archie had something serious on his mind. The Gamemaster did something which stunned

Archie, who had never seen such a thing happen in his life, and which Archie later loved to remember: He unpinned his badge and set it on the little table beside them. "For ten minutes, I'm not," he said. "Now talk."

-10-

Play Again?

He made faces at the ugly eagle shield on the monitor, but stopped before Lieutenant McAllen's image appeared. When she saw who was calling, her expression became guarded. Her eyes narrowed and her voice took on a reserved tone. "Mr. Chamberlain. What can I do for you?"

"Are you in more trouble?" he asked.

"Yes." Enough said.

"Then I don't suppose you'd let me ask for another favor," he said in his humblest voice, "perhaps even letting me buy you dinner at some place without as much salt and grease...?"

"I really don't think so. But thank you." Her tone was undoubtedly final.

"Well, that's that, then." Archie let his face show his disappointment. Then he brightened. "How about if I could give you some juicy gossip about Recover to take home with you?"

"Some j— what are you talking about?" she asked, obviously caught off guard.

"Ah, no more out of me. Do you like Brazilian?"

"I love Brazilian," Lt. McAllen said immediately and decisively.

"Good. Poki's at 1800 hours and I hope you've got a recording device on you, because I hate repeating myself," Archie said cheerfully, and shut the monitor off before she could beat him to it.

The busy hum of quiet conversations, clatter of dishes, and the trotting of waiters at Poki's made a nice background cover for private conversation. Dinner was the house specialty, a lovely seafood dish which cooled unnoticed as Archie gave McAllen a complete report of their capture in the Neptune Yards. To the best of his ability, he included physical descriptions of young persons unknown, and positively identified the one Recover commando now residing at Building 1 West Alpha. Archie skated over many details, such as the eventual fate of the *Albatross*. He was not making a recording to land his boss in prison, just to outline their recent adventures. Anyway, unless Lt. McAllen was supremely stupid (and he doubted that), she could figure out that part out for herself. Thanks to the Gamemaster, earth orbital position L5 would never contain an ECM War Memorial as planned.

"So why are you telling me all this?" she asked suspiciously.

"So you can leak it back to your boss," Archie replied pragmatically. "You could probably use the good press, and I owe you. It might also convince your folks that it's on the up-and-up, because it is."

"You're making a ghastly accusation about officers' children all over the Solar System."

"I'll bet if you take that information back home with you, somewhere in your organization, you'll find a department that's not all that surprised," Archie predicted.

She sighed. "I'm so afraid you're right, I almost don't want to do it," she confessed.

"But you will. Loyalty is not a bad trait. Changing loyalty is." He sipped wine.

"I suppose it's never been an issue for you."

Archie cocked an eye at her. "Want the truth? It'll shock you. Never. Absolutely never crossed my mind. I spent six years as a schoolteacher, trying to pretend I wasn't 'born to the purple,' so to speak, and found out I was a lousy liar. Especially to myself. I was a Gee-9 born, not made. While I got some excellent experience out there, I was only postponing the inevitable."

"You knew right from the start you'd be a Gamemaster?"

"I knew I'd end up getting sucked in by the Company. I didn't want it to happen."

"And here you are."

"And here I am," he agreed.

"Won't you-know-who be pissed off— excuse me, won't he be annoyed, when he learns one of his chosen employees has leaked confidential information?"

Archie chuckled. "Who do you think told me to leak it?"

There was no answer to that but a stare.

"They're kids, Lieutenant," Archie said softly. "Kids. None of us want to hurt kids. It's going to take all our combined efforts not to."

"Oh, God," said Lt. McAllen. She closed her eyes and took a deep breath. "You're right, I'll report back to Captain Jahnik, and he'll probably pass it on."

"You said 'probably.' Will he or won't he?"

Lieutenant McAllen reached up to touch something on her collar. "Well, I'm not the steadiest soldier in that department."

"Was that the off button for your recorder?" Archie asked.

"Um, yes, it was."

"Well, now I'll say, don't tell Captain Jahnik, tell Commander Marsden."

McAllen shook her head. "I can't go over his head."

"You can if you tell him you have a private message for him from Archie Chamberlain, and you are cordially invited to use my name to do so. Lieutenant, I don't understand politics, but I do understand you're in a bad spot."

"What do you mean?" she asked, but her eyes didn't have a matching expression of innocence.

"Well, if I did work for the ECM and had the data I found using palimpsest programs on those press releases, I'd be talking to Internal Affairs right now."

Lieutenant McAllen shook her head again. "I can't do that."

Archie spread his hands. "It's your call. I just wanted to give you the leeway to do it if you wished. I really did owe you, and I was thankful for your help."

"And you-know-who said it was okay?" she demanded disbelievingly. "Why?"

"I think I know why, but I can't really explain it."

Sheila McAllen leaned across the table and looked him straight in the eye. "Try."

Archie felt his breathing stop. In that moment, things became very clear.

It must have been the wine, Archie decided the next morning, as he walked to work. Never touched the stuff during the work week, normally. Yet he hadn't been drunk— the realization that he was in love with Sheila McAllen had kept him stone cold sober. Sheila McAllen! What the hell was wrong with him? There was a chasm between them as big as Valles Marmeris. Here he'd been blathering on about the lieutenant's problems, and all the time, both Gee and Trann must have been thinking, Chamberlain's head over heels and doesn't know it. Not even Gennaro had commented on it. And if anyone was going to comment, particularly rudely, it would have been Gee. He hadn't said a thing, while Archie told him about McAllen and her troubles.

Well, he thought unhappily, he didn't like living alone. That was the crux of the matter. This coming home to nobody and nothing got old fast, and he could understand why so many of his single counterparts were never home. But he liked home. He liked his life. Maybe Luki had meant more than he'd said in his marital prediction.

And, he confessed to himself, he didn't want a dull wife. Day-to-day life was pedestrian enough without that. He had even more in common with his father than he'd realized. Life with Peggy Chamberlain wasn't dull for father or son. But Sheila McAllen! Her rah-rah-ECM attitude got on his nerves after a while, and was in direct opposition to everything he'd grown up with. And, when you came right down to it, despite a certain something in her attitude, she was just an aspiring paper-pusher. He could talk himself out of his infatuation with Sheila if he tried hard enough, but dammit. He'd be heading toward a professional matchmaker in another year if he couldn't get himself under control.

A goddamn crush! Well, thank you for your tolerance, gentlemen, Archie told Trann and Gee silently, but I'm sober now. I'm too good a Gamemaster to waste time on a hopeless game like Lieutenant McAllen. I will watch my step from here on.

He entered the Gee-9 lab, nodded to Trann, got his second cup of tea, and slid comfortably into his seat like he had never left it. "Rise and shine, Max."

"Good morning, Archie."

"What's on my priority list?"

"Elsa Grayson plans to take you to lunch. You have a reminder to take another shot at the Three Rivers game today. President Carson asks you to return her call. General MacKenzie has a query about emergency medical kits. The Surgeon General of West Meg wishes to speak to you. After these matters have been settled, Trann would like to reassign you to new material."

"Confirmed on all." Archie took another sip.

"Alert, Archie. Priority message coming in."

There was only one priority message level above any of those. Archie sighed. "What's on Gee's mind?"

"He promised Alec de Bruyter he'd go scouring for Tens and wants your company on the one with the medical nanotechnology application. Drop in anytime in the next two days."

"Right. Tell him, glad to." Archie took another sip. "Now let's get to work."

Once again, Archie dove into Three Rivers. He absorbed himself in vanishing boat hooks and murderous pirates for three hours. When holes started appearing in the bottom of the raft, he caught on at last. "Oh, hell. Max, tell me this program wasn't created on a machine with a faulty clock."

"What shall I check to verify?"

"Match my error chart and frequency-of-error chart against standard battery decay formulae. Do I have any possible matches?"

"Yes, you do." Patterns of data flashed before Archie's eyes.

Archie groaned. "That's a kindergarten problem. The clock should have been tested back in the Gee-One stage. How did this error get all the way to me? Give me background on the Gees who passed it up to me, and on the author. I'm damned if I will bounce back something I've already said is good, especially not without due cause."

"I'm doing background work now. Approved by Gamemaster Eight Andy Andrews. Approved by Gamemaster Seven Alice MacKinnon. Approved by Gamemaster Six Leo Leonard. Approved by Gamemaster Five Sin Kyung Hee. Approved by Gamemaster Four Dolzin. Approved by Gamemaster Three..."

Archie sighed again. "Stop, Max. Tell me about the author." He hoped it was someone he could snub, someone already comfortably well-off.

"Emilio Nagueia. Managua, Nicaragua. Aged fourteen. Address: American Orphanage at Managua..."

"Stop, Max." Archie frowned. "Bloody hell. Get Trann."

"On his way."

Trann stood at Archie's shoulder. "What is the problem?"

"I'm in deep, Trann." He showed the Gee-9 Lab Manager the charts and records. Trann said some bad words in what might have been Polynesian. "Mm-hm, we've been handed a hairball. Everyone thought someone else had cleared all the preliminary work, and passed this game on because they couldn't get it, so it must be too sophisticated. I doubt anyone examined it for more than twenty minutes before it reached me."

Trann's voice was like ice. "It is high time for another project monitoring workshop for Lab Managers." In which he would have plenty to say, Archie suspected, especially to Gee-8 Lab Manager Shiera Walton.

"I have an idea how to deal with it, if you're on. I don't like having egg on my face any more than you do."

"I'm listening. I'm pissed. Every damn problem child per level had this game. No wonder the flaws got by."

"Yes, but I can work with Andy and Shiera. The worst we can get is good publicity for rewarding a hard-working orphan. In fact, Andy would make an ideal partner, since he's spending half his time in the Emergency Room with Diane. He'll be perfectly willing to leave everything to Shiera and me. Andy's stubborn enough to stick by his approval and that will help. He won't be able to concentrate on anything, anyway, until Diane has that baby. At best, he can be our PR man, and otherwise we spread the blame around and Shiera will owe you one."

"You can try. That is one of your good points, Archie. You never present a problem without a possible solution."

"Yes, it's one of my charms. Do I have your permission to go beat up on the Gee-Eight lab later?"

"My blessings." Trann lumbered off.

"Okay, Max. Now President Carson."

When he signed off his conversation with the President, a voice behind him said, "I don't suppose 'Eunice' might be the President of Eastern Seaboard in her spare time?"

Archie looked up at bright blue eyes and, most amazingly, a smile. Elsa Grayson looked more like an angel, with her halo of golden curls and comfortable light-blue-and-white clothes. "Yep. Known her since she was a freshman politico. Hello, poppet. How's life with Damiel?"

"Wonderful. We're making great strides."

Archie looked doubtfully at his desk. "You're doing better than I am today, then."

"What about lunch? I heard you know all the best places."

"Oh, no, no. You don't invite me for lunch and then put the onus of choosing a restaurant on me."

Elsa laughed. "All right. Sabad's."

"Not for anything. Giardino's."

She laughed again.

As they walked to the restaurant, Archie noticed the Gamemaster company badge. Nothing splashy, just general corporate. "So you signed a contract."

"Mm-hm. Gamemaster Management. I'm old enough. Gee says on my worst days, which he's seen, I'm still more mature than a lot of Gamemasters."

"Right enough." They walked without speaking for a few moments, then he asked, "Forgive the intrusion— was there anyone to brag to?"

She stared into the distance as they walked through Miklin Park. "Nobody. Mom was an only child. My grandparents are dead. Uncle Marc was a UN construction worker on Ganymede. Since they were trained in military procedure, not space construction, they died in construction accidents by the score out there." She glanced up into Archie's eyes. "Seems easy to tell you that."

"That's me. Everyone's uncle. You'll get used to it. Got a place yet?"

"No, I'm still in a guest room in the penthouse. Shirley from Contract is going to find me one."

"Shirley from Contract is being nosy. It's the job of Personnel to find you an apartment. Tip them the wink and they'll tell Shirley to butt out."

"Thank you. I was wondering about that."

Archie's favorite Italian lunch spot was busy but not bustling. As they examined their menus, Archie commented, "So you and Damiel are playing the game."

"Mm-hm. I'm logged in permanently as a market tester. If that held correctly, I'll never be capable of becoming a combatant, just an advisor, and only have limited access to the program. Which is fine by me." She returned to her menu. "Pasta Primavera looks like it."

"With all these choices? Are you a vegetarian?"

"No." Her cheeks reddened. "I don't understand a word of this menu except 'pasta.'"

"Here, I'll help," Archie said kindly. "Don't pick the only thing you know. Get some of the alcohol-free Lambrusco, since you'll have a busy afternoon, and try one of these three, down here."

Elsa smiled, showing her dimples once again. "That was the other reason I wanted to go to lunch with you. I've never been out to lunch."

"Oh, my." Archie's blue eyes opened wide. "Of course you haven't. ECM creches and military cafeterias. I'd be delighted to take you to restaurants and things."

"I was afraid that you'd say no," Elsa told him, "that you wouldn't want to be accused of being a cradle robber."

"My friends know better. My enemies shall be envious. I shall have the best of both worlds."

Elsa dissolved into laughter. It made him grin, too. Archie couldn't have imagined the cold, vicious kid in the red spacesuit turning into such a charmer.

"You would scorn me," said Archie, "if I told you I thought you were turning into the joyful person you were meant to be."

Elsa stopped laughing. "You're the second man to use that expression to me."

"Mmph. We learned it from the same school." Archie helped her with the menu, and then they slid them into the slot under the red checkered tabletop to start their order. "Now. What's on your mind besides lunch?"

"Damiel. The game. All this." She waved a hand around the busy restaurant, full of laughter and jabbering. "He's just given me a badge and turned me loose. Does he really expect that computer to keep me under control?" "He" was obviously not Damiel.

"It's what he calls 'the long leash' and no, he doesn't." At her look of surprise, he explained further. "Max is everywhere, or at least everywhere that a computer can manage to be. He's a tool, Elsa. That's all. He's what Gee has in lieu of a puppy."

"Well, then, what's to prevent me from stealing secrets and trashing the place?"

"You really don't know, do you?" The wine rose from the table hatch. Archie tasted it. "Another hint— always make sure your lunch wine is nonalcoholic. With the crowd you'll be associating, you may be hopping all afternoon and most of the evening."

"I'll keep that in mind. Answer the question."

"I'll answer it by asking another one. Do you realize how much you've been smiling the past couple days? What did they dope you up with?"

"'They' didn't dope me with anything."

"That's what others might assume," Archie pointed out.

"Well, they'd be wrong."

"I know that. The question still on the floor is, Why are you smiling so?"

"My God, why shouldn't I be? I'm helping with a computer program that might end all warfare!"

"But if you told me that— and I was a Recover agent— I would just say, Elsa, you've been lied to, it's brainwashing, such a program doesn't really exist. Come let us straighten you out. Now, wouldn't I?"

"That's ridiculous. I haven't been brainwashed." He heard the hesitation.

"Pretend I'm Recover and convince me." Archie crossed his arms.

Elsa Grayson sat back in her seat unhappily. It was a tribute to her grey matter that she was taking the time to examine the issue carefully. She rose three notches in Archie's estimation in those three minutes.

At last, she sighed. "I couldn't convince you, could I? Brainwashing is just behavior modification of the most drastic kind, and I've drastically modified my behavior in the past few days." Another pause. "And the program doesn't really exist. Not yet. Just my hopes and dreams for it." Another pause, as Elsa further examined the furniture inside her head. "And I am unreasonably, foolishly happy."

"Damiel," Archie suggested.

"You think I'm in love?"

"Unreasonably, foolishly, happily." He felt a pang of something in himself, but it was too vague to describe.

Deep thought didn't keep Elsa from munching on a very good salad, but there was plenty of quiet at their table. Archie didn't mind. The company was good. "Even without Damiel," Elsa said slowly, "I think I'd be happy here. But Damiel... he's a Gee-Ten and he can't see it, can't imagine how far this thing could go. Gee knows that I can see it, can't he? Just like him and you. That's why he's glued me to Damiel. Not that it took much glue," she amended.

"Horrible old mind-benders, aren't we?"

"I feel like this was supposed to have been my place all along."

Archie was terribly familiar with that feeling.

"My God," Elsa said, "I can't go back."

Archie knew that feeling, too.

They kicked their way through garbage in a dark alley in Augusta. They found a half-broken down wooden door that only Max would have been able to locate. Thanks to the three-hour time difference, it was almost sunset here, but alley visibility was near zero. The place gave Archie the jimjams. Gee, one step ahead of him, pounded on the door. Apparently the bolts and hinges were sturdy, even if the door looked like something left over from an ancient raid.

A horrid mechanical voice, far worse than the Earth Combined Military's welcome screen, squawked into the night. "GO. AWAY. YOU GODAM KIDS. OR I WILL CALL COPS (squawk)."

"I refuse to speak to yard-sale doorbells." Gamemaster pounded again.

"STATE YOUR (squawk)."

"I presume that was 'State Your Name,'" Archie suggested.

"Take a look at us," Gee replied sharply to the door.

If Archie hadn't expected a high-tech response, he would have been surprised at the hum of the motor, the sound of a restraining bar lifting automatically, the door swinging open with no one at the threshold. They stepped inside. The door swung shut behind them and relocked securely.

A dark-skinned woman in a print top, white pants, and nurse's shoes stood there with her arms folded. She wore a name badge that said LANA N.A. "Who the hell are you, wandering around South Augusta this time of night?"

"Who," said the Gamemaster, "do I look like?"

The nurse glowered at them suspiciously.

"May I see Mr. Bonner, please?" the Gamemaster said.

"I'll see. He ain't much for talking. It's too much trouble." She did not move.

Gee was unperturbed by the faceoff. "Let's see if we can make it worth his while, shall we?"

Reluctantly, she left them while she stepped to the back room. There were no windows. It was fairly clean, which spoke of the efforts of the aide. Archie watched Gee tap the door-opening device approvingly. He glanced at the jerry-rigged observation system that helped Mr. Bonner maintain his decrepit two-room home as his castle.

"He say come on in."

They stepped into the bedroom. It was neat but stale, the room of an occupant who never left it. A grey-haired white man sat in an old-fashioned wheelchair. His hair was gathered back in a substantial ponytail. He wore thick spectacles. His mouth twisted to one side, and one hand seemed to be in a permanent cramp. Archie saw the scars of a formidable accident. The man's one good hand gripped a wheel, to turn him away from his desk. The nurse reached over to help him. His eyes focused on Gamemaster through the great fisheye lenses.

The ghastly mechanical voice issued from a box attached to the wheelchair arm. Various consonants twanged, the volume raised and lowered, static noise cut in. "CAN'T BE TWO looking like YOU. WHAT. CAN. I DO FOR YOU."

"I should introduce my employee, Gamemaster 9 Archie Chamberlain."

The eyes moved to focus on him, looking almost green through the great lenses. "HOW do YOU DO. (squawk) saw LIVER TECHNOLOGY TRANSPLANT."

Archie could guess at that one. The Surgeon General of the Confederate States of America and Archie had been in the news for the opening of the new Liver Technology Unit at the University of the CSA.

"He had better tools than you had here." Gamemaster looked around.

"COULD ALSO STAND. up"

It was a callous sort of humor meant to embarrass the non-handicapped. Archie recognized it as the test it was, and grinned. "Nah, I'm just taller than you are."

The nurse grinned, too. Bonner's mouth twisted in something that might have been a smile, for just a moment. The ice was broken.

The great fish-eye lenses focused on Archie. "YOU COME DOWN. here ABOUT. NANO."

Gee sat down on the bed and let Archie carry the ball, since this was nano talk. Archie took the only chair in the place. "That, too. Also some of your suggestions for space exploration. They're solid work, and worth some money."

"GOOD IF SOMETHING. does COULD USE THE MONEY"

"Oh, I intend to adapt your nanotechnology work for medical applications, almost at once," Archie replied. "Trann— my lab manager— sent me your specs because of the liver work I've been doing. Your power-source idea is superb, far better than anything I've been getting from Walter Reed West."

"HAVE NOT seen about PATENT."

"Not an issue. We'll register you for the patents involved. Or you can register."

"no MONEY FOR REGISTER or research PATENT."

"Mr. Bonner's on ECM disability," Lana felt obliged to explain. "Spends most of it on in-home care, and food— "

"GOOD LOOKING NURSES."

"Pooh. An' if he gets any change, he orders more electronic stuff delivered, so he can work on them electronic bugs."

"Does the government of the Confederate States of America contribute anything toward your support?" Gamemaster asked, in a tone that sounded more businesslike than sympathetic.

"No," said Lana and the squawkbox almost in unison.

Gamemaster regarded Lana. "I presume you work the night shift because of the shift differential. Do you have other jobs?"

"That's none of your business," said the nurse.

Bonner, though— who was very quick on the uptake, apparently— butted in. "L.A.N.A."— as if it were audible Ameslan sign language, Bonner's jerry-rigged voice system could produce a word but not a proper name— "good Nurse ONLY ONE RIGHT NOW eight twelve hours SOMETIMES on credit LOST JOB NURSING HOME WHEN kids GOT sick KICKED OUT (word not available)"

"Insubordination," suggested Gamemaster.

"AFFIRMATIVE."

"You shut up, Joseph Bonner," she said.

For someone who wasn't supposed to be much for talking, Bonner did quite well with the box. "THREE kids nursing home said US FIRST kids take care of themselves"

Archie remembered one of old Gentian's favorite lines, often quoted by his son as well: "Insubordination is acceptable if it is accompanied by initiative, imagination, and results." Archie suspected he himself was the third man in this room to pick up a liking for Lana, and to see insubordination as an endearing trait.

"Excuse me," Gamemaster interrupted again. "I can't listen to that any longer. Max, what news of the world?"

"Standing by, Gamemaster," said Max's familiar voice, through the squawky speaker. The tone improved wonderfully. Archie saw the grimace he hadn't quite yet learned to interpret on Bonner's face.

"Surely there are archival tapes somewhere of Joseph Bonner's pre-accident voice. Military reports, family albums, something. Find them, and match them up with his originating signals on this abysmal signal box."

"Retrieving now, Gamemaster. Sorting. Matching. Calibrating. Testing. Finished."

"Do I dare speak?" said Joseph Bonner.

Through the fisheye lenses, Archie saw his eyes widen. The nurse looked like she'd just seen voodoo magic.

"Good God. It sounds like me. It really does. Inflection and everything. I can YELL! Hey, — Lana!"

"You j-just s-said my name," Lana stammered.

"As I was saying," said the Gamemaster, as if he hadn't dropped a brick, "the nanotechnology you created is very innovative."

"I was not hampered by what had been done because I didn't know it. I could only get some journals when I was aboard ship, not the esoteric ones. So I don't know them now, either," Bonner said.

"That could be part of your charm. I read your background information. I found myself wondering what you could do if you had some tools."

"Did you come here to give me some tools?"

"Not at all," the Gamemaster replied, still in that hard, business-like voice.

"I applied for a Gamemaster Inc. research grant. Is that it?"

Now the Gamemaster allowed himself to appear annoyed. "Don't waste my time with trivia. I don't appreciate it."

"You will have to say it. I am poor. I am a cripple. I can't even see. You must confirm the reason that you are here. Lana should hear, also. She has spent a long time— wiping my behind for me."

"Very well. When you applied for the grant, as you well know, you tested out."

"That means," Archie explained to Lana, in answer to her puzzled look, "that he took something like an IQ test, something we use to screen for Gamemasters."

"Oh, I've heard of that," Lana said in comprehension. "Lots of people test for the GCODE when they take the Armed Forces tests and stuff." She turned to Bonner. "Didn't you already take it?"

"Mr. Bonner entered the Army of the Confederate States of America at age 17 as rank-and-file and opted not to take the GCODE at that time." Gamemaster's tone was dry. "Do your stint, drink your beer, have a good time."

Bonner's teeth showed in what was, for him, a broad grin. Lana snorted disapprovingly.

"However," Gee continued, "a candidate for a Gamemaster Inc. research grant must take the GCODE test battery as part of the application." He focused again on Bonner. "I presume you know how the system works."

"Of course I do."

"Are you interested in becoming a Gamemaster and moving to West Meg?"

"Hell yes."

"Good. I will contact Personnel and have them complete the arrangements to have you and all your personal possessions moved to the new location within three days."

Lana gasped. "Ain't there visas and stuff?"

"Personnel will take care of that." He dismissed it.

"What about my personal care?" Bonner asked. "I have needed a nurse ever since the accident."

"That will be your call. I think that with the robotics and arrangements in our assisted-living apartments, you'll be self-sufficient."

"Try it for a few days," Archie suggested, in the voice of experience, "and if you're not satisfied, call on Personnel. It's their job to satisfy your every whim."

"I can not believe you are doing this. I am a cripple."

"The part I want to put to work isn't crippled," Gee replied. "It just created the most innovative piece of technology since the vacuum tube."

"Self-sufficient. I did not even know for certain if I could pronounce the word. I am afraid, I think. But I am thrilled. But why did you come here?"

"To give you your badge. It's difficult moving cross-country, let alone with a physical disability. I thought it would be helpful." Gamemaster stood, and pulled the badge from his pocket. Archie grinned like a fool while Gee pinned it on Bonner's shirt.

The entire chair started to shake. At any other time, Archie might have been afraid the patient was having a seizure; but he recognized it for what it was. Static emerged from the speaker.

Finally, the speaker began to form words. "It says Ten. I am a Ten! Hoot! Hoot! Hoot! Hot damn, by the time I am done reprogramming this sucker, it will be able to give a Rebel Yell."

The Gamemaster told him, "You will report to Alec de Bruyter after you're done with Personnel."

"The Lab Ten manager. I have read about him."

Wishful thinking, Archie bet himself, *never knowing the dream could come true.*

"I think he is even happier than you are that you're a Ten. Good-bye. I'll see you in a few days."

Joseph Bonner's good hand clamped the badge. "So I am a Ten, am I?"

"Yes, you are." Gee's voice showed that he knew what was com-ing next.

"So what if I said Lana and her kids are part of the package."

Gamemaster never batted an eye. "I would ask how quickly they could pack, and I might recommend an apartment for Lana near the schools."

"Lord a'mercy," Lana gasped, dropping into a seat and clasping one hand to her heart.

"You hear that?" Bonner said to her. "Help me pack tonight and when it's daylight and safe to walk home, you go get all three kids and what you can carry from that shithole you live in."

"S'pose it don't work out?" she asked Gee.

"Would you rather be stranded in West Meg or here?" Gee asked. There was no answer to that conundrum.

Lana escorted them to the front room. Suddenly, she grabbed one of Gee's hands and squeezed. "I can't find anything to say except God bless you."

Gee shook his head. "I didn't do it. His mind did. The man is brilliant."

"The man is crazy. I thought you had to be a nurse to see why. He'll be awake all night, packing them bugs into boxes."

"There are worse ways to spend the night," said Gee. For the first time, he smiled. The smile transformed his face, as usual. Still clasping his hand, the nurse was drawn into that smile.

"Don't I know it. I'm afraid he'll wake up in the morning and find it was all a dream."

"That's the other reason I brought along the badge." Gee patted her hand, and released it. "Any time he thinks his senses are failing him, he can just ask Max."

"I bet Max will earn his pay confirming his senses for the next week or so."

The Gamemaster replied, "There are worse ways for Max to earn his pay, too."

Archie was aware of shadowy forms following them as they left, and understood why Lana stayed bolted in the little apartment until morning. Gamemaster never changed his leisurely pace. They were almost out of the raunchy little alley when they heard the sound of feet running toward them. A voice said, "Hey. Rich boys. I got a gun. Gimme the credit bars! Now! Now!"

They didn't even look back. They kept walking, knowing full well what the creaking sound was: the turning of valves. The sudden blast of water from the computerized city hydrant system surprised only the potential gunman as it slammed him against the wall of the alley.

"I've been working like stink, to use your phrase," said Elsa, twirling a cellophane noodle around her chopstick like a pro, after only the third attempt. "Technically, I'm in Marketing, assigned 'for advisory purposes' to Gamemaster Ten Damiel Deutreil. I'm doing my best to live up to it."

"You're fourteen. You're entitled." Archie was not nearly as fond of Asian as of European dinners, but he owed Elsa a little experience with all of them. Later they would try offworld cuisine.

"I started taking a calisthenics session before breakfast. I tried to get Gee to join." The dimples appeared. "Not a chance."

"He does his exercises with his early-morning meditations." Archie sipped tea. They did make good tea here.

"But I really like the routine. I go down to the local cafeteria for breakfast when I haven't dated you up. I miss the morning news that way, though, but I do get company."

"Start a breakfast club. Get 'em all checking the news."

"That's a thought. Then I report to the Assignments Chief in the Marketing Department, to prove I'm still alive, and check for mail. Then I go see Damiel."

Although he felt it had been a challenge, Archie did not ask her to elaborate on "check for mail." He was almost certain Elsa hadn't broken her illicit connections. On the other hand, he was sure Gee knew it, too, and there was nothing so low that Gee couldn't turn it to his advantage.

"Damiel knows his business. I edit copy and make recommendations. If we have lunch together, we take half the afternoon. And, everybody stops to chat. But you know what part of the day I like best? You'll laugh."

"Sunset," Archie guessed, thinking of the view through Gee's office window.

She nodded. "He's always in the corner, by the statue, with his eyes closed. He's a different person then, isn't he?"

"Think you're right," Archie agreed, sipping more tea. Her tone sounded almost worshipful. If he told either one of them that Elsa had adopted Gee as her dad, they'd both be shocked. He'd heard some of their conversations, ranging from small to intense, held during their regular afternoon tea. Gee treated her like an adult, yet his was the final word. Elsa strove to do her best.

In passing, Archie thought that of course some of the other Recover members had spotted Elsa by now. It would be ludicrous to think they hadn't. Everyone, including himself, was maintaining a tactful silence about the obvious.

"Can I ask you something else? It's personal."

"You mean, the rest of this wasn't?" Archie kidded. "Ask away."

"He said you died."

"Well, he did too," Archie hedged. The peaceful feeling, that he'd done well and so everything was settled and good, revisited him for a moment. Yes, everything was fine. It was all right to fall for an Army woman and just sit back and enjoy the sensation.

"He doesn't remember what it was like. Do you?"

"Not a thing. But I certainly remember waking up." Archie described the strange bearded man beside his cot, learning from the voice alone that it was Gee.

"Did you ever solve the riddle?" Elsa asked.

"Yes, we did. We found the monkey. And it was— "

"Excuse me, Archie."

"What is it, Max?"

"Trann interrupting. Urgent."

"All right. Go ahead, Trann."

The familiar manager's voice. "We've got a problem. Go see Shiera Walton immediately."

"Can I finish my luncheon?"

"*Now*." Trann never said things like that, nor cut off the transmission.

Archie stood up and dropped his napkin on the seat. Elsa, alarmed, stood too. "I'll go with you."

"No." Archie was firm. "Stay here and settle the bill. To me, of course. I'll be in the Gamemaster Eight Lab, if you want to follow."

"What's wrong?"

"I can't imagine," Archie said, on his way out the door.

-11-

Reshuffle

Archie took a taxi across town, to Miklin Square. From there it was easier to walk to Building 3 West. If it had been a true emergency, Trann would have had a taxi waiting for him before he'd called, so the damage had been done already. Trann was organizing mop-up. Archie entered Building 3 West, an open, spacious white building full of windows and sunlight. He crossed to the escalator, rose two levels, then walked down corridors, past the signs, to the Gamemaster Eight Lab. There was no reason to wonder if he was in the right place. People were standing around as if there had been a traffic accident. He didn't get it, but he had been told to see Shiera. Her office was at the far end of the Gee-8 lab, with sliding doors to shut her off from the cacophony if she wished.

Shiera could have been a Broadway chorus girl. She was tall, leggy, and beautiful. And, in fact, she had done time in the footlights, as a dancer in a chorus line. The gorgeous Gee-8 Lab Manager was sitting at her desk. She was not numb from shock, like everyone else, but working. She looked up when Archie stepped inside her inner sanctum.

He saluted her with, "What's going on, love?"

"Did Gee send you?" she demanded.

"Trann did." Same difference. "What happened?"

"Andy Andrews just tried to kill himself, here in the lab."

"My God!" He stopped short, on his way to her guest chair, to stare at her.

Shiera shook her head. "There was no way we could have guessed what he was thinking."

"Didn't Max detect anything?" He was moving again, to sit in the chair.

"He had pills, not weapons. Diane died an hour ago."

"WHAT?" Archie dropped in the chair, stunned, just staring at her.

Shiera Walton brushed her dark hair back. Now she looked as haunted as anyone else. "Friggin' Alternative Childbirth Suite got caught with their pants down. Blood clot, straight to the brain. The baby lived. A little boy."

"God in Heaven."

"I had four Eights retire this week, and now Andy does this. I swear to God I'll run away and join the circus." Even in stress, she spoke like a Lab Manager.

Archie stiffened his legs, got up and walked to the little table against the wall behind her desk. He brought the porcelain coffee filter back to her. Shiera rose and began fixing the filter and heating water. The handmade cuppa coffee was a tradition, a guarantee of normalcy. It was a bond of long personal friendship between them. Shiera had grown up in West Meg, at least the earlier part of her life, like Archie. Then, like him, she went East, but only to the Atlantic coast. She often joked she'd only ever accepted one backstage proposition, knowing full well it would lead to her ruin— Gentian's, to become Lab 8 Manager, and now look at her.

Shiera's back was toward him as she made the non-processed coffee. Her voice was muffled. "Max caught Andy's body changes with the pills. The Chief came tearing in here with the medics like Andy was the only Gee-8 on Earth."

"God bless him," murmured Archie.

"Yeah. And my people started to freak. Not Tenian or Janet or any of the stable ones, but I've got a few loose fuses. So I did damage control on them while the Chief went off to the hospital with Andy. The only thing the Chief said was that he'd have someone down here to help me in two shakes. Then you show up, so I guess you're it."

"I must be." Archie raised his voice. "Max, what news of the world?"

"Standing by, Archie."

"Do I have administrative powers?"

"Yes, temporarily, to assist Shiera Walton, for three days."

"Why not one of her own Gee-8's?"

"Andy Andrews was on three projects related to yours. Mark Cyprian and Tellen Ges, other logical choices, are off-planet. You are not heavily booked. You can contact Shiera Walton easily when you have questions. Do you need additional reasons?"

"No, I've got the picture. Thanks, Max. Where do you want me, Shiera?"

She finished the coffee. "Here at my desk, after we've had our cuppa. I'm going up to Maternity."

"How about psychotherapy for Andy?"

"Already on it, of course. The way he tore in here, the Chief will probably be better therapy than they are." Shiera poured the two white porcelain cups, handed him one, and sat down again. She sipped hot coffee. She looked tired. Such was the lot of a Lab Manager.

"You need me to tell Alan anything?"

"Nobody needs to tell Alan anything. We've split." When Archie sighed, she observed, "You don't seem too surprised."

"I was there the night he forgot to open the passenger door and drove off without you, remember?"

She turned her scowl into a smile. "Oh, yeah. You were."

"Did the airhead ever notice you weren't beside him?"

"Somewhere around Seattle. He did come back. By then, of course, I'd got a ride home and had no intention of going to Vancouver with him. I was asleep when he came home. He threw a very dramatic fit." She sighed. "I just got very tired of dramatic fits."

"No doubt," Archie agreed. "They throw such wrenches into your otherwise sedate life."

Shiera finished the coffee, put down her cup, and kissed the top of his head on her way out the door. "I'd marry you if it didn't seem too much like work."

"God forbid," said Archie piously.

Archie was sifting through the last of Andy Andrews's projects when a voice said, "Well! And an administrator besides. How do you rate?" Elsa plopped into the guest chair.

"Nearest body not actually engulfed in flames," Archie replied.

"Oh, come on. There are hundreds of manager wanna-bees here, and they chose a manager don't-wanna-bee."

"That's why. Also, most of Andy's projects were on their way to me." He finished the current notes. "And that, my girl, is that."

"Those bitches wouldn't even speak without a guarantee." There was a tremor in Elsa's voice.

Archie understood that she referred to the nurses at The Childbirth Alternative. "They knew someone would sue the pants off 'em otherwise. Why, was it on the news?"

"It's all over the place." Elsa averted her gaze. "Shiera and Gee and Andy with the baby. David Maclachlan Andrews. Named for Diane's father."

Archie answered the tone rather than the words. "You shouldn't watch those things if they hurt you so."

"Everyone else was watching."

"If everyone else jumped off a bridge, would you do it, too?" Archie was trite, deliberately.

"I was close to it." Elsa Grayson admitted.

"I was afraid you were," said Archie. His fingers ran over Shiera's console, tapping in silent commands. "Look, poppet, I'm not the Almighty. I know your own family was ripped from you. I can't kiss it and make it better. All I can say is, I know you are one tough girl, and I rely on that toughness to keep you from folding up like an old tent. So does Gee. It's why he wants you here. You know that."

"I know."

"What would you be doing if you weren't picking up the tab for me and watching another Gamemaster Inc. tragedy on the news? Which, as you may have noticed, just garnered the Company a huge amount of positive publicity, and don't think your esteemed employer has missed that fact, no matter how genuine his concern for his employees?"

She acknowledged the truth in that "editorial aside" with a rueful smile. "Running simulations with Damiel."

"Don't you think he's going to miss you? Surely he's aware that you and he have even greater work to do."

"I told him I was coming here, to see you."

His work-console was flashing back a silent reply. **I was concerned. Shall I come down?** To which Archie answered, **Yes.**

"How is the project progressing?"

It was a leading question, designed to move to pleasanter and more important things, and they both knew it. Archie was a ready and patient listener, as usual.

A voice at the door said, "Elsa?"

She turned, eyes shining, as if it were the only voice on Earth. Perhaps it was, for her.

"I was worried," said Damiel. "Come on. Let's go to the island."

They left together. Archie silently promised one more favor to Damiel.

Saturday meant at least one cricket game. Archie, stepping out of the shower, reached for his towel and addressed the bathroom speaker. "Max, see if Elsa Grayson still wants to go to the cricket game with me today."

"Doing it now, Archie." There was a pause, then Max told him, "Elsa is also in the shower and plans to attend. She will be ready by the time you reach her apartment. Her new address is 473 Gehman Heights, Suite 3C." That surprised him; that area didn't run to single-person apartments. Max added, "She wishes to know if her roommate may accompany her."

"Certainly." *What the devil?*, he wondered, as he combed his hair and dressed. Elsa hadn't said anything about moving. She couldn't have moved in with Damiel— the only thing that would make Gee hit the roof faster would be if she moved in with Shirley from Contract. When it came to Elsa, Gee was almost a daddy-like prude, and Archie sympathized. And not Malasha— Archie had met her roommate, an Irish girl who worked for Gamemaster Renditions.

Although many taxis still had human attendants, this one did not. Max kept an eye on Archie's gear in the taxi while he went inside. Archie found that 473 Gehman Heights had a surrounding wall and a front iron gate and looked very secure. The gate opened for him; he was expected.

Inside the lobby, he recognized faces— three or four people from the company. They smiled and gave their warmest hellos. The impersonal lobby and corridor decorations looked like a cross between a Pacific Coast tribal art gallery and a hotel.

Leaving the elevator, he found the entire third floor consisted of only four apartments. Waiting for him, at the door of 3C, was the roommate— and Archie gave her the full blue-eyed stare. "Well, of course," he said. "It makes perfect sense."

Bet Berensen grinned, and welcomed him inside. "Now *I* can give *you* the grand tour." They left the little foyer for a gigantic living room with a fireplace big enough to accommodate a Scout meeting. Archie noted the wood-framed prints approvingly; she had followed his advice for a print shop and framer. They were nature scenes, not a religious one in sight. The furniture and other accessories would have blended nicely with those in his own flat.

Elsa blew in like a white breeze, still toweling her hair. "Was that Archie? Oh, yes, it was. What do you think? Am I going to be a bad influence on her?"

"My word, no." He looked at the bright-eyed blonde before him, in light blue leggings and undershirt with white overshirt, her blue eyes twinkling. Then he looked at Bet's similar black and dark-blue, and quipped, "You two are salt and pepper, if ever there was."

They both laughed. It was the sound of two very happy girls, he realized. He saw two sleeping bags stuffed next to the expensive leather sofa and guessed that they spent their nights here, with a fire going, talking, not asleep in their luxurious bedrooms.

It was shy Bet who quipped in return, "Really? Which is which?"

"I'm amazed you asked Elsa to join you," Archie told her.

"She took her courage in her own two little hands," Elsa announced, "and did it. And we've been having fun ever since."

"True words." Bet nodded. "Anyway, I wanted you to see the place first. You're practically family."

"I'd be glad to— Oh, Lord, no, I wouldn't. Come on, girls, come on! We're running late now."

They looked at each other, and spoke together. "Cookies later."

"What do you mean?" asked Archie.

"Birthday cookies," Bet announced, popping a package into her carryall. "My birthday today. Sixteen. Elsa's tomorrow. Fifteen."

"Oh, of course it is, and I've forgotten." He grimaced. "But now— run, run! I will *not* be late for one simple morning innings."

It was while he was sitting on a bench, waiting his turn at bat, that he first noticed the young man sitting alone. Usually, spectators did not arrive solo. He wore a dark jacket, too, although it was a hot summer day. "Max," he murmured to his badge, "man alone on the top of the stands. ID, please, possible threat."

"Bet Berensen transmitted the same request, Archie," the badge replied in a muted vibrato. "Chief Robinson has been notified."

Archie looked across the pitch at Bet in the stands. Her expression was steady, a symbol that she was a survivor. She had lasted for sixteen years with no aid but her grandmother and a librarian. Bet could have been watching him, or watching the game. "Is the young man a local?" he murmured.

"Affirmative. Name, Joshua Brown. He is a resident of West Meg, a member of the New United Christian Church, and the son of a retired ECM soldier."

"Oh, hell. He could be making trouble for anyone here. Weapon?"

"Just located. Disposable one-time-use firearm." Max paused. "Security detail is in position."

Archie's eyes had been on the game while the rest of his attention was given to Max. A batsman had been run out, and it was his turn. "I never thought I'd be grateful for a fast bowler, because they usually make a fool of me at bat. But I'll keep all eyes on me if you want to get that fellow removed quietly. OK with everyone else?"

"Understood by all," Max replied in a tone only Archie could hear. "When McEwan bowls to you it will be Bet's signal to step out in clear view." That would determine if Bet was the target.

"Now, don't talk to me until I'm out, unless it's an emergency." Archie focused on the bowler and moved on to the business of batting. Normally, he was not a showy batsman, but he knew that delay would cause observers to stare elsewhere. Patiently he dusted off his bat, checked his equipment, and braced himself. He was conscious of all eyes on him.

Amazingly, he managed to hit the ball almost immediately. He and the non-striker ran to score, twice, and lasted almost two overs. He was finally run out. There was plenty of cheering and yelling during the action. Nonetheless, it was almost a relief to return to the bench. A glance showed him that the young man was gone. "What happened, Max?"

"Joshua Brown pulled the gun from his pocket when Bet Berensen stood up, Archie. However, Elsa Grayson stood to applaud your run at the same time. It is impossible to determine which girl was his target. A West Meg police officer quietly removed the gun from his hand when it appeared. Joshua Brown is in custody, but his lawyer has already been summoned by his parents. Lucretia Danvers predicts he will be charged with public nuisance infractions, but nothing more. He is fifteen years old."

"The same age Elsa will be tomorrow," Archie sighed.

As he left the locker room, Timberlake said, "What, two more girls! And not the same ones. Aren't they a little young for you?"

"They're family," Archie retorted, as he strode out to meet them at the empty stands.

Elsa was glum. "Bet told me all about it. I never saw a damn thing."

"But I did," Bet told her consolingly. "That's all that matters."

Archie nodded. "You'll learn, poppet. It'll become reflex soon." He put an arm around Elsa's shoulder. "Now. Are you going to let me take you both out to celebrate?"

"Celebrate?" Elsa blinked. "Your team lost."

"Your birthday."

"No, I— I think I'll just go home." She sounded discouraged.

Bet and Archie locked gazes for a moment. There was plenty he could have said about Bet's experience watching her back versus Elsa's experience as a soldier kid. None of it was worth declaiming now. "If you want," Archie replied carefully. "But I'm coming along for tea and biscuits, then. And I want to try out that oversized leather chair I saw." He frowned at himself. "A comfy chair and a nice cuppa tea. I'm turning into my father," he sighed.

That made Elsa laugh. "Is that bad?"

"I suppose not," he admitted, but it made him think about the facets of his father's life he hadn't known.

Elsa's smile faded slowly. She looked up into his face. "I want to ask you a question because I know you'll give me an honest answer."

Uh, oh, he thought. "Of course, Elsa."

"If Gee promised me that I could go somewhere and— do something confidential and he wouldn't trace me or eavesdrop— would he keep his word?"

Good Lord, thought Archie. What am I getting myself into? Best to let my conscience be my guide, since my face betrays me anyway. "Absolutely not. It's his job to know everything he can possibly know." Bet, standing silently nearby, nodded corroboration.

Elsa also nodded, satisfied with the answer. He reflected that, had he given any other, he would have lost her trust. "I figured."

"Did you have something illegal in mind?"

She loosened herself from Archie's arm. "Not exactly illegal. But he's— well, you know— expressed an interest in meeting some people I know. It's not the sort of thing you can arrange via Max communications."

"Certainly not. Not to belittle your friends, poppet, but— they don't seem to mind dying much, and taking us with them if they can."

"It's the long view that's important," Elsa replied earnestly, as they walked toward the exit. "If killing a child horrifies some soldier, and makes him think twice about implementing a destructive device, that's a step in the right direction, don't you see? That's why I also hope the War Game can work the same way."

"As a cautionary tale," Bet supplied. Bet was a supremely good listener, Archie reflected. There couldn't be two better-matched roommates.

"Exactly. I don't even have to be a peacenik, or an Isolationist, or even a member of Recover, to want the game to do that. But Recover has a lot of inside dope on war, soldiers, actions, that came from military families involved. Stuff that could hurt. Stuff that could make people think. That's what I want to use. That's what Gee wants. But the thing is, they won't trust him."

"They'd be fools to." Archie waved to an automated taxi, which slid over to the curb.

"They might be fools even to trust me. As you pointed out, I've been brainwashed. But— if nobody ever takes the chance— it's guaranteed not to happen."

Archie saw her point, but he didn't like it. Glimpsing Bet's tight mouth, he suspected she felt the same. "Just because you see the War Game as Recover doctrine put to work, doesn't mean Recover will see it that way."

"They don't. I'm doing my best. But I think that, sooner or later, I'll have to go there."

"Where?" Bet asked.

"Where they are." Elsa clamped her jaw as if she expected controversy.

Archie slid back upon acquired wisdom and did not press the issue. "Have fun while you can, then."

Her jaw unclenched, and she smiled. "I will. Thanks for understanding, Archie." Her voice shook a little as she added, "You guys are the only family I've got, you know." She climbed in, and Bet followed.

"Everyone's uncle, that's me." Archie climbed into the taxi after them, and plopped his gear on the floor. "There is no charge."

Bet was staring straight ahead. It was not her thinking stare; Archie knew that well by now. He saw her jaw move, as if she were trying not to cry. Then she looked at Archie. "We need more than cookies. What was the name of that Italian restaurant? Giardino's? The only Italian food I've ever had is spaghetti at the Magnolia Diner."

"Oh, I've got it, I've got it!" Elsa was recovering quickly. "And we're dressed for it. The Alpha Tea Room."

"Hold it," Archie objected, alarmed, "*I'm* not dressed for it. These are my Saturday slumming rags."

"Oh, you look good in anything. They'll let you in. And besides, Luki Drost is sweet on you. He thinks you're the most charming straight guy he knows. Come on, let's do it! Max, see if Gee's available to join us. We'll make the place buzz."

Archie looked into Bet's face, his eyes widening slightly as a question. The answer was an equally slight nod. "All right," said Archie, "I'm in. Let's go beat up the Alpha."

"Gee will come, too, and we'll have a great time," Elsa predicted, and she was absolutely right.

Elsa did not know how to dance, which limited Archie, in a way. He liked a good dance floor with a decent partner. The restaurants therefore had a drawback— he had to watch how much he ate, since they wouldn't dance it off and might sit for hours, talking.

On the other hand, Elsa had picked up a taste for concerts and live theatre from Gee, so they might attend a program instead. This was more agreeable to Archie's conscience. It also got him out of his rut and viewing shows he otherwise might not see.

After the theatre, a week later, they walked through Chrysalis Park. It was one of West Meg's most beautiful parks, a few blocks in size, near enough to the theaters for a pleasant detour. The park lights were dull enough to make colors indistinguishable, but Elsa's gold curls glinted occasionally. Even at night, they could smell the roses and hear the dull thrum of an occasional bumblebee losing its footing on a flower in the shadows.

"I think I've worn this outfit more times since I've met you than I have the rest of my life," Archie commented. Elsa clasped his elbow, matching his slow pace. Occasionally they saw others just as dimly in the comfortable anonymity.

Elsa's next words had nothing to do with his. "Why are you so normal, Archie?"

"In what way?"

"No artistic temperament, no center-staging, can't often tell that you've even entered the room, no tantrums, none of that stuff Gamemasters are supposed to do. How on Earth did you become a Gee-9, and survive?"

They kept the easy pace together. "I think a great deal of my behavior comes from my training as a teacher. Mutual respect, and all that, gets one much further than laying down the law. This isn't the military. Give someone an order and you'll get a reply to bugger off, which you deserve."

"Not what other people say, Archie. You."

Archie stared up at a darkened rhododendron ahead of them. "I'm an ordinary man in extraordinary circumstances, Elsa."

"You are the only person I've met who thinks you're ordinary. Normal, yes. Ordinary, no."

"Well, thanks for the compliment." There was a long silence punctuated only by the slow, steady beat of their footsteps on the walkway. "You're really asking what makes me a Gamemaster and not part of the common herd. Is that it?"

"Yes. It is."

"The truth is, I don't know. I'm certain of only one thing, that there has been no genetic tampering in my family. I have my father's word on that."

"So. Only child; stable childhood; smart virtuous parents; clean living; and just hanging around the Gamemasters for a couple of generations."

"That seems to be it."

"But you wondered enough to ask your dad, didn't you?" Elsa asked.

"Yes, I did." Archie felt a vague uneasiness, anticipating her next words.

"Did you ever ask your mother?"

"No," Archie replied, "I didn't."

"I wanted to ask my dad once." Elsa clamped his elbow tightly, and drew his arm closer. He knew it wasn't a come-on; it was tension, the same tension he felt about the topic. "I couldn't. It was just... I couldn't do it. That's more frightening than knowing, isn't it?"

He returned the pressure on his arm. "Yes. It is."

It still felt strange to be back at his own desk after three intense days in the Gee-8 Lab. Archie leaned back and soaked in the normalcy of his own office cubicle. He looked at Shiera Walton's image as she said, "All right, I've been in touch with Emilio in Managua. Nice kid. I don't think it's going to take him too long to figure out that we screwed up. But I'm going to tell him we're buying the Three Rivers game, and then see about employing him in the Games Division. If, of course, he doesn't test out as a Gamemaster. In that case, I'll have to tell him we screwed up."

"If he doesn't figure it out, some market analyst will in a few years," Archie concurred. "In the meantime, he'll eat."

She nodded. "Yeah, that's the bottom line. That's what I hope they put on my tombstone. 'She screwed up, but people ate.'"

Archie grinned. "And that wraps up the Three Rivers game. Every mention of it has been a jinx to me. I am greatly relieved to get it off my board."

Shiera said wryly, "Don't forget there will be at least one marketing party. So it will come back to haunt you."

Just then, Max interrupted, "Excuse me, Archie, priority message coming in."

Shiera lifted a brow. "You said it was a jinx, Archie. Love ya. Stay cool." Shiera's image vanished, to be replaced by the Gamemaster.

"What's on your mind, Gee?"

"Where, exactly, is Oxford in relation to the rest of the England Historic District?"

"Rather eastern border. Oxford hits it, but London and Cambridge miss it. Why? You could look that up on any map."

"I'd like you to come up in half an hour. Some of my Security people are going to be in the England Historic District, and they could use some advice from a native."

"I may have been born there," Archie demurred, "but I didn't return until my public school years. If I moved tomorrow and lived the rest of my life there, my children would be known as the children of a West Megger."

Gee acknowledged this truism with a twitch of his lips and said, "Close enough for Gamemaster work. Come anyway."

"All right. I'll see you then."

He entered the sumptuous office half an hour later, and recognized five out of seven of the Gamemaster Inc. Security officers sitting there. Haviland, the butler, added one final chair for him. Usually the office did not have this many seats laid out for business. For more than five, Gee generally used a conference room nearby. Robinson must have brought more Security conferees than had been expected. What was going on?

Chief Robinson was speaking. "We've been dealing all right with the lack of communications, but everyone knows everyone there, and they know they don't know us. Luckily, Blodgett has turned out to be a darts wolf."

Archie raised a brow at Danny Blodgett. The young security officer grinned back.

"So he's been hitting up the local pubs and standing 'em drinks when he wins and smacking his lips about the local ale when he loses. We've got a little apartment— excuse me, flat— over the local stationer's, and Blodgett's been staying there off and on. But that's the only luck we've been having."

Archie tried to catch up. "What town are you set up in?" he inquired.

"Shipperton Vale. Know it?"

Archie whistled. "Coat-closet sized. Everyone knows everything that goes on. You're lucky you've been able to get as far as you can, then."

"Don't I know it," said Robinson. He turned back to the Gamemaster. "The signals end somewhere in that area, no matter what direction we come in."

Archie frowned. "Can I ask? What signals?"

"The tracer from my probe," Gee filled in.

Archie stared. Of course! "Blue One" had nicked Gee's nice new probe when he locked them in the *Albatross* brig. And of course it had one of Damiel Deutreil's revolutionary Kapi tracking sensors in the handle, so you could find your tool anywhere you misplaced it on Earth. It had never occurred to Archie that the Gamemaster might be pussyfooting around, looking for his unique property tag. Apparently, he found it, somewhere in the England Historic District.

"Any tips or hints you might pass on?" Gee asked Archie.

Archie thought deeply. "Well, that region loves their horses. It's the sort of place where an American girl with a passion for dressage might go to see genuine English horsemanship, I think."

"Works for me," muttered Maria Sanchez, taking notes.

"You might not have to do a thing to your hair." Archie motioned toward Sanchez's thick black shoulder-length mane. "I think there's also gypsies in that area. You might be mistaken for one by the village, and the gypsies might mistake you for a villager."

"That's two ideas. Thanks," said Maria.

"Nature study might work, too," said Archie. "Someone might be working on a college herbarium or insect collection."

"You knew the name," Gee observed. "Why?"

"I'd ridden past the signs for the turnoff with my parents. Shipperton Vale itself is not on a main road."

"Are there mines in that region?" Robinson asked. "There certainly aren't buildings big enough to hide their stolen spaceships."

Archie searched his memory. More than the countryside, he remembered many blissful hours in rented Land Rovers with his parents. It was the heady atmosphere of holidays spent in England with their only child, leading the kind of life they wanted to live permanently. Knowledge and remembrance of the three of them together, in great happiness, was what remained from those days. Stopping at the wayside for an inexpensive picnic. Hot, milky tea from a thermos being held by his Mum, or green trees flashing by while he sang harmony with his Dad. "Max could tell you better than I. I seem to recall seeing tourist signs somewhere to explore some mine when I was a kid, but I don't remember where. It could have been anywhere from Cardiff to Cambridge."

Robinson grunted and made a note. Then, another security officer asked a question about pub etiquette, then another about asking people up to the flat, when was it proper; another about the local restaurant. The questions Archie was answering told him that these folks were indeed doing their homework. Security had been staking this place out for a while now.

Why they were marking time, instead of moving, also became clear. "Well, we'll see how Elsa does," Gamemaster said. "I'm fairly certain she headed for some place in western Europe." So she did take off to meet her old cronies, as she threatened, thought Archie. And as Bet already knew, he reminded himself. It was probably Bet who had told the Gamemaster.

"And we don't have this ready-to-go," said Robinson, indicating his notes, Maria's notes, the notes on the great black desk. "We're not even close to having a top-to-bottom operation in there. The best equipment and resources in there right now are what the Earth Combined Military of the England Historic District has, and we aren't able to tap into it. We don't have an 'in.' The few agents we've got in place are all information-gatherers, not active employees."

"Historic Districts are usually closed systems." The Gamemaster concurred. "They are generally administered by trusts, not governments. I remember the Euro government going into the Cote d'Azur Historic District a few years ago. The U.N. judge slapped their hands. It was very like invading an American Indian reservation, as far as the U.N. was concerned. My policy has always been to treat them the same way I treat Chinook Land and the other reservations. So far, it's worked well."

Robinson nodded grim agreement. "For a choice, if we must tangle with the group, I'd rather do something silent and 'way off-the-record, or present the U.N. with a pile of evidence even it couldn't overlook."

"My thoughts exactly. Still, I'd rather have agents on the spot. Two or three of your people in different places in the village, perhaps with a friend or two they brought back with them from West Meg. Don't push it, yet. We have more pressing problems."

There was a little more back chat. Archie remained after the Security people left. Haviland, waiting nearby, returned to pull seats back into discreet corners. "I'd forgotten all about that probe."

"I never mentioned it. I wanted Elsa to forget about it, too."

"Judging by what I heard, I'd say she had." He gazed out the great window at the Pacific Ocean in the afternoon sun. "I'd also say that, when you pop up knowing what you've known all along, it will be exactly what she expects from you."

"She told me what you'd said about me. I told her you were perfectly correct." He added, with a twinkle in his eye, "Thank you. I have a standard to maintain."

Archie chuckled, and spoke up. "A decent cup of tea, Max."

"Mr. Chamberlain," the butler objected, "please allow me to— "

"Sorry, Haviland. I didn't think. Old habits are hard to break. Next time, you may bring tea." Archie lifted the cup out of the hatch.

The butler's response was drowned out by the sudden loud clank of metal.

The door to the office anteroom, and the door to the inner apartments, swung shut and locked audibly. The big picture window vanished as reinforced metal double-doors slid up from opposite corners and locked diagonally. The overhead lights shut off, and the room plunged into darkness, relieved only by one remaining sconce on the wall perpendicular to the vanished windows. As Archie watched, the white light of that sconce turned red. Under other conditions, Archie would have expected to hear the klaxon for liftoff. Instinctively, he set down the cup of hot tea and jumped away from it, as the contents rose from the cup and splashed against the sideboard.

He could barely see Gee grip his desk, but heard the command, "Hang on!"

Archie felt the floor drop beneath him, as if he were descending in an express elevator. He grabbed the desk, too. Vaguely he understood that some emergency mechanism had kicked in. He remembered John Arrow's explanation: "He moves the rooms."

Haviland exclaimed, "What's happening?"

"Hang on, Haviland," said Archie. "The tower's been attacked."

"Be quiet," ordered the Gamemaster.

Were the tremors they felt caused by the mechanism, or had there been explosions? Here, in the dark, they were safe, but blind.

Blind, but not deaf. Archie began to hear transmissions. First was Robinson's voice. The Security Chief was on the job. The blaring announcement would drown out everything else in the area. "Alpha Building, evacuate at once. Repeat, everyone in Alpha Building, evacuate at once. Ladies and gentlemen in Gamemaster Incorporated Building One West, please exit immediately through any lit doorway. Alpha employees, escort visitors to lit entryways. This is not a drill. Repeat, this is not a drill. Alpha Tea Room Kitchen Staff, your causeway is the emergency exit. Escort all guests through the Kitchen to the underground exit. All personnel remove to Building Two West repeat, Building Two West. Use exits at the rear of Alpha Building ONLY, repeat, rear exits only."

The announcement was plain enough— something had crashed into the top or front of Alpha itself. Debris was falling into the front courtyard. Since it had the most non-employee visitors, the staff of the various offices, retail stores, and businesses were escorting them out first, then taking cover themselves. It was a massively organized evacuation.

Another voice said, "Crash teams one, two, three on the roof, please. Fire crews are arriving on Early Street and Caiphill."

Robinson's voice said, "Security, block off Caiphill, Delmont, and Second Street."

"What the hell hit us?" Archie wondered aloud. Gee shushed him.

Another voice said, "Acting Administrator is at secondary station." He heard Gee grunt approval in the dark. Archie understood. The Gamemaster was fine, but he was going to give the AA and his emergency teams some on-the-job practice.

Yet another voice said, "The Gamemaster is secure. Repeat, the Gamemaster is secure."

"Earth Combined Military troops are entering Early Street and Main Street. They are offering assistance."

Robinson's voice, with authority. "Let the ECM forces secure Main Street, Early Street, Delmont, and Caiphill. They can also escort non-employees out of the area. Bring our Security people in from those areas to secure Alpha Building and assist the crash teams."

"Acting Administrator has transmitted these instructions to ECM troop leaders with appropriate maps and authority."

"Chief Robinson, this is Chief Adamson, Fire Disaster. I'm bringing in an engine containment flight from Artemis Fission Management."

"Read you, Chief Adamson. Clear all nonessential personnel from the roof and top floor of Alpha immediately."

Engine containment. It had been a spaceship hitting the building, crashing into the roof and so into the top floor. A suicide attack on the Gamemaster was the most likely explanation, but even that seemed insane. Any flyer would have had to pilot the ship through thousands of kilometers of friendly area first. Archie listened to the chatter of the containment team as they prepared to scoop up the dangerous engine and take it back to the moon.

Through it all, the three men in the darkened office maintained silence. Gee's gaze was intent on his desk. Archie concentrated on the voices. Haviland glanced back and forth at the two men, almost invisible in the red darkness. Gee's silence was logical; rather than cutting in on precious radio time to ask what the hell happened, he was letting his professionals deal with the disaster and informing himself of their progress as it occurred. When he heard the quiet plip of tea hitting the carpet, Haviland came forward with a napkin. He was as well-trained for mopping it up as Archie for setting it down. Archie stayed where he was, hands barely touching the desk, as Haviland moved around behind him.

After an interminable amount of chatter and instructions, adjusting and readjusting loads and lifts and angles of takeoff, Chief Adamson's voice announced, "The engine has been removed. Artemis Fission Management ship is clear. ECM West Meg ships are escorting her home."

"Alpha top levels are clear of radiation. Electrical systems have been disabled and the fire is contained," said Adamson's voice. "Complete extermination in twenty minutes. Structural assessment teams to roof and top floor of Alpha."

"This is Public Relations. We have reporters and citizens at the perimeter, being restrained by ECM soldiers. We need information and clearance."

"Acting Administrator says you get visuals of the ship hitting the building and that's all, PR. A Gamemaster Inc. employee shuttle missed the Alpha landing pad and struck the building. Incident is still under investigation. You'll have to make do."

A Gamemaster Inc. employee, flying a solo shuttle. Archie sank into a chair, guessing which employee. He felt sick.

"Top floor is not, repeat not, clear. Structural damage has occurred. Repeat, top floor is not, repeat not, clear."

"Max, move the sealed box to Level 13," said Robinson's voice.

Their room started to move.

Gamemaster spoke, to the air, for the first time. "The Acting Administrator may stand down."

Robinson responded almost immediately, "Acting Administrator is standing down. Secondary station is closed, sealed, and secure. We are back on line, ladies and gentlemen."

Archie thought he could hear cheering in the background, and wondered how they could cheer. The mysterious AA had gone, things were normal, hooray.

Haviland knew it, too. His voice was shocked. "Oh, sir, it was Miss Elsa."

The room moved laterally. There was a clank of locking mechanisms. The doors swung open. Archie could see the rooms beyond, not ones he normally associated with Gamemaster's suite.

"She was— " Archie cleared his throat, and tried again. "She was a stubborn little cuss. She must have been trying to pilot the ship back manually, to hit the building."

"Confirmed, Archie." Max had been listening in. "She commanded me to leave it on manual rather than assume control." He did not offer apologies or explanations— how could he? Why should he? "It was a sudden misnavigation that caused the shuttle to strike the building." Death throes, Archie thought, biting his lip. She hit a switch as she died. He couldn't sit down and think about it, not yet. There were still things to do.

The great diagonal metal shutters slid open with a bang. Instead of a panoramic view, there was black wall with one small plexiwindow. The view was lower, no longer facing the sea, but another building. Archie realized with a jolt that they were eye-level with Building 1 East Publishing. There were no windows directly opposite. Of course not, he thought. They were on Floor 13. Everyone thought it was omitted through superstition, but it was really the floor that held the extra space for shifting rooms around.

"This is temporary," Gamemaster told Haviland, who was peering uncomfortably into a strange bedroom. "Only the office moved from the top floor, because that's where I was."

"I understand, sir." A good butler never let a little thing like the disappearance of his entire domain get him down. "I shall consult Chief Robinson regarding the security of the remaining rooms and the schedule of our return."

"Good. Do that." The Gamemaster stood. His face was a mask as he said to Archie, "Come on. Down the lift with me, and on out the front door."

Archie understood. The residents of West Meg had to see for themselves that Gamemaster was all right. He remembered Elsa calling it "the king thing." Well, yes, it was. They stepped into the lift, as familiar as always, and stepped out again in the equally familiar Alpha foyer, now empty and abandoned. Their footsteps echoed across the silent great golden hall as they crossed it to the front door.

Gamemaster Inc. Security was mixed with ECM soldiers, all in security equipment including helmet and anti-radiation goggles. They guarded the perimeter of the front plaza, although people were gathering at barricades about a hundred meters beyond the edges of the plaza. Cheering began as the Gamemaster appeared.

The burnt-electrical smell made Archie want to hold his breath. He could smell the remains of fire-fighting chemicals, too. He looked down at the scraps of unidentifiable blackish masses upon the tiles of the plaza and tried not to think of their source.

Gee murmured, "Don't look down."

As they approached the barricades, an ECM officer, standing amid his troops, turned toward them. Gee held out his hand. The anti-radiation goggles hid the man's eyes, but Archie knew the shape of that mouth and chin. He recognized the smile before he saw the name badge and insignia. It was Commander Scott Marsden. "Good to see you again, sir."

"Thank you for supporting us. And please thank General Carpenter as well."

"He was more than happy to assist, I assure you, Gamemaster." Marsden's helmeted head gave a quick nod upward. "Will you need our assistance on any of the investigation? We would be willing to do anything in our power."

"Since my investigators haven't yet reported to me, I have no idea of the situation," Gamemaster replied, "so I do not know what will be needed."

"The offer remains open," said Marsden. "Particularly if we can share files and come to conclusions faster." It was pretty plain that he knew whose ship it was, and what had probably happened. ECM Special Services must have monitored the strange craft, even more closely than Gamemaster Inc. They had trusted Max instead.

"I'll keep it in mind," said the Gamemaster.

Archie watched him move to the perimeter and start talking to various guards, both ECM and Gamemaster Inc. It was the royal touch, all right. As he approached the crowd, hands reached out to shake his, as if he were a pop star.

They certainly had got a scare. Another ECM squad came trotting up Delmont. Obviously, the barricades were down, and Miklin Square was back in business. It took Archie a moment to realize this helmeted, goggled, flak-jacketed squad leader was a woman. He stepped up to join the Gamemaster. The squad leader had joined Marsden and Gee, locking her rifle and slinging it back over her shoulder. A tough young chick, he thought, to be doing this job. Then her jacket name patch slid back into view: MCALLEN.

Archie caught his breath again. He felt his heart thud once or twice and settle down. With those lips and the wisp of blonde hair peeping out from behind the helmet and goggles, she looked like a recruitment poster girl. She might have been looking at him, but with the opaque goggles in place, he couldn't tell. It was a relief to hear Gee's voice. "McAllen. What are you doing here?"

Marsden's smile flashed once; McAllen did not smile. It was Marsden who replied, "She volunteered. She had us organized and ready to move out before I had clearance."

"Thank you," said the Gamemaster to her.

"You're welcome." Still she did not smile. Now she looked plainly at Archie. Her voice sounded flat. "Are you all right?"

"Yes," he replied, "thank you."

She nodded and left to get her troops back in the transports. Behind them, cleaners were clearing the last of the debris from the plaza tiles.

Archie asked Marsden, "And she's going to pay for this, isn't she?"

It was impossible to see his expression behind the goggles. Archie had no idea if he was telling him something new, or something old. "She'll take care of it."

Marsden also left. People started walking by them, going back to the Alpha, back to work. As they walked inside, Gee said, "Would you be terribly offended if I gave you some advice?"

"Depends on what it is," said Archie.

"Let McAllen fight her own battles. Otherwise, she'll never know her limits and abilities."

"That's good advice," Archie admitted, adding, "I just hate seeing people get screwed. It's a weakness. It's not like I'm romantically involved with her, you know."

"I'm not, either. Still, it takes a lot of nerve to stand up to me, and I like her for it. I promised you I'd take no official notice, remember?" He departed for the elevator, leaving Archie stunned with the realization that Lt. Sheila McAllen had his boss solidly in her corner as well.

"If you hadn't been on company business when you got locked in, I'd dock you for the entire frigging afternoon," Trann said. It was his emptiest threat, since no one was ever docked as long as the work got done.

"Sorry. Sorry!" Archie threw his hands in the air. He could play the game, too. "I'm yours, then. What do you want me to do?"

Much mollified, Trann pointed to his console. "Something. Anything. Here's the list."

"Which do you want me to do first?"

"The VR college text set."

"I'm there. I'm sorry."

Archie threw himself into textbook editing. It was just grind, but it kept him from thinking. He knocked off work in time for a late supper at a café on Rhodalia Row, and went home to bed.

He kept his mind on textbook editing to keep it off Elsa. It was too easy to remember the walk in the park, the game, the time at Bet's apartment, a dozen little silly things about her. It occurred to him that someone, somewhere, ought to be arranging a memorial service, but that was not his problem. He bent his mind to his work.

He was deep in textbook editing, next day, when he heard his name. He pulled out to see Bet standing at his cubicle door.

Wordlessly, he stood and held out his arms. Bet came over for a hug, then accepted a seat. There were rings under her eyes.

"Gonna be a memorial service for Elsa tomorrow morning at 1100," she said. "He's planning a big one, an omnichannel broadcast. He'll speak, and General Carpenter will, but he wants you'n me in the front row as mourners. And Damiel. ECM will be sending representatives, too, and the U.N. Elsa and Damiel covered a lot of ground."

"Are you worried about it?" Archie asked her. There were probably CSA fanatics who would like to use the same treatment on her, if they identified her. That was another thing she and Elsa had had in common.

She shook her head. "He wants to rub their noses in it. I can't say I blame him."

"Do they know exactly what happened?"

"She'd been shot, apparently in the chest. She didn't want to radio anyone that she was injured, she just wanted to get to Gee and tell him something important. It was a miracle she got back into our airspace at all. I think Elsa manually diverted the ship from its automatic landing sequence for the usual pad, and aimed for Alpha because she knew she was out of time."

"And she was right," Archie said softly. It occurred to him that Bet had more information on this sensitive topic than mere roommates were usually given. He saw Bet rub her eyes. "You're dead on your feet, love."

"It'll pass."

Archie made a decision. "Tomorrow night, we'll see a show or a concert, something totally mindless. Then I should teach you how to dance."

A smile broke through the clouds. "What a hedonistic Christian you are."

"Yep. Are you on?"

"I'm on," she confirmed. Then she added, "Elsa taught me how much fun roommates can be. I don't like living alone."

"No one does."

"If it's any consolation to us— " Bet stopped, and frowned. "An' to think I laughed when you complained you were soundin' like your poppa. I just had Momma jump out at me."

"Did she say anything good while she was there?"

"Yeah. She did," Bet admitted. "She said if it's any consolation to us, Elsa affected a whole lot of lives for the better."

"Including one man who will not forget," said Archie.

Her frown deepened. "That's the part that scared me. That's the line the Fundamentalists always tack onto the end of that speech to legitimize their next martyr."

"Oh. Yes, I see the problem. Don't worry. We'll do our best to keep him humble and alive."

Bet smiled, not a full smile. "Still too raw for me to joke about, I guess. Also— an' I hope I'm not tellin' tales out of school— there was a last transmission from Elsa. I think maybe you should see him and talk about it."

"If he wants me to know, he'll tell me," Archie demurred. "I'm not a psychiatrist or a social worker."

"You nudge him about that riddle. Why not this?"

"That's different. That's an obligation from John Arrow. 'I alone am the audience' on this one. I've been left one half-clue to try to keep him on track. No one else can do it. We found the stone monkey in Tibet, and I think we've pretty much wrapped up the dead bird with the game found on the *Albatross*." Archie rubbed his nose. "I'm not sanguine we have enough data for the last part, and every time I get called upstairs I'm half in fear he'll announce he's on the trail of the brass mouse. But I know we've got to do it."

"You wrapped up the dead bird with an unfinished simulation," said Bet thoughtfully.

"Pretty much so, I think."

Bet did not change expression, but she tilted her head to one side. Archie had come to recognize that movement. It signaled that Bet Berensen's brain had kicked into high gear, and whatever emerged from her mouth would be a finished product. She stared at Archie for a long moment. Then she said, "You are playing a terribly risky game, Archie."

Yep, she had it, all right. "Not I. I'm just watching."

"What if it isn't finished?"

"It's still a move forward."

"And if something happens to you?"

"You finish it, Bet."

"I'm probably the one person who couldn't, Archie."

Now, it was Archie's turn to stare and let the gears work. "Good Lord. You're the A.A."

No one else would have guessed it. Nonetheless, Bet did not appear surprised or flustered by his deduction. It was as if she expected him to be exactly that intelligent. It struck him how perfectly Bet fit the part Gee had cast for her, the Acting Administrator. "Don't let yourself get killed before you complete this good work, Archie."

"I won't. But no one's understood it before you."

"We have similar backgrounds in that regard." The words sounded strange to him, in that gentle drawl. "And I have always understood and worked well with teachers."

"I suppose so. I'm ashamed of myself. I thought you were in love with the man, and that was why you spent so much time with him and thought everything here was so wonderful."

"No. Don't mean I swear men off forever, though. Don't also mean I still can't think everything here is wonderful." The broad smile returned. "'Cause I do think it."

-12-

Marking Time

"All right. Twelve VR texts, signed, sealed and delivered. Happy?" Archie asked.

"Delighted. Ecstatic," Trann replied serenely, helping himself to the guest seat in Archie's cubicle and therefore signaling this was more than a brief stop. "Thought you might be interested in a little gem I picked up at the Managers' Meeting this morning. ECM West Meg has been shopping."

"Oh? What did they buy from us?"

"A very exclusive set of palimpsest deciphering programs that, apparently, are going to be in the Special Services office. I don't suppose you said anything to Marsden."

"I don't think I told him anything he didn't already know or suspect," Archie replied frankly.

"Not our fault, then, if he starts checking internal documents just for fun, and finds tampering," Trann said, as sedately as before. "I have the impression— not backed by any facts, just manager's instinct— there are wheels within wheels, and we've only seen a spoke or two. Apparently the McAllens have a solid military background that goes back generations. But they have been infantry, groundpounders, not officers. That could be the root of the discrimination, in my opinion. I'm sure you've encountered discrimination before."

"Most certainly I have. It would explain a lot," said Archie thoughtfully. "Thanks for telling me."

"You're welcome. Now. Another item off the pile?"

"Lead me to it," said Archie. "Whatever you want. I haven't got an agenda."

"You're spoiling me rotten," Trann sighed blissfully. "When I leave here, there will be twenty struggles ahead of me to get projects done, and I haven't worked up to speed with you."

Archie grinned. "Serves you right. I have no sympathy. Take what you can get."

"All right. Operating system for computers for Marianas City, my old home town. The new waterproof hardware can't handle some alloys— here's the list— and this is creating speed and conductivity problems. Reports here from the engineering department, too. We put some Gamemaster Sixes and Sevens on a new operating system to accommodate the changes. They recognized a need for something beyond their programming abilities and kicked it up to Shiera Walton. She put Tenian on it, and he's done a lovely job. Now it needs polishing, so that's where you come in. Try to finalize it. We're tired of kicking this up levels, and the waterdome wants their product."

"Can't blame them. I'll try to wrap it up." Archie turned to the software, and Trann padded off happily. Archie loved Tenian's work. The Gamemaster 8's crafted product was always smooth as silk, no loose ends and no questions to ask. Archie could lean back and look at the big picture, knowing the details were attended to. He let his mind wander around the charts, tables, and vocabulary lists, seeing nothing much to tweak, getting a couple of ideas for minor changes and supplements. It was pretty obvious that the Venan had just wanted a double-check by someone more familiar with water than he. The pressure-domes of Venus were desert-like, since water was a precious commodity. Tenian probably couldn't imagine being surrounded by an ocean of it, and couldn't imagine it leaking into a computer system and causing trouble. Archie made a memorandum of changes Tenian would want to know about, sent it to him, and OK'd the product.

He looked at the time. Three hours, and another major item off Trann's list. Trann *was* getting spoiled. But knowing the Gamemaster, something would come along soon to upset the tranquil life of the Gee-9 Lab.

"There are three kinds of dancers," Archie said to Bet Berensen, who held his arm comfortably as they walked along the sidewalk in the declining light of a West Meg summer day.

Bet wore her usual simple black dress and slippers. Over the dress she had draped violet webbing, a beautiful shawl that was, in fact, a gift from Archie. "Tell me," she said.

"I've heard said that you dance best with the person you sleep with, but I don't think that's so." He felt her grip tighten, then relax. Archie was not surprised by her reaction to talk about sex. "The first kind, well yes, they've been around the track maybe, or at least sex isn't new to them. They're the ones who are actually there to dance, and aren't intimidated by their own bodies or anyone else's. The second kind, dance might be a come-on for sex, or perhaps they fondly hope. The third kind lie. Every movement of their bodies says they hate dancing and don't want to be there. Yet they dance. And they don't acknowledge, or aren't aware of, the fact that you cannot lie on a dance floor."

They stepped into the elevator in the Gamemaster Inc. Recreation Building 9 West before Bet said, "You always say you're a bad liar."

"I'm afraid I fall squarely into the first category," Archie admitted. "Give me a partner who's there to dance as much as I am, who's going to do her best to keep up with me every step of the way. I don't care about her sex life or mine.

I will happily dance until dawn. But it gives you new insight on people you thought you knew, right enough."

They emerged in the Gamemaster Inc. Grand Pavilion, a brilliant ballroom festooned with patterns of rainbow lights and darks. It was jam-packed with people. Archie listened approvingly to the music, and sought out faces he knew at tables. Luki Drost, towel over his arm and tray balanced as though it had grown on his hand, served cocktails at a whirlwind pace and never stopped chatting as he flitted from table to table. While it was true that the Summer Dance was one of the few required activities of the year— no attendance, no bonus— it was like a summertime Christmas party, as well. People came because it was fun.

Archie didn't bother looking for a place to sit, or a drink. He never did. Once they were inside the ballroom, he took Bet's hand. She lifted her arm gracefully to his shoulder. Those dance lessons really paid off for her, Archie thought approvingly, as they moved onto the dance floor. They tried a few steps. She trod on his toe once, but her slippered feet were hardly noticeable, and she found her step again in the music.

True to his word, Archie concentrated on dancing. Bet followed suit. She was not a natural, but she had learned. Some of the other dancers were people who knew either Bet or Archie; there were glances of greeting as they passed. Archie felt Bet grow more comfortable with him as they danced. She became less stiff leaning against his body, letting him take the lead, coming along a calculated beat behind. When the music stopped, he nodded, satisfied. "You'll be good with practice," Archie said judgmentally.

"You weren't kiddin'," said Bet, "about the three categories. I couldn't see much 'cuz I was busy, but I saw what you meant."

In unison, their gazes moved to the front of the ballroom. Archie didn't have to ask who in particular she had observed. That dark dancer was bowing to his partner, seating her, speaking cordially to her, getting her a glass of champagne. The woman was a visitor, probably European, undoubtedly rich and titled. She was a well-dressed blonde, still a little breathless from the dance. Here, probably unlike anywhere else on earth, she was merely the date of the evening. She was completely interchangeable with a thousand other women who had had the same partner at various other times in the past ten or fifteen years.

Archie knew the routine. Now Gee would dance with the Employee of the Year, and the Countess would get another dance or two and then be foisted off on the more diplomatic members of management or City of West Meg public servants.

"Category three," Bet murmured, in the same interested tone. "He hates being here. Simply hates it."

"Loathes it," Archie concurred, "to the bottom of his heart. And doesn't care if every employee in the place picks up on it. I'm sure the chick-of-the-day catches on after a while."

Bet frowned. "What a waste."

"What? Waste? Who?" Archie wondered briefly if today's Countess was someone Bet actually knew.

"Him, of course. He's the warmest man I've ever met, and here he is, building ice palaces."

"Are we talking about the same man?" Archie asked disbelievingly.

"You think they just pulled a name like Gennaro out of the air?" Bet queried.

Archie had to admit that he'd never thought about Gee, or family background, or how he might behave privately with girls he liked, such as Bet. It would give him something new to think about, he realized— but not right now.

A woman stood up at one table, apparently to make herself visible. It would have been difficult to miss her, anyway— hair in three shades of bottled blond, fluorescent blue dress, drink in her hand and plenty of attitude.

"There's Shirley," Bet murmured.

Archie nodded, murmuring as well, "No point in postponing the inevitable." They joined the ten or twelve at the table. They were all from Contract, or Accounting, and their spouses.

"Didn't know if you two would be exempted after that horrible funeral thing," Shirley said. "I was ready to put on a black armband if you gave up dancing, Archie baby."

"No, we weren't exempted. But we did our part," said Archie. "Not a dry eye in the house."

"You said it. Damn, he was good." When you were at a table with a group of Gamemaster Inc. employees, there was only one He. "The part about young Elsa Grayson being a Recover agent finding a weapon she could use— the War Game."

"And about the hopes of the solar system," another contributed.

Without thinking, Archie clamped Bet's hand again, and felt her return the pressure. Like him, he was certain, she was thinking of the painful two hours in the front row of the West Meg Auditorium, with camera remotes flitting around their heads like June bugs, listening to eulogy after eulogy about the violent death of someone they had grown to know well and to love. For them, it had been no performance. It would have been useless to say so here.

"And when he panned in on you two, and Damiel started crying— " Shirley shook her head admiringly. "He had every top cameraman and visual artist and sound man from the entire west coast there, you know it? I'm surprised Recover isn't standing in line to drop their weapons and apologize."

"I think he expected to hear something, at least," said someone else, "and he hasn't."

"They're fools to take him on," Shirley declared.

That, of course, was one point of view.

Chief Robinson eyed Archie across his desk. "I am still," he said, "living down the Himalayas thing." While the Security Chief exuded comfortable police experience, there was a dash of focussed corporate executive in him as well.

"Oh." Archie, ensconced comfortably in Robinson's guest chair, pursed his lips. He had never thought about their adventure in the light of Robinson's Security office. "I understand. Still, you were not the one who had to be rescued by your boss, and carried like a baby through a blizzard."

Robinson's sheepish grin acknowledged their mutual pride.

Archie finished, "And I am sorry about walking in on his tirade in Alpha, truly I am."

Robinson sat back more comfortably in his chair. "If I had a credit for every time he's fired me for insubordination, I'd be rich. He knows it's my job to rain on his parade. I made my worst mistake on letting him go to Lhasa unaccompanied, except by you. No offense. But you aren't trained security. And you were being dragged there."

"True. But you must also understand, Chief, that he takes risks. It's not only in his job description, it's in his genes. He really *can* go further and faster than you or I. And— " Archie hesitated— "if you'd prevented bad things from happening to him in Lhasa, you'd have prevented the good things from happening, too."

Robinson thought about that for a minute. "I admit it's a tightrope."

"Yes, it is. I don't doubt for one minute you feel like a fool, having to live down the fact that your primary charge was stranded two months in Tibet. I'm saying— excuse me, this sounds so pompous— swallow it, because it might be a better thing for Gee and the Company in the long run."

The Chief sighed. He did not take offense, obviously having learned to roll with the punches. "Or having Harry Goto take him quietly up to the Neptune Yards and dragging the War Game back with him. I know. But goddamn it, it's my job to keep him secure."

"It's your job to keep the company secure, not him. It's his job to take risks," Archie returned. "The moment a Gamemaster stops taking risks, this becomes an ineffectual company, and you know it." He rubbed his nose. "I'm sorry, Chief. You have a damnable job, and I know you must strike a happy medium."

"I don't feel this Recover business and the England Historic District are in the same category as Tibet or even the Neptune Yards." Chief Robinson got to the point. "Taking on a bunch of armed radicals in a civilized area is a mighty different proposition. And that does fall in my department. I know damn well that what he wants to do is sneak into the England Historic District, yank his tools out of there, and snag anyone and anything attached to 'em. Well, it's not going to be that easy. The EHD is a heavily regulated area, and if it's Recover pussyfooting in and out of there, they'll be watching out for people doing exactly what we're doing. I don't have much intelligence information, but it does strike me that there's been some odd disappearances in the EHD put down to a number of causes I'll bet I could reduce to one."

"Long noses?"

"You got it," the Chief confirmed. "What I'm asking you to do is let me know if he wants you to go gallivanting off with him again."

"If I say I will tell you, I will also tell him you asked me to do it," Archie warned.

"You think he wouldn't ask you to go along, then?"

"I think it wouldn't even slow him down. He'd ask anyone anything. He'd just have to adjust to the fact that you'd know, too."

"That's fair, if you really do tell me if he asks you along."

"If I say I will, I will," said Archie.

Again, the Chief nodded, satisfied, and said something that pleasantly shocked Archie. "That's your reputation. Now, about this Shipperton Vale." He pulled forward a notepad. "Population 400, plus or minus. No possible way of sneaking in. The number of our ops there, now, totals all the newcomers they'd get in a year. If it was a question of just calling up the Queen and making an appointment to discuss Recover, that would be easy. But it's not. The British Government has a long history of letting the Trustees of the England Historic District govern the district themselves. Even their branch of the Earth Combined Military is separate from the British Army— I'm not sure why."

"That dates from the old Sandhurst scandal," Archie commented.

"Yeah? See, you know that kind of information off the top of your head. I don't. That's why I was hoping to keep you on tap, both for data on the area and on the boss. Also— " he hesitated— "you were fond of the girl. She was some kid. I thought you might have a vested interest."

"As a matter of fact, you're right," Archie replied quietly, "and I'm glad to give you whatever help I can."

"Good. I'm hoping that, eventually, he'll ask the Trustees of the England Historic District to meet with him. I don't know what evidence he'd present to them, seeing how he wants to keep our prowling around Shipperton Vale to himself, but he ought to be able to come up with something to make it worth the trip. Someone has got to convince them this isn't a fairy tale— they've really got Recover tiptoeing around their district."

"The English are very good at disbelieving things."

"Don't I know it," said the Chief, with feeling. "My nerves are already on edge having Bet Berensen on planetwide media, not to mention Damiel Deutreuil and you. At least with Damiel and you, the furthest you usually go is job-related or that cricket field, and you've both got Max in the corner of your eye when you're there." Archie hadn't realized Robinson knew of his security habit, nor that he appreciated it. "Bet, thank God, doesn't leave the immediate area hardly at all, except for church." He shifted again, moving his uncomfortable holster to one side. It was his only tacit announcement that Gamemaster Security was on alert. "It's like this, Chamberlain. Miss Elsa's death pissed off the Gamemaster, and everybody knows it. Recover knows that he's aware of them and has some idea of where to go looking. He's not the only man in the world with tracer signals in the handles of his tools. Anybody could copy that little signal. Something is going to blow. I'm just trying to stay on top of it."

"I think you're absolutely correct."

That was the right thing to say. "I wish more people would think that, more often. None of these are short-term problems. If the CSA's mythological Christian Council declares a 'cleansing' on Bet, that'll be in place until she dies. If Recover is made up of kids, they've got their entire adulthood to try to nail the Gamemaster. And I wish to hell I knew what Elsa had meant in her last transmission when she said it's all a lie."

Archie frowned. "Is that what she said? I hadn't heard. Is all what a lie?"

"Well, *that's* one of the thousand things I don't know. She said, 'Gee, it's all a lie.' And then she was gone."

It's all a lie, Archie thought. "Knowing Elsa— "

"Yes?"

"She was a Recover diehard. She felt it was worth dying for. To come tearing back here to Gee, to tell him that— it had to be that Recover was a lie."

"That possibility is being explored as well," said the Chief dryly. "However— judging from the attacks they're making on targets, Recover still seems real enough to me."

Trann entered the cubicle with a look in his eye that Archie knew from long experience: Whatever the subject he was about to broach, Trann expected to win the argument. "What's on your mind?" Archie asked cautiously.

"Before you go off again, I want you to get a communications implant," the Lab Manager told him.

"A communications implant? Me? I've got a badge."

"You had one in the Himalayas, too. I realize that the England Historic District is not as backward as Lhasa was, in terms of communication, but the Company has learned a hard lesson. No Gamemaster is going anywhere that is free of Gamemaster products without some means for Max to warn him of trouble."

"It was purely coincidental..." Archie began.

"You had a low-grade infection that became high-grade in an area where Max was mute." Trann overrode him. "Max, unknowingly, put you in more danger while trying to contact you. You are too valuable an asset to the company to let that happen again." His tone sounded final.

Archie could sound just as final. "No. I am aware that you have them, Trann, and that they don't inconvenience you. However, they are not natural to me, and I will not take a chance with them. What Max can use in my favor, anyone else can use against me. It is far too easy for implants to become infected, and I don't want anything in my ears where they could just as easily affect my balance or other bodily functions. You know perfectly well that no unmodified human being is as well-mapped as a gene-mod."

"That's the trouble with you donkeys," Trann complained.

"Excuse me. Donkeys?"

"Unmodified humans. You haven't heard it before? It describes both attitude and genes, I regret to say. Now, hear me out. First, nothing goes in the inner ear. Everyone acknowledges the danger in that. It's actually attached to the skull or jawbone. The sound carries just as well by bone conduction, and you're in no danger. Second, it can be removed either by computer programming or by magnets." There was a glint in Trann's eye, and Archie braced for the clincher. "Best of all, it is new nanite technology, proven harmless because it is based upon the research of one Archie Chamberlain."

Hoist on his own petard. "Attaching nanites to the jawbone of an ass?"

"Please note I never said that," Trann said calmly, handing him a small packet. "You will report to your own physician, Dr. Barnett, who is expecting you. These are the nanites and the instructions. Bon voyage."

Once again at his desk, Archie rubbed his chin, dissatisfied. He really couldn't feel anything. He knew that the crawling sensation along his jaw was only his imagination. Still, he didn't like it. Dr. Barnett assured him that in another day he would forget all about the implant, and Archie knew perfectly well he was right. But the crawling, bad feeling remained.

So he was not particularly surprised, in the middle of this mood, to see Security Chief Robinson's face pop up on his monitor. "No," said Archie flatly. "Don't tell me you've lost him."

"So I won't tell you. Figure it out for yourself. Have you seen him?"

"I haven't been looking. What does Haviland say?"

"The butler? He says The Gamemaster gave orders not to be disturbed. Max says he's not in the building, not in West Meg, and not in North America. Think you'd have any better luck with Haviland?"

"Not in the slightest, and I wouldn't try. Good butlers who follow orders are too rare to corrupt. Let me ask around, though. There might be someone who heard him make a comment about a trip." He thought of Luki in the Alpha Tea Room. "Or even some gossip."

Robinson's tone was disbelieving. "And he didn't tell you where he was going?"

"No, I tell you, dammit. If you don't believe me, why are you calling?"

"Unfortunately, I do believe you. I wouldn't have called, either, if my five-day marker hadn't popped up."

"Max has lost track of him *for five days?*"

"Max has *not* lost track of him. He just won't tell me where he is. Max simply says that he's not in North America, and as his goddamn Security Chief, I would really like to know where my boss is," Robinson replied in an exasperated tone.

Despite himself, Archie grinned. "All right. I'll take a shot at finding the lost lamb— or black sheep, I guess."

"Not funny. Good-bye."

Archie wandered over to Bet's cubicle. He waited while she worked, became aware of his presence, and pulled out of her current project. She merely looked inquiringly at him. "Anything wrong with Gee?" Archie asked softly.

"Not to my knowledge."

"Have you talked to him within the past five days?"

"No."

That was good news. Archie thanked her and left. If there were a crisis, Bet would be the one to know. There was nothing wrong.

He found Luki Drost in the Alpha Tea Room. It was midmorning, a slow time there, a good time to chat. "Luki, heard any good gossip lately?"

"Nothing." Luki sighed. "Dull as dishwater."

"Ditchwater," Archie corrected. "What news from the top floor?"

Luki stared at him. "My good man, he's been gone for a week. Didn't you know that?"

"A week? I'd heard five days. Any Earl Grey? I don't keep it at home."

Luki motioned him to a seat near his post. "In a jiff. Milk and sugar, as I recall?"

"Yes. –so did he pack a lunch?"

"Archie! Not hardly. He had a rucksack, that's all. Dressed so casually I didn't recognize him. He wasn't wearing black." Luki arched his brow. "An Indian cotton shirt in a shade of purple so nice I asked him where I could get one. And grey hiking slacks and brown boots. Not his usual style at all."

"And he walked through here?"

"I'll bet half the people didn't recognize him, out of his usual clothes." Then Luki caught on. "Oh, that was the idea, wasn't it? He was testing the waters to see if he *would* be recognized, out of his usual clothes. He was scrapping the trademark Gamemaster black to go undercover."

"Sounds like it," Archie agreed.

"You don't suppose he's got a special friend somewhere?" Luki asked. "He's the right age for it, you know. Twenty-eight to thirty-two years old. It's in the book."

Archie recognized the reference not as a real book, but as the euphemistic book of Gamemaster behavior. "It may be in the book, but I don't think this is it."

"What do you think it is?" Luki wanted to know.

"I'm not sure yet." Archie lifted the cup to his face and inhaled the aroma. "What is it about oil of bergamot that makes it fade so fast in this climate? I can't keep any zing in my tea at home."

"Do you want the truth?" Luki asked rhetorically, then explained, "This really is oil of bergamot. Our Earl Grey is real. The stuff Max finds, or you buy in local stores, is ersatz Earl Grey."

"Who the devil would want ersatz tea?" Archie asked, surprised.

"Nobody's making Earl Grey any more. There were only two companies left, anyway, one in India and one in England. The Indian one just folded, and the English one has cut back drastically. We pay for this in blood, and it's reaching a point of diminishing return. In another ten years, you won't find Earl Grey anywhere, unless a fad comes in for it."

"That's sad," said Archie. "It's been around since the heyday of the British Empire."

"I know," Luki agreed regretfully. "At the same time, I remind myself, you close a window and a door opens. Something else will come along to take its place that will be sensational. People still want tea, on the whole. There's an atmosphere and a culture with it. I don't think that will fade." He brightened. "But you didn't come here to talk shop. You came to ask questions about the Chief's vanishing act, didn't you? Well, pardon me if I think it was a romance nonetheless. They may not have recognized him in those clothes, but hearts were going pit-a-pat throughout the place. Including my own, and I know better."

"Knowing what a cynic you are," Archie observed, "that's high praise."

Archie put his feet up on his desk, leaned back in his seat, and glowered at the ceiling in thought. Dressed casually, keeping it low-key, keeping Robinson out of it. Of course he was headed for the England Historic District, whether or not he had a line on his missing probe or just wanted to prowl around unobserved. But saying he was in the England Historic District didn't narrow it down much. That covered a good portion of central England and even a bit of Wales. In the south, it included a portion of Greater London. An army could hide out there.

Army. That made him think of Lieutenant McAllen. He wondered how she was doing with her anti-Infantry discrimination. Free-associating made him think of the Earth Combined Military of the England Historic District. Wouldn't they have records of strange ships and airplanes in their airspace? How much did the different regional ECMs work together? The Sandhurst Scandal had rocked the military world twenty years ago and probably put the England Historic District's force on the defensive; the communication between the EHD's ECM and the others was probably as restricted as possible. Why would anyone go to the England Historic District, anyway, unless one had family there, went to university, or wanted to hide out? Archie lowered his gaze back to the level of his desk and entryway, and saw Trann standing there. Without preamble, Archie demanded, "If you were going to the England Historic District, why would you be going?"

Trann, who by this time was accustomed to irrational and totally unrelated questions from any of his thirty-seven eccentric charges, did not bother asking why he should care or even what that had to do with business. He merely answered the question. "I would be buying antiques."

"Hah," said Archie, to Robinson on the monitor, "got him. He's antiquing."

"Is that a verb or an adjective?" Robinson inquired.

"Verb. He's a tourist on a buying trip for antiques. He's been in two different antiques shops in Coventry, both a couple of days ago. I rang up and said I was looking for my West Meg partner, who had mentioned visiting their shops, and they said oh yes he was here. He hasn't been as far south as Oxford, to my knowledge."

"I'd be inclined to try much further north," Robinson murmured, referring to Shipperton Vale, well at the north end of the England Historic District.

"No doubt. Perhaps he just wanted to lay a foundation, in case someone questioned his itinerary. If I were doing it, I'd have a Land Rover from one of the rental places, and I'd be hitting the back roads which, theoretically, antiques hunters might have missed."

"Good cover," Robinson admitted. "I wonder what he's using for a name. I'd rather not hit the rental places with an APB for a nameless dark-haired West Megger who looks a lot like The Gamemaster."

"Well, I just asked for my partner Gennaro, without getting into last names. But you're right, they'll ask. Anyway, I've done all I can do."

"Yes, you have. Thank you." Already Robinson looked preoccupied with the next step in his puzzle. Ah, well, thought Archie, it's good for his brain.

It was strange, but now that Archie knew Gee wasn't in the penthouse, he felt his absence. One always knew Gee was there, working on something, planning something, meeting with someone, getting in the news again.

He missed him.

It was a peculiar feeling. It was not as though they spent much time together. An argument over the communications link, a quick message in passing— that was the norm.

Oddly enough, he noticed a difference in Trann, too, a subdued mood. The eighteen Lab Managers were, so to speak, extensions of their Chief's ego. Without him present, they could still function, certainly, and always did. After all, what made a good lieutenant was the ability to understand intuitively how your commander would want any situation handled, and they were good lieutenants. But the spark was missing.

Just as odd, to Archie, was that when Gee's name was mentioned (he was officially "on a business trip"), it was mentioned fondly. Usually, with a smile. Archie thought: You sure as hell wouldn't have heard them talk that way about Gentian. Perhaps it was the same mold, but the final product had turned out quite differently.

Archie was sound asleep when he heard a voice right beside him, as clear as day: "Archie, wake up."

It took him a long minute to realize that it was Max, talking to him via the new implant. Max never did that; they spoke by intercom as they had always done. The implant was for emergencies. Max had deliberately awakened him. "What's the problem, Max?"

"Security Chief Robinson will have two officers at the front entrance to your apartment building in ten minutes. Please be ready to travel with them. There is a matter of some urgency. The Chief will explain to you en route. He is certain his explanation will convince you that this trip is necessary."

It would be more difficult to argue with Security than to comply, Archie thought, rising out of bed hurriedly. Robinson had also forestalled most of his questions. Archie changed his clothes as he spoke. "Max, is this an overnight trip, or longer?"

"I have no data, sorry, Archie. Shall I pack your overnighter, just in case?"

"Yes, please." Archie finished dressing. He glanced at the chronometer: 02C3. Two in the goddamn morning. Archie felt his chin and decided that he might as well look as though he'd just been rousted out of bed, since he had.

"Your overnighter is just outside the apartment door, Archie." Max was still programmed to avoid letting Archie see any robot packing his bags. Archie grabbed a jacket from the rack inside the door, scooped up his overnight bag, and headed for the elevator.

When he reached the lobby below, he saw two Gamemaster Inc. Security officers standing outside, in the street. The royal blue uniforms blended easily into the night, except for the occasional metal glint of the badges attached to their belts. A vehicle waited also. Rhodalia Row was silent at two on a Thursday morning. "Hello, gentlemen," Archie greeted them in a subdued voice.

"Morning, Mr. Chamberlain." They greeted him just as quietly, bundled him and his bag into the floater, and left. Since they did not comment on the luggage, Archie felt that his hunch to take it had been wise.

They were all silent. Robinson would brief him. Archie saw that the floater was headed for the main company spacepad, again not surprising.

The Security men accompanied him from the floater right to the ship. The ship was dark-colored and unmarked, confirming Archie's remaining suspicions. The two guards followed him into the ship.

Robinson looked up from a table near the front of the ship, just behind the open cockpit. The pilot and co-pilot were in place. The Chief motioned Archie to a seat just opposite his. Eight of the ten passenger seats were occupied by Security people. Archie sat down and yawned. The pilot commenced liftoff.

Robinson did not apologize for interrupting his rest. "I got a message from the Security Chief at Bel Aire Shipyards six hours ago. You know the Boss has a lot of friends there."

Archie, remembering how the Hilo division scuttled the *Albatross* in record time on his say-so, could find no fault with that statement. "They think the world of him."

"And I understand the feeling is mutual, which is damned lucky in this case. Dock workers are the last men to bring things to the attention of Security, any Security, even their own. They're suspicious as hell of anything with a badge. From what I gather, talking with Chief Kane, the rank-and-file had a meeting of the entire goddamn union before they came to him. I also gather that they came to him with a whopper of a problem. A worker discovered a piece of a known ship in a funny place— as part of another ship he was dismantling. The dock workers starting comparing notes, and finding a *lot* of funny parts."

"Define 'funny,'" said Archie.

"Lost, strayed, or stolen," Robinson replied. "Much of it that could be traced to locations where Recover has been spotted. Those boys know ships like the backs of their hands, you know that. What might not be a 'system of identity' to some second-hand buyer is as clear as day to them. Anyway, the workers got worried because they were seeing recycled Gamemaster Inc. parts, and knew the Gamemaster wasn't recycling them. They were materials the Boss rejected or scrapped. Someone else had hijacked 'em and was selling 'em second-hand. The workers wanted it stopped before someone got killed, so they took it to Bel Aire Shipyards Security. Of course, now, their management is in a panic, hoping we won't sue the bejesus out of 'em for selling pirate parts."

"Which they didn't sell anyway." Archie frowned.

"No, and even their own goddamn employees are telling 'em so, which is why I won't give 'em a Gamemaster Inc. guarantee."

"Good for you. I wouldn't, either, not in a foolish situation like that."

Robinson nodded. He seemed preoccupied. "Anyway, with the descriptions of parts Kane gave us, we started working backward. I've had people tracing sales until they can't be traced any more. I want to tell you, we've traced back a long way, a lot of parts, to dealers all over the solar system, until we reach points of no return. Junkyards, salvage heaps, excess inventories, you name it, all kinds of places these parts were supposed to have come from, and they didn't come from there. We're not talking a few salvaged ships here, Mr. Chamberlain. The magnitude of these sales shows a large money-making operation. This underground business isn't as big as Gamemaster Inc., but it could put a dent into the universal economy. If this all traces back to Recover— as I suspect it does— we're talking billions."

-13-

Tagged

Archie stared at him. "Those kids?"

"...Have got an incredible amount of money socked away. The stuff they've stolen on raids? Plowed back into the economy, would be my guess. We've been wrong about them all along. These aren't a bunch of idealistic kids, trying to rehabilitate the military. If my guess is right, they've got enough profit to make a Gamemaster proud."

Archie thought of Elsa. "'It's all a lie.'"

Understanding the quote, Robinson nodded. "I don't think she knew until the end that they were a profit racket, not a threadbare resistance movement. She got the rug yanked out from under her, on the last trip."

Archie closed his eyes. Everything was making sense. Somehow, he knew that Robinson had caught on to part of the truth, at least. He also suspected that Blue 1, the unnamed leader of the Albatross boarding party, was a gene-mod, a Gamemaster in the bud, and might be building his own empire up from scratch. Just as the original West Meg Gamemasters had done, centuries ago.

Robinson continued, "On that premise, the Boss is in real danger, Mr. Chamberlain, and I want him out of there. You can talk him out faster than I can. This isn't a bunch of idealistic kids, holed up with some second-hand equipment, trying to change the military. This is a business enterprise as well-organized as our own company, top to bottom, with real mercenaries hiding in it, watching after their own asses."

"You don't have to talk any more to convince me," said Archie.

"I hoped I wouldn't have to. Want to take a look at some of the business analyses, anyway, so I can show I'm not making it up?" He passed a notepad across the table. "We have an hour and a half before we reach England, and I want to get some sleep."

Archie relaxed in a flight seat beside Robinson, and leaned back. Robinson's team had gathered and plowed through a remarkable amount of information in six short hours. Archie paged through the results, stopping from time to time to examine data. While it was true that Archie had indeed majored in classical literature while Gee had studied Advanced Business Analysis, as Gee commented on the Tibet trip, Archie had nonetheless taken his share of Business Analysis courses. His random checks into Robinson's report could find no fault with his figures and suppositions. Eventually, he turned off the notepad and fell asleep.

It was noon in the England Historic District when they arrived. The Security Chief was too anxious to wait for nightfall. "What I want to do," he explained to Archie, "is land at the Manchester Spacepad, as if we were just ordinary Gamemaster Inc. business, like you've got a valuable cargo for some local industry so we're accompanying you. If that's all right by you."

"I'm a lousy liar," Archie objected, "when it comes to making up these kinds of stories from scratch."

"That's all right. Let me do the talking." Robinson smiled. "Blodgett will meet us there, with a transport. He's been busy, too. From Manchester, we can head south into the EHD. Since that's a normal route for out-of-district business to take, we won't attract attention. We could be headed for anywhere in the EHD, or even as far as London or Cambridge. You just need to look like a Gamemaster on business."

"That's one role I do play well," commented Archie.

He stood idly on the landing pad, waiting with the Security people, while Robinson chatted with Manchester Security. He had his overnight bag over his shoulder and his jacket folded over his arm. God knows where the confidential and expensive material was supposed to be located. A minibus pulled up near the hangar, and Blodgett hopped out, in uniform. Oh, if Shipperton Vale could see him now, thought Archie.

Robinson returned. "We're set. In case anyone asks, we're on our way to Leicester with an experimental fuel core."

"Sounds good," Archie agreed. Their parade, led by Robinson, made its way to a hangar exit near Blodgett's floater. Blodgett shook Archie's hand and displayed a surprising sense of humor. "Nice to see you again, Mr. Chamberlain. Sorry to drag you out in the wee hours like this." They climbed on board.

Once inside, with one of Blodgett's operatives at the controls of the bus and the vehicle in motion, Robinson and Blodgett were all business. "Took me a hell of a long time to find him, sir. He was even laying low from us, a damn good trick in Shipperton Vale. He's in North Shipperton, which is even smaller than Shipperton Vale, and I didn't think that was possible."

"I've never heard of North Shipperton," said Archie.

"Seven miles north of me, up a single-lane road that ends right there. Three houses and an inn. I kid you not. The inn only has four guest rooms, and this antiques shopper booked two of them, one for him and one for his merchandise. I guess that's not so unusual, either. I wouldn't have heard about him if it wasn't for the pub. Some of the girls caught sight of him, scouting around, and got talking about this good-looking fellow with the West Meg accent. Made me wonder if it was the boss before I even heard from Chief Robinson."

Robinson muttered, "If you were wondering, others were wondering."

"Yeah." Blodgett watched the road out the front panel. "If you're right about this gang being a quantum level above what we thought, he's in real danger. I'd be willing to haul him out myself. I hope you can reason with him, Mr. Chamberlain."

"Sometimes Reason and the Gamemaster occupy two different buckets," said Archie doubtfully, "but I'll try. I think that report you assembled is going to be the clincher, though, Robinson. It sure as hell convinced me."

"We didn't know then what we know now," Robinson said grimly, "and he still doesn't know it. It may be a battle."

Archie and Robinson watched the roads and turnings carefully. Neither man had ever been in Shipperton Vale before. And certainly not beyond it, down a quiet country lane which one would never guess led to more than a couple of residences.

Actually, to call North Shipperton "a couple of residences" was charitable. At first, Archie mistook it for a cottage farm. Then he realized he was looking at an inn— *The George*, said the sign— with three cottages and some outbuildings a little further back. He saw a scooter parked in front of one cottage. Another had a small electric automobile behind it. In front of the inn was a vehicle as well.

"We don't even know if he's here," Robinson muttered.

"He's here," said Archie. He indicated the vehicle. "Land Rover. That's the universal tourist vehicle in the England Historic District. They've got a concession."

"One thing in our favor, then." Robinson turned to his team. "You two come with Chamberlain and me. Blodgett, I want this town secured. This team will know where every living thing in North Shipperton is, and what it's doing right now, within ten minutes."

Their bus pulled off to one side of the road before it reached the inn. Its passengers climbed out. Archie, the Chief, and three Security personnel, two men and a woman in royal blue Gamemaster Inc. uniforms, made their way silently up the grassy path to the inn. "Who runs the inn?" Robinson asked Blodgett.

"An old man and his wife. They probably won't be here, though. This is market day. Everyone heads for one of the picture postcard villages, to sell their produce for ten times what it's worth."

"Fine by me." By now, they were at the front door. Robinson reached for the handle, which opened easily to reveal a darkened room. He stepped inside, with Archie behind him. Blodgett followed.

It took Archie's eyes a moment to adjust to the interior darkness. They were in a low-ceilinged room with a few tables and a sort of wooden-and-plaster bar. This room encompassed much of the ground floor of the inn. An archway to the right revealed a tiny parlor, with slightly finer-looking furniture— a couple of tables and upholstered dining chairs.

The man sitting at one of these tables had set down his book to glare at them. It was, alas, a glare they knew quite well.

"What the *hell* are you doing here?" demanded the Gamemaster.

Archie stepped past Robinson. His tone was not apologetic. "I think we've got enough data to convince even you that this is not a healthy place to be. Robinson's penetrated their cover, Gee. These aren't a bunch of sweet kids on a crusade. It's a heartless money-making operation with a lot more savvy than we expected."

Gee stood. His face and voice were angry. "You have blown over a week's worth of careful spadework by showing up here, you goddamn jackass."

"Jackass I may be," Archie replied firmly, "but you are at risk and we are here to haul you out of here to comparative safety, physically if necessary. Then we'll discuss issues, but not before." He might have been speaking to a rebellious teenager at Mars-Isidis Preparatory School. "This is not a safe place for you. We can prove it."

"Why shouldn't it be safe? Especially, as I suspect, if you have just secured the entire goddamn village and blown my project wide open."

Robinson looked as adamant as Gee, but he let Archie do the talking. "This is not a good time to debate security issues. The point is, Recover's in this district, and we've got enough data now to take it before the United Nations. Which is where it needs to be." Archie was unfortunately aware he was not moving his audience. "This isn't a matter of West Meg versus the world. This is a system-wide problem which must be dealt with on an Earth-wide level."

The Gamemaster's voice was like cold iron. "By the time we appealed to the U.N. for a hearing and took the information I have gathered to them, Recover will have vanished like smoke. I do not wish that to happen. They have much to answer for, including the death of Elsa Grayson and the damage to my city. I will take steps *now*."

"For Christ's sake, we don't have the manpower here to take steps. As Robinson says, we've been pussyfooting here. We don't have a single full Security team up and running, let alone enough to take out an army. The

United Nations has issued orders to their military units not to attack Recover because it's now known that they're children. So ECM England Historic District, without orders to the contrary, would join in the attack on us. We're vulnerable," Archie argued. "This is Shipperton Vale, not West Meg. Gee, they've got their own pirate network set up. They've got Blue 1, a young version of a Gamemaster, in charge of it. They're not doing anything that hasn't been done before – or *you* wouldn't be here. It's a textbook piracy and takeover, which you'll see the moment you start looking at Robinson's notes."

"Vulnerable" was a word usually carrying a restorative effect on the Gamemaster's mule-headedness, and to Archie's great relief, he saw a difference his glare. The Gamemaster looked fully at Robinson for the first time. Apparently he understood why Robinson had let Archie talk— the Security Chief had selected the Gee-9 as the best weapon in his arsenal of the moment. "What's your recommendation?"

"My first one," said Chief Robinson, "is to get somewhere more secure than this. Then we hop on communications, before we jump back in. I'm not saying go home, boss. Don't get me wrong. I think you're right— we'll never get this close again. You got something, didn't you? Something good."

The Gamemaster actually smiled for a moment before he replied, "This is why I hired you, Robinson. Yes. I think I've found a weak link. I've been trying to cash in on it, but it is most difficult."

"Why didn't you let someone know where you'd gone?" Archie asked bluntly.

"Because you would have disapproved," his dark friend replied, just as bluntly. "You play a fair and honest game, Archie, I don't. If I have to hurt a few people to win this round, I didn't want you on my shoulder, nagging me. As you have so impolitely pointed out, this is pirate versus pirate."

Robinson grinned.

"And you think I would nag you? Are you doing something that reprehensible?"

"I'm flying under false colors. Gennaro, tourist, asking naïve questions of the locals while hunting for antiques and realia."

"And looking for suckers," Robinson murmured.

"And perhaps finding them," Gee agreed. "They may have a hidey-hole nearby, and their cover is somewhat vulnerable."

"And you're dead sure they don't know who you are," Archie accused.

"I'm not dead sure about anything. I am feeling my way," Gee answered. "The last thing I need is you or Security showing up, sticking your noses in." The look in his eyes was both challenging and a warning. Again, Archie recognized the signs when he saw them, and pulled back.

"Let Robinson show you what he's got. I think he's one hundred per cent right," Archie said quietly. "You must let— "

Robinson's hand went to his holster. "What's that?"

Archie realized he'd been ignoring a background noise. With a sinking heart, he knew he'd ignored it because it was a sound he associated with the ordinary buzz of the Gee-9 lab, with virtual war games that did not interest him: the *zat, crack, thung* of weaponry.

Robinson recognized it, too, and moved. "Behind the bar," he ordered the two Gamemasters, turning toward the door with his gun drawn.

The door smashed inward. Archie saw weapons. The Security personnel jumped into action, toward the door. Immediately Archie closed his eyes, threw himself against Gee and knocked him behind the rude wooden bar. There was the deafening sound of weapons fire, a burnt smell, noises of men yelling— and the grunt of men being hit. Blinding flashes of light coruscated about the room. Gee was still and silent beneath him.

The bar wasn't much cover at all. Archie knew it. No miracle would save them. Masked, rifle-carrying strangers peered around the bar and saw them.

Further back, someone spoke urgently, not to him. "Gunfire outside!"

"All right." That was a familiar voice. "Fall back. We've got him." That masked soldier— surely Blue 1— had spotted them.

"Max— " said Archie, too late. A final bright blast knocked him into darkness.

He awoke in stabbing, full-body pain that started in the back of his neck and traveled up his head and down into his spine in great waves. Every nerve was clanging. He could see nothing but fireworks. The blinding pain made him cry out.

Someone grabbed him as he sat up. "You'll be all right," a man's English voice said. "You've just experienced a stunner blast at close range."

The voice was friendly. Archie gasped back, "I can live without it."

"Here." The man shoved something in his mouth. "Put this under your tongue." Archie shoved it in place and felt the difference immediately. The waves of pain subsided, although a dull thrum remained. He closed his eyes, sat still, and let the medication work. The man, recognizing the reaction, said, "Good. You'll be all right. Can you open your eyes yet, Mr. Chamberlain?"

His heart sank. The stranger knew his name. That meant time had passed. Archie tried to force his eyes open. "Hurts like hell."

"He's blue-eyed." A woman's voice cut in, from a little further away. "Blue eyes take longer."

"Good Lord," gasped Archie, eyes still shut, "I was never so glad to hear a West Meg accent in my life. It *is* Lieutenant McAllen, isn't it?"

"It is," the man confirmed. "And I am Commander Dyvim Sang of the EHD ECM." England Historic District Earth Combined Military.

"Did they get him?" Archie blurted.

"Who?" asked Sang, at the same moment McAllen growled, "Shit."

Archie groaned. His eyes watered, whether due to pain or shock he did not know. He heard Sang say to McAllen, "You were right."

His eyes stung too painfully to open. "Lieutenant," said Archie, "what are you doing here?"

"Apparently," the Commander replied mildly, "saving your life against our strongest arguments."

They helped Archie to a seat at a little wooden table. Through his watery eyes, he saw the surroundings of the pub. He hadn't been moved, so he wasn't unconscious for long. His hearing worked better than his vision. He heard the sounds of troops running, a chopper passing overhead, orders being called out. There was military activity all around them. His second thought was, They wouldn't be this active if they had been successful.

Sheila McAllen sat on his right hand, Commander Sang on his left. McAllen reached out to grip Archie's wrists and pull his hands away from his face. Archie fought loose, fumbled for a handkerchief and wiped his stinging eyes. Now he could see her face, with a grimness in it he had never before encountered. But she looked active, and competent. It was not a polite paper-pusher's expression.

"Mr. Chamberlain," McAllen said, "we've got dead Gamemaster Inc. Security men all over the place."

"Robinson?" he choked.

"The Security Chief? Major internal injuries. They medevac'd him to London. He's the only survivor besides you, and he may not make it."

"This was a well-organized raid," said Sang, "with a definite goal. However, we didn't know what the goal was, until just now. They kidnapped the Gamemaster, did they not?"

Archie could see him now. There was nothing English in Commander Sang's looks; he was as Oriental as God made them. Instinctively, then, Archie trusted in his abilities, because to get as far as he had in the England Historic District, with that against him, he had to be damned good. This cancelled out his concern that the man's name was Sang, the name of the most famous torturer of three centuries. This Sang was here, and he was working for England. "They heard weapons fire just as they reached us."

"That was me," said McAllen. "I was hoping to upset the show enough to leave one witness. It looked too much like a LNS situation to me." He understood that LNS meant Leave No Survivors. "I didn't know it was you in there. And I definitely didn't know about him. What the hell is going on?" Her voice was reasonable, like someone filling in information. Not like she had just charged in and saved his ass ten minutes ago.

"I don't know. What are you doing here?" he repeated.

"Stop trying to figure the angle and start talking," she countered. "Most kidnappers leave survivors to tell the tale. Someone just kidnapped the most famous man alive, with a standing no-ransom policy, a blitzkrieg."

"Goddamn it, you know perfectly well who it was." Archie's head started pounding again. "Just as I do. Why, I have no idea."

"Perhaps to prove they could," Sang murmured.

"That would be my guess," Archie replied. "Nothing else makes sense." His eardrums were pounding too.

"Here, take this." McAllen had a pill in her hand.

"I will not. You people and your damnable pills!" Archie lurched to his feet, and staggered to the bar. Underneath, he found an ice bucket and a barman's towel. He wrapped some of the ice in the towel and applied the compress to the back of his neck.

Sang and McAllen, who had risen from their seats to watch him, sat down. Now Sang grinned. "I recognize an old Oxford hangover cure when I see one."

"Can't be any less effective than the dope you gave me." Holding the ice pack to the back of his neck, Archie settled again in the chair. He glimpsed soldiers with rifles inside the door.

Following his glance, Sang explained, "We're waiting for a Gamemaster Inc. Recovery unit. They radioed us to say they'd be picking up the bodies. We've bagged them, but that's all. Shipperton Vale only has one policeman, and he contacted the Foreign Office and us. The Prime Minister ordered him to give me temporary authority here."

"How long was I out?"

"Three-quarters of an hour. We came in on Lt. McAllen's signal, too late to trace the attackers."

Archie groaned, "Because she'd come to tell you about it and no one thought she was serious."

"Not quite like that," said McAllen. "Don't forget, if it was Recover— we've got U.N. orders to withhold fire."

"Lieutenant McAllen followed fighter exhaust trails to this location. All we know is that they were McAllister crafts, which means British made. She hoped a handgun would only wound, not kill, from the distance, but she took a terrible risk nonetheless."

Archie forgot that both eyes felt like ice picks stabbed through them. He stared at her. "You took on a Recover attack unit with your handgun?"

"Well, I had good cover," she demurred, "and I just wanted to scare them away. It worked, thank God."

"Or I wouldn't be here. I understand that. Thank you," said Archie. "But that still doesn't explain how you ended up here to begin with." Irresistibly, he added, "A question you've now ignored three times."

"I came out here for a briefing," she replied tersely. "It seemed more appropriate to send me— regarding information you gave me."

Archie set down the ice pack and demanded, "It seemed more appropriate to whom?"

He saw her jaw set. "To General Carpenter."

"Uh-huh." Archie had the picture. "Whom you were forced to go to over the head of that ass of a commander of yours, after I'd given you a bucketful of true facts straight from the stable. Right, Lieutenant?"

Her jaw remained stiff. "Captain Jahnik merely pointed out that we had absolutely no substantiation whatsoever for these allegations— "

"— which, nonetheless, caused the United Nations to ban shootouts with Recover on the ground that they were children— " Archie shot back.

She overrode him. "— causing General Carpenter to decide that a verbal briefing with EHD ECM would be more appropriate than a written report— "

"— and you're on remand for what this time? Insubordination?"

The jaw didn't change. "Excuse me, but that is none of your business."

"Excuse *me*, but, Yes, it is. We're in a life-threatening situation and the ECM decide it can all be solved by calling you a liar. I am a patient man, but I am reaching my limit."

"Yes," said McAllen suddenly, "you are a very patient man."

It was not the response he was expecting, and it caught him short. He rubbed his hand over his aching face. "Oh, hell, I'm sorry, Lieutenant. I'm scared and I hurt." Archie turned to Commander Sang. "You could have stopped our argument at any time."

Sang merely smiled. "I'm getting educated. This is the most enlightening exchange I've heard in days."

"I have orders to keep this visit as unofficial as possible," said Lieutenant McAllen.

Archie asked McAllen, "You said you followed fighter exhaust trails here. Is that so? Do you have a location pinpointed? Can we get Gee out?"

"What makes you think he's alive?" McAllen asked.

"My badge would have let me know of a change in management," said Archie. For some reason, he was loath to tell her about his recent implant.

Sang concurred. "They would not have used a stunner gun otherwise. You are a fortunate man, Mr. Chamberlain. Your loyalty saved your life. If you hadn't jumped to protect your commander and been stunned with him, you would be dead now. In any other position in the room, you would have been killed by ordinary weapons fire."

A grim smile touched McAllen's lips. "You said, once, it wasn't even an issue."

"I guess not," Archie admitted quietly.

"To answer your question," said McAllen, "I know you don't know much about ships, because you said so. But have you ever been down to San Diego and seen the antique jet shows?"

"Not live, but I've seen them onscreen."

"Well then, you've seen jet trails. At first they're very clear, then they dissipate," she said. "Fighter exhaust fumes are composed of a mess of things used to keep the fission engines functioning smoothly, and are just as clear to detection equipment as jet streams are to the naked eye. Usually, though, left to themselves, fighter fumes don't dissipate. You need an additional— exhaust gadget— to do that."

Archie smiled ruefully. "Thank you for dumbing it down to my level. I think I recognize some of my own vocabulary in it."

"You should. Anyway, even if you dissipate it— if you fly over the same area repeatedly, dissipation or not, you're bound to leave a buildup."

"And the buildup is around Shipperton Vale?"

"You could slice it with a knife. I didn't need to try pinpointing anything, though, when I saw actual McAllisters pop up from somewhere and drop right here." McAllen, Archie and Sang looked up at the sound of more engines. Her tone changed. "They're here," she said. "That was fast." A look passed between her and Sang. Archie rose with the two officers and went outside.

Three ships had landed: two marked GAMEMASTER INC., one marked CITY OF WEST MEG CORONER'S OFFICE. The business of putting the sealed body bags in the ships had already commenced.

The dark green bags crinkled as two men lifted each onto a floating gurney. Large black box letters were stenciled on each one— just a word. Belatedly, Archie realized they were names. The moment he realized it, unfortunately, was when he saw one labeled BLODGETT.

It was too much for him. He saw a vision of the dancer Selina, the nice dinner— "Oh, God!" He turned and careened into Lieutenant McAllen.

She understood what happened and gripped his shoulder, unfazed, while he stood gasping and shaking.

"A friend?" Commander Sang's voice came from behind him. Archie managed a nod. "Lieutenant, take Mr. Chamberlain to that grass patch over there, with a real cold pack. We shall need him functioning."

"Yes, sir."

Archie let himself be led to a green, grassy thatch near a wooded area. He sat down. He heard the zip of a prepared package. Lt. McAllen knelt down beside him and pressed the icy pack into his face. He clasped it in both hands and pressed it against his aching eyes.

It was a struggle to recover himself. He felt McAllen's hand rest on his shoulder. He tried not to think about Blodgett, the dinner, or Bet's rescue. He tried to focus on the situation around him, what to do next. He kept the pack over his eyes.

Lieutenant McAllen's hand never left his shoulder. She spoke quietly. "It's okay to lose it, Archie. Lord knows I have. You've just got to remember that there's still a job to do and that people are depending on you. It doesn't hurt to remember promises you made, either."

"I suppose that's true." Archie got his breathing under control. "You talk as if you were on the front lines."

"I was. Mercury and Ganymede." She kept her hand on his shoulder. There was an unemotional tone in her voice that was somehow comforting. "Enlisted when I was eighteen, just like my five brothers before me. The sergeant-major— that's my dad— was pissed. It never occurred to me that he expected greater things of me." She was talking on, just to distract him, he realized. "He pulled every string he had to get me into OTS— officer training school— and into a desk job in West Meg. That's where I've been ever since. Thanks to my dad, who didn't want me to be a groundpounder all my life, like him."

Archie understood. "So that's what you're living up to, in that nest of cats."

"You don't even know them." She sounded amused.

"I've worked in enough offices in my life."

McAllen grinned, and took her hand from his shoulder. "You're definitely back to normal now."

"I think I am, thanks." Archie wiped his eyes, and examined his handkerchief. It was covered with blood, dirt, tears, and worse. "I hope I don't have to lend this to anyone."

"Only you would even worry about that, Mr. Chamberlain," said the Lieutenant. "Now, come on, let's talk. How did you end up here?"

"Max was blocking out Gee's itinerary to keep Robinson off his back. Robinson asked me if I could locate him."

"I don't envy Robinson his job."

"No, it's a rough one, providing enough security for a famous daredevil without getting in the way. Anyway— " Archie blew his nose on the disgusting handkerchief— "I followed the gossip lines instead, which are much more reliable."

"You are worth your weight in platinum to that outfit. And you found him?"

"I made a good guess, supported by damn little evidence, that Gee was in Shipperton Vale somewhere. He had a Kapi tracer in the handle of one of his tools that Robinson managed to get close to. So we came to see."

"And what had he been doing?"

"Playing bloody tourist. Now you ask me where, and *that's* the part I don't know."

"Let's talk with Commander Sang. He might have an idea where tourists go around here. The Gamemaster saw those ships, Mr. Chamberlain, and he's a pilot. If he got a visual on them, he could've followed them with one eye. It would have been easy."

"Mmph." Archie rose with her. "But what he saw with the other eye is the problem. How much can Sang help us— pardon— help me?"

"Us," she clarified. "I'm in this with you." Then she frowned as she answered his question. "Damn little. The UN has issued orders to avoid harming the children in Recover. All they can do is sit on their hands, really."

"You're not sitting on yours." Archie was relieved to see that the mortuary ships had moved out. Commander Sang was using the bonnet of Gee's Land Rover as a desk.

"No. I'm not. I'm afraid I've said some things that I am going to regret. Later. Not now." She stared at some inner vision for a long moment. Then she looked at him again. Apparently, she decided to let a few more details out of the bag. "I'm not easy with the idea of children being killed. It's bothered me since the Neptune Yards incident. We picked up the frozen remains of children's bodies for months after that. And if what Com— " She stopped.

"Commander Marsden?" Archie filled in the blank. His was the one name that had not yet appeared in any conversation.

"Off the record," she said uncomfortably.

"As you wish," Archie agreed.

"I think he's Commander Sang's source, probably without ECM West Meg permission."

"'And if what Commander Marsden suspects is true,'" Archie prompted, and she glanced at him sharply.

She did not, however, contradict him. "Then there's more to Recover than meets the eye and we have to get to the bottom of it before more children get killed. And adults."

That certainly jibed with Elsa's last transmission, too. "Are you working for Marsden, then?" Archie asked.

"I only wish. I tested but didn't qualify for Special Services. No, I am just an insubordinate smartass junior groundpounder putting on airs. It's very likely, Mr. Chamberlain, that when you return to West Meg, you'll be dealing with someone else. Captain Jahnik let General Carpenter know, in no uncertain terms, that he has had quite enough of me. I'll be pushing on." She didn't sound nearly as regretful as she had that day on the cricket field.

"I'm sorry," said Archie. "I know it's not your fault."

"Well, thanks," said Lieutenant McAllen, "but let's deal with one crisis at a time."

Commander Sang looked up from his notepad. "Feeling better?" he asked Archie.

"Much, thanks." Archie leaned on the dirty yellow bonnet of the ancient Land Rover, as the Commander did, and stared at Sang's portable screen. It held a map of the region. He could see colored areas— concentrations of the exhausts, he suspected. He realized that any move forward was completely his responsibility. "I've been thinking. Gee was pretending to be interested in antiques. That rather says he was interested in well-to-do houses and little off-the-road locations, doesn't it?"

"Certainly it does," said Sang.

"Well, I've already called a couple of places in Coventry and sung 'em a song about how I was looking for my antiques partner from West Meg who had gone off his itinerary. I could just as easily drop into places around here and do the same, couldn't I? And if they didn't believe me, they can check out Coventry and find I have background."

Sang nodded. "I can give you a list of possibilities in the region. Little antiques shops and nice manors directly under the heaviest concentrations of exhaust. I'll attempt to prioritize it." He shot a sharp glance at Archie. "Do you have any idea how long we have before he's written off as dead?"

"Twenty-four hours," Archie replied.

Sheila McAllen took in a deep breath. "That's not very long."

Commander Sang also took a deep breath, but his gaze remained serene and undisturbed. "Mr. Chamberlain, I am not certain you realize the seriousness of the situation. The Board of Trustees of the England Historic District is convening this afternoon at the request of the United Nations. West Meg has demanded action against the attackers of Gamemaster Inc. employees within EHD boundaries. The Gamemaster Inc. Acting Security Chief and her squad have been denied entry to the England Historic District on U.N. orders. They are appealing to the U.N. We could be on opposite sides of a battle zone within twenty-four hours."

Archie remembered the look between Sang and McAllen in the inn, and understood it now. They had realized Gamemaster Inc. Security was on high alert to respond that quickly, and they were ready for a fight. "Then I'd better hop on this list as soon as you can hand it to me."

Commander Sang handed him a hard-copy. "Here's the list. Now we have to get you some civilian transportation. All we've got here are armored personnel carriers." He scooped his remaining desk materials off the Land Rover's bonnet.

"We can use this Land Rover— " Archie stopped, remembering the jingle he'd heard when Gee stood up in the Inn. "Oh, hell. No. Here's the perfect tourist vehicle, and Gee had the keys in his pocket."

Lieutenant McAllen demanded, "Can you drive one of these?"

"Yes, I can, but not without keys."

To his amazement, Sheila McAllen hopped into the passenger seat and reached under the dashboard. She pulled wires from beneath the dash and started tinkering with them. "If I can't hot-wire one of these antiques, the UN has wasted a lot of good money on my training." There was the scuffle and rip of wires, then the sound of the engine turning over. McAllen looked satisfied.

Archie had the presence of mind to run back to Blodgett's bus and grab his overnight bag. Good for you, he told himself, your brain's not completely gone. Robinson's notepad had been next to his bag and wasn't there now. Whether the EHD ECM realized it or not, the "mortuary van" had shaken down this bus. There might even be a tracer in Archie's bag— although probably not, seeing how they could find him in a moment with his badge. He ran back to the Land Rover, engine still purring, and climbed in.

Archie shifted gears and accelerated, and they were off. She watched him for a while as he drove, then sat back, satisfied. "You do know how to drive," she said.

"Yes. And you do know how to get by, don't you?"

"It's nice to be able to impress you," she said. "I've batted a row of goose eggs for as long as I've known you."

"Now is not the time to debate that untruthful statement." Archie concentrated on the road. "Who are our prime candidates?"

McAllen consulted the list. "There's two big estates. General Mason Abbott, Retired, and Mrs. Sarah Chase." She looked up. "Your turn to hit up a General. I shook up my own General yesterday."

"Who's nearest?"

"About the same. They're both northwest of Shipperton Vale." She scowled at the notepad. "We don't have to go all the way back there to pick up a highway, do we?"

"Yes, we do."

"This 'quaint little road' stuff has its disadvantages, doesn't it?"

"Yes, it does." Archie kept his eyes on his driving.

Archie envied McAllen's ability to sleep soundly in the Land Rover while he drove, despite all the bumps and curves. Well, he reflected, she learned to sleep in personnel carriers, caves, and worse places, while in full armored airsuit. This was probably a nap in the park.

He passed the inn where Blodgett used to hang out in Shipperton Vale, and had second thoughts. He swung around and pulled up in front of it.

McAllen woke up when the movement stopped. "What is it?"

"It's tea and I need something to eat."

"You're stopping for a cup of *tea*?" she asked incredulously.

"No, idiot, tea is the only meal that will be available until dinner at eight, and I haven't had a bite to eat since dinner yesterday."

"Oh. Good point. I think I remember breakfast at an EHD canteen, but that was a long time ago, too."

Archie examined the Land Rover's panel. It had a fuel cutoff switch, as well as an ignition. "Do I dare shut this off?"

"Sure, go ahead. Piece of cake to re-start." She admitted with a smile, "Speaking of cake. Now I am hungry."

He shut off the switch. The engine died. He glanced at her jacket. "It might be a good idea for you to leave that in the vehicle. Your West Meg accent will stick out enough without color illustrations."

"Right." She slid it off, folded it carefully, and leaned back to set it on the rear seat. Her shoulder holster followed, stowed into the metal toolbox on the back floor. Archie noticed once again how nicely that white turtleneck fit her, and held back a comment with effort. Timberlake was perfectly justified in saying the line could form on the left. Even more embarrassingly, she caught his glance, smiling and saying nothing.

"Come on," said Archie. "Now I have the opportunity to treat you to a truly decent meal. I'm not going to waste it."

-14-

Bishop and Queen

"Lordy," sighed McAllen, leaning back and patting her stomach, "I needed that."

They were alone in the inn's little parlor. They could hear voices and footsteps in the bar, but there had been no other tourists needing tea. Sophisticated tourists would have gone to finer places.

Archie poured another cup of tea. He had seen her looking interestedly at everything, but she'd let him do the talking. The landlord, Mr. Callender, and his wife had been happy to oblige with cake and good tea. They talked about the local dairy and had eventually ended up with homemade bread, butter, crackers and cheese.

"Have you been following any of the conversation from the bar?" Archie asked in a low tone.

"Every word I could hear," she replied, just as quietly. "Did you see one guy glance in here?" Archie nodded briefly. "I thought it was your badge, then I realized he was looking at me. He'd done his time. Recognized my uniform."

"They'd have to be deaf and blind to not hear the fuss in the north," Archie murmured back.

"I also heard the name Blodgett," she said, watching him carefully.

"He's the local darts champion," Archie answered.

Her mouth tightened. What she said was totally unexpected. "Wish I'd known him."

"Green as grass. First big assignment, came through with flying colors. Chief was impressed, put him here." Archie kept his nose in his teacup.

"Sucks," said McAllen.

"Yes, it does." He was discovering that he liked McAllen's way of looking at things— not who's to blame, not how can you fix it, just an appreciation of the moment. "Tell me what happened with General Carpenter."

McAllen shifted uncomfortably. "Captain Jahnik was downplaying all this stuff about 'the children' like we were talking about naptime. I finally said if he was uncomfortable with it, I'd be willing to take the information to someone who wasn't so embarrassed dealing with children." She frowned and played with a crumb of bread. "Right now, I can't recall what he said that made me stand up and head for the door. All I really had in mind was walking down to the General's office and making an appointment with the secretary that I'd probably cancel later. But Commander Marsden was standing with the General himself in the outer office when I got there. Like they'd planned it."

"They probably did. I don't think much gets by those fellows. Didn't Jahnik stop you?"

A scornful grunt. "I'd like him to try. He trailed me all the way down the corridor. He apologized to the General for my behavior. He said he'd put me on remand, he'd cut my pay, he'd had enough of me and I was out of there." She frowned at the bread crumb in remembrance. Then she met Archie's gaze. "You know, I didn't care what any of them thought right then, and I told them so. I said they knew perfectly well that Recover was full of military brats with an agenda, and I wanted to see there were as few deaths as possible because we were talking about our own children here. And suddenly General Carpenter told me to come in to his office and sit down."

"Did Marsden come, too?"

"Sure did. I said what you said, and Marsden and Carpenter started consulting back and forth like I'd just submitted a regular report. Marsden asked me if I'd be willing to take a chance in the EHD and go in unofficially. I said sure, this needed to be reported and stopped. Carpenter himself said their hands were tied as a unit, but an individual might get somewhere. So here I am."

"So you came here to give Commander Sang a report and get the lie of the land," Archie said thoughtfully.

She nodded. "That was all. But the exhausts are so thick here, a blind man could see where they were leading. My report was the icing on what Sang was already checking out. You about ready to push on?" she asked.

"Not quite so fast." He stood up. "Let me pay Mr. Callender for our meal, and chat him up a bit."

"Have you got a plan?" she wanted to know, rising.

"After a fashion," he replied.

She followed him through the entryway to the bar. There were about ten people there besides the landlord and barman. The conversation dropped to nothing when they saw Archie, but he would have expected that in any village pub when a stranger appeared.

He stepped comfortably on the footrail and placed his credit bar on the counter. "We'll be moving on now. Thanks for that bread and cheese, it was a lifesaver."

The landlord's plump hand swiped up the credit bar. "You're welcome, sir. Staying here long?"

"No. I wish I could." Archie sounded regretful.

The man standing beside him said, "That's a Gamemaster badge, isn't it?"

"Yes."

"You like working for 'em?"

"Very much."

Another curious soul was bold enough to ask, "How did you get a job like that?"

Archie turned to her and answered, in just the right tone, "Oxford. It does wonders." The entire bar burst into laughter, and he clarified with a smile, "Seriously, though. I was teaching, and liked it, and had a chance to get into educational work with Gamemaster Inc."

The ice was broken. "Young Blodgett used to work there, I think," the first man said to Mr. Callender, who was handing Archie's credit bar back to him. Then he turned to Archie. "Young Danny Blodgett. You ever met him?"

Archie hesitated, wondering whether to answer with a truth or a lie, and realized his hesitation had been an answer and Mr. Callender had seen it. "Yes, I did."

"Hang on a bit," someone said, "he'll be here for darts this evening, to defend his title."

"I don't think you'll see him tonight," said Archie quietly. He turned and met the landlord's gaze. "Thanks once again, Mr. Callender."

"I'll see you folks out to your car," the landlord offered, as Archie expected. Lt. McAllen stepped quietly out ahead of them, to the vehicle.

The sun was setting, but Mr. Callender could easily see McAllen hotwire the Land Rover. He said dubiously, "No problem with your credit bar, but most people have keys to their vehicles."

"We've lost them, but Sheila can hotwire anything. I think your crowd figured out her employer."

"That they did. I got the impression you wanted me to come out, sir," said the landlord frankly.

"I didn't want to announce in a room full of strangers that Danny Blodgett is dead," said Archie, and heard the landlord take in his breath. "Someone shot him this afternoon."

"Anyone told the Sergeant?" Mr. Callender asked.

Before he could reply, McAllen cut in. "The ECM is working with Scotland Yard and the United Nations to find out what happened. Mr. Blodgett wasn't on assignment in England. This was a vacation."

"He'd never been out of West Meg before," Archie concurred.

Mr. Callender made the connection himself. "All that ruckus up in North Shipperton?"

"They sent for us to identify the bodies," said Archie.

"Lord! His lads, too?"

"The lot."

Mr. Callender took in another breath, appalled. "There wasn't a penny-worth of harm in any of them, great gawking West Meg boys on holiday."

"I know. They loved your pub, too. You'll probably know, better than I, who ought to be told. And I think it goes without saying that anyone with information, no matter how scanty, ought to tell the police."

"Doubt they will," said Mr. Callender.

"I doubt it, too," said Archie.

"I wondered if you were doing the right thing to tell him." McAllen donned her holster and jacket without difficulty in the jouncing vehicle. "Then I realized if anything was going to come from Shipperton Vale, it would only come from local public outrage. You don't think a damn thing will happen, do you? Inertia."

"If someone does report something to the police, the military, or the company, it will be worth reporting. Now. How close are we?"

"The first right takes you to General Abbott's. It's closest. Beyond that, a mile or so on the left, is the turnoff for Mrs. Chase's estate."

Suddenly, Trann spoke, as clearly as if he sat in McAllen's lap. Only Trann would transmit via the implant, unannounced, simply because he was so used to it himself. "Archie. I've been monitoring your incoming mail. You just got an anonymous message from Shipperton Vale. An uneducated man's voice, saying that shouldn't have happened to young Blodgett and the place where troublemakers hang out in this region is Bowman House. Voice scan says it's a genuine message, and looks untampered and truthful. I looked up Bowman House. It belongs to a woman named Sarah Cordelia Chase. It's about three kilometers beyond your current position."

"We're going for Chase," Archie said to the Lieutenant. "I have a hunch."

McAllen, who of course did not hear voices in her head, eyed him curiously. "If you say so."

Archie swung left at the next fork, down the road for Mrs. Chase. The road degenerated to a one-lane set of tire tracks. They passed fields where the grass and greenery seemed overgrown and untended.

"Looks a little tatty," said McAllen.

"She doesn't keep livestock, that's all. Sheep and cattle would cut this back." The road curved, and the mansion house appeared.

"Wow," said McAllen. "Now, that's fancy."

"Isn't it?" Archie agreed.

Mrs. Chase's home had large, well-tended front and back lawns. The great house itself appeared to Archie to be 18th century, with some modern modifications. The glint of the windows suggested that they were self-cleaning, and while he saw chimneys and fireplaces, he also suspected a modern heating system. Mrs. Chase was not a farmer. Archie wondered what was in the rolling fields behind the house, out of sight.

"There's money here," Lt. McAllen murmured.

"Some, at least." Archie pulled into the carriage circle, near the front entrance, and stopped. He regarded the Lieutenant meditatively. Since he was just fishing, what role should he suggest for her?

" I'll wait here," said McAllen, solving his problem.

Archie climbed out, brushed off his jacket, and straightened it. As his feet crunched up the walkway, he saw a curtain move. He saw a doorbell, and pressed the button. He heard chimes within. As a butler opened the door, he said, "Hello. Mr. Archie Chamberlain to speak to Mrs. Chase, please."

"What is the nature of your business, sir?"

"I am searching for a missing associate who planned to call on Mrs. Chase regarding the purchase of some antiques. He's needed urgently," Archie added truthfully, "and I have traced him this far. I hope to determine if I am still on his trail."

"Your associate's name, sir?"

"Gennaro Gochak."

"I do not recall a visitor by that name, sir."

No wonder, since Archie made it up. Tibetan for "lock," and what name would be better? "May I speak to Mrs. Chase, just in case she had an inquiry? It is quite important we locate him."

"I shall determine if Madam is available, sir." The butler ushered Archie into a small salon immediately on the right. He had only a glance of a great hall and fashionable staircase as he entered the room. They had been in shadow, but this little drawing-room was well-lit by windows, a pleasant reception room for tea and conversation. The pale blues and whites spoke of wealth and taste. Archie was not an expert on fine furniture, but he suspected these chairs and sofas weren't reproductions of anything— they were the originals.

There were no pictures on the mantelpiece, on the nice white grand piano, or anywhere else in the room. There was no personal memorabilia of any kind. The paintings on the wall were conventional, known artists. Not an item in this room gave clues to the identity of the person who owned them. It was a polar opposite to his parents' jumbled, loving house.

"Mr. Chamberlain?" A low feminine voice caused him to turn in surprise.

Mrs. Sarah Chase appeared. He was astonished to discover that she was only about his age. Her dark hair looked effortless, her dress and jewelry simple and tasteful. Mrs. Chase was beautiful, in a European fashion. However, when she approached him close enough to look up into his face, he found her gaze unpleasant.

"Mrs. Chase," he greeted her. "Forgive me for troubling you. I am searching for my missing associate. Was Gennaro here?"

"Gennaro...?" she asked politely.

"Gochak." He smiled, and added, "I should think the number of Gennaros in this region are limited, Mrs. Chase."

She returned his smile politely, but there was something hard in her discomfiting gaze. "That is quite true, Mr. Chamberlain. I have not communicated with a Mr. Gochak. Are you certain of your information?"

"Quite certain, Mrs. Chase. Have you received any visitors from West Meg recently?"

"Pardon me, Mr. Chamberlain, but my visitors are certainly not your business." Her voice was civil but objecting. She had no difficulty meeting his gaze, either. At that moment, one of old Gentian's maxims occurred to him: "When someone maintains constant eye contact with you, they're trying to keep you from looking around."

He dropped his gaze for a moment. The brief respite gave his brain a chance to absorb other odd details. Then, he looked at her again. "I am well aware of that, ma'am. Please understand the awkwardness of my position. Gennaro has undoubtedly vanished. His vehicle and luggage have been found, but not the man himself. I am attempting to retrace his steps. His family has asked me to take one last look before they turn this matter over to the police."

"His vehicle and luggage?" She raised a brow.

"I drove here in his Land Rover. There's no question of his absence. It does not appear to be voluntary."

"Then by all means, you should consult the police," she said, still only politely concerned. "I am certain I do not know your friend."

"I am sorry you have taken this attitude." Archie's tone was gentle but final. "I have proof he made it this far. The police investigation may very well spark an international incident you will indeed regret."

Her voice hardened. "Sir, are you threatening me?"

"Not in the least, Mrs. Chase."

"I think you should leave, Mr. Chamberlain."

"So sorry to trouble you, then." Well, he had tried. What else was he supposed to do? She escorted him firmly into the dimly-lit front hall.

He had no choice but to leave the way he came. "Believe me, Mrs. Chase," Archie said, "I would not have invaded your privacy had I not considered this urgent." Even as he stood in her front hall, he felt the unspoken push out the door. "I am looking for a missing man who may have been kidnapped. If he has, time is running out rapidly because no ransom will be paid. His kidnappers are equally merciless."

"I'm sorry, but you are under some misapprehension, Mr. Chamberlain," the woman replied firmly. "No one lives on this estate but myself. If you are trying to incriminate me, I assure you, this will be actionable in a court of law."

"That certainly is not my intent," Archie replied. "I have never— " Then, something caught his eye— something on the wall, above his head, opposite him.

When he first entered the house, he had noticed that the dim hallway contained odd bits of Historic District memorabilia— shovels, a wooden plough blade, an ox yoke— fastened to the walls above their heads. These were meant to be visible when the hall lights were on, when people were going upstairs. Unlike the pretty, sterile salon, this hallway held the flotsam and jetsam of this family, he presumed. But now, one piece had his full attention.

"Oh, Lord," said Archie Chamberlain, in sudden understanding.

Mrs. Chase, puzzled, turned to see what had caught his gaze.

A board was fastened to the wall above their heads. Plainly, it had once been the sign outside a shop. The words, and the metal design hammered into it, had taken Archie's breath away. The Brass Mouse Antiques.

"I beg your pardon?" said Mrs. Chase.

It was an effort for Archie to make his tone commonplace. "Can you tell me about that sign, the one over your head?"

"It was the sign over the door of my antiques shop. What does it matter?"

"And then you closed down the shop?"

"We'd been married about five years when I closed it down, yes, when my mother died and we moved here. It was just too much to handle, with my baby sons as well as my husband." Was it Archie's imagination, or had her jaw stiffened and her tone changed when she spoke of babies and husband? No.

"Has anyone else asked about that sign lately?"

That hit the bell. The answer, whether she said it aloud or not, was yes. "What can it matter to you?"

"Mrs. Chase, if my friend was here, and saw that sign, and you lied about it, you are abetting criminal activity. You will soon be accessory to murder. I have a nice mind, and I wouldn't like— I really wouldn't like— to call you up to trial as a witness in a murder investigation." He pushed and kept his voice urgent, but nonetheless, he had never seen blood drain from a face so quickly. "There's no doubt Gennaro would have asked about that sign." Good Lord, Archie thought, what did Gee do to bring on such a strong reaction? "Mrs. Chase, if he was here, I beg you to tell me quickly. Let me get an unofficial investigation underway. Once the authorities are called in, there will be no way to prevent someone getting hurt."

"I don't know what you're talking about," she said whitely.

Her gaze. Those eyes. Trann had said Bowman House. Inspiration struck him again. A bow man shot arrows. "What relation are you to John and Richard?" he demanded. "Sister? You look enough like them. Two of the best men on earth, and here you are, acting like this. I won't begin to guess what they would have to say about it."

"How dare you walk in here and discuss my dead family!" He had no idea if her outrage were feigned or real. She was still deadly pale. Her voice sounded hoarse.

"It would be pointless, since neither is of the earth earthly. Mrs. Chase, you are making a mistake, and putting a good man in serious jeopardy. Not only that, you are allowing these children to kill each other. It's already started. True Recover idealists are already finding that they've been dupes for dirty little Sandhurst power games, and being shot like dogs when they object. Surely you've seen the news. Elsa Grayson was Blue Five. She's dead because she found she was aiding and abetting felonies, not noble causes."

The look on Sarah Chase's face was extremely unpleasant. For a moment, it reminded Archie of Gee somehow, the look he got when he talked about his training. But then, she shook her head, recovered her voice, and opened the door. "Good day, Mr. Chamberlain," she said firmly.

There was no point in getting himself dragged out of the building. He bowed to the inevitable. "Good day," he said, and left.

Sheila McAllen waited in the Land Rover. "Well?"

"Well all hell," Archie replied sourly. "Gee was here and she won't say anything. I said talk to me before I split for the authorities, and still nothing."

"Protecting somebody, do you think?"

"I do think. Probably either husband or babies— except the husband's dead and the babies must be twenty by now. Oh, hell." Archie rubbed his eyes. "I need to think about what to do next."

"I think you should report it to the authorities next," said Lt. McAllen, in a different voice.

"Oh." Archie took a good look at her. "I just did, didn't I?"

"Yes. I think we need to bring Commander Sang in on this. Have you got any proof that the Gamemaster was here?"

"Nothing I could take to court, dammit, certainly not to The Hague," Archie replied. "But there's something on the wall in there he'd have to be blind not to notice. When I asked her if anyone else had been asking about it lately, she nearly fainted, and told me no. Then I asked how she was related to the Arrow family, and she told me none of my business."

As matter-of-factly as if all vehicles started that way, Sheila McAllen hotwired the Land Rover again. She indicated a higher altitude with a covert glance. "We're being watched, but I don't think they can lip-read," she said. "That cliff yonder would be a nice vantage point, if you can figure out the road to get up there. A little privacy for my report wouldn't hurt, either."

"Gotcha." Archie put it in first gear and left the estate circle for the lane back to the main road.

"Good work, both of you," said Lt. McAllen's lapel radio. "And yes, you're correct on your guess, Mr. Chamberlain. Mrs. Sarah Chase was born Sarah Cordelia Arrow. Captain John and Mr. Richard Arrow are indeed her brothers. But... that's not the worst of it."

"The 'Chase' part has been worrying me for some time," Archie said to her lapel. "I was young enough to be thinking of my own future career when the Sandhurst Scandal broke."

Lt. McAllen's eyes widened. "Jumping Jesus! That slipped right by me. Lieutenant-Colonel Chase of Sandhurst Military Academy!"

"Nailed it in one," Sang's voice confirmed.

"They made the old U.S. Navy Tailhook Scandals look like tea-parties," she remembered with the summary indifference of a girl too young, half a world away, unaffected by the news of that era. "Enforced eugenics, virtual slavery, concubines, torture chambers, and I don't know what else. Chase was prosecuted as the brains behind it all."

"Mrs. Chase and her sons were not charged because it was clearly demonstrated they were not involved in activities at Sandhurst," the Commander supplied. "An officer named Allyson took some of the blame, but mainly, it rested upon Chase. Still, it must have been humiliating to discover one's husband was keeping women cadets for breeding stock. Not to mention the tortures discovered in the buildings there for testing 'new generations' and eliminating the unfit. They were in the second and third generations of gene-mods for the perfect soldier when the crematorium was accidentally discovered and the whole business blown open."

Archie remembered, too. He had watched and listened to the news at home, with his parents. He remembered their shock and disbelief. "Sandhurst has always been the soul of honor. Even parts of the Military Academy couldn't believe such a thing was happening there. They never recovered from the blow. It shook England to the foundations. I've always felt it was part of the reason the England Historic District is such a howling success. Going back to a time before such a horror could happen meant going back to a better England. At least, that's how a great many people felt about it."

Lt. McAllen glanced at him sharply. Her vested interest was obviously different from his. "Is Mrs. Chase a gene-mod, or are her kids? If I have to take any of them on, I would like to know."

"It's not the sort of thing that shows," Archie replied.

"No, but use your brain. How would she act if she had such a dirty secret, and did she act that way?"

Archie cast his mind back to their brief altercation. He remembered that odd grimace, so reminiscent of Gee himself. "If I had to pick no or yes, on a gut feeling with no data— I would say yes. If she's not a gene-mod, then the kids certainly are."

"If she's a gene-mod," McAllen continued, still looking at him carefully, "were John and Richard Arrow, too?"

Archie was thunderstruck. It had never occurred to him to question the rapport between the Arrow men and Gennaro, or the Arrows and himself.

"I don't know," he said slowly.

"You do know," McAllen contradicted him. "Yes."

"And what Gee saw," Archie said, just as slowly, "was himself, and realized the illegal eugenics of Sandhurst were still going on. Only now, it's not being done by Sandhurst. It's being done by Recover."

"We don't know that," McAllen's lapel protested, but McAllen herself was leaning back and folding her arms as if convinced.

Archie's mind leaped ahead. He was thinking about snippets of Gee's behavior, which took on entirely different meanings now. When he looked at Sheila McAllen again, he realized that she was right with him. "I've been stupid, haven't I?"

"No," she answered. "We wouldn't know if you hadn't talked to Sarah Chase."

Archie closed his eyes, trying to remember. "It's no good. Flying has never interested me. I wouldn't know a West Meg T-11 from a McAllister X-21. But Gee would. He must have seen that those unmarked ships— in fact, all the Recover stuff we've seen— had English influence. He would recognize the dregs of Sandhurst."

"I'm getting people to call up the images and examine them, even as we speak," said Commander Sang. "Recover seems to have bases all over the world, however, so I imagine there are many different designs, depending on what was stolen from where."

"But it's logical that a major base might be here, in the England Historic District," Archie argued, "simply because there would be no monitoring equipment keeping an eye on them. Max and similar computer systems are very limited in the EHD."

"Pretty likely the base is on this little estate right here, I'll bet," McAllen predicted. "I haven't seen much of this English territory, but I have seen tourist signs for old mines. This area's like Swiss cheese. There could be a planetful of stuff hidden underground."

Archie climbed out of the Land Rover, and stepped away from McAllen and the vehicle. He stared at the vista below them. He saw cliffs with occasional odd pockmarks, dark spots he couldn't identify. They could be underground ship hangars. But mainly, he was recalling the news stories. The Sandhurst geneticists were breeding the perfect soldier. Not much different from what the Gamemasters did to themselves in North America. Except— the Gamemasters had all the money in the world, and went into this voluntarily. The Gamemasters experimented only on themselves and their families. If Sandhurst had kept to that, it would probably have been considered noble. But no. That had been part of the horror.

Sandhurst was smuggling vouchers through the government, conscripting labor to build the underground caverns, and actually kidnapping and enslaving geneticists and human lab animals. Most of those involved in it were not volunteers, not hardly. The project was destroyed by three factors— the massive shame attached to the revelations about the human genetics performed there, the virtual slavery of so many involved, and the fact that now they had no money. Archie spoke in a low tone. "Max. Give me Bet, please."

"I'm right here, Archie," her voice said, far too quickly. His heart sank.

"Have you been listening in?"

"I've got a fair portion of it."

"Who's— in charge right now?" He held his breath.

"I am, Archie. He deactivated his badge. I don't know if he's dead or alive. His last location is somewhere near you. I'm getting data from Max now. He says you're within five kilometers of his last known location— but— diagonally. Either you're on a cliff, or he's underground."

"A combination of both. Listen, Bet. He's worth just as much money to them, dead or alive. They're not interested in his job. They're selling the body. I don't know who's doing the eugenics research, whether it's them or the highest bidder. I'd lay odds of fifty to one the kidnappers are Recover. I think it's controlled by our old friend, Blue One, and that he is a budding, primitive Gamemaster, a figment from the Sandhurst Scandals. He's ready to build up an empire and he's equipped with no scruples whatsoever. I think they're all in mines out here, right below us. But I can't prove a damned thing. We couldn't get so much as a search warrant on what we've got. Have you got SOP for a situation like this?"

"I do for me, but not for you. In twenty-four hours I wake up Genoa, and we get that body, one way or another." She paused. "You realize, by then, I won't be in charge any more. I don't know what Genoa will do, but I can guess. He in't no Gennaro. Historic District or no, he'll go through that area like drain cleaner, and not care who gets hurt. 'Less you want that to happen, Archie, you got to take chances."

"All right, Bet," said Archie quietly. Then he added, "If this doesn't work and Genoa takes over, will you run away to Mars with me?"

"Like a shot," she answered. "I'm prayin' for you, Archie."

Archie took a deep breath, and walked back to Lt. McAllen. She had waited patiently in the Land Rover, probably thinking that he was having a conference with himself— or maybe a short prayer. "McAllen, tell Commander Sang to get his troops moving in this general direction. Even if he can't do anything, I'd greatly appreciate the appearance of force. They should be equipped with riot gear, just in case. I want to take one more crack at Mrs. Chase before I write her off."

McAllen duly transmitted his request. Then she objected, "I don't see what you can say now that you couldn't say before."

"That's my problem." He gestured to the bonnet. "Will you do the honors?"

She smiled wryly, and obliged. "If I practice this much longer, I can run away to Mars and be a transport thief."

"I may be running with you," Archie said.

Archie saw Sarah Chase, standing at a window, as the Land Rover swung into the curve of the entrance. He stopped the vehicle. He hoped against hope that his absence had given her time to become afraid, for Gee's sake if not for her own. "Do me a favor and lurk out here. Make yourself conspicuous."

"I'm good at that." Lt. McAllen slid out of the vehicle and stood beside it, checking her weapon.

Once again, the butler answered the door. Archie had expected a polite stonewalling. Instead, the butler showed him into the salon and left to fetch Mrs. Chase. Archie felt his heart leap. There was something wrong here.

He was even more certain when she appeared. In the brief time since he had seen her last, her face had become haggard. There were rings under her grey eyes, and she looked ten years older. Her voice, too, was strained. "Mr. Chamberlain, who is the young woman waiting with your vehicle?" she asked, coming straight to the point.

"I would have thought that was obvious. She's an ECM West Meg officer, and she'll soon be joined by EHD ECM soldiers."

"She— and they— have no right on my private property."

"That is true, under ordinary conditions," Archie agreed. "But when it comes to a question of Recover, they would rather undertake clearing the area than letting Gamemaster Inc. Security do it. West Meg is within a day of invading the England Historic District." He felt obliged to add the fact he had realized when he had broken his gaze with her. "You didn't even look at my badge. It was something with which you were familiar."

"You are mistaken," she said, white to the lips.

"For God's sake, Sarah, I'm trying to help you. Do you know who Gennaro is? You must. Don't you realize what they want him for? It isn't ransom. There's a policy of no ransom for the Gamemaster."

"The Gamemaster!" she breathed. To her, it had just been a company badge. It seemed she hadn't known it was special. "No— he's not. He works for Gamemaster Inc.— "

"They want the body, Sarah. They may have killed him already, but I doubt it. When they find a buyer, they'll want it fresh."

"No!" she croaked.

"You're a gene-mod, aren't you? He must have recognized that. Your kids are, too, aren't they? Pirate ones? Are they still testing and torturing each other, to see what they can take?"

"He's not!"

"He." Archie picked up on the pronoun. "You have two sons. Where's the other one?"

"One of my sons is dead."

"And how did he die? Oops, a test failed?"

"A swimming accident."

"With his brother?" Archie pressed.

She was silent for a long moment. Perhaps it was just occurring to her that the answer to that question might be Yes. "You're wrong about Gennaro."

"I hope I am. If he's still alive, he— "

"I don't mean that. I mean why he was here. It wasn't to do with Recover. He came here because of me. We were— " she swallowed, and suddenly turned from white to crimson. "We were lovers."

Archie stared at her, speechless.

"He said he was a Gamemaster Inc. employee, on vacation. He'd noticed this place, and— wanted to know more about it. I— " she took a deep breath. "I invited him to dinner, and he stayed. And then went— I don't know where."

Archie found his voice. "How can you stand there and tell me such a parcel of lies? And you didn't see him leave? And you don't know where he went? Sarah, this isn't pure Recover doctrine. They aren't trying to raise money to fight militarism. This is Sandhurst all over again. Somewhere, there's a kid who thinks the eugenics tyrants were doing the right thing, and wants to pick up where they left off. And the cost-effective method of doing that is an autopsy— "

"Sandhurst, oh God." She shut her eyes tight. Again, her face twisted into that horrid expression.

He overrode her to finish his sentence. "-an autopsy on a body that's three or four generations ahead of them."

She groaned and sank into a chair and covered her face with her hands. Archie was aware that he was watching her world— what world it was, he wasn't certain— come crashing down. He would have been more sympathetic if he had time.

"Sarah, are you working with Recover?" Archie asked, sinking into a chair to face her.

"This can't be happening. Why would they do something like this?"

"They're desperate, Sarah. It's unraveling. The true Recover believers are discovering they're being used, and the Sandhurst holdouts are trying to hush them up by killing them."

"They said it was kidnapping, quick money— they needed it to repair the old ships— "

Oh, Lord, she'd been in deep. Unless he was being exceptionally dense, Gee must have seen this. Archie answered, "They knew better. They don't need money. They've already stolen themselves a fortune. They identified Gennaro. When they saw him on their trail, their group leader— I don't know his name, but his codename is Blue One— recognized him as a pilot they thought they'd killed at the Neptune Yards. It didn't take them long to figure out that he was the Gamemaster, to whom Elsa Grayson had pledged allegiance after he pulled her out of there. They murdered Elsa to prevent her telling Gennaro that Recover was a lie from start to finish." Archie reached out and pulled her hands away from her face, and held them. Her hands were outdoors rough. Her eyes remained tight shut, but she did not weep. Something was hurting too deep for tears.

"Sarah," he insisted, "I'm only guessing at everything, and I would really appreciate some corroboration. What I think is that Gennaro came to the village as a tourist, and started looking around. He soon heard spaceships in the area, and found that their trails matched the Neptune Yard trails. He found out where they seemed to be landing, came here, saw you and spoke with you. He knew he was on a hot scent. They, on the other hand, saw him out here, saw him with you, and said divert him, and we'll take it from there." He had his answer in the way she clasped his hands and yet avoided looking at him directly. "Sarah, please. I've got less than twenty-four hours before the sky starts falling."

"You don't know— " she started.

"About how you diverted Gennaro? That's crap. Knowing him the way I do, I doubt it was as you said. I can't imagine him as either seducer or seduced."

"Not that." She shook her head. "Sandhurst. You can't know. You can't know what it was like. How it started. Or how— it didn't end."

He waited. The ghost of that horrid expression remained on her face— too frighteningly like the Gamemaster's.

"It wasn't just the concubines. Us too. A generation previous. John and Richard as the soldiers. Me as the — breeding ground for the next generation. My father— our father— was Colonel John Allyson. Not Arrow."

The pieces fell into place with a thud. "The commanding officer." That was why the name Arrow hadn't rung any bells. It was a commander named Allyson who had been tried and found not guilty. His second in command, Jonas Chase, proved to be the force behind the wild genetics schemes.

She nodded. "Jonas was his lieutenant. And wild for the project. But he came in on the second generation. My father started the first."

"And proclaimed no knowledge of it when the fireworks went off."

She nodded miserably. "Compared to— what can be done now— we were rough drafts. Amateurish attempts. It wasn't fast enough for Father, or good enough. Between his impossible standards, all the secrecy and lies, Mother reached her limit. Mother divorced him, and took us with her. She changed our name to Arrow." Again, she clasped his hands. Her grip was like iron.

"What happened, then?"

"Mother died. John and Richard ran. I didn't. He was my *father*. He introduced me to Jonas. I didn't realize— " Her voice had risen frantically. Aware of it, she took a breath, and brought it down to normal. "No, that's not true. I thought it didn't matter that the training went on. I was proud. Proud of producing better children!"

"That's not a sin by itself," Archie said gently. He might as well not have been there. She could have been talking to the piano. She was unloading, perhaps for the first time in her life. What had triggered this? Thoughts of Gee? Bet had told Archie there was a gentle caring side to Gee that Archie had never seen. Could he possibly have seduced this miserable woman, after all?

She talked on. "But there was always a wall between us. I thought it was me, being an overprotective mother. It wasn't until Marco declared himself legally independent of me— at age seven— that I understood *they* were making the wall, *they* were keeping the secrets. It was still going on. I reported Sean's death as a swimming accident. I could sit on a police detection chair and not set off an alarm, because I believed it true." Her glance flicked up at him questioningly. That gaze no longer frightened him. Archie had finally recognized John Arrow's dead eyes, just as he had seen them in Tibet, in Richard. "Why didn't I understand that?" she mused.

"Perhaps you did." It would explain the lack of a single family picture. He still held those rough hands. "Perhaps."

"Is your son Marco still involved in Recover?"

"You said so."

"*I* said so?" he echoed, startled.

"Yes. Blue One."

Archie winced. "Still building the better soldier, at Recover expense. He's at the bottom of it all, Sarah, no question about it."

Sarah Chase gazed at their clasped hands. "Until Gennaro came, I—" She closed her eyes. She really did look miserable. "You're saying he knew who I was."

"I have no idea," he replied truthfully, "but I'm inclined to think he didn't strike up an association with you blindfolded."

"It was so nice," her voice sounded almost wistful, "to talk about ordinary things like antiques and— the weather— with someone who didn't know who I was— Jonas Marshall Chase's widow, the foolish faithful wife."

"Who, apparently, was no more foolish than the man who spoke with her about ordinary things."

She looked Archie in the eye. "You don't believe he seduced me."

He smiled. "Holding your hands makes it seem more likely," he admitted, "but not by a very long shot."

"What's wrong with him, then?"

"Nothing. It's what's right that matters. I can probably count the women he truly admires on one hand and have fingers left over. Even the most likely of those are youngsters he treats with gentlemanly chivalry. I've known him all my life and never seen him jump the fence."

She shook her head. "I've never known a man to act like that, especially not a gene-mod."

Quietly, seriously, Archie replied, "You've been hanging out with the wrong crowd, then. All gene-mods are not like the ones you've met. Even your brothers learned better than that."

She was startled, but before she could speak, there was the sound of a door opening. The butler was there. "A visitor, madam." He glanced at Archie.

Archie understood. "In a uniform, I imagine." The butler's face said yes. He turned back to Mrs. Chase. "EHD ECM. In about five minutes, it's all going to be taken out of your control."

Sarah Chase took a deep breath. A striking transformation occurred. In a twinkling, she became steady, clear-eyed, and purposeful. She released Archie's

hands, and stood. "No," she said, as if she were making a regretful decision, "no."
To Archie, she said, "I am going to change my clothes. Then I will go with you."

Archie had stood, too. "As you wish."

She told the butler, "Show the Commander and— what is your friend's
name, Mr. Chamberlain?"

"Lieutenant McAllen."

"— Lieutenant McAllen to this room, to wait with Mr. Chamberlain. I shall
join them shortly."

"Very well, madam."

Archie waited, alone, until the sitting-room door opened. Commander Sang
and several officers entered, Lt. McAllen with them. They were looking around
alertly. "She's changing her clothes," Archie told the commander. "She's going
with us."

-15-

Tunnels and Trolls

They waited in frigid silence, under the butler's watchful eye, until Mrs. Chase returned to the salon. She had changed to slacks, boots, and a dark turtleneck, and looked uncomfortably like the perfect female soldier. Apparently, too, she knew the Commander. "Dyvim Sang, grandson of Sang the Torturer. You are even less welcome here than any other officer of the Earth Combined Military."

"I am well aware of that, Mrs. Chase. Please feel free to contact your solicitor if you wish us removed."

The niceties had been exchanged, the opening guns fired. Mrs. Chase demanded, "Do you have authority to be here?"

"Not in the least," replied Sang cheerfully. "I only hope that, as a law-abiding citizen and property owner of the England Historic District, you will allow its military body to survey your property for missing materials. An itemized list is available if you or your solicitor wish to inspect it." As if unveiling another card, he continued, "If you prefer to lodge a complaint about my behavior with the commanding officer of the Earth Combined Military England Historic District, you are welcome to do so. Unfortunately, it will be some time before an investigation may take place, as we are rather short-handed. There will be four or five other panels of inquiry before mine."

"I see," said Mrs. Chase icily.

McAllen's shoulder barely touched Archie's. No doubt she was letting him know these developments were new to her, too. She hadn't known that Commander Sang was actually related to the Torturer, but he had been validated by his work and record. He had also been involved in the efforts of the Earth Combined Military of the EHD to do a little housecleaning in their own ranks. Of course it was logical that the current ECM should have some Recover sympathizers, and just as logical that someone like Sang had been assigned to ferret them out— with, Archie suspected, help from other sources like Commander Scott Marsden. They must have a nice file on Sarah Cordelia Chase and her objectionable family. *Did John Arrow manage to eliminate himself and Richard completely from that file?*, Archie wondered.

Archie cut in, deliberately keeping his tone neutral. "Sarah, you promised to help us. That's all I'm asking now."

"That's all I can give," she answered, sounding far more kindly to him than to Sang. She was not the miserable wreck he'd spoken to only a while ago.

He actually smiled at her. "You'll do fine. I recognize the signs."

There was something firm in her voice as she spoke, mainly to Archie. "It will end," she said. "It will end today." He recognized her words as a statement of fact, exactly as he would expect to hear from Gee himself. Someone was about to get blindsided; he only hoped it was Sang, not him.

The exterior of the nice house had changed drastically. The greenery had been plowed back and shoved out of the way by armored personnel carriers, parked anyplace they would fit. There were digging equipment, defense equipment, ordnance and supply vehicles, anything that could be construed as a military defensive weapon.

Sarah stopped cold, and stared at everything. "My home."

"Was it ever?" Archie asked quietly.

Sarah Chase did not reply. She stepped forward, toward the Land Rover. Something in her pocket clanked. He was certain the noise came from rifle cartridges. Archie noticed for the first time that she had picked up a rifle from the hallway. The accompanying officers moved toward other waiting personnel, except McAllen, who stayed at Archie's side.

Archie kept pace with Sarah as she moved. It felt strange to be with her like this, more like he was briefing Gee on a diplomatic situation. "For all this show of force, their hands are tied, Sarah. The U.N. now knows that Recover is comprised of the children of military, and has prohibited return fire."

Her gaze swept the Land Rover, the waiting soldiers, her lawn. "Sparing the children of heroes, no doubt." There was an unpleasant tone in her voice.

Lt. McAllen took in the exchange between them, but said nothing.

"Well, yes. I suspect they know one rebel from another, but that wouldn't matter in a firefight." Archie paused, wondering if he should press further. "It would be nice if this cell of resistance could be taken out with a minimum of bloodshed. And... if it didn't mean the end of the fight. Gee was sympathetic to the cause, as I expect you know. I imagine he was as disappointed as Elsa."

Sarah turned to look at him again, fully. He hoped she comprehended the magnitude of his message.

McAllen spoke for the first time, very quietly. "I'll settle for anything that will keep war from breaking out within twelve hours. Mr. Chamberlain and I are on the wrong side of the line when it does." Archie felt grateful to her for speaking.

Commander Sang appeared beside them, again looking at Sarah Chase. "Mrs. Chase. How much cooperation may we expect from you?"

"My full cooperation, Commander."

He blinked. That was obviously not the answer he expected. "Do you know ways and means into the Recover locations?"

"No. I met— the children— at locations previously agreed upon, or they came to my house."

He looked puzzled. "But if you had information to convey to them?"

"I never summoned them. They always found me. You must understand, Commander— they did not trust me. As it turns out, with good reason— but it limits my usefulness to you. Yes, they are using the mines and tunnels. The only mine entrances, three of them, are the entrances they must use, if they wish to drop a ship in. I don't know what supplies and materiel are stored there. I can show you the various paths and routes I used in hunting and hiking, on my own property in my own time. But that is almost all the help I can give."

He still appeared puzzled. "What support did you give them, Mrs. Chase? I was under the impression that money, material, and information changed hands."

"Most of my purchases were foodstuffs and ammunition. I was not aware they had other funding sources until Mr. Chamberlain told me, Commander. I have gone without so that they could survive." She looked around at the ill-kept fields and untidy roadways.

So did Commander Sang, who shook his head and winced. "Not knowing they could survive very nicely without you."

"It was a play on my sympathy that worked quite well," she agreed. "I was completely deceived."

Archie realized in surprise that she had thrown her lot in with them completely. He asked her, "Why take my word for it so easily?"

"What would it matter if you were lying?" Sarah Chase replied.

McAllen insisted that Archie drive them to some great oaks a considerable distance away from the ECM soldiers, ostensibly for food, but mainly for a chat. "I'm surprised someone didn't offer to accompany us," she muttered, taking a bite of something from a packet, "seeing as how we'll be POWs in half a day." She made a face at the packaged food, a far cry from cakes and tea.

"It hasn't happened yet." Archie sipped tepid water through a tube that reminded him too much of Tibet.

"You know, I like her. She's totally whipped, yet she's managing to keep her head up. That's the gene-mod thing, isn't it?"

"I think you're right," said Archie. "It doesn't hurt to meet some people who see you for what you are and still support you, though."

"In other words, you think she likes us, too."

Archie clenched his fists. "I wish I could think of something to do!"

To their surprise, they heard shots. McAllen left their bower of trees, looking sharply in one direction, then another. At last, she reported, "Crap. They sent in a team while we were over here dining, that's what they did. She pointed out mine entrances to them, and they decided on a frontal assault."

"I thought they weren't going to shoot kids!" Archie looked out, too. He could see that the personnel carriers were moved or absent.

"They probably didn't." McAllen shook her head. "They went in with riot gear, I'll bet." A ship with red cross/red crescent markings flew directly over their heads and landed in a field somewhere beyond the clump of trees. McAllen watched it until it dropped out of sight. "They've got casualties, then, thanks to their screwing around. The best they're going to get out of this is wounded."

"Blue 1 won't be merciful to anyone, not even his mother," Archie muttered worriedly. "As far as he's concerned, she just became a traitor. I wonder if she feels the same way about him."

McAllen jumped as Archie started to walk away from her. "Where are you going?"

"To think. I won't go far." He climbed the next little hillock.

In one direction, near the house, he could see very little action. Most of the personnel carriers and military equipment had moved on. He could see their progress in another direction— the only large, open expanse for miles. The rest of the local landscape was hilly; this was so flat it was obviously man-made. For ages, miners had scraped away this soil, and dug tunnels like ants; then, with the failure of the mines, it had all grown over green. Some bare areas still protruded. Archie remembered the dark little holes and molehills he had seen from the top of the cliff. He looked beyond his current vista, at the cliff he'd once mounted with McAllen, and calculated distances.

"Bet, are you there?"

"I'm here. News says you-all just got casualties out there, but that's it. What happened, army try to go in the front door?"

"I think so. They sent McAllen and me off to supper, and made tracks in the meantime."

"And got their behinds kicked," said Bet.

"Yes." He bit his lip. "We're screwed, Bet. I don't have any ideas left. I don't know what to do next."

"You sound pretty desperate, Archie."

"I am."

"Desperate enough to try something that probably won't work?"

"What are you talking about?" He felt a cold stone in his stomach, and his breathing changed.

"I've got one possibility that requires a large amount of desperation. If you've still got any other options, this is not the one to go for."

Archie was silent. He did not know what to say to her.

"Go talk with the EHD Army and see how bad it is."

"Bet, I can't just walk in and ask for— "

"That's an order, Archie. Before we try something as damn-fool as my last option, I have to know there's no alternative. Now, move."

He had never heard Bet cuss or command.

He walked back to McAllen.

"Lieut— " he cleared his throat. "Lieutenant. Let's go see how bad the damage is. Quickly."

She looked puzzled, but merely walked back with him to the Land Rover and jump-started it once again.

He didn't have to ask if there were casualties as they pulled up to the new base of operations. The medics were plainly busy. Worse yet, there were body bags.

"What the hell happened?" McAllen asked a fellow lieutenant, loud enough for Commander Sang to hear without swearing at him directly.

Sang turned to reply, jaw tight. "We made one last attempt to subdue youthful rebels, Lieutenant. I have casualties to show we attempted it in good faith. Now we know exactly how well-guarded their compound is, and how secure. I have three dead, seventeen wounded, and miscellaneous destroyed equipment. To the best of our knowledge, the rebels sustained no casualties whatever."

"So there's no chance of taking them head-on, that's what you're saying?" McAllen summarized for Archie's benefit.

Sang shook his head. "Nor from any other direction. Except for the air shafts, which they guard, they are completely secure."

"And knocking out the air shafts wouldn't get you inside and wouldn't force them out, because they've got an entire space-station in there. Life support systems and guns big enough to blast their way out once they get tired of being confined." She frowned in thought. "How about once they're spaceside?"

Again, Sang shook his head. "The diplomatic situation. They are minors. It is against U.N. orders to shoot them down, although they suffer no similar compunction. If ships leave here for outer space, neither Earth Combined Military nor Federal Law Enforcement Agency will bear the onus of shooting children. If they remain in sub-atmospheric flight, the situation becomes even touchier. There are at least eight different governmental bodies with sub-atmospheric jurisdiction, depending on where a plane or ship goes." He glanced at figure in the middle distance— Sarah Chase. "But they have no need to go anywhere, if they wish not. They are safe, secure, and well-supplied here."

"In other words, we're stuck," said Archie.

McAllen agreed. "We're stuck."

Archie walked off again, ostensibly to consult with himself. He climbed back to the little hillock from which he'd previously conversed with Bet. "They can't get them, Bet. The rebels are secure."

Bet sounded frustrated. "I wish I was there," she said. "This is life-threatening for you and him. But, Archie, I need to know if you're in on this. Once I give you this information and you commit yourself, there's no turning back."

He took a moment to give his answer. Truthfully, though, it was obvious. He hadn't gone so far— with the children at Mars-Isidis, with the riddle, with Arrow and all the medical research, with Gee through the Himalayas, with Elsa through all her trials— to bail out now. "You know the answer, girl. Tell me what you want me to do."

"Listen, Archie," Bet's voice said. "I wouldn't even suggest this to anyone else to try. They've taken Gee's badge, too. But as far as Gamemaster Inc. is concerned, there's still one template down there as a screen for VR modification. Gennaro himself."

Archie felt his mouth go dry. "You can't be serious. Modify— morph— a live human being?"

"You know why examining Gennaro's DNA won't get them far?" Bet asked.

"I've suspected an answer or two." His main suspicion was that whatever made the Gamemasters unique wasn't located in their DNA; that was a decoy.

"Max, tamp this transmission down as secure as you can make it," Bet directed. Was it Archie's imagination, or did the sound quality improve? "This is between you and me, and thank God you're there and not me. You were talking about it one evening. Remember saying, 'The ocean is the motion'?"

Archie's research had been almost completely in animal-based cells, Bet's in plant-based cells. The joke had been, she could move walls, cell walls; his human cells were animal-based, full of motion that came from their evolution from ocean life. The ocean was the motion. Those were the two factors that separated plant cells from animals. But the main contributor to the difference in animal cells was that they contained mitochondria, almost cells within cells, still a cellular mystery being explored. The mitochondrial controversy had gone on for centuries— were they actually sub-microscopic life that had adapted themselves to live inside animal cells?

"Gennaro's generation is the first to have artificial mitochondria— almost completely a Gamemaster Inc. project, created by Alpha Genetic to act like the real thing," Bet told him. "So— you've got a VR screen inside every cell of his body. God, I hate tellin' you that."

"That can't be so. On such a level— that's just a pipe dream," he croaked.

"Tell it to Alpha Genetic. You have to be within a hundred meters to use it," her small voice continued. "I don't know if you can sidle in that close. I might be able to, but I'm sneakier'n you are. And I suspect it's immensely painful to him. The mitochondria create a VR grid for the transformation, and then...light him up. The thing is, even if I could get to you, and sneak in close enough for reliable VR transmission, I'm a plant hacker. Not an animal hacker. Technically, you aren't either, but you've got more experience in medical research than I do. Your hacks, no matter what you do to him, will be excruciatingly painful, and all guesswork."

"But if it's that or losing him..." Archie could barely speak.

"My thoughts exactly. It's a desperate measure. I've just turned over experimental control to you for six hours. There's yourself, and Max, and his organic material. Bear in mind, it's not virtual, it's real. Anything you do has to come out the same weight and volume. You can't turn him into a mouse, or something."

"Meaning I could kill him myself."

"Archie," Bet Berensen said, "The reason he chose me for this job was because I could see pain and death as an option. I can grit my teeth and make some ugly choices, because I've shown that I can. This don't mean it's fun, believe me. And I wouldn't even tell anyone else. All I'm sayin' is, the option's there if you can use it."

"Let me think. Maybe I can. Thanks, Bet."

Desperately he turned ideas over in his mind. Then he consulted with Max, with Bet listening in to double-check his work, and put three or four options in place, at a rate calculated to give any Gamemaster brain-fever. Then he bade goodbye to Max and Bet.

Sarah Chase had now joined the military group. Lt. McAllen must have seen how pale he was, because she demanded at once, "What's wrong?"

"Nothing's wrong. The AA— acting administrator— suggested something that might get him out alive."

"Acting administrator?" McAllen demanded.

"They took Gee's badge. His badge, when you remove it, is immediately deactivated. The industry safeguards for the entire company have kicked in. The Acting Administrator has assumed command of Gamemaster Inc. until either Gennaro reactivates his badge or until we report finding his body."

"God." It was Sarah Chase speaking, looking just as pale as Archie.

"But you're saying the company's safe," McAllen said. The Commander, too, looked alert.

"The company," Archie told them, "is always safe. It is provided for. No ransom to kidnappers is policy. So, if we dick around here and they kill him, all that happens is the arrangements are made for another Gamemaster to take his place. It will not be Gennaro. My best friend will be dead. The new Gamemaster will be a stranger, who won't give a damn about John Arrow and his riddles, or my friendship with his predecessor, or what we've gone through to get this far. He will simply install himself in the office, make a few cosmetic changes to the company, and drop a Gamemaster Inc. Security team in here to clean out this mess."

"It won't be Gennaro," Sarah repeated dully.

He turned to her. "It can't be Gennaro. There's only one Gennaro. He's unlike anything before or since. He's the only one of them who's ever acted like a goddamn human being— and this is the thanks he gets!" Archie's voice broke. He turned away from her, and took a deep breath. When he spoke, it was to the soldiers. "The AA gave me an idea how to rescue him, if you're game. I'm scared shitless that it might not work. But if I could physically sneak somehow within a couple hundred meters of where they're holding him, I might— and I stress *might*— have the ability to create the illusion that he's vanished from his cell. A prisoner escape ought to be distraction enough from within to let you attack efficiently from without."

"Without his badge?" McAllen asked alertly. "Doesn't everyone know it takes Max, a Gamemaster, and a badge to create the whole show?"

"Except for him," Archie replied. He took a deep breath. "And— without the badge— if it works— it's still life-threatening to him."

Lt. McAllen looked at the Commander. "The air shafts?"

The Commander nodded. "They're guarding the crucial ones."

"I'm not shy about taking out one or two kids to get him back." McAllen slipped out her pistol and took the safety off. "You can't pick out individuals underground, but you could get us infrared for area population density, can't you?"

"That I can do," the Commander said. "But killing any Recover operative is directly against standing orders from the U.N."

"Good thing you've got me here, then," said McAllen. "I've busted so many rules in the past week, I'm already dead. One more won't matter."

The Commander grinned. "I'll manage that you accidentally get an opportunity to see all sorts of things you're not supposed to see, then. However, my hands are still tied. I can't give you any backup."

Snick went a rifle bolt.

Sarah Chase was not smiling. "I am not bound by ECM regulations."

"Can you shoot?" McAllen asked her.

"Sharpshooter first class, Sandhurst," Sarah replied in a cold voice.

Lt. McAllen nodded at her, satisfied, and turned back to Sang. "All right, Commander, here's what I want you to leave around accidentally for me to steal. I want a flak jacket and decent helmet for Archie and for me. I need climbing ropes, hooks, and clips. You can pick those out, Archie, you know what we need."

"I can. Thank God, something to do." Archie went off with one of the soldiers and started selecting ropes, clips, and climbing gear. Another soldier gave him a stout pair of boots that fit perfectly. When he came back with the equipment, he found McAllen and the Commander bent over the charts. Lt. McAllen nodded approval.

"We've found the most likely air shafts, the ones that used to lead to corridors near vaults in the old days," she told him. "They're probably using the vaults as prison cells. I know I would. By the infrared density, sheer number of bodies, it looks like those shafts are being best guarded. So we won't have long to drop and start trouble. It'll start the minute they hear a shot or a sentry doesn't report. I was thinking," she added, in a different tone, "Even if you can't do what you want to do, we can probably make trouble with your VR capabilities. They've stolen enough military equipment, and Gamemaster Inc. stuff, for you to put on a nice show if you got close enough to it with your badge."

"Making their tools come to life, and so on," Archie nodded. "I was thinking that as well."

The Commander looked serious. "We'll be in there as fast as we can, with stunners, gas and billies, if you create the distraction," he said to McAllen and Archie, "anything to keep them from rallying, getting inside their ships, and closing the hatches. But I want you to understand your danger. All they have to do is spot your ropes from the top, or locate which shaft you're in, and they will shoot you like fish in a barrel."

"You are telling me things I'd rather not hear," said Archie, "and as a mere civilian, I request that you stop it right now."

Both McAllen and the Commander grinned, that tense pre-action expression so common to soldiers.

McAllen had two thick white disks. She attached one to her belt, and then clipped one to Archie's. "Anti-grav cushions. They're minimum strength. All they'll do is make our landing lighter if we fall, so we'll only have broken bones instead of being killed." She eyed him. "If you can bring yourself to trust new ECM technology."

"I'll try," said Archie in a humble voice, which brought back her smile.

"Sarah Chase went off hunting for a location, like a good sniper," the Commander said. "Truthfully, she worries me more than they do."

McAllen nodded. "I know. Mr. Chamberlain and I will be at her mercy. I don't like it, either. I can't believe that any mother can give up on her kid like that. She might still finish us off to save Marco."

"I don't think so," Archie contradicted. "I was afraid they'd burnt out her core until there was nothing left inside, but no. I'm sorry I got a little emotional earlier, but— on the other hand— I think I moved Sarah Chase, and I think we're going to need her. She met Gee, and liked him."

Sheila stared at him. "That was a show? You rat! I was feeling sorry for you!"

"I didn't say anything I didn't mean. I'm a lousy liar and always have been. But I will admit I poured it on just a bit, to see if there was anything left of Sarah Chase. There is."

"Does it matter?" Lt. McAllen asked incredulously.

"It will," Archie promised.

Lt. McAllen led the way stealthily through the scrubby undergrowth, up a low hillside. Archie moved carefully behind her. He was not a soldier. He didn't want to be a liability. He stopped when she held up her hand, and eased himself to the ground.

She slid back to lie beside him. Her lips touched his ear. "Two sentries ahead. Wait. Come fast when you hear shots." He nodded. She crept forward carefully.

He heard two quick shots, got up, and ran forward through the brush. He halted immediately when he saw a great hole in the ground in front of him. He was in a clearing, on a rocky expanse with many of these circular drilled holes in it, like wells.

McAllen held her pistol and made a face. There were two dead youths on the ground, a boy and a girl. She looked up suddenly as someone appeared on the profile of the nearest ridge, and lifted her pistol. But, before she could fire, a shot from elsewhere hit the newcomer and knocked him back over the ridge. Sarah Chase was indeed in position.

"Quick," said McAllen urgently. She counted holes, recalling something she had memorized, and pointed to one. "Come on. We've got no time at all."

Feverishly, Archie pounded in mountaineering clamps, secured the ropes, and slid into the shaft. McAllen was right with him. The ropes ran together and their bodies bumped as they rappelled carefully and silently as possible.

Lt. McAllen's watch glowed as she checked the time while she descended. Again, she spoke into Archie's ear. "We don't have time. We've got to drop." She clamped her arms around his body.

Archie gasped as the extra weight made him lose his grip. Instinctively he let go the rope, rather than burn his gloves and hands to cinders. It was a terrifying sensation, dropping at that uncontrolled speed in the well.

She said, "I'm letting go. Grab hold."

He felt her release him. He grabbed his rope again, and stopped with a jerk. "If we get out of here alive, I'm going to kill you," he gasped.

"*If* we do. Now. Can you do it?"

They could hear voices below them now.

"Max," he whispered, "are we within a hundred meters of the Gamemaster?"

"You are two hundred thirty seven meters from the Gamemaster," Max replied.

"Oh, damn," Archie breathed in dread, "Sheila, do it to me again."

She grabbed him. They dropped. "I'm letting go."

He grabbed. "Max, distance."

"One hundred two meters."

"Time," said McAllen. They heard a change in the noises down below, as if something from somewhere else might be getting their attention. The attack at the front had begun. If they didn't move soon, Sang's forces would be beaten back again.

Archie slid down the last two meters, took a breath, and prayed. If only he and Max had got this right. "Max, initiate my quilt sequence."

Somewhere below them came a cry of agony. It was a man's cry, cut off suddenly. A few moments passed. They waited.

They heard voices: exclamations, shouts, a yell.

Then they heard a klaxon. "Escaped prisoner." McAllen's lips touched his ear. "It worked. C'mon, do magic."

"Max, I need any tools you can reach below us to appear to be crawling away like animals. I need weapons in your reach to appear to have safety locks that won't come off. I need vehicles to turn into dinosaurs of similar appearance."

A shot rang out above them. "We gotta go," McAllen said, grabbing him again. Again they went into free-fall. Their heavy boots hit a metal grid at last, smashing it as they broke through. Archie hit the floor and nearly lost consciousness.

But Lt. McAllen came up shooting. After three shots, she barked, "Drop 'em! Against the wall, NOW!"

When he looked up, he saw what looked like seven or eight children in flak jackets, placing their hands against the wall. Two more lay on the cavern floor.

"McAllen, I've got to find him fast," Archie gasped. He could see a spanner crawling along the floor. "Max, talk to me. Where's Gee?" The spanner stood up and pointed. Archie staggered to his feet and ran. Behind him, he could hear the sounds of McAllen's voice, and the creaking of metal. He guessed that she was dumping the weapons in a great metal box he'd seen.

This section was empty. The door to a room was open. Sheila caught up with him at the door.

The room was a shambles. The bed had been tipped over, the quilts and blankets kicked to the floor. There were burn marks around the air shaft, as if they had shot up it in the hopes their escapee had somehow fit his way up the tiny air tube.

She stared as Archie righted the bed and feverishly began putting it back together. "This is a hell of a time for morning duty!"

"Oh, shut up and help me fix it up," Archie sobbed. After he had the last sheet in place, he picked up a bundle of quilts from the floor. Sheila helped him lift it to the bed, her eyes wide with surprise at the heaviness of them. She gaped when she realized that there were scraps of cloth littered in it. "Get 'em out, get all the cloth scraps and dirt out," Archie babbled, as he did so himself. "Got to get 'em out of all the folds..." Like him, she brushed, picked, scraped, until the bundle of quilts was free of all foreign material. "Oh, please God, please. Max. This is it. Reformat to original."

Lt. McAllen stared at the bundle of quilts metamorphosed— into a naked, dark-featured man crying in agony.

Archie hurriedly wrapped him in the sheets. McAllen ran back to the doorway, in case of unwanted visitors.

"Archie," he gasped.

"Oh, thank God." Archie nearly wept. "I was so scared."

"Oh, God. Pain. Never felt— any like— this. Thrown about— " he gasped. "Dust and dirt in the reformat— ." He cried out.

"Max. Tell the AA that Gamemaster is alive. The meta-material transformation worked. Tell Commander Sang that Gamemaster is alive and we need a medical team as soon as he can get one to us. Tell the Gamemaster Inc. Medical Division we need Alpha Genetic here fast."

"Acknowledged, Archie."

Lt. McAllen fired a shot down the corridor. There was return fire. She ducked inside, dropped, shot again. He saw blasts of light, heard deafening explosions, saw McAllen shooting grimly from her prone position in the doorway. Archie huddled over Gee desperately. At last, the shots stopped.

Then they heard yells. McAllen kept her pistol in position until she heard words more clearly. "ECM came down the air shaft, too. They've got 'em from both sides."

Just then, her radio kicked in. "Lieutenant McAllen. We're in the front door. We're sending medevac for the Gamemaster."

"Home in on my signal," the Lieutenant directed. "He's hurt badly. You should be hearing from Gamemaster Inc. in a few minutes. Mr. Chamberlain called for the specialists."

"Can we do something about the goddamn dinosaurs?" McAllen's radio interrupted.

Archie spoke up. "End the dinosaurs and moving tools distractions, Max."

"Simulations ended, Archie."

Despite his uncontrollable spasms, Archie felt Gee laugh. "Dinosaurs?"

"Best I could do on short notice." Archie held him firmly in his arms, guarding him against his own throes of pain, with McAllen still at the door. Archie could well imagine the dust and debris of this filthy underground room, trapped inside Gennaro's cells, stinging every nerve in white-hot agony. "Breathe," urged Archie. "Control your breathing."

Gee nodded briefly, and closed his eyes. Archie felt his body relax as he concentrated on the meditations he had learned from the Abbot.

After another eternity, McAllen moved to one side of the doorway. Two medics maneuvered a floating gurney inside. They slid the gurney expertly to the side of the cot.

"No," said Gee, in a different voice now. "Don't touch me. I've got massive nerve damage. I'll slide myself over." He sat up, and slid from the cot to the gurney without help. He lay still. They slipped one light sheet up to his waist.

Archie stayed with them on the longest trip of his life, out of that mine, up innumerable shafts and lifts. The pace was slow, almost unendurable. They moved gently, so as not to bump him. But around the next pitch-black corner would be only another shaft, or a rough-hewn lift. Every bump made him cry out in pain. Lt. McAllen also stayed with them every inch of the way. She still had not sheathed her pistol. Archie was glad of that.

An ambulance waited immediately outside the mine entrance. Archie didn't pay attention to specifics, but realized that the medics were treating Gee like a third-degree burn victim, on his instructions. He lay almost naked in the watery sunlight as they labored over him, giving anaesthetic and rehydration medicines.

Sarah Chase stood nearby, watching. Archie got out of the way of the medics and went over to her. "Thank you for your help. I hope we got to him in time."

"Will he be all right?" Her eyes never left the view of Gee and the medics.

"Truthfully, I don't know. My trick may have saved his life at the cost of doing physical damage to his nervous system. When Gamemaster Inc. Medical and Alpha Genetic get here, they'll do a full brain scan— to see if he's still capable of being the Gamemaster."

"I don't understand." Like Archie, Sarah could hear his voice from here, answering the medics' questions. "He sounds like he'll be fine, in time."

"He's a very finely-tuned instrument, Sarah. He can't snap back, the way we scratch-feds can. He hasn't got any undocumented emergency reserves. He's a fifth-generation gene-mod. He can still have brain damage enough to prevent him from functioning properly. He was created to do one and only one thing with his life— be the Gamemaster."

"And if he can't?" Still, her gaze never left the scene before her.

"It's not even an issue. He'll die."

An engine suddenly thrummed overhead. A white space vehicle appeared above them. It settled to the ground near the ECM vehicles. On its side, in black letters, read the words GAMEMASTER INC. ALPHA GENETIC TOP PRIORITY. It was a fact that whenever Alpha Genetic was called, it was top priority, so why not say so permanently? Archie was surprised to see his own physician, Dr. Barnett, climb out of the hatch first, and come over to him.

"Hello, Archie, how are you?" the elderly doctor greeted him.

"Lots better than he is." Archie indicated Gee.

"I was briefed on the way," said Dr. Barnett, "but I want to look at both of you. Dr. Andre and the Alpha Genetic team were planning to scout for hospital facilities, but there's none nearby."

Sarah Chase spoke. "There's Bowman House. My home. The mansion five miles southeast of here. Would it do?"

"Admirably. The ship is compact and self-contained, but it helps to be able to spread things out. Thank you. I'll tell Andre." The doctor went back to the ship.

"Thank you," Archie said to Sarah Chase.

"It wouldn't have been worth it." Sarah looked at him as if she were awake for the first time. "For the price our children would have had to pay. It wouldn't have been worth it."

"I often wonder if it is," Archie replied frankly. "Then, at other times, I see Gee in action, and think, there, that's genetic engineering when it's done right. But when it's done right, not jumble-sale genetics."

"Jumble-sale genetics," Sarah repeated. For the first time, he saw her lips tremble in something that almost might have been a smile. "That may be the story of my life."

"Your life has hardly started," said Archie. "Please think about that. All you've got right now are some clear ideas of the ways you don't want to live. Gee and I don't think much alike, but I know I'm speaking for him when I say if you're even one-tenth as fine as your brothers, you have the ability to make an incredible change for good in the world." He saw Dr. Barnett returning to him.

"I've got to go. Barnett won't be happy until he makes sure I'm sound. I'll see you at the house."

"I'll go with you," she volunteered. It surprised him.

Barnett, Sarah, and Archie moved to either side of Gee's gurney as the medics moved him over to the ship. Archie kept pace at a position near Gee's left shoulder. "How's the pain?" Archie asked him.

"More bearable now. Thanks for sticking with me."

"Thank me?" Archie shook his head to make a joke of it. "Don't thank me. You might set a precedent you can't keep."

"I've been damaged, Archie." For a moment, Archie saw a shadow behind his eyes. "Cryo is on standby."

Archie felt a chill, but merely replied, "You don't know to what limit you're damaged. It could be recoverable— like appendicitis in Tibet."

He smiled, and admitted, "It may."

"Then don't quit on me. I'll tell Dad."

"All right. I won't."

He neither spoke nor looked at Sarah Chase, walking on the other side behind Dr. Barnett and an attendant. It might have been because he didn't, or couldn't, see her in his current condition. Nor did she bring herself to his attention. No matter what happened next, it would be rough on Sarah Chase. But Archie wondered what was foremost in her mind, this man who might as well have stepped out of a storybook, just to manipulate her, or her missing son, well-known to her, who had treated her in the same fashion.

They loaded the gurney aboard the ship. Gee was strapped into the central analysis chamber. Dr. Andre clamped electrodes to the base of his neck. There was no one who scared Archie more than the demonic-looking French geneticist, even though Archie knew he was probably the best scientist on earth. Sarah's eyes widened when she saw Andre run tubes to an already-existing, nearly invisible shunt in Gee's body. More than anything, that seemed to make it plain to her that the Gamemaster spent so much time being fine-tuned that the attachments were permanent and ever-ready.

Archie hated this. Instinctively, he turned away, and found himself looking instead at Dr. Barnett. Barnett smiled. "Come sit up in the cockpit with me. Ask the lady to join us."

"Oh." Archie realized he was being asked for an introduction. "Mrs. Sarah Chase, Dr. Lionel Barnett. She's an Arrow, Doc, John's sister."

"This is indeed an honor," said the gentle old physician, with a smile. He clasped her hand kindly. "Now, come up front." He opened the hatch to the cockpit, and followed them through.

Archie stared at the pilot. "Harry?"

Harry turned long enough to nod, then got to the business of getting them up and flying. "Willard owed me a favor, so I wangled this job. It was right."

"Harry," said Archie, touched, "if the Samurai were still around, you'd be one."

Harry did not look away from his controls. "The code of honor is still there. The Chief's one in a million, Mr. Chamberlain. But I don't have to tell you that."

"You don't," said Archie. He sat down between Sarah Chase and Dr. Barnett, and closed his eyes.

"Archie." Sarah's voice was soft in his ear. He felt her hand on his cheek. He forced his eyes open. "Archie. We're here."

"Sorry. Dozed off." To his consternation, he realized he was resting his head against Sarah's shoulder, and hauled himself vertical. "Oops. Taking liberties. Apologies."

Sarah Chase smiled at him, as friend to friend. "It's all right, Archie. Dr. Barnett and I were trying not to wake you. He was telling me about your last few days."

"There's nothing wrong with you that twelve hours of unbroken sleep won't cure," Dr. Barnett told him cheerfully, putting away his kit. Obviously, he had run his diagnostics on the sleeping Archie. They stood, and passed back through the hatchway.

The first thing Archie saw was Gee, stiff and unconscious. "Oh, God," he choked. But then, he saw Dr. Andre's smile, and his hopes rose.

Andre confirmed the hope. "Brain fluid is almost completely clear, and the cerebral cortex and spinal fluid are clearing up rapidly."

"And everything else is icing." Archie's knees nearly buckled.

Dr. Andre nodded. "The exchange fluids are taking out the coal dust and other wastes. Then natural healing processes can handle everything else. It is good you changed him back as fast as you did. You had no idea they would turn him practically inside out in their search for him. The coal dust is the worst offender. I'm going to do a complete fluid exchange when we set up inside. We will look at the recordings of what you did to turn him into an inanimate object later, because obviously, you did it right."

Sarah Chase stepped forward to look at the inert body on the table. "He looks so cold." Her voice was gentle, thoughtful.

Dr. Andre nodded. "I've shut the body down almost completely while the repair equipment works on the nervous system." He spoke as if Gamemaster were part of the machinery, which was probably the reason Archie didn't care for him. "But it won't last more than an hour. Then I'll bring him back up and let him eat and drink."

There was a bustle getting people and things off the ship and organized. Sarah directed her startled household staff to clear certain bedrooms, start meals, help the Gamemaster Inc. personnel with power cables, and so on. She directed a housemaid to show Archie to a guest room. The little maid escorted Archie upstairs, to a warm room with a ready-made bed. Archie thanked her, shut the door, slipped off his boots— and that was all he remembered.

He woke in the dark, remembered where he was, and felt around for a bedside lamp. In its dim light, he found his boots again, and struggled to his feet. The feeling took him back in time, as if he were once again at Oxford or Mars-Isidis and it was his turn for night duty.

He straightened out the clothes he fell asleep in, and left the room.

He stopped in the corridor of the tasteful, colorless English mansion, and listened. He homed in on a dull buzz and followed it down a corridor, across a landing, and up another few steps.

Two ECM soldiers stood in the dim corridor, on guard. Apparently, this wing was blocked off. As one guard made eye contact with him, Archie asked, "What time's it?"

"0230, sir."

It had been one hell of a day, that was certain. "Am I allowed in?"

"I'll check, sir." He spoke to his lapel radio. "Lieutenant, Mr. Chamberlain's here." Pause. "Go on in, sir, Second door on the right."

"Thanks." He found the door and opened it. Bright lights, a loud bass hum, and an antiseptic smell nearly knocked him backward. He stepped inside and closed the door behind him. Sheets draped over much of the furniture, and the bed had been moved to the center of the room. The laboratory-like effect was staggering, like something from an old monster film.

"Christ," said Archie, rubbing his eyes.

McAllen stood up from one of the sheet-covered chairs. She did not seem surprised to see him here at two in the morning. Like him, her gaze turned to the white bed.

The sheets were wrapped up to his chest now, but he was wide awake and looking straight at Archie. Archie came over and sat on the edge of the bed, where there was already an indentation. Sheila McAllen hadn't sat there; she was in charge, and kept an eye on the door. Archie suspected it was Sarah, looking down at the sleeping man and trying to organize her remaining thoughts. McAllen returned to her corner. Gee's voice was weak, but otherwise normal. "We're square now, aren't we?"

"Very much so," Archie smiled, speaking in a voice as low as his. "We don't owe each other anything now. But this is doing it the hard way, Gee."

Gee returned the smile. Then it faded. "You saw the sign nailed to the wall?"

"Yes, I did."

"We've finished the riddle." He could hear palpable disappointment in Gee's voice. "The brass mouse ended with a muffled squeak."

"No." Archie shook his head. "It hasn't ended. Will you take my word on this?" At Gee's surprised look, he continued, "The sign had the words The Brass Mouse in it, but it's only a clue. We're on the right road, but we're not there yet."

"How do you know?"

"I know. When you've got the final answer, you'll know, too."

"All right." His energy seemed to fade with the words. He closed his eyes. "Hate this lethargic feeling. Damn Andre and all his magic. At least Sarah Chase has had a chance to sit here and see how bad it can be, when the experiment *does* work properly. That's one consolation from this."

"Oh?" Archie queried. Oddly enough, he felt his heart lighten. "How do you know she wasn't just sitting here because you're nice to look at, and you have been treating her decently?"

"And you can't figure out why I didn't want you here?" Gee returned bitterly, opening his eyes. "It can't be news to you that no gene-mod is decent. They don't have to be. They do anything they want, no matter how callous or depraved, simply because they can."

"You're decent," Archie contradicted mildly. Gee stared at him. "In fact, you're one of the most decent men I know."

"You moron," Gee said, sounding touched nonetheless, "get out of here."

"I shall." Archie stood up. "You should get some sleep. Tomorrow— this morning— is going to be a rough day. We need you at your ugliest and most controversial."

"That's what I do best. Now go!" Gee rolled over onto his side, looking much more human with the movement.

Archie left. He wanted Bet here, to dance with.

Oh, it was a lovely dream, it must have been, with Sheila McAllen in it, saying his name. "Archie. Archie." Then he realized that someone was indeed saying his name. Not only that, it was Sheila McAllen.

He stared up into her face. The room was full of sunshine. "What time's it?"

"0845. The whole shootin' match is assembling in Mrs. Chase's dining room in fifteen minutes. The Gamemaster told me not to come back without you."

Archie groaned, and sat up. "How do I look?"

"Like you slept in your clothes and haven't had a shave for two days." She looked as rough as he did. "I've been with Sarah Chase the rest of the night, in the recovery room."

"Did either of you get any sleep?" He saw a hairbrush on the night stand, and used it.

"We took turns." McAllen gave him an odd smile. "Sarah sat on the edge of the bed whenever she was awake. I had to convince her I'd keep an eye out while she napped. All she did was stare at him as he slept."

"I imagine she's feeling as wrecked as he is."

"Maybe. Now he's awake, and uglier than hell. He claims he's still too sick to move much. Then a warrant officer showed up for me, from West Meg HQ. He ordered one of his security people to escort him off the property. I am in *so* much trouble."

Archie patted her hand. "Relax, girl. Apparently you've got the meanest man on Earth feeling he owes you a favor, which is not bad."

"I think I know why he never fazes you. You're English and you're used to royalty."

"What an atrocious thought. Let's go see how bad this shindy will be."

-16-

The Reformat

There was no question that Bowman house had been commandeered. ECM soldiers stood in every corridor, coming smartly to attention when Lt. McAllen went past. "So you're a hero," Archie murmured.

"Great documentation for my court martial." McAllen was not impressed. "I was out here for a twenty-four hour job and it's been seventy-two, with no report to base. So I'm AWOL and Captain Jahnik will have me for lunch."

"I imagine someone has reported back by now."

"Reported. Uh-huh. Wait till you see Commander Sang," she predicted, opening a downstairs door.

This room was full of people, mainly in ECM uniforms. It might have been a brightly-lit, sunny breakfast room at other times, possibly the dining room, judging by its size. Sitting midway down one side of the table was the Gamemaster, dressed in borrowed clothes. He merely glanced at the newcomers. His dark eyes, unusually ringed with illness and exhaustion, focused again on soldiers on the opposite side of the elegant pale-blue table. Archie wondered if Sarah liked pale blue and white, or if the house had come furnished that way. Archie and McAllen stopped at the nearest end of the table and remained standing.

Sarah herself sat further down the table. She glared at Sang. Her dark, well-spaced eyes were very good for glaring. Soldiers standing at either side of her chair made it very clear that she was under arrest. Directly opposite the Gamemaster sat Commander Sang, and, as Lt. McAllen had observed, Archie hadn't seen him yet. He wouldn't have recognized him without her warning, because he was obviously raging. The Gamemaster, as usual, was unperturbed.

"Thank you, Mrs. Chase," Gee was saying, "but I do not think a criminal action will be necessary, so you shouldn't need your solicitor. Nor should the Commander speak of a warrant officer, nor should I mention Lucretia Danvers." That alone told Archie how serious matters were. The greatly-renowned Lucretia Danvers was Gamemaster Inc. Legal Division's equivalent of a doomsday weapon.

It was quite clear that nothing short of a doomsday weapon would distract Commander Sang now. He exclaimed furiously, "By all means, get her, and we'll take this to trial, Gamemaster! Mrs. Chase is an accomplice in treasonous activities. The extent of her complicity is yet to be discovered, but by now, with the mines thrown open to the CID, MI6, and the EHD ECM, and the evidence within them— "

"I do not care if you throw the entire alphabet at me," Gamemaster said tiredly. He lifted a pile of report cartridges with one hand. "What your warrant officer is going to discover, in time, is that you do not have a case. You cannot possibly take Mrs. Chase to trial on these charges and find evidence to back them up. The witnesses are dead."

Commander Sang leaned forward. "What I will find," he grated, "is evidence that the shots that killed Marco Chase and his companions came from the rifle I have impounded." He turned his glare to Mrs. Chase. "Your rifle, madam. The World Court will see that you would sacrifice your own son to promote treason." Again, the glare at Gee. "A child-murderer and a seducer. The Court will see that she is not the only one who has overstepped the bounds of legality or propriety here." His searing rage was palpable. Yes, Sang had indeed been broadsided, as Archie had expected. Archie could have warned him, and been nicely thanked and ignored for his trouble.

"Names, names," said Gee, far too mildly. He was at his most dangerous when he sounded mild. "I sneaked out here to trail space ships and bitched up your surveillance game, is that it?" Commander Sang was silent; but if glares could fry flesh, the Gamemaster would already be Well Done. "You have arrested twelve members of Recover, and recovered eight bodies, and ECM Dependent Services are already notifying their parents and pressing charges against the living. You have rousted one of the Recover field stations entirely, and this is completely to your credit. It is certainly not my fault that another Recover field station retaliated against ECM West Africa only this morning. Nor is it my fault that you cannot put detainees from this England Historic District operation through the third degree to see what information you can squeeze out of them."

What on earth?, Archie wondered. Then he thought: The questioning by the United Nations would be torture for these children. Gene-mods are bred to understand and resist torture. Mrs. Chase is a gene-mod. The children were not. So: Being a gene-mod and a crack shot, she prevented the need for them to undergo torture by utilizing the method she knew best.

"Call it preventive detention," the Gamemaster said, "call it intensive questioning, debriefing, anything you wish. It would occur with or without the presence of a lawyer, night and day. It would be what they used to call it in the old days, 'the old Syria game,' where so-called sophisticated governments step out and turn responsibility over to governments still promoting torture. Whatever you call it, it would be bullying, gut-wrenching torture of children."

"I am not a torturer." Commander Sang's mouth was tight. "Nor does the United Nations sanction child abuse."

"Dyvim Sang," said the Gamemaster, still mildly, "perhaps you personally are not, but I know better. I know your family and I know what your grandfather did. The so-called 'Doctor Sang of Shanghai.' People like him are, in large part, responsible for the training of Gamemasters as it is today. They are also responsible for people like Marco Chase, and just as responsible for the method of his death as well as his life training."

There was a deadly silence. Sang and McAllen had gone very still.

Gee's gaze never left Sang's face. "Your father spent his life living down his father's reputation as the best torturer of modern time, and you have spent your life atoning for it. I, for one, spent my childhood learning how to resist your grandfather's specialty, and it has poisoned my life. I can hardly throw stones at Mrs. Chase for recognizing the need to protect her children, even by death. I think she was wrong. I hope she was wrong. But I'm not sure enough to stand in judgment."

Archie wanted to run away, wanted to stop this ugly speech somehow, knowing that Gee only spoke the truth. The expression on his face, the expression he'd seen on Sarah's face that had told him she too was a gene-mod, came from learning to resist torture. That was what Archie saw every time a gene-mod spoke about his childhood. Betrayal by his parents, the heartless utilitarianism of it, family and love ripped away because if you don't have it, it can't be used to hurt you.

John Arrow had devised this idiot riddle to help a man who had a chance at recovering something they had lost.

"Sarah." Archie hardly dared speak. "You shot them?"

Sang exploded. "All of them! One bullet apiece, right through the heart, every one!"

"All right, all right," Archie said to him, waving a vague hand in his direction, "I was just getting up to speed. I saw this coming. If I'd warned you this would happen, Commander, you would have said thank you very much for your opinion, Mr. Chamberlain, wouldn't you?" Sang regarded him in stony silence. Archie's voice was as mild as Gee's had been. "I'll tell you some other things now, if you're willing to listen. Of course, you can say thank you very much for your opinion, Mr. Chamberlain, and waltz off, no one the wiser. But perhaps I can help, and perhaps we can avoid a nightmare of a court case."

There was an understanding expression in Gee's eyes. He did not know what Archie was going to say, but he could live with it. He pulled out one of the chairs and motioned Archie to it.

Archie sat. Lt. McAllen, oddly enough, preferred to stand at his shoulder. She still gave him this feeling of being protected, or defended, God knew why. "Genetically modified humans have no concept of right or wrong, good or evil. They spend their days being tested and reinforced against all the weaker emotions. But to them, those aren't weaknesses. They've never seen these dangers. They're just another part of life. They aren't resisting torture. They aren't responding to stimuli because they've never seen the stimulus. The only life they know is the life of the laboratory. Not a real life, Commander.

"From babyhood, they are trained to build up reactions to situations completely unlike reactions of normal humans versed in the ways of the world. A good gene-mod's behavior seems to come from nowhere. A bad gene-mod's behavior comes from reacting to the psychological baggage of their trainers. Gene-mods have no moral sense of their own because of their deliberately scripted laboratory life. Do you want to get into court and discuss their psychology? It's very likely the decision will go against you, especially when the court reaches the point of discussing baselines of moral and ethical standards. You know how risky an insanity defense can become. This will be quite along the same lines. There will be six Dr. Andres on the witness stand, showing graphs and charts of biotechnological reactions to prove their sanity, talents and abilities. There will not be one demonstration of belief in God, loyalty to a friend, or plain old love."

"You're belaboring the obvious," Sang growled, but his tone was different.

"You and I," said Archie, "have plenty of psychological burdens to thank our parents for, but compared to a gene-mod, those are isolated incidents.

"The good gene-mods, like Gennaro and his father Gentian before him, or like John and Richard Arrow, Sarah's brothers, have found a way to regain what they have lost and become— I hate to say it— decent people again. They're interacting with the rest of the human race, and learning to care. They have to be protected, so that the human race won't take advantage of them, which is frankly why Gamemaster Inc. exists. And perhaps the Karpo Gompa, too, though it had been around a few centuries before Richard Arrow. And, they need to learn what it means to be decent people. They learn from the human beings they hire or work with. I'm as much a product of Gamemaster Inc. as Gennaro is. My folks have been caring for the Gamemasters for two generations now. Many families I know are into three or four generations. It's not a kingdom, it's a trust.

"Think. Think before you unleash this dreadful legal and public maelstrom, and give the gene-mods a couple of generations to undo the terrible damage they've done to themselves."

Archie saw the expressions on the faces around him. Probably no one in the universe had ever considered genetic modification to be terrible damage, no more than a robot could be anything but a helpful tool. Maybe he was wrong. But what mattered, right now, was making sure that progress for all of them, gene-mod and scratch-grown, didn't stop here.

There was a moment's silence. Quietly, the Gamemaster said, "All right, Archie. I've got the point."

"Then you should apologize, for starters," Archie told him.

Gamemaster turned to Sang as if Archie's request had been the most natural in the world, and spoke accordingly. "I could not argue a case more eloquently, neither Sarah's nor mine. I am indeed— sorry— for the bedlam I have caused. What Mr. Chamberlain observed with a teacher's eye is true, the common-sense next step for me was not his. I offer no excuse nor reason beyond what he himself has said." He shook his head. "I apologize to you. The things I said to you were low blows, and unethical. Perhaps Mr. Chamberlain feels he should not let me down, but that feeling is reciprocated. We owe each other our lives. I shall back up your judgment in this matter— " he took a deep breath— "with my personal guarantee. So, please, be careful what you wish for, because you will indeed get it."

It was the first time in his life that Archie could ever remember Gee apologizing to anyone for anything, and it had indeed been a regal apology. He could feel the atmosphere of the room change.

Apparently, Commander Sang recognized the seriousness of the Gamemaster guarantee. He thought and moved slowly. "Mr. Chamberlain has been of material assistance in this operation. Since he has asked a favor, I am inclined to grant it. However, the death of Marco Chase is another matter. There is evidence enough to prove his complicity in several deaths involving subversive Recover activities. He acted as a unit commander. As he was a minor, his mother, Mrs. Sarah Cordelia Chase, being very much alive, is still responsible for his actions. In a criminal case, it doesn't matter if he has declared personal independence."

Sarah Chase pounded the table with both hands. In a voice too exhausted to vent more emotion, she croaked, "I don't *want* responsibility for my son's actions. Can't you see? I was wrong, wrong from beginning to end. I *never* made a correct choice for my sons. Jonas didn't, either! Oh, he *knew* how to raise our children, and *I* didn't. I didn't but *he* didn't, either! Don't tell me it's my business or my motherly responsibility, because it's not! Marco signed a Statement of Independence years ago, so I could eat his dust. Oh, for a world where I could give a man children that would *not* be my responsibility! Every decision I've made has been wrong, wrong, *wrong*." She pounded the table.

Archie saw Gennaro start, and stare at Sarah Chase as if he were seeing her for the first time.

Archie knew he should feel sympathy for Sarah as the ceiling tumbled in upon her world. Instead, to his own surprise, he felt a smile coming to his face in the middle of this catastrophe.

Gee was not looking at Archie. His eyes were intent upon Sarah. He leaned back, both voice and pose deceptively normal. "So do you consider yourself an evil woman, or merely a stupid one?" he asked, as if the question were not the most important one of his life. Oh, please, thought Archie, let her answer be...

"Stupid," she snarled at him. "Stupid to let Jonas ruin my life, stupid to let Sean die, stupid to believe Marco, stupid to rescue you. Stupid, stupid, stupid!" She buried her face in her hands.

It's not my fault, Gee had said, *I haven't found a woman stupid enough to marry me...*

"You're on a streak," Gee said agreeably. "Care to go for five out of five?"

Archie stifled a grin. He stood, grasped Sheila McAllen's arm firmly and spoke. "We have to take the Land Rover back to the rental place. Come on, Lieutenant."

The Gamemaster looked at them as if he had forgotten they were in the room.

Archie met Gee's gaze and told him, "If you come back alone, I'll kick you myself."

The light danced in Gee's tired eyes. "I won't come back alone. We'll meet you where?"

"My folks' place on Saturday. That will give you three days to thrash it through."

"Done. Now get out."

"We're gone," said Archie, dragging McAllen out the door and closing it firmly behind him.

Sheila McAllen watched uncomprehendingly as he did a little dance step in front of the closed door, in the darkened hallway. "What the hell is going on?"

"Marriage proposal, I hope. Two stupid people together for all eternity, alleluia."

"Her— and *him*?" McAllen stared. Archie had never heard the pronoun for Gamemaster stretched to three syllables before this.

"Yes, yes, and the end of this damnable riddle, thank God! Didn't you hear her? She would like nothing more than a faithful husband, and children that weren't her duty to raise single-handedly. And there's a man who's head over heels in love with her! Oh, God be good to them, make them best friends forever, and that's a real prayer!" Archie walked swiftly down the darkened corridor and back outside.

Lieutenant McAllen hurried out behind him. It wasn't like Archie not to let the lady go first, and maybe she had sensed something else in his emotional speech. Outside, she clasped his shoulder. "Are you all right?"

He stopped, and drew in a deep breath. "No— yes. Tired, that's all. Glad to see the end of this riddle, that's for dam'-sure. Sarah Chase is the Brass Mouse, Lieutenant. It was the name of the antiques shop she was running when she married Jonas Chase, but it was obviously the nickname her brothers gave her. The only chicken with a gun." He looked into her face, not quite eye-level, into the bold blue eyes. He felt something stir again, and reminded himself that had all been decided. He would return the Land Rover, visit his folks, and wait for Gennaro and Sarah. By then, Lieutenant Sheila McAllen would be back in her world, ECM West Meg, dealing with important military things.

Sheila McAllen leaned against the bonnet of the vehicle on the passenger side, facing him. "So you're going to take the Land Rover back?"

Archie jingled the ring. "I have keys now. I can start it the old-fashioned way. I'm sure you can call for ECM transport from here, if you wish."

"I thought I'd ride with you, anyway," McAllen said. "If it's okay by you."

Archie wanted to say, No, it will make things harder and hurt a hell of a lot more when you go. He looked at her rumpled uniform and mussed hair. There was a smudge on her cheek. The boyish golden pageboy haircut glittered in the remaining sunlight. He opened his mouth, and found himself saying, "I'd like that." How many times had he been told that anyone could read the truth in his face?

She stayed where she was. "I'm going to get written up again. AWOL, this time."

"I could ask Max to straighten it out. Or at least inform them where you are."

"No, it's my responsibility."

"I rather thought you'd say that," Archie replied, "or I would have offered before. I didn't want to hurt your pride."

"Thank you for realizing I have some." She gazed down at the bonnet for a moment, then back at him. There was an odd smile on her lips. "I'm the good little rule-abiding Public Relations officer, and I'm going to get busted for sure on this one."

Archie knew his face was betraying him, felt breathless, wondered what she was telling him. "Sorry it wasn't worth it."

"I never said it wasn't worth it." Her little smile remained. "It would be good for us to drop by your folks' place, anyway. I should probably meet my future in-laws."

He protested, "I haven't asked you to marry me!"

"I know." She flung herself into the passenger seat. Archie climbed more carefully into the driver's. "You've been slow on that. Why? Is it the braid? No problem, I'm about to lose it all. Is it marrying an ECM officer? Again no problem, I'll be rank-and-file before this is over. Or is it marrying a criminal? 'cuz I'm headed for that when I get back, fer sure." He had never heard Californian in her voice before.

Archie pushed the key in the slot, but did not start the engine. "None of that," he answered quietly. "It was the thought of asking you to marry a boring old desk jockey, perfectly content with his afternoon tea and weekend cricket and church on Sunday with the family. I'm neither a hero nor an adventurer, Sheila. I never will be."

Sheila's smile never faded. "We're both selling ourselves pretty short, aren't we? The worst thing that could happen to us is that we're both perfectly right."

"I suppose so," Archie said. His breathing still felt strange. It was very difficult to look her in the eye. "The truth is, I've been your man for a long time."

Her smile grew. "I know. It hit me at the cricket match, how well we fit." She ran her hand up the inside of Archie's thigh. Apparently she liked what she felt, because the smile got sunnier.

Archie leaned over to kiss her. He put his heart into it, and he had no idea how long the kiss lasted. When they broke, he managed to say, "I think I'm going to have trouble driving if you do that."

"Adjust," said Sheila McAllen, and she kissed him again.

Archie woke up to Sheila against his shoulder. He slipped his arm around her and nestled her close against his body. The soft golden pageboy hair fluttered against his skin.

He didn't know what they would meet when they left the England Historical District, but one thing was certain: they would cope with it together. No woman had ever made him feel like this, that everything was absolutely right and he would not regret it in the morning. It was morning, and he was not regretting it. Not one iota. He had given his heart. He used to think that was just a figure of speech.

Sheila stirred. She ran her hand down his chest and murmured sleepily, "Whoever said that Englishmen were cold fish obviously didn't know the right Englishman."

He smiled. "I was thinking the same about you."

She nodded, looking almost shy. "One of my friends in OTS, from Colorado, used to say, 'You want to succeed in this man's army, keep your saddle on and your cinch tight.'" She draped an amazingly muscular arm across his chest. "You were so— passionate last night, you would've blown me away if only you'd given me time to think about it."

"I hope you realize that, heat of passion or not, I meant every word of it," said Archie. "I do want to marry you. I don't give a damn if I have to visit you in prison. I want us to have some kind of a life together, any kind of a life together, I'll take whatever I can get as long as you're in it."

"My God," she said. "Men aren't supposed to be like that. It's the morning after, and you're still serious about it."

"Damn serious."

Her eyes grew big as saucers with this new emotion. "Archie— " She rolled over atop him to kiss him again and again.

And that, of course, was when the lapel radio went off.

"EHD HQ to Lieutenant McAllen. Lieutenant McAllen, please respond."

"God DAMN," they cursed together.

Sheila rolled for her uniform jacket, placed neatly on the back of a chair (even in love, habits remained), detached the radio from her collar, and rolled back into position in bed.

"EHD HQ, this is McAllen," she said.

"General Dumont to speak to you. Stand by."

"General Dumont? As in EHD High Command General Dumont?" she asked disbelievingly.

"Well, I'm glad *you've* heard of me," an older, sharper English voice snapped.

"Of *course* I have, sir." She sat straight up in bed. If she saluted her radio, Archie would punch her. Though, admittedly, the view from this angle was simply lovely.

"What's your current location?"

"Um— Woodford, sir, the Golden Lion Inn."

"Ah. Obtaining a reward for your work, I hope."

"You might say so, sir," Sheila replied formally. Archie thought he heard him chuckle.

"Lieutenant, you may be West Meg and I may be England Historic District, but I am still a general and you are still a lieutenant in the Earth Combined Military. You will remain within the confines of the England Historic District until you receive further orders *from me*. Am I clear?"

"Yes, sir," she said. "May I ask why?"

"You may. There is some disagreement among various divisions of the ECM as to your future. A conference is scheduled later today. One of my staff will meet with you tomorrow to brief you."

"Where do you want me to report, sir?"

"He'll come to you. Right now, I am the only one who knows where you are, and I prefer to leave it that way."

"Excuse me, sir, but Captain Jahnik is my commanding officer. It's my duty to report to him." Then, she added hastily, "Unless, of course, you tell me why I shouldn't, sir."

"Refer Captain Jahnik to me," he said brusquely. "You will remain in Woodford until further notice. Over and out."

Sheila set down the radio on the nightstand. "One might think he had already spoken with the Captain."

Archie concurred. "One might also think the Captain hadn't recognized his name and said something tasteless before he found out who he was talking to."

Sheila giggled. "One might think so, mightn't one?" She lay back down again and wrapped her arms around Archie. She shook her head. "*They'll come to me!*"

"I wonder if you're a hot property and don't know it."

"I never was before."

"You never led a commando raid or had a Gamemaster eating out of your hand before," Archie pointed out.

"True," she admitted. Then her stomach rumbled loudly. She looked surprised. "When was the last time we ate?"

"I don't remember," Archie admitted.

"You can't just ask Max to conjure up stuff for us, can you?" Sheila asked. "I am dying for a toothbrush and a change of underwear. And I can't leave Woodford."

"No, we've got to shop for them the old-fashioned way," Archie answered. "It'll be fun, love, you'll see." He watched her stand up and start dressing. "Maybe get you some decent civs, too."

"And we can't go to see your folks."

"Well, they're not that far away. I'll ring them and ask if they'd like to run up to us. Max, get my folks on the phone."

A moment later, the phone lit up with Peggy Chamberlain's face. She broke into a sunny smile when she saw her son. "Archie, baby! How are you? Where are you phoning from?"

"Fine, Mum." He could see his Dad now, too. "I'm in Woodford, actually, but I can't get down to meet you. I was wondering if you'd like to take a run up and have lunch with us."

"'Us'?"

"Er— yes. Sheila's part of the reason I can't leave Woodford. Sheila McAllen. She's under house arrest by the Earth Combined Military. We're planning to marry very soon, preferably before her court martial. Would you care to join us for lunch at the Golden Lion around 1300 hours?"

In the background, George Chamberlain broke into a broad grin. Peggy merely stated decisively, "We'll be there."

"Looking forward to it," said Archie. "Lots of love." They broke the connection.

Sheila commented, "I thought you said your mum had heart trouble."

"If she didn't even blink through what I just told her," Archie replied, "she's good for another fifty years."

-17-

Happy Beginning

They pulled the Land Rover into a tiny driveway behind another Land Rover. "Well, they're here," Sheila pointed out.

"Mmph," Archie agreed, "or at least, some tourists are."

The front door opened, with both Peggy and George Chamberlain framed in the entryway. Archie smiled and slid the keys in his pocket. He and Sheila trod the tiny walkway to where Peggy waited to kiss them both. George clasped his son's hand and tapped his own cheek for Sheila to kiss. If Sheila and his parents hadn't won each other in Woodford, they had now.

Peggy hustled them into the tiny kitchen, parked them on stools, and started pouring coffee. A thud from somewhere in the house sounded like workers or moving men. It warmed Archie's heart to realize how quickly and completely his parents had accepted Sheila, merely on their son's word. Well, maybe not, knowing them both as well as he did, and thinking of his father's years at Gamemaster Inc., doing a job he did not mention. Maybe they had taken the liberty of a few background checks, but that was their prerogative. "So you're all back in the ECM's good graces, then?" Peggy asked Sheila, sitting opposite her, coffee cup in hand.

"Yes." Sheila sipped hot coffee and found it good. "Some paper-pusher came up from EHD ECM HQ to guarantee it would all be smoothed out."

"Apparently General Dumont has turned this into a personal project," Archie supplemented. It occurred to him that the thuds and bumps were above them, off and on. He glanced upward toward the ceiling, a glance which his father caught.

"The furniture movers," George explained in a low voice.

Peggy had a different agenda. "If you two are going to be married, we should meet your parents, Sheila."

Sheila McAllen merely observed, "It will be interesting to have you and the Sergeant-Major in the same room." She was catching on to his family's understated humor.

George's smile flashed, and Archie thought, *And Dad will be there to tamp down the fireworks.* Aloud, Archie asked, "Who's moving furniture?"

"We don't have a guest room, in a house this small," Peggy explained apologetically to Sheila.

The one spare room had a narrow bed that was usually given to Archie. He caught on immediately. "I see. Shall we go watch other people work, then?"

Peggy's smile was brilliant. "Let's." First, she poured two small glasses of apple juice from the icebox, then led the way up the back stairs. Her movers, as Archie well knew, rarely drank coffee.

They followed Peggy up the twists and turns of the back kitchen stairway all the way to a tiny attic door. She shoved it open with her elbow. Archie swore he heard a feminine giggle just before Peggy announced in a loud voice, "Company coming! Are you decent?"

"As decent as we'll ever be," said a well-known male voice, as they clambered into the attic room.

This low-ceilinged room had been cleaned and swept, and was now lit by a couple of lamps. Under normal circumstances it would be a dim attic storage area, but now it was a makeshift guest bedroom. In its center was a platform bed with two rough end-tables. Against the walls on every side were the previous contents of the room— trunks and large pieces of furniture whose change in position bespoke of the physical strength of the movers.

The furniture movers, themselves, looked more like they were doing this for fun than for exercise. Dressed in black tee-shirts and loose pants, they were very comfortable and quite unfashionable-looking. Archie noted with approval that Sarah wore no makeup and looked sexy in the scrubby outfit. She also looked as though she had grown ten years younger. Love will do that, he thought.

The object of her affection looked no different from ever, except for the casual wear. Oh, and the smile. He wore slippers Archie recognized as Tibetan, although Sarah was barefoot. They both bore evidence of the previous grime of the little attic.

Archie and Gee's gazes met across the room. There was no need for a further greeting. But Sheila said, "Hey, bud," to Sarah, implying that the two women had had a long talk— or were going to. It also warmed Archie's heart to see the two dark guests accept glasses of juice from Peggy as docilely as if she were truly their mom.

"It's looking good," said George Chamberlain.

"I'm excited. We've never had this many kids here at one time," said Peggy. Sheila grinned, realizing, as Archie did, that as far as Peggy Chamberlain was concerned, she and Sarah weren't marrying into the family; George and Peggy were adopting two girls. The grins and twinkles getting passed around the room showed that Peggy's comment hadn't been lost on anyone.

"Come on downstairs and get the dust out of your lungs," Archie suggested, "and tell us what's happened."

Gee and Sarah washed up and joined the others in the living room. The man who hated to be touched, and was leery of all women and their lures, pulled

Sarah bodily against him on the couch. She lifted her bare feet up onto the seat and rested on his body, as comfortable as any newlywed. She moved her feet for Sheila, who lifted herself over the back of the couch and sat cross-legged on the end, still sipping coffee.

"So are you legally married?" Archie asked them.

"Legally, as by the law of West Meg, I'm as married as I ever will be," Gee replied. "And Sarah had a military wedding once."

"You have to do the right thing," Archie said.

"I knew you were going to say that. St. Ethelred's sound all right?" That was the Anglican church in West Meg that Archie sometimes attended.

"Sounds fine, but it's not your bride's parish, you know."

"I will not return to Sandhurst, not even to visit," said Sarah quietly.

Archie looked at her for a long moment, and an old Bible verse popped into his head, Ruth: "Wherever you go, I will go; Wherever you live, so shall I live. For your people shall be my people, and your God my God."

"What are you thinking?" Sheila asked him.

"I was wishing Bet was here. She'd have the right Bible verse and I wouldn't have to explain it to her."

"We need to talk about Bet," said the Gamemaster, his gaze straight at Archie.

"Well, we can't." Archie leaned back in his chair. "You didn't tell me how much stuff she did was confidential, so I can't tell you what Bet and I discussed, either."

"Blow that," said Gennaro, not one of his usual expressions but good enough for polite company, "I hate to think how much confidential information has been wafting about your cubicle, and you consorting with the enemy."

"Yeah, you should know," Sheila agreed in a matching tone, and again Gennaro's smile flashed.

However, Gee continued, "Bet told me that you knew the answer to John Arrow's riddle, had known it all along, and at least one other person had figured it out besides you."

Archie stared into his cup for a long moment. "Well, yes. Bet, the Dalai Lama, and Richard Arrow all knew the answer, but left me to lead you on."

"The riddle?" Sheila stopped suddenly, and looked at Gee, puzzled. Then she looked at Archie, as if in confirmation. Then, to them both, she asked, "You're kidding, right?"

Archie didn't even have to guess if she had the right answer. He settled back in his chair, and remained as silent as George Chamberlain beside him. This moment, he had become an observer like his father. It was a strange feeling.

Both Gee and Sarah looked at Sheila questioningly. Gee, particularly, looked surprised. However, he said, "No, I'm not kidding. I never have found the answer to Arrow's riddle. McAllen, are you saying that you understand it?"

"Well, yeah," said Sheila, looking at Archie for guidance. "It was so obvious, I thought you were putting me on."

"I wasn't," Archie replied quietly, fully aware that Sheila felt she was letting the cat out of the bag. He didn't mind at all if Sheila said it, he discovered. She was not some Gamemaster displaying her brilliance to the boss. She was a human being, saying what the rest of the world would say.

At that moment, he felt his father's hand on his shoulder. George Chamberlain, just as silent, watching things.

Lt. Sheila McAllen reached inside her uniform jacket, and pulled from an inner breast pocket a little book with a tin cover. Tin. Bulletproofing, from the old days.

"I didn't know the military still issued tin-plated Bibles," George Chamberlain observed. Archie felt an additional pressure on his shoulder— Peggy Chamberlain standing behind them, placing her hand upon her husband's.

"They don't. This belonged to my grandfather," Sheila said, handing it to Gee. "Here. First letter of Paul to the Corinthians. 1 Corinthians 13:13."

Gee handled the little tin-covered book as gently as he handled the Dhammapada readings, or as Archie handled the great leather Bible. His long, delicate fingers probed and turned the pages as carefully as they unlocked the great computer on the *Albatross*. At last he smoothed down a page, and read: "In short, there are three things that last: faith, hope and love; and the greatest of these is love."

"There, that's it," said Sheila McAllen. "I'm just a military paper-pusher, and not a good one, so I figured I must have been wrong and I didn't say anything. But those three things, Gee, you've been just clobbered by them. It's hard to miss."

Gee's gaze moved to Archie. In a tone Archie had never before heard, Gee said, "So he marked the Bible."

"Just a crease. Nothing noticeable," Archie replied.

"And you saw the crease, guessed part of it, and hoped for the rest."

"Well, yes," said Archie, "I did."

Sarah touched Gee's arm. It seemed the motion of a woman reminding a man of a prior discussion. Gee asked Archie, "Did you mean what you told Dyvim Sang?"

"Every word of it."

Gee's gaze remained thoughtfully upon the Chamberlains for a long moment. Then he asked, "Teaching Gamemasters. Is it worth it?"

"Always has been," said George Chamberlain.

"Always will be," said Archie Chamberlain.

Peggy Chamberlain turned her head suddenly, as if to hide a tear, but her gaze fell on the television, alit with the sound turned off. "Oh, no, the ECM are taking over your estate, Sarah."

They turned as one to the television, and Peggy put the sound up. They heard the familiar chuk-chuk-chuk of soldiers' feet, and the blathering of some news reporter.

"I shan't miss it," said Sarah quietly.

Sheila McAllen looked at her, and smiled. "You'll be all right, bud." Archie knew he couldn't fall in love with Sheila any further than that moment. There was a new world out there for them all to explore, and Archie didn't want to miss a minute of it.

The End

CPSIA information can be obtained at www.ICGtesting.com
Printed in the USA
BVOW030413120612

292382BV00001B/10/P

9 781604 594812